DOVER · **GIANT THRIFT** · EDITIONS

Resurrection

LEO TOLSTOY

English translation by
LOUISE MAUDE

DOVER PUBLICATIONS, INC.
Mineola, New York

DOVER GIANT THRIFT EDITIONS

GENERAL EDITOR: PAUL NEGRI
EDITOR OF THIS VOLUME: T. N. R. ROGERS

Bibliographical Note

This Dover edition, first published in 2004, is an unabridged republication of the translation into English by Louise Maude of Воскресение (Voskresenie) that was originally published by Oxford University Press, London, in 1916. Воскресение was first published in Russian in 1899. The editor has prepared an introductory Note specially for this edition.

Library of Congress Cataloging-in-Publication Data

Tolstoy, Leo, graf, 1828–1910.
   [Voskresenie. English]
   Resurrection / Leo Tolstoy ; English translation by Louise Maude.
      p. cm. — (Dover giant thrift editions)
   Originally published: London : Oxford University Press, 1916.
   ISBN 0-486-43216-5 (pbk.)
   I. Maude, Louise Shanks, 1855–1939. II. Title. III. Series.

PG3366.V7 2003
891.73'3—dc22

2003059546

Manufactured in the United States of America
Dover Publications, Inc., 31 East 2nd Street, Mineola, N.Y. 11501

Note

LEV NIKOLAYEVICH TOLSTOY (1828–1910) was not satisfied with just being one of the greatest novelists who ever lived; what was more important to him was to be a good person, a person who lived rightly. His good works and his lucid, persuasive philosophical writings led him to be honored worldwide as a sage and moral leader, and for many inside Russia his moral authority rivaled that of the tsar. But to the government and the church he was a dangerous man. Because he rejected many of the practices and dictates of Russian Orthodoxy, this searching, complex man was not only never designated a saint—as might have seemed appropriate to his admirers—but in 1901 was excommunicated.[1] A large part of the reason for his excommunication was his publication of *Resurrection*.

By the time he came to write this novel, Tolstoy—impelled by the same moral imperatives as those his alter ego, Prince Nekhlyudov,[2] wrestles with in its pages—had given up much of his land and had given up the copyrights on his published works. Though he had evidently been working on *Resurrection* on and off for ten years, he had pretty much put his fiction on the back burner while he focused on what seemed to him a more pressing concern: educating the people through essays such as his 1893 "The Kingdom of God Is Within You."

But suddenly the need for money presented itself. Not money for him or for his family, but for the transplantation to Canada of the members of a peace-loving, Quaker-like sect—a sect that had been

---

[1] Tolstoy's own form of Christianity, based on the Sermon on the Mount, rested primarily on five tenets: the suppression of anger, the rejection of sex outside marriage, the refusal ever to use oaths of any sort, the renunciation of resistance to evil, and the love of one's enemies.

[2] He had introduced Nekhlyudov years earlier in such autobiographical stories as the 1856 "A Landlord's Morning" (in which the nineteen-year-old prince writes to his aunt that he's quitting his studies in order to try to remedy the living conditions of his peasants) and the 1857 "Lucerne" (an excerpt from the prince's diary).

derogatorily dubbed "Dukhobortsi," or spirit wrestlers, by a Russian Orthodox archbishop of a century earlier. These Dukhobors were hard-working communal farmers, pacifists who rejected meat eating, the use of tobacco and alcohol, and the worship of icons. Such heresies, not far removed from Tolstoy's own, led to recurrent persecution by both the tsarist government and the church. To help these people move to Canada (as the government had finally allowed after extensive lobbying by Tolstoy), Tolstoy needed quick money—and the way to get it, though it seemed to him like a pact with the devil, was to write and copyright a piece of fiction. After looking through his uncompleted manuscripts, he decided on *Resurrection* as the one most likely to sell widely. He went to work feverishly (telling his wife that he had not felt so strongly gripped by the creative impulse since *War and Peace*), sending chapters out as soon as they were finished, for serial publication not only in Russia but in magazines throughout the world, all of which were thrilled to get their hands on a new piece of fiction by the author of *War and Peace* and *Anna Karenina*.[3]

The plot of *Resurrection* had come to Tolstoy from his friend, the brilliant jurist Anatoly Fedorovich Koni. A man who had come to Koni for legal aid confessed that as a youth he had seduced a pretty sixteen-year-old whom one of his relatives had taken in after her parents' death. When this girl became pregnant, she was turned out, and after fruitless attempts to earn a living by other means, she became a prostitute. She was arrested after stealing money from one of her drunken clients, and, in an astonishing coincidence, the man who had seduced her found himself on her jury. He made up his mind to marry her; and they did in fact get married, but soon after she finished serving her four-month prison sentence, she died of typhus. For Tolstoy this story was painfully resonant: he himself, as a young man, had similarly taken the virginity of a servant in his aunt's house, a girl named Masha, who as a result was dismissed from service and perished. Tolstoy urged Koni to publish this story; when he did not do so, he asked his permission to use it himself. Ten years later, prodded by the Dukhobors' plight, he finished *Resurrection* (in December 1899), and 7,400 Dukhobors went off to their new lives in Saskatchewan.

Resurrection certainly is not as great a novel as Tolstoy's earlier masterpieces. The novel's structure is flatter, the characters less gripping, and the plot more linear than those of *War and Peace* and *Anna Karenina*, and some chapters seem driven more by the author's beliefs than by the story he is telling. The ending is weak, and though the cen-

---

[3] In Russia the novel underwent heavy censorship; the first complete, uncensored Russian text did not appear until 1936.

tral character, Nekhlyudov, is always a living, believable presence, to many readers he may seem to have too few real problems to fully engage their empathy, and occasionally may seem annoyingly priggish and self-righteous.

But, even given all those caveats, this is a book that is worth reading—a book that only Tolstoy could have written. Its pages are rich with depictions of humans and events set forth so precisely and accurately as to seem not merely scenes in a fictional world but windows miraculously opening into the real one. And some of the windows Tolstoy opens are achingly beautiful. In particular, the scenes of Nekhlyudov's first love are as lovely, powerful, and honest as anything he ever wrote. In *What Is Art?*, Tolstoy set forth his belief that the essence of art is a "sense of infection with another's feeling—compelling us to rejoice in another's gladness, to sorrow at another's grief, and to mingle souls with each other." In the best parts of *Resurrection* he succeeds in doing that. Though the scenes of young love bring to life the smells and sights and sounds of the nineteenth-century Russian countryside in summer, spring, and fall, their passionate reality is rooted not in a specific time and place but in the boundless immensities of the human heart.

Unbracketed footnotes in the following text are mostly by the translator; a few, marked "L. T.," are by Tolstoy. Those in brackets are by the editor of this Dover edition.

Contents

NAMES OF CHARACTERS

(Marked to show on which syllable the accent falls)

Máslova, Katerína Mikháylovna (Katúsha, Lubóv, Lúbka)
Sophia Ivánovna, *her godmother* ⎱ *Nekhlyúdov's aunts*
Mary Ivánovna, *Sophia's sister* ⎰
Nekhlyúdov, Prince Dmítry Ivánich (Mítya and Mítinka)
Agraféna Petróvna, *Nekhlyúdov's housekeeper*
Michael Petróvich ⎱ *Judges*
Matthew Nikítich ⎰
Brevé, *Public Prosecutor*
Baklashóv, Peter, *a merchant*
Peter Gerásimovich
Nikíforov
Ivanóv, Iván Semënich
Dánchenko, Captain Úri Dmítrich
Kuleshóv, Gregory Efímich, *a merchant* ⎰ *Jurymen*
Kartínkin, Simon Petróv, *a peasant* ⎱ *prisoners*
Bóchkova, Euphemia Ivánovna, *chamber-maid* ⎰ *on trial*
Smelkóv, Therapónt, *a merchant who has been poisoned*
Tíkhon, *Nekhlyúdov's aunts' man-servant*
Schönbock, *an officer*
Matrëna Pávlovna, *old servant to Nekhlyúdov's aunts*
Korchágin, Prince, *a retired General*
Kólosov, Iván Ivánich, *his friend, a bank director*
Pétya, *Korchágin's son*
Telégin, Michael Sergéyevich (Mísha), *Missy's cousin*
Korchágina, Princess Mary (Missy)
Korchágina, Princess Sophia Vasílyevna, *Missy's mother*
Catherine Alexéyevna, *a Slavophil maiden lady*
Stephen, *the Korchágins' butler*
Philip, *the Korchágins' footman*

Kitáeva, Caroline Albértovna, *keeper of a brothel*
Kornéy, *Nekhlyúdov's man-servant*
"Khoroshávka" ⎫
Korablëva ⎬ *women prisoners*
Birukóva, Theodosia ⎭
Scheglóv, *a prisoner*
Iváshina, Mary Kárlovna, *a warder*
Sídorov, *a prison attendant*
Fanárin, Anatole, *an advocate*
Vasílyev ⎫
Nepómnyashchy, *a tramp* ⎬ *prisoners*
Petróv ⎫
Fedótov ⎬ *jailers*
Máslennikov (Micky), *a Vice-Governor of the city*
Anna Ignátyevna, *his wife*
Dúkhova, Véra, *a political prisoner*
Menshóva, *a woman prisoner*
Menshóv, *a prisoner, her son*
Shchetínina, Mary Pávlovna, *a political prisoner*
Kólya, *a boy prisoner*
Medíntsev, *a visitor to the prison*
Tilyáevskaya, Madame ⎫
Chernóv ⎬ *visitors at Máslennikov's*
Fináshka, *a boy in prison*
Vasíly Kárlich, *a German steward*
Matrëna Khárina, *Katúsha's aunt*
Láska ⎫
Fédka ⎬ *peasant boys*
Anísya, *a peasant woman*
Chárskaya, Countess Catherine Ivánovna, *Nekhlyúdov's aunt*
Chársky, Count Iván Mikháylich, *her husband, an ex-Minister*
Mariette, *wife of General Chervyánsky*
Chervyánsky, General
Wolf, Vladímir Vasílich, *a Senator*
Kiesewetter, *an Evangelical revivalist*
Vorobëv, Baron, *an influential official*
Kriegsmuth, General Baron, *of German descent, Governor of the Petropávlov Fortress Prison*
Bay ⎫
Nikítin ⎬ *Senators*
Skovoródnikov ⎭
Selénin, *Public Prosecutor*
Bogatirév, *an aide-de-camp to the Emperor*

Shústova, Lydia, *a political prisoner, released*
Zakhárov, *Lydia's cousin*
Toporóv, *Procurator of the Holy Synod*
Rogózhinskaya, Nataly Ivánovna (Natásha), *Nekhlyúdov's sister*
Rogózhinsky, *her husband, a jurist*
Fëdorov, *a gifted prisoner*
Okhótin, *a humorous prisoner*
Birukóv, Tarás, *Theodosia's husband*
Ósten, *a diplomat*
Mávra, *a peasant woman*
Símonson, Vladímir ⎱ *political prisoners*
Kriltsóv, Anatole ⎰
Buzóvkin, *a convict*
Aksútka, *his daughter*
Fédka, *a blind prisoner*
Bernóv, *an orderly attending on convoy officer*
Dévkin, Makár, *a peasant convict*
Rántseva, Emily ⎱ *women political prisoners*
Grábets ⎰
Novodvórov, *a political prisoner*
Kondrátyev, Markél, *a factory hand and political prisoner*
Nabátov, *a peasant, political prisoner*

"Then came Peter, and said to him, Lord, how oft shall my brother sin against me, and I forgive him? until seven times? Jesus saith unto him, I say not unto thee, Until seven times: but, Until seventy times seven." — MATT. xviii. 21–22.

"And why beholdest thou the mote that is in thy brother's eye, but considerest not the beam that is in thine own eye?" — MATT. vii. 3.

"He that is without sin among you, let him first cast a stone at her." — JOHN viii. 7.

"The disciple is not above his master: but every one when he is perfected shall be as his master." — LUKE vi. 40.

BOOK ONE

Chapter I

THOUGH HUNDREDS of thousands had done their very best to disfigure the small piece of land on which they were crowded together: paving the ground with stones, scraping away every vestige of vegetation, cutting down the trees, turning away birds and beasts, filling the air with the smoke of naphtha and coal—still spring was spring, even in the town.

The sun shone warm, the air was balmy, the grass, where it did not get scraped away, revived and sprang up everywhere: between the paving-stones as well as on the narrow strips of lawn on the boulevards. The birches, the poplars, and the wild cherry trees were unfolding their gummy and fragrant leaves, the bursting buds were swelling on the lime trees; crows, sparrows, and pigeons, filled with the joy of spring, were getting their nests ready; the flies were buzzing along the walls warmed by the sunshine. All were glad: the plants, the birds, the insects, and the children. But men, grown-up men and women, did not leave off cheating and tormenting themselves and each other. It was not this spring morning men thought sacred and worthy of consideration, not the beauty of God's world, given for a joy to all creatures—this beauty which inclines the heart to peace, to harmony, and to love—but only their own devices for enslaving one another.

Thus, in the prison office of the Government town, it was not the fact that men and animals had received the grace and gladness of spring that was considered sacred and important, but that a notice, numbered and with a superscription, had come the day before, ordering that on this, the 28th day of April, at 9 A.M., three prisoners now detained in the prison, a man and two women (one of these women, as the chief criminal, to be conducted separately), had to appear at the Court. So now, on the 28th of April, at eight o'clock in the morning, the chief jailer entered the dark, stinking corridor of the women's part of the prison. Immediately after, a woman, with curly grey hair, and a

1

look of suffering on her face, came into the corridor. She was dressed
in a jacket with sleeves trimmed with gold lace, and had a blue-edged
belt round her waist.

The jailer, rattling the iron padlock, opened the door of the cell—
from which there came a whiff of air fouler even than that in the corridor—called out "Maslova! to the Court," and closed the door again.

Even into the prison yard the breeze had brought the fresh, vivifying
air from the fields. But in the corridor the air was laden with the germs
of typhoid, and the smell of sewage, putrefaction, and tar. Every new-
comer felt sad and dejected in it. The woman warder felt this, though
she was used to bad air. She had just come in from outside, and entering the corridor she at once felt weary and sleepy.

From inside the cell came the sound of bustle and women's voices
and the patter of bare feet on the floor.

"Now then, hurry up!" called out the jailer, and in a minute or two
a small young woman with a very full bust came briskly out of the door
and went up to the jailer. She had on a grey cloak over a white jacket
and petticoat. On her feet she wore linen stockings and prison shoes;
and round her head was tied a white kerchief, from under which a few
locks of black hair were brushed over the forehead with evident intent.
The woman's face was of that whiteness peculiar to people who have
lived long in confinement, and which puts one in mind of shoots that
spring up from potatoes kept in a cellar. Her small broad hands, and
the full neck which showed from under the broad collar of her cloak,
were of the same hue. Her black sparkling eyes, one with a slight
squint, appeared in striking contrast to the dull pallor of her face.

She carried herself very straight, expanding her full bosom.

With her head slightly thrown back, she stood in the corridor looking straight into the eyes of the jailer, ready to comply with any order.

The jailer was about to lock the door when a wrinkled, stern-looking
old woman put out her grey head and began speaking to Maslova. But
the jailer closed the door, pushing the old woman's head with it. A
woman's laugh was heard from the cell, and Maslova smiled, turning
towards the little opening in the cell door. The old woman pressed her
face to the hole from the other side, and said in a hoarse voice:—

"Now mind, and when they begin questioning you, just go on repeating the same thing and stick to it; say nothing that is not wanted."

"Well, it could not be worse than it is now, anyhow: I only wish it
were settled one way or another."

"Of course, it will be settled one way or another," said the chief
jailer, with the self-assured wit of a superior. "Now then, get along!"

The old woman's eyes vanished from the opening, and Maslova
stepped out into the middle of the corridor. The chief jailer in front,

they descended the stone stairs; passed the still fouler, noisy cells of the men's ward, followed by eyes looking out of every one of the holes in the doors; and entered the office, where two soldiers were waiting to escort her. A clerk sitting there gave one of the soldiers a paper reeking of tobacco, and pointing to the prisoner, remarked, "Take her."

The soldier, a peasant from Nizhny Novgorod, with a red, pock-marked face, put the paper into the sleeve of his coat, winked, with a glance towards the prisoner, to his companion, a broad-shouldered Chuvash,[1] and then the prisoner and the soldiers went to the front entrance, out of the prison yard, and through the town up the middle of the roughly paved street.

Cabmen, tradespeople, cooks, workmen, and Government clerks stopped and looked curiously at the prisoner. Some shook their heads and thought, "This is what evil conduct—conduct unlike ours—leads to." The children stopped and gazed at the robber with frightened looks; but the thought that the soldiers were preventing her from doing more harm quieted their fears. A peasant who had sold his charcoal and had had some tea in the town, came up, and, after crossing himself, gave her a kopeyk. The prisoner blushed and muttered something. Feeling the looks directed towards her, she gave, without turning her head, a sidelong glance to everybody who was gazing at her: the atten-tion she attracted pleased her. The comparatively fresh air also glad-dened her, but her feet had become unused to walking, and it was painful to step on the rough stones in the ill-made prison shoes. Passing by a corn-dealer's shop, in front of which a few pigeons were strutting about unmolested by any one, the prisoner almost touched a grey-blue bird with her foot; it fluttered up and flew close to her ear, fanning her with its wings. She smiled, and then sighed deeply as she remembered her position.

Chapter II

THE STORY of the prisoner Maslova's life was a very common one.

Maslova's mother was the unmarried daughter of a village woman employed on a dairy-farm belonging to two maiden ladies who were landowners. This unmarried woman had a baby every year, and, as often happens among the village people, each one of these undesired

---

[1] Chuvash—one of the Asiatic races subject to Russia.

babies, after being carefully baptized, was neglected by its mother, whom it hindered at her work, and was left to starve. Five children had died in this way. They had all been baptized and then not sufficiently fed, and just allowed to die. The sixth baby, whose father was a gipsy tramp, would have shared the same fate, had it not so happened that one of the maiden ladies came into the farmyard to scold the dairy-maids for sending up cream that smelt of the cow. The young woman was lying in the cowshed with a fine, healthy, new-born baby. The old maiden lady scolded the maids again, for allowing the woman (who had just been confined) to lie in the cowshed, and was about to go away; but seeing the baby, her heart was touched, and she offered to stand godmother to the little girl. Pity for her little goddaughter induced her to give milk and a little money to the mother, so that she should feed the baby; and the child lived. The old ladies spoke of her as "the saved one." When the child was three years old her mother fell ill and died, and the maiden ladies took the child from the old grand-mother, to whom she was only a burden.

The little black-eyed maiden grew to be extremely pretty, and so full of spirits that the ladies found her very entertaining.

The younger of the ladies, Sophia Ivanovna, who had stood god-mother to the girl, had the kinder heart of the two sisters; Mary Ivanovna, the elder, was rather hard. Sophia Ivanovna dressed the little girl in nice clothes and taught her to read and write, meaning to edu-cate her like a lady. Mary Ivanovna thought the child should be brought up to work, and trained to be a good servant. She was exacting; she punished, and, when in a bad temper, even struck the little girl. Growing up under these two different influences, the girl turned out half servant, half young lady. They called her Katusha, which sounds less refined than Katinka, but is not quite so common as Katka. She used to sew, tidy up the rooms, polish the metal cases of the icons with chalk, and do other light work, and sometimes she sat and read to the ladies.

Though she had more than one offer she would not marry. She felt that life as the wife of any of the working men who were courting her would be too hard for her, spoilt as she was by an easy life.

She lived in this way till she was sixteen, when the nephew of the old ladies, a rich young prince and a university student, came to stay with his aunts; and Katusha, not daring to acknowledge it even to herself, fell in love with him.

Two years later this same nephew stayed four days with his aunts before proceeding to join his regiment, and the night before he left he seduced Katusha, and, after giving her a one hundred ruble note, went away. Five months later she knew for certain that she was pregnant. After that, everything seemed repugnant to her, her only thought being how to escape from the shame awaiting her; and she not only began to serve the ladies in a half-hearted and negligent way, but once, without knowing how it happened, she was very rude to them, though she repented afterwards, and asked them to let her leave. They let her go, very dissatisfied with her. Then she got a housemaid's place in a police-officer's house, but stayed there only three months, for the police-officer, a man of fifty, began to molest her, and once, when he was in a specially enterprising mood, she fired up, called him "fool" and "old devil," and pushed him away so vigorously that he fell. She was turned out for her rudeness. It was useless to look for another situation, for the time of her confinement was drawing near, so she went to the house of a village midwife and illicit retailer of spirits. The confinement was easy; but the midwife, who had a case of fever in the village, infected Katusha, and her baby boy had to be sent to the foundlings' hospital, where, according to the old woman who took him there, he died at once. When Katusha went to the midwife she had a hundred and twenty-seven rubles in all, twenty-seven she had earned and the hundred given her by her seducer. When she left she had but six rubles; she did not know how to keep money, but spent it on herself and gave to all who asked. The midwife took forty rubles for two months' keep and attendance, twenty-five went to get the baby into the foundlings' hospital, and forty the midwife borrowed to buy a cow with. Some twenty rubles went just for clothes, sweets, and extras. Having nothing left to live on, Katusha had to look out for a place again, and found one in the house of a forester. The forester was a married man, but he, too, began to beset her from the first day. She disliked him and tried to avoid him. But he, besides being her master who could send her wherever he liked, was more experienced and cunning, and managed to violate her. His wife found it out, and catching Katusha and her husband in a room all by themselves began beating her. Katusha defended herself and they had a fight, and Katusha was turned out of the house without being paid her wages.

Then she went to live with her aunt in town. Her uncle, a book-binder, had once been comfortably off, but he had lost all his customers and taken to drink, and spent all he could lay hands on at the public-house. The aunt kept a small laundry and managed to support herself, her children and her wretched husband. She offered Katusha a place as assistant laundress; but, seeing what a life of misery and hardship her aunt's assistants led, Katusha hesitated, and applied to a registry office. A place was found for her with a lady who lived with her two sons, pupils at a public day school. A week after Katusha had entered the house, the elder, a big fellow with moustaches, threw up his studies and gave her no peace, continually following her about. His mother laid all the blame on Katusha, and gave her notice.

It so happened that after many fruitless attempts to find a situation Katusha again went to the registry office, and there met a woman with bracelets on her bare, plump arms and rings on most of her fingers. Hearing that Katusha was badly in want of a place, the woman gave her her address and invited her to come to her house. Katusha went. The woman received her very kindly, set cake and sweet wine before her, then wrote a note and gave it to a servant to take to somebody. In the evening a tall man, with long grey hair and white beard, entered the room and sat down at once near Katusha, smiling and gazing at her with glistening eyes. He began joking with her. The hostess called him away into the next room, and Katusha heard her say, "A fresh one from the country." Then the hostess called Katusha away and told her that the man was an author, and that he had a great deal of money, and that if he liked her he would not grudge her anything. He did like her, and gave her twenty-five rubles, promising to see her often. The twenty-five rubles soon went; some she paid to her aunt for board and lodging, the rest was spent on a hat, ribbons, and suchlike. A few days later the author sent for her and she went. He gave her another twenty-five rubles and offered her a separate lodging.

Next door to the lodging rented for her by the author there lived a jolly young shopman, with whom Katusha soon fell in love. She told the author, and moved to a small lodging of her own. The shopman, who had promised to marry her, went off to Nizhny on business without mentioning it to her, having evidently thrown her up, and Katusha remained alone. She meant to continue living in the lodging by herself, but was informed by the police that in that case she would have to get a yellow (prostitute's) passport and be subjected to medical examinations. She returned to her aunt. Seeing her fine dress, her hat, and mantle, her aunt no longer offered her laundry work. According to her ideas, her niece had risen above that. The question as to whether she was to become a laundress or not did not occur to Katusha either. She looked with pity at the thin, hard-worked laundresses, some already in consumption, who stood washing or ironing with their thin arms in the fearfully hot front room, which was always full of soapy steam and very draughty; and she thought with horror that she might have shared the same fate. It was just at this time, when Katusha was in very narrow straits, no "protector" appearing upon the scene, that a procuress found her out.

Katusha had begun to smoke some time before, and since the young shopman had thrown her up she was getting more and more into the habit of drinking. It was not so much the flavour of wine that attracted her, as the fact that it gave her a chance of forgetting the misery she suffered, making her feel unrestrained and more confident of her own worth, which she was not when quite sober: without wine she felt sad and ashamed. The procuress brought all sorts of dainties, to which she treated the aunt, and also wine, and while Katusha drank she offered to place her in one of the largest establishments in the city, explaining all the advantages and benefits of the situation. Katusha had the choice before her of either going into service to be humiliated, probably annoyed by the attentions of the men and having occasional secret sexual connection; or accepting an easy, secure position sanctioned by law, and open, well-paid regular sexual connection—and she chose the latter. Besides, it seemed to her as though she could, in this way, revenge herself on her seducer, and the shopman, and all those who had injured her. One of the things that tempted her and influenced her decision, was the procuress telling her she might order her own dresses: velvet, silk, satin, low-necked ball-dresses—anything she liked. A mental picture of herself in bright yellow silk trimmed with black velvet, with low neck and short sleeves, conquered her, and she handed over her passport. That same evening the procuress took an *izvozchik*[1] and drove her to the notorious house kept by Caroline Albetovna Kitaeva.

From that day a life of chronic sin against human and divine laws commenced for Katusha Maslova, a life which is led by hundreds of thousands of women, and which is not merely tolerated but sanctioned by the Government, anxious for the welfare of its subjects; a life which for nine women out of ten ends in painful disease, premature decrepitude, and death.

Heavy sleep until late in the afternoon followed the orgies of the night. Between three and four o'clock came the weary getting-up from a dirty bed, soda water, coffee, listless pacing up and down the room in bedgowns and dressing-jackets, lazy gazing out of the windows from behind the drawn curtains, indolent disputes with one another; then washing, perfuming and anointing the body and hair, trying on dresses, disputes about them with the mistress of the house, surveying one's self in looking-glasses, painting the face, the eyebrows; rich, sweet food; then dressing in gaudy silks exposing much of the body, and coming down into the ornamented and brilliantly illuminated drawing-room; then the arrival of visitors, music, dancing, sexual connection with old and young and middle-aged, with lads and decrepit old men, bache-

---

[1] *Izvozchik*, the nearest Moscow equivalent to a cabman. The same word is used both for the driver and for the vehicle.

lors, married men, merchants, clerks, Armenians, Jews, Tartars; rich and poor, sick and healthy, tipsy and sober, rough and tender, military men and civilians, students and mere schoolboys—of all classes, ages, and characters. And shouts and jokes, and brawls and music and tobacco and wine, and wine and tobacco, from evening until daylight, no relief till morning, and then heavy sleep; the same every day and all the week. Then at the end of the week came the visit to the police station, as instituted by the Government, where doctors—men in the service of the Government—sometimes seriously and strictly, sometimes with playful levity, examined these women, completely destroying the modesty given as a protection not only to human beings but also to animals, and gave them written permissions to continue in the sins they and their accomplices had been committing all the week. Then followed another week of the same kind: always the same every night, summer and winter, work days and holidays.

And in this manner Katusha Maslova lived seven years. During this time she had changed houses backwards and forwards once or twice, and had once been to the hospital. In the seventh year of her life in the brothel, when she was twenty-eight years old, there happened that for which she was put in prison and for which she was now being taken to be tried, after more than three months' confinement with thieves and murderers in the stifling air of a prison.

Chapter III

WHEN Maslova, accompanied by two soldiers, reached the building, wearied out by the long walk, Prince Dmitry Ivanich Nekhlyudov, who seduced her, was still lying on his high bedstead, with a feather-bed on the top of the spring mattress, in a fine, clean, well-ironed linen nightshirt, smoking a cigarette and considering what he had to do to-day and what had happened yesterday.

Recalling the evening he had spent with the Korchagins, a wealthy and aristocratic family whose daughter every one expected he would marry, he sighed, and, throwing away the end of his cigarette, was going to take another out of the silver case; but, changing his mind, he put down his smooth, white legs, stepped into his slippers, threw his silk dressing-gown over his broad shoulders, and, walking heavily and quickly, passed into his dressing-room, which smelt of eau-de-Cologne and fixatoire. He there carefully cleaned his teeth (many of which were stopped) with tooth-powder, and rinsed his mouth with scented wash.

After that he washed his hands with perfumed soap, cleaning his long nails with particular care, washed his face and stout neck at the marble wash-stand, and went into a third room where his shower-bath stood ready. Having refreshed his plump, white, muscular body and dried it with a rough bath-sheet, he put on his fine under-garments and his boots, and sat down before the glass to brush his black beard and his curly hair, which had begun to get thin above the forehead.

Everything he used, everything belonging to his toilet—his linen, his clothes, boots, necktie, pin, studs—was of the best quality, very quiet, simple, durable, and costly. From among ten different ties and scarf-pins he took the first he happened to lay his hands on. There was a time when all this was new and attractive to him, but now it had become perfectly indifferent.

Nekhlyudov put on his clothes that were brushed and lying ready for him on a chair; and clean and scented, if not quite refreshed, he went into the dining-room. A table, which looked very imposing with its four legs carved in the shape of lions' paws, and a huge sideboard to match, stood in the oblong room, the floor of which had been polished by three men the day before. On the table, which was covered with a fine, starched cloth with a large monogram, stood a silver coffee-pot full of aromatic coffee, a sugar-basin, a jug of hot cream, and a bread-basket filled with fresh rolls, rusks, and biscuits; and beside the plate lay the last number of the *Revue des Deux Mondes*, a newspaper, and several letters.

Nekhlyudov was just about to open his letters, when a stout, middle-aged woman in mourning, a lace cap covering the widening parting of her hair, glided into the room. This was Agrafena Petrovna, formerly lady's maid to Nekhlyudov's mother. Her mistress had died quite recently in this very house, and she remained with the son as his house-keeper. Agrafena Petrovna had at different times spent nearly ten years abroad with Nekhlyudov's mother, and had the appearance and man-ners of a lady. She had lived with the Nekhlyudovs from the time she was a child, and had known Dmitry Ivanich when he was still called Mitinka.

"Good morning, Dmitry Ivanich!"

"Good morning, Agrafena Petrovna! What is it?" Nekhlyudov asked.

"A letter from the Princess—either from the mother or the daughter. The maid brought it some time ago and is waiting in my room," answered Agrafena Petrovna, handing him the letter with a significant smile.

"All right! one second!" said Nekhlyudov, taking the letter and frowning as he noticed Agrafena Petrovna's smile.

That smile meant that the letter was from the younger Princess

Korchagina, whom Agrafena Petrovna expected him to marry. This supposition of hers annoyed Nekhlyudov.

"Then I'll tell her to wait?" and Agrafena Petrovna put away a crumb-brush which was not in its place, and sailed out of the room.

Nekhlyudov opened the perfumed note and began reading it.

The note was written on a sheet of thick grey paper with rough edges; the writing looked English. It said:—

"Having assumed the task of acting as your memory, I take the liberty of reminding you that on this the 28th day of April you have to appear at the Law Courts as juryman, and, in consequence, can on no account accompany us and Kolosov to the picture gallery, as, with your habitual flightiness, you promised yesterday; *à moins que vous ne soyez disposé à payer à la cour d'assises les 300 roubles d'amende que vous vous refusez pour votre cheval,*[1] for not appear-ing in time. I remembered it last night after you were gone, so do not forget.—Princess M. Korchagina."

On the other side was a postscript:—

"*Maman vous fait dire que votre couvert vous attendra jusqu' à la nuit. Venez absolument à quelle heure que cela soit.*—M. K."[2]

Nekhlyudov made a grimace. This note was a continuation of that skilful manœuvring which the Princess Korchagina had already prac-tised for two months in order to enmesh him tighter and tighter with imperceptible threads. But, besides the usual hesitation of men past their youth to marry unless they are very much in love, Nekhlyudov had very good reasons why, even if he did make up his mind to it, he could not propose at once. It was not that ten years previously he had seduced and forsaken Maslova; he had quite forgotten that, and he would not have considered it a reason for not marrying. No! The rea-son was that he had a liaison with a married woman, and though he considered it broken off, she did not.

Nekhlyudov was rather shy with women, and his very shyness awak-ened in this married woman, the unprincipled wife of the *Maréchal de noblesse* of a district where Nekhlyudov was present at an election, the desire to vanquish him. This woman drew him into an intimacy which entangled him more and more while it daily became more distasteful to him. Having succumbed to the temptation Nekhlyudov felt guilty,

---

[1] Unless you feel disposed to pay the Court of Assize a fine of 300 rubles, the price of the horse you denied yourself.

[2] Mamma wants me to tell you that your place will be kept for you till night. You absolutely must come, whatever the time may be.

and had not the courage to break the tie without her consent. And this was why he did not feel at liberty to propose to the young Princess Korchagina even had he wished to.

Among the letters on the table was one from this woman's husband. Seeing his writing and the postmark, Nekhlyudov flushed, and felt his energies awakening, as they always did when he faced any kind of danger.

But his excitement passed at once. The *Maréchal de noblesse* of the district in which his largest estate lay, wrote only to let Nekhlyudov know that there was to be a special meeting towards the end of May, and that Nekhlyudov was to be sure and come to *donner un coup d'épaule*[1] at the important debates concerning the schools and the roads, as strong opposition from the reactionary party was expected.

The *Maréchal* was a Liberal, and with some who shared his views he struggled against the current of reaction that ran strong under Alexander III, and was so absorbed in this struggle that he was quite unaware of his family misfortune.

Nekhlyudov remembered all the dreadful moments he had lived through in connection with this man: he remembered how, one day, he thought that the husband had found him out and was going to challenge him, and how he made up his mind to fire into the air; also the terrible scene he had with the woman when she had run out in despair into the park intending to drown herself, and he had gone to look for her.

"Well, I cannot go now, and can do nothing until I hear from her," thought Nekhlyudov. A week ago he had written her a decisive letter, in which he acknowledged his guilt and his readiness to atone for it, but at the same time pronounced their relations to be at an end, "for her own good," as he expressed it. To this letter he had as yet received no reply. This might be a good sign, for if she did not agree to break off their relations she would have written at once, or even come herself, as she had done before. Nekhlyudov had heard that some officer was paying her marked attention, and although this tormented him by awakening jealousy, at the same time it encouraged him in the hope of escape from the lie that was tormenting him.

The next letter was from his steward. The steward wrote to say that a visit to his estates was necessary that Nekhlyudov might enter into possession, and also, to decide whether, in future, the land was to be managed as it had been when his mother was alive, or whether, as he (the steward) had represented to the late lamented Princess and now

---

[3] Lend a helping hand.

advised the Prince, he had not better increase his stock, and himself
farm all the land now rented by the peasants. The steward wrote that
this would be a far more profitable way of managing the property; at the
same time, he apologised for not having forwarded the three thousand
rubles income due on the 1st. This money would be sent on by the next
post. The reason of the delay was that he could not get the money out
of the peasants, who had grown so untrustworthy that he had to appeal
to the authorities. This letter was partly disagreeable and partly pleasant. It was pleasant to feel that he had power over so large a property,
and yet disagreeable, because Nekhlyudov had been an enthusiastic
admirer of Herbert Spencer. Being himself heir to a large property, he
was specially struck by the position taken up by Spencer in *Social
Statics*, that justice forbids private land-holding, and, with the straight-
forward resoluteness of his age, he had not merely argued that land
could not be looked upon as private property, and written essays on that
subject at the university, but had acted up to his convictions: considering it wrong to hold landed property, he had given to the peasants the
500 acres he had inherited from his father. Inheriting his mother's large
estates, and thus becoming a landed proprietor, he had to choose one
of two things: either to give up his property as he had given up his
father's land some ten years before, or silently to confess that his former
ideas were mistaken and false.

He could not choose the former, because he had no means but the
landed estates (he did not care to serve in a Government position);
moreover, he had formed luxurious habits which he could not easily
give up. Besides, he had no longer the same inducements; his strong
convictions, the resoluteness of youth, and the ambitious desire to do
something unusual were gone. As to the second course, that of denying
those clear and unanswerable proofs of the injustice of land-holding
which he had drawn from Spencer's *Social Statics*, a brilliant corrobo-
ration of which he had at a later period found in the works of Henry
George—such a course was impossible to him. And this was why the
steward's letter was unpleasant to him.

Chapter IV·

WHEN NEKHLYUDOV had finished his coffee, he went to his study to
look up the summons and see at what hour he was to appear at the
Court, as well as to write his answer to the Princess. Passing through his
studio, where an unfinished picture stood facing the easel, and a few

studies hung on the walls, a feeling of inability to advance in art, a sense of his incapacity, came over him. He had often had this feeling of late, and explained it by his too finely developed æsthetic taste; still, the feeling was a very unpleasant one. Seven years before this he had given up military service, feeling sure that he had a talent for art, and from the height of his artistic standpoint had looked down with some disdain at all other activity. And now it turned out that he had no right to do so, and therefore everything that reminded him of all this was unpleasant. He looked at the luxurious fittings of the studio with a heavy heart, and it was in no cheerful mood that he entered his study, a large, lofty room fitted up with a view to comfort, convenience, and elegant appearance. He found the summons at once in the pigeon-hole labelled "Immediate," of his large writing-table. He had to appear at the Court at eleven o'clock.

Nekhlyudov sat down to write a note in reply to the Princess, thanking her for the invitation, and promising to try to come to dinner. Having written one note, he tore it up, as it seemed too intimate. He wrote another, but it was too cold; he feared it might give offence, so he tore it up too. He pressed the button of an electric bell, and his servant, an elderly, morose-looking man, with whiskers and shaved chin and lip, wearing a grey cotton apron, entered the room.

"Send for an *izvozchik*, please."

"Yes, sir."

"And tell the person from Korchagin's who is waiting, that I am obliged for the invitation and will try to come."

"Yes, sir."

"It is not very polite, but I can't write; no matter, I shall see her to-day," thought Nekhlyudov, and went to get his overcoat.

When he came out of the house, an *izvozchik* he knew with rubber tyres to his trap, was at the door waiting for him. "You had hardly gone away from Prince Korchagin's yesterday," said the man, turning half round, "when I drove up, and the Swiss[1] at the door says, 'Just gone.'" The *izvozchik* knew that Nekhlyudov visited the Korchagins, and had called there on the chance of being engaged by him.

"Even the *izvozchiks* know of my relations with the Korchagins," thought Nekhlyudov, and again the question whether he should not marry Princess Korchagina presented itself to him, and he could not decide it either way, any more than most of the questions that arose in his mind at this time.

In favour of marriage in general, besides the comforts of hearth and

[1] The hall-porter in a Russian house is usually called the "Swiss."

home, was the consideration that it made it possible to live a moral life, and chiefly that a family—children—would, so Nekhlyudov hoped, give an aim to his now empty life. Against marriage in general was the fear, common to bachelors past their first youth, of losing freedom, and an unconscious awe of that mysterious creature, a woman.

In this particular case, in favour of marrying Missy (her name was Mary, but, as is usual among a certain set, a nickname had been given her) was the consideration that she came of good family, and differed in everything—manner of speaking, walking, laughing—from the common people (not by anything exceptional, but by her "good-breeding"—he could find no other word for this quality though he prized it very highly); and besides, she thought more of him than of anybody else and therefore evidently understood him. This understanding of him, that is, the recognition of his superior worth, was a proof to Nekhlyudov of her good sense and correct judgment. Against marrying Missy in particular, was the consideration that, in all likelihood, a girl with still higher qualities could be found, that she was already twenty-seven, and probably he was not her first love. This last idea was painful to him. His pride could not reconcile itself to the thought that she had loved some one else, even in the past. Of course she could not have known that she would meet him, but the thought that she was capable of loving another offended him. So that he had as many reasons against marrying as for it; at any rate, they weighed equally with Nekhlyudov, who laughed at himself and called himself the ass of the fable, undecided which haycock to turn to.

"At any rate, before I get an answer from Mary Vasilyevna [the wife of the *Maréchal*], and finish completely with her, I can do nothing," he said to himself. And the conviction that he might, and even must, delay his decision was comforting. "Well, I shall consider all that later on," he said to himself, as the trap drove silently along the asphalt pavement up to the entrance of the Court.

"Now I must fulfil my public duties conscientiously, as I am always in the habit of doing, and as I consider it right to do. Besides, they are often interesting." And passing the doorkeeper, he entered the hall of the Law Courts.

Chapter V

THE CORRIDORS of the Court were already full of activity. The attendants, out of breath, shuffling their feet along the ground, hurried backwards and forwards with all sorts of messages and papers. Ushers, advocates, and law officers passed hither and thither. Plaintiffs, and the defendants who were not in custody, wandered sadly along by the walls or sat waiting.

"Where is the Law Court?" Nekhlyudov asked an attendant.

"Which? There is the Civil Court and the Criminal Court."

"I am on the jury."

"The Criminal Court, you mean. Here to the right, then to the left—the second door."

Nekhlyudov followed the direction. At the door mentioned two men stood waiting. One of them, a tall, fat merchant, a kind-hearted fellow, had evidently had some refreshments and something to drink, and was in most jovial spirits. The other was a shopman of Jewish extraction. They were talking about the price of wool, when Nekhlyudov came up and asked them if this was the jurymen's room.

"Yes, my dear sir, this is it. One of us? On the jury, are you?" asked the merchant, with a merry wink.

"Ah, well, we shall have a go at the work together," he continued, after Nekhlyudov had answered in the affirmative. "My name is Baklashov, merchant of the Second Guild," he said, putting out his broad, soft, flexible hand: "One has to work! . . . With whom have I the honour?"

Nekhlyudov gave his name and passed into the jurymen's room.

In the room were about ten persons of different sorts. They had only just arrived, and some were sitting, others walking up and down, looking at each other and making each other's acquaintance. There was a retired colonel in uniform; some men in frock-coats, others in morning-coats, and one wore a peasant's dress. Their faces all had a certain look of satisfaction at the prospect of fulfilling a public duty, although many of them had had to leave their businesses, and most of these were complaining of it.

The jurymen talked among themselves about the weather, the early spring, and the prospects of business: some having been introduced, others just guessing who was who. Those who were not acquainted with Nekhlyudov made haste to get introduced, evidently looking upon this as an honour; he taking it as his due, as he always did when among strangers. Had he been asked why he considered himself superior to the majority of people he could not have given an answer; the life he had been living of late was not particularly meritorious. He knew quite well that the fact of his speaking English, French, and German with a good accent, and of his wearing the best linen, clothes, ties, and studs, bought from the most expensive dealers in these goods, could not serve as a reason for claiming superiority. At the same time he did claim superiority, accepted as his due the respect paid him, and was hurt if he did not get it. In the jurymen's room his feelings were hurt by disrespectful treatment. Among the jury there happened to be a man whom he knew, a former tutor of his sister's children, Peter Gerasimovich. Nekhlyudov never knew his surname, and even bragged a bit about this.[1] This man was now a master at a public school. Nekhlyudov could not stand his familiarity, his self-satisfied laughter—his vulgarity, in short.

"Ah, ha! You're also trapped." These were the words, accompanied with boisterous laughter, with which Peter Gerasimovich greeted Nekhlyudov. "So you couldn't wriggle out of it?"

"I never tried to wriggle out of it," replied Nekhlyudov, gloomily, and in a tone of severity.

"Well, that's what I call being public-spirited. But just wait until you get hungry or sleepy; you'll sing to another tune then."

"This son of a priest will be saying 'thou'[2] to me next," thought Nekhlyudov, and walked away with a look of sadness on his face, that might have been natural if he had just heard of the death of all his relations. He came up to a group that had formed round a clean-shaven, tall, dignified man who was recounting something with great animation. This man was talking about the trial going on in the Civil Court as of a case well known to himself, mentioning the judges and a celebrated advocate familiarly. He was saying that it seemed wonderful how the celebrated advocate had managed to give such a clever turn to the affair that an old lady, though she had the right on her side, would have to pay a large sum to her opponent.

"The advocate is a genius," said he.

The listeners heard it all with respectful attention, and several of them tried to put in a word, but the man interrupted them, as if he alone knew all about it.

Though Nekhlyudov had arrived late, he had to wait a long time. One of the members of the Court had not yet come, and everybody was kept waiting.

---

[1] Nekhlyudov liked to show that his acquaintance with the tutor was so slight that he did not even know his surname. It must be borne in mind that in Russian the surname is hardly ever used in addressing people.

[2] In Russian, as in many other languages, "thou" is used among people very familiar with each other, or by superiors to inferiors.

Chapter VI

THE PRESIDENT of the Court had arrived early. He was a tall, stout man, with long grey whiskers. Though married, he led a very loose life, and his wife did the same, so neither stood in the other's way. This morning he had received a note from a Swiss girl who had formerly been a governess in his house, and who was now on her way from South Russia to Petersburg. She wrote that she would wait for him between five and six in the Hotel Italia. This made him wish to begin the sitting and get it through as soon as possible, so as to have time to call before six o'clock on the little red-haired Clara Vasilyevna, with whom he had begun a romance in the country last summer. He went into a private room, latched the door, took a pair of dumb-bells out of a cupboard, moved his arms twenty times upwards, downwards, forwards, and sideways, then, holding the dumb-bells above his head, lightly bent his knees three times.

"Nothing keeps one going like a cold bath and exercise," he said, feeling the biceps of his right arm with his left hand, on the third finger of which he wore a gold ring. He had still to do the *moulinée* movement (for he always went through those two exercises before a long sitting), when there was a pull at the door. The president quickly put away the dumb-bells and opened the door, saying, "I am sorry to have kept you waiting."

One of the members of the Court, a high-shouldered, discontented-looking man with gold spectacles, came into the room.

"Matthew Nikitich has again not come," he said in a dissatisfied tone.

"Not yet?" said the president, putting on his uniform. "He is always late."

"I can't think how he's not ashamed of himself," said the member angrily, sitting down and taking out a cigarette.

This member, a very precise man, had had an unpleasant encounter with his wife that morning. She had spent her allowance before the end of the month and had asked him for some money in advance; but he would not give way to her, and so they had quarrelled. The wife told him that if he was going to behave like that, he need not expect any dinner; there would be no dinner for him at home. At this point he had left, fearing that she might carry out her threat, for she was capable of anything. "This comes of living a good moral life," he thought, looking at the beaming, healthy, cheerful and kindly president, who, with elbows far apart, was with his fine white hands smoothing his thick grey whiskers over the embroidered collar of his uniform. "He is always contented and merry, whereas I am suffering."

The secretary came in with some document or other.

"Thanks very much," said the president, lighting a cigarette. "Which case shall we take first?"

"The poisoning case, I should say," answered the secretary indifferently.

"All right; the poisoning case let it be," said the president, thinking that he could get this case over by four o'clock and then get away. "And Matthew Nikitich; has he come?"

"Not yet."

"And Brevé?"

"He is here," replied the secretary.

"Then, if you see him, please tell him we begin with the poisoning case."

Brevé was the public prosecutor who had this case in hand.

In the corridor the secretary met Brevé, who, with uplifted shoulders, a portfolio under one arm, the other swinging with the palm turned to the front, was hurrying along the corridor clattering his heels.

"Michael Petrovich wants to know if you are ready?" the secretary asked.

"Of course; I am always ready," said the public prosecutor. "What are we taking first?"

"The poisoning case."

"That will be all right," said the public prosecutor, but did not think it all right. He had spent the night at an hotel, playing cards with a friend who was giving a fare-well party. Up to five in the morning they played and drank, so he had had no time to look at this poisoning case and meant to run through it now. The secretary, happening to know this, advised the president to begin with the poisoning case. The secretary was liberal, even radical, in opinion. Brevé was a Conservative, particularly devoted to Orthodoxy; and the secretary disliked him, and envied him his position.

"Well, and how about the Skoptsy?"[1] asked the secretary.

"I have already said that I cannot do it without witnesses, and so I shall say to the Court."

"Dear me, what does it matter?"

"I cannot do it," said Brevé, waving his hand emphatically; and he ran into his private room.

He was putting off the case of the Skoptsy on account of the absence

---

[1] A religious sect.

of a very unimportant witness, his real reason being that if they were tried by an educated jury they might possibly be acquitted. So by agreement with the president this case was to be tried at the coming session in a provincial town, where there would be more peasants, and therefore more chances of conviction.

The commotion in the corridor increased. The people crowded most at the doors of the Civil Court, in which the case that the dignified man talked about was being heard.

An interval in the proceeding occurred, and from the Court emerged the old woman whose property that genius of an advocate had found means of getting for his client, a person versed in law, who had no right to it whatever. The judges knew all about the case, and the advocate and his client knew it better still, but the move they had invented was such that the old woman's property had inevitably to be taken from her and handed over to the person versed in law.

The old woman was stout, well dressed, and had enormous flowers on her bonnet. She stopped as she came out of the door, and spreading out her short fat arms and turning to her advocate she kept repeating: "What does it all mean? The idea!"

The advocate was looking at the flowers in her bonnet, evidently not listening to her but considering some other question.

Following the old woman out of the door of the Civil Court, his broad, starched shirt-front glistening from under his low-cut waistcoat, came the celebrated advocate who had managed to arrange matters so that the old woman with the flowers lost all she had, and the person versed in the law, who paid him ten thousand, received more than one hundred thousand rubles. He walked quickly and his face was beaming with contentment and self-satisfaction, and, feeling all eyes directed towards him, his whole bearing seemed to say: "No expressions of deference are necessary."

Chapter VII

AT LAST Matthew Nikitich also arrived, and the usher, a thin man, with a long neck and a kind of sideways walk, his lower lip obtruding to one side, came into the jurymen's room. This usher was an honest man and had had a university education, but could not keep a place for any length of time, being subject to fits of drunkenness. Three months before, a certain Countess who patronised his wife had secured him this place, and he was very pleased to have kept it so long.

"Well, sirs, is everybody here?" he asked, putting his pince-nez on his nose and looking round.

"Everybody, I think," said the jolly merchant.

"All right; we'll soon see." And taking a list from his pocket he began calling out the names, looking at the men, sometimes through and sometimes over his pince-nez.

"Councillor of State[1] I. M. Nikiforov!"

"I am he," said the dignified-looking man, well versed in the ways of the Law Court.

"Ivan Semenich Ivanov, retired Colonel!"

"Here!" replied a thin man, in the uniform of a retired officer.

"Merchant of the Second Guild, Peter Baklashov!"

"Here we are, ready!" said the good-humoured merchant, with a broad smile.

"Lieutenant of the Guards, Prince Dmitry Nekhlyudov!"

"I am he," answered Nekhlyudov.

Looking over his pince-nez, the usher bowed to him politely and pleasantly, as if wishing to distinguish him from the others.

"Captain Uri Dmitrich Danchenko; Gregory Efimich Kuleshov, merchant," etc., etc. All but two were present.

"Now, please to come to the Court, gentlemen," said the usher, pointing to the door with an amiable wave of his hand.

All moved towards the door, pausing to let each other pass. Then they went through the corridor into the Court.

The Court was a large, long room. At one end, with three steps leading up to it, was a raised platform, on which stood a table covered with a green cloth trimmed with fringe of a darker shade. At the table were placed three arm-chairs with very high, caved oak backs; and on the wall behind these hung a full-length, brightly-coloured portrait of the Emperor in uniform and sash, with one foot advanced, and holding a sword. In the right corner hung a case with an icon of Christ crowned with thorns, while beneath it stood a lectern, and, on the same side, the public prosecutor's desk. On the left, opposite the desk, was the secretary's table; and beyond, nearer the public, an oak railing, with the prisoner's bench, as yet unoccupied, behind it. Besides all this, on the right side of the platform there were high-backed chairs for the jury, and on the floor below, tables for the advocates. All this was in the front part of the Court, divided from the back by a railing.

The back was all taken up by seats in tiers. Sitting on the front seats

---

[1] Dignities such as this are common in Russia and mean little.

were four women—either servants or factory girls—and two working men, all evidently overawed by the grandeur of the room and not venturing to speak above a whisper.

Soon after the jury had entered, the usher came in with his sideward gait, and, stepping to the front, called out in a loud voice, as if he meant to frighten those present:—

"The Court is coming!"

Every one got up, and the members of the Court stepped on to the platform. First came the president, with his muscles and fine whiskers. Next came the gloomy member of the Court, now more gloomy than ever, having met his brother-in-law, who informed him that he had just called in to see his sister (the member's wife), and that she had told him there would be no dinner there that day.

"So that evidently we shall have to call in at a cookshop," the brother-in-law added, laughing.

"It is not a laughing matter," said the gloomy member, and became gloomier still.

Then, last of all, came the third member of the Court, that same Matthew Nikitich who was always late. He was a bearded man, with large, round, kindly eyes. He suffered from a catarrh of the stomach, and by his doctor's advice had this morning begun a new treatment, which had kept him at home longer than usual. Now, as he was ascending the platform, he wore a meditative air, resulting from a habit he had of deciding, by different curious means, all sorts of self-put questions. Just now he had asked himself whether the new treatment would be beneficial, and had decided it would cure his catarrh if the number of steps from the door to his chair would divide by three. He made twenty-six steps, but managed to get in a twenty-seventh just by his chair.

The figures of the president and the members, in their uniform with gold-embroidered collars, looked very imposing. They seemed to feel this themselves, and, as if overpowered by their own grandeur, they hurriedly sat down on the high-backed chairs behind the table with the green cloth, on which were a triangular article with an eagle on the top, two glass vases—something like those in which sweetmeats are kept in refreshment-rooms—an inkstand, pens, clean paper, and newly-cut pencils of different kinds.

The public prosecutor came in with the judges. With his portfolio under one arm and swinging the other, he hurriedly walked to his seat near the window and was instantly absorbed in reading and looking through the papers, not wasting a single moment, in hope of being ready when the business commenced. He had been public prosecutor but a short time, and had prosecuted only four times before this. He was very ambitious and had firmly made up his mind to make a career, and therefore thought it necessary to secure a conviction whenever he prosecuted. He knew the general outline of the poisoning case, and had already formed the plan of his speech, but he still wanted a few facts, and these he began hastily noting down.

The secretary sat on the opposite side of the platform, and, having got ready all the papers he might want, was looking through a newspaper article prohibited by the censor which he had procured and read the day before. He was anxious to have a talk about this article with the bearded member, who shared his views, but he wanted to look through it once more first.

Chapter VIII

THE PRESIDENT, having looked through some papers and put a few questions to the usher and the secretary and received affirmative replies, gave the order for the prisoners to be brought in.

The door behind the railing was instantly opened and two gendarmes, with caps on their heads and holding naked swords in their hands, came in, followed by the prisoners: a red-haired, freckled man and two women. The man wore a prison cloak which was too long and too wide for him. He stuck out his thumbs and held his arms close to his sides, thus keeping the sleeves, which were also too long, from slipping over his hands. Without looking at the judges he gazed steadfastly at the bench, and, passing to the other end of it, sat down carefully at the very edge, leaving plenty of room for the others. He fixed his eyes on the president, and began moving the muscles of his cheeks as if whispering something. The woman who came next was also dressed in a prison cloak, and had a prison kerchief round her head. She was elderly, her face was sallow, with no eyebrows or lashes, and with red eyes. She appeared perfectly calm. Having caught her cloak against something, she detached it carefully, without any haste, and sat down.

The third prisoner was Maslova.

As soon as she appeared, the eyes of all the men in the Court turned her way, and remained fixed on her white face, her sparklingly brilliant black eyes, and the swelling bosom under the prison cloak. Even the gendarme whom she passed on her way to her seat looked at her fixedly until she sat down, and then, as if feeling guilty, hurriedly turned away, shook himself, and began staring at the window in front of him.

The president paused until the prisoners had taken their seats, and when Maslova was seated turned to the secretary.

Then the usual procedure commenced: the counting of the jury, remarks about those who had not come, the fixing of the fines to be exacted from them, the decisions concerning those who claimed exemption, and the appointing of reserve jurymen.

Having folded up some bits of paper and put them in one of the glass vases, the president turned up the gold-embroidered cuffs of his uniform a little way, baring his hairy wrists, and began, with the gesture of a conjurer, drawing the lots one by one and opening them. Then, having pulled down his cuffs, the president requested the priest to swear in the jury.

The old priest, with his puffy yellow-pale face, his brown gown, his gold cross, and little medal, laboriously moving his stiff legs beneath his cassock, came up to the lectern beneath the icon. The jurymen got up and crowded towards the lectern.

"Come up, please," said the priest, pulling at the cross on his breast with his plump hand, and waiting until all the jury had drawn near.

This priest had been in office for forty-six years, and was preparing to keep his jubilee in three years' time, in the same manner as the archdeacon had kept his a short time before. He had served in the Criminal Court ever since it was opened, and was very proud of having sworn in some scores of thousands of men, and, in spite of his venerable age, of still continuing to labour for the welfare of the Church, of the Fatherland, and of his family, to whom he expected to leave, besides his house, thirty thousand rubles in interest-bearing papers. The fact that the business of hearing men swear on the Gospels, in which all oaths are distinctly forbidden, is a bad occupation, never occurred to him. It did not at all trouble him; on the contrary, he liked this familiar occupation of his, through which he often got to know nice people. It was not without some pleasure that he had now made the acquaintance of the celebrated advocate, who inspired him with great respect by having received ten thousand rubles for that one case against the old lady with the enormous flowers on her bonnet.

When they had all ascended the steps of the platform, the priest passed his bald grey head sideways through the greasy opening of the stole, and having rearranged his thin hair he again turned to the jury. "Now raise your right arms in this way and put your fingers together thus," he said in his tremulous old voice, lifting his fat dimpled hand, and putting the thumb and two first fingers together as if taking a pinch of something. "Now, repeat after me, 'I promise and swear by Almighty God, by His holy gospels, and by the life-giving cross of our Lord, that in this work which,'" he said, pausing after each phrase—"Don't let your arm down; hold it like this," he remarked to a young man who had lowered his arm—"'that in this work which . . .'"

The dignified man with the whiskers, the Colonel, the merchant, and several others, held their arms and fingers as the priest required of them, very high, very exactly, as if they liked doing it; others did it unwillingly and carelessly. Some repeated the words too loudly, and with a defiant tone, as if they meant to say, "In spite of all, I must and will speak out!" Others whispered very low and not fast enough, and then, as if frightened, hurried to catch up with the priest. Some kept their fingers tightly together, as if fearing to drop the pinch of invisible something they held; others kept separating and closing theirs. Every one save the old priest felt awkward; but he was sure he was fulfilling a very useful and important duty.

After the swearing-in, the president requested the jury to choose a foreman, and the jury, thronging to the door, passed out into the debating-room, where almost all of them at once began to smoke cigarettes. Some one proposed the dignified man as foreman, and he was unanimously accepted. Then the jurymen put out their cigarettes and threw them away, and returned to the Court. The dignified man informed the president that he was chosen foreman, and all sat down again on the high-backed chairs.

Everything went smoothly, quickly, and not without a certain solemnity. And this exactitude, order, and solemnity evidently pleased those who took part in it; it strengthened the impression that they were fulfilling a serious and valuable public duty. Nekhlyudov, too, felt this.

As soon as the jurymen were seated, the president made a speech on their rights, obligations, and responsibilities. While speaking he kept changing his position: now leaning on his right, now on his left hand, now against the back, then on the arms of his chair, now putting the papers straight, now handling his pencil, now the paperknife.

He told them that they had the right to interrogate the prisoners through the president, to use paper and pencils, and to examine the articles put in as evidence. Their duty was to judge not falsely but justly. Their responsibility meant that if the secrecy of their discussion were violated or communications were established with outsiders they would be liable to be punished. Every one listened with an expression of respectful attention. The merchant, diffusing a smell of brandy around him and restraining loud hiccoughs, approvingly nodded his head at every sentence.

Chapter IX

WHEN HE had finished his speech the president turned to the prisoners. "Simon Kartinkin, rise."

Simon jumped up, his lips moving more rapidly.

"Your name?"

"Simon Petrov Kartinkin," he said rapidly, with a cracked voice, having evidently prepared the answer.

"What class do you belong to?"

"Peasant."

"What government, district, and parish?"

"Tula government, Krapivensky district, Kupyansky parish, the village Borki."

"Your age?"

"Thirty-three; born in the year one thousand eight——"

"What religion?"

"Of the Russian religion, Orthodox."

"Married?"

"Oh no, sir."

"Your occupation?"

"I had a place in the Hotel Mauritania."

"Have you ever been tried before?"

"I never got tried before, because, as we used to live formerly——"

"So you never were tried before?"

"God forbid! never."

"Have you received a copy of the indictment?"

"I have."

"Sit down."

"Euphemia Ivanovna Bochkova," said the president, turning to the next prisoner.

But Simon continued standing in front of Bochkova.

"Kartinkin, sit down!"

Kartinkin continued standing.

"Kartinkin, sit down!"

But Kartinkin sat down only when the usher, with his head on one side and with preternaturally wide-open eyes, ran up and said in a tragic whisper, "Sit down, sit down!" He then sat down as hurriedly as he had risen, wrapped his cloak around him, and again began silently moving his lips.

"Your name?" asked the president, with a weary sigh, without looking at the prisoner, but glancing over a paper that lay before him. The president was so used to his task that in order to get through it all quicker he did two things at a time.

Bochkova was forty-three years old and came from the town of Kolomna. She, too, had been in service at the Hotel Mauritania.

"I have never been tried before, and have received a copy of the indictment." She gave her answers boldly, in a tone of voice as if she meant to add to each answer, "Yes, Euphemia Bochkova, and have received the indictment, and don't care who knows it, and won't stand any nonsense."

She did not wait to be told, but sat down as soon as she had replied to the last question.

"Your name?" said the woman-loving president, turning with special politeness to the third prisoner. "You will have to rise," he added, softly and gently, seeing that Maslova kept her seat.

Maslova got up quickly, and, with her chest expanded, stood looking at the president with a peculiar expression of readiness in her smiling black eyes.

"What is your name?"

"Lubov,"[1] she said quickly.

Nekhlyudov had put on his pince-nez, looking at the prisoners while they were being questioned. "No, it is impossible," he thought, not taking his eyes off the prisoner. "Lubov! How can it be?" he thought to himself, after hearing her answer.

The president was going to continue his questions, but the member with the spectacles interrupted, angrily whispering something. The president nodded, and turned again to the prisoner.

"How is this?" he said; "you are not put down here as Lubov."

The prisoner remained silent.

"I want your real name."

"What is your baptismal name?" asked the angry member.

"Formerly I used to be called Katerina."

"No, it cannot be," said Nekhlyudov to himself; and yet he was now certain that this was she, that same girl, half ward, half servant, with whom he had once been in love, really in love, and whom he had seduced in a moment of delirious passion, and then abandoned and never again brought to mind—because the memory would have been too painful, would have convicted him too clearly, proving that he who was so proud of his integrity had treated this woman in a revolting, scandalous way.

Yes, this was she. He now clearly saw in her face that strange, indescribable individuality which distinguishes every face from all others; something peculiar, all its own, not to be found anywhere else. In spite of the unhealthy pallor and the fullness of the face, it was there, this sweet peculiar individuality; on those lips, in the slight squint of her eyes, in the voice, particularly in the naïve smile and the expression of readiness on the face and figure.

---

[1] ["Love" in Russian.]

"You should have said so," remarked the president, again in a gentle tone. "Your patronymic?"

"I am illegitimate."

"Well, were you not called by your god-father's name?"

"Yes, Mikhaylovna."

"And what is it she can be guilty of?" continued Nekhlyudov in his mind, unable to breathe freely.

"Your family name—your surname, I mean," the president went on.

"They used to call me by my mother's surname, Maslova."

"What class?"

Meshchanka."[2]

"Religion—Orthodox?"

"Orthodox."

"Occupation? What was your occupation?"

Maslova remained silent.

"What was your employment?"

"I was in an establishment."

"What sort of an establishment?" asked the spectacled member severely.

"You know yourself," she said, and smiled. Then, casting a hurried look round the room, she again turned her eyes on the president.

There was something so unusual in the expression of her face, so terrible and piteous in the meaning of the words she had uttered, in this smile, and in the furtive glance she had cast round the room, that the president was abashed, and for a moment there was absolute silence in the Court. The silence was broken by some one among the public laughing, then some one said "Ssh!" and the president looked up and continued:—

"Have you ever been tried before?"

"Never," answered Maslova softly, and sighed.

"Have you received a copy of the indictment?"

"I have," she answered.

"Sit down."

The prisoner leant back to pick up her skirt in the way a fine lady picks up her train, and sat down, folding her small white hands in the sleeves of her cloak, her eyes still fixed on the president.

The witnesses were called, and some sent away; the doctor who was to act as expert was chosen and called into the Court.

Then the secretary got up and began reading the indictment. He read distinctly (though he pronounced the *l* and *r* alike) with a loud

----

[2] Working-class town-dweller, corresponding in class to a country peasant.

voice, but so quickly that the words ran into one another and formed one uninterrupted dreary drone.

The judges bent now on one, now on the other arm of their chairs, then on the table, then back again, shut and opened their eyes and whispered to each other. One of the gendarmes several times repressed a yawn.

The prisoner Kartinkin never stopped moving his cheeks. Bochkova sat quite still and straight, only now and then scratching her head under the kerchief.

Maslova sat immovable, gazing at the reader; only now and then she gave a slight start as if wishing to reply, blushed, sighed heavily, and changed the position of her hands, looked round, and again fixed her eyes on the reader.

Nekhlyudov sat in the front row on his high-backed chair, without removing his pince-nez, and looked at Maslova, while a complex and fierce struggle went on in his soul.

Chapter X

THE indictment ran as follows:—

"On the 17th of January 188—, the proprietor of the Hotel Mauritania in this town gave notice to the police of the sudden death, which had occurred in his hotel, of Therapont Smelkov, a Second Guild merchant from Siberia.

"The local police doctor of the fourth district certified that death was due to rupture of the heart, caused by the excessive use of alcoholic liquids. The body of the said Smelkov was interred. On the fourth day after Smelkov's death his fellow-townsman and companion, the Siberian merchant Timokhin, returned from Petersburg, and when he heard of the death of his companion, the said Smelkov, and the circumstances that attended it, notified his suspicion that Smelkov's death was not due to natural causes, but that he had been poisoned by the undermentioned persons, who had stolen the property, some money and a diamond ring, that had been in Smelkov's possession but were not found when an inventory of the property of the deceased was made. In consequence of which an inquiry was instituted, and the following facts brought to light:—

"1. That the said Smelkov must have had in his possession three thousand eight hundred rubles which he had received from the bank; that this was known to the proprietor of the Hotel Mauritania, and also to the clerk of the merchant Starikov, with whom the said Smelkov had had some business transactions on his arrival in the town, but in the port-manteau which had been sealed after Smelkov's death, and in his purse, only three hundred and twelve rubles and sixteen kopeyks were found.

"2. That the said Smelkov spent the whole day and night preceding his death with the prostitute Lubka, who came twice to his room in the hotel.

"3. That a diamond ring belonging to the said Smelkov was sold by this prostitute to her mistress.

"4. That the chambermaid, Euphemia Bochkova, deposited one thousand eight hundred rubles on current account at the bank on the day following Smelkov's death.

"5. That according to the deposition of the prostitute Lubka, the hotel servant, Simon Kartinkin, gave the prostitute Lubka some powder, advising her to give it to the merchant Smelkov dissolved in brandy, which the prostitute Lubka did, according to her own confession.

"When cross-examined, the accused prostitute, nicknamed Lubka, stated that while the merchant Smelkov was in the brothel where she 'works,' as she expresses it, she was actually sent by the merchant to the Hotel Mauritania to get him some money, and that, having unlocked the portmanteau with a key given her by the merchant, she took out forty rubles, as she was told to do, but had taken nothing more; that Bochkova and Kartinkin, in whose presence she unlocked and locked the portmanteau, could testify to the truth of the statement.

"She further gave evidence that when she came to the lodging-house for the second time, she did, at the instigation of Simon Kartinkin, give Smelkov some kind of powder, which she thought was an opiate, in a glass of brandy, hoping he would fall asleep and that she would be able to get away from him; but that she had taken no money, and that Smelkov, having beaten her, himself gave her the ring when she cried and threatened to go away.

"When cross-examined, the accused Euphemia Bochkova stated that she knew nothing about the missing money, that she had not even gone into Smelkov's room, but that Lubka had been busy there all by herself; that if anything had been stolen, it must have been by Lubka when she came with the merchant's key to get his money."

At this point Maslova gave a start, opened her mouth and looked at Bochkova.

"When," continued the secretary, "the receipt for one thousand eight hundred rubles from the bank was shown to Bochkova, and she was asked where she obtained such a sum, she said that it was her own earn-ings for eighteen years, and those of Simon, whom she was going to marry.

"The accused, Simon Kartinkin, when first examined, confessed that he and Bochkova, at the instigation of Maslova, who had come with the key from the brothel, had stolen the money, and divided it equally among themselves and Maslova. He also confessed that he had supplied the powder in order to get Smelkov to sleep. When examined the second time, he denied having had anything to do either with the stealing of the money or giving Maslova the powder, accusing her of having done it alone. Concerning the money placed in the bank by Bochkova, he said the same as she—that is, that the money was given to them both by the lodgers in tips during eighteen years' service.

"It was found necessary for the elucidation of the circumstances to examine the body of the merchant Smelkov, and an order was given for the exhumation of the corpse, and for an examination of the contents of the bowels, and of the changes that had taken place in the organism. The examination of the bowels showed that Smelkov's death was actually due to poison."

Then followed an account of the examination of the prisoners when they were confronted, and the depositions of the witnesses. The indictment concluded:—

"The Second Guild merchant Smelkov was addicted to drunkenness and debauchery. He entered into relations with the prostitute nicknamed Lubka in the house of Kitaeva, and, having taken a particular fancy to her, he sent the said Lubka, on the 17th of January 188—, when he was in Kitaeva's brothel, with the key of his portmanteau, to the room he occupied, to fetch money, to the amount of forty rubles, which he required to pay for refreshments he was ordering. When, having arrived at the Hotel Mauritania, Maslova was getting the money in his room, she agreed with Bochkova and Kartinkin to steal all Smelkov's money and valuables, and to divide the same among themselves. This they did."

Here Maslova gave another start, and even rose, blushing scarlet.

"Maslova received for her share a diamond ring," continued the secretary, "and probably a small sum of money, which she either hid or lost, being that night in an intoxicated condition. In order to conceal their crime, the accomplices decided to entice the merchant Smelkov back to his lodgings, and there to poison him with arsenic, which Kartinkin had in his possession; with this object in view, Maslova returned to the house of Kitaeva, and there persuaded Smelkov to go back with her to the Hotel Mauritania. When Smelkov returned to the hotel, Maslova, having received the powder which Kartinkin supplied, dissolved it in brandy, and gave the brandy to Smelkov to drink, which caused Smelkov's death.

"In consequence of the aforesaid, the peasant of the village Borki, Simon Kartinkin, thirty-three years of age; the *meshchanka* Euphemia Bochkova, forty-three years of age; and the *meshchanka* Katerina Maslova, twenty-eight years of age, are charged with having, on the 17th of January 188—, jointly stolen from the said merchant, Smelkov, money to the value of two thousand six hundred rubles, and of having given the said merchant, Smelkov, poison to drink, with intent to deprive him of life, in order to conceal their crime, and of having thereby caused his death.

"This crime is provided for in Article 1455 of the Penal Code. Therefore, in accordance with Article so and so of the Criminal Proceedings the peasant Simon Kartinkin, the *meshchanka* Euphemia Bochkova, and the *meshchanka* Katerina Maslova stand committed for trial by jury at the District Court."

Thus the secretary concluded the long act of indictment, and having folded the papers he sat down in his place, smoothing his long hair with his hands. All sighed with relief at the thought that now the investigation would commence, and that all would soon be cleared up and justice be satisfied. Nekhlyudov alone did not share these feelings; he was entirely absorbed by horror at the thought of what this Maslova, whom he had known as an innocent and charming girl ten years ago, could have done.

Chapter XI

WHEN the reading of the indictment was over, the president, after consulting with the members, turned to Kartinkin with an expression that plainly said: "Now we shall find out the whole truth down to the minutest detail."

"Peasant Simon Kartinkin," he said, stooping to the left.

Simon Kartinkin got up, stretched his arms down his sides, and leaning forward with his whole body, continued moving his cheeks without speaking.

"You are charged with having, on the 17th day of January 188—, together with Euphemia Bochkova and Katerina Maslova, stolen money from a portmanteau belonging to the merchant Smelkov, and then, having procured some arsenic, persuaded Katerina Maslova to give it to the merchant Smelkov in a glass of brandy, thus causing Smelkov's death. Do you plead guilty?" said the president, stooping to the right.

"Not nohow, because our business is to attend on the guests, and——"

"You may say all that later on. Do you plead guilty?"

"Oh no, sir. I only——"

"You'll tell us that afterwards. Do you plead guilty?" asked the president quietly and firmly.

"Can't do such a thing, because that——"

The usher again rushed up to Simon Kartinkin and stopped him in a tragic whisper.

The president moved the hand in which he held the paper and placed the elbow in a different position, and with an air that said: "This is finished," turned to Euphemia Bochkova.

"Euphemia Bochkova, you are charged with having, on the 17th of January 188—, in the Hotel Mauritania, together with Simon Kartinkin and Katerina Maslova, stolen some money and a ring from the merchant Smelkov's portmanteau, and, having shared the money among yourselves, of giving poison to the merchant Smelkov, thereby causing his death. Do you plead guilty?"

"I am not guilty of anything," boldly and firmly replied the prisoner. "I never went near the room, but when this baggage went in she did the whole business."

"You will say all that afterwards," the president again said, quietly and firmly. "So you do not plead guilty?"

"I did not take the money nor give the drink, nor go into the room. Had I gone in I should have kicked her out."

"So you do not plead guilty?"

"Never."

"Very well."

"Katerina Maslova," the president began, turning to the third prisoner, "the charge against you is that, having come from the brothel with the key of the merchant Smelkov's portmanteau, you stole from his portmanteau some money and a ring." He said all this like a lesson learnt by heart, leaning to the member on his left, who was whispering into his ear that a jar mentioned in the list of the material evidence was missing. "Stole out of his portmanteau some money and a ring," he repeated, "and shared it. Then, returning to the Hotel Mauritania with Smelkov, you gave him poison in his drink, and thereby caused his death. Do you plead guilty?"

"I am not guilty of anything," she began rapidly. "As I said before I say again, I did not take it—I did not take it—I did not take anything, and the ring he gave me himself."

"You do not plead guilty to having stolen two thousand six hundred rubles?" asked the president.

"I've said I took nothing but the forty rubles."

"Well, and do you plead guilty of having given the merchant Smelkov a powder in his drink?"

"Yes, that I did. Only, I believed what they told me, that it was a sleeping-powder, and that no harm could come of it. I never thought, and never wished. . . . God is my witness, I never meant this," she said.

"So you do not plead guilty of having stolen the money and the ring from the merchant Smelkov, but confess that you gave him the powder?" said the president.

"Well, yes, I do confess that; but I thought it was a sleeping-powder. I only gave it to make him sleep; I never meant and never thought of worse."

"Very well," said the president, evidently satisfied with the results attained. "Now tell us how it all happened," and he leant back in his chair and put his folded hands on the table. "Tell us all about it. A free and full confession will be to your advantage."

Maslova continued to look straight at the president in silence.

"Tell us how it happened."

"How it happened!" Maslova suddenly began rapidly. "I came to the hotel and was shown into the room. He was there, already very drunk." She pronounced the word "he" with a look of horror in her wide-open eyes. "I wished to go away, but he would not let me." She stopped, as if she had lost the thread or remembered something else.

"Well, and then?"

"Well, what then? I remained a bit, and went home again."

At this point the public prosecutor raised himself a little, leaning on one elbow in an awkward manner.

"You would like to put a question?" asked the president; and having received an answer in the affirmative he made a gesture inviting the public prosecutor to speak.

"I want to ask: Was the prisoner previously acquainted with Simon Kartinkin?" said the public prosecutor, without looking at Maslova, and having put the question he compressed his lips and frowned.

The president repeated the question. Maslova stared at the public prosecutor with a frightened look.

"With Simon? Yes," she said.

"I should like to know what the prisoner's acquaintance with Kartinkin consisted in. Did they meet often?"

"Consisted in? . . . He invited me for the guests; it was not an acquaintance at all," answered Maslova, anxiously moving her eyes from the president to the public prosecutor and back to the president.

"I should like to know why Kartinkin invited only Maslova for the guests, and none of the other girls?" said the public prosecutor, with half-closed eyes and a cunning, Mephistophelian smile.

"I don't know. How should I know?" said Maslova, casting a fright-ened look round, and fixing her eyes on Nekhlyudov. "He asked whom he liked."

"Is it possible that she has recognised me?" thought Nekhlyudov, and the blood rushed to his face. But Maslova turned away without distin-guishing him from the others, and again fixed her eyes anxiously on the public prosecutor.

"So the prisoner denies having had any intimate relations with Kartinkin? Very well, I have no more questions to ask."

And the public prosecutor took his elbow off the desk and began writing something. In reality he did not write at all, but only traced over with his pen the words of his notes: having seen *procureurs* and advo-cates, after putting a clever question, enter a remark into their notes which should subsequently confound their adversary.

The president did not address the prisoner at once, because he was asking the member with the spectacles whether he agreed that the questions (which had all been prepared beforehand and written out) should be put.

"Well! What happened next?" he went on.

"I came home," said Maslova, looking a little more boldly, but only at the president, "gave the money to the mistress, and went to bed. Hardly had I fallen asleep when one of our girls, Bertha, woke me. 'Go, your merchant has come again!' I did not wish to go, but Madame ordered me to. He"—she again uttered the word "he" with evident horror—"he kept treating our girls, and then wanted to send for more wine, but his money was all gone, and Madame would not trust him, and he sent me to his lodgings and told me where the money was and how much to take. So I went."

The president was whispering to the member on his left, but in order to appear as if he had heard he repeated her last words.

"So you went. Well, what next?"

"I went, and did all he told me; went into his room. I did not go alone, but called Simon Kartinkin and her," she said, pointing to Bochkova.

"That's a lie: I never went in," Bochkova began, but was stopped.

"In their presence I took out four notes," continued Maslova, frown-ing, without looking at Bochkova.

"Yes, but did the prisoner notice," again asked the prosecutor, "how much money there was when she was getting out the forty rubles?"

Maslova shuddered when the prosecutor addressed her; she did not know why it was, but she felt he wished her evil.

"I did not count it, but only saw some one-hundred-ruble notes!"

"Ah! The prisoner saw one-hundred-ruble notes. That's all."

"Well, so you brought back the money," continued the president, looking at the clock.

"I did."

"Well, and then?"

"Then he took me back with him," said Maslova.

"Well, and how did you give him the powder? In his drink?"

"How did I give it? I put it in and gave it him."

"Why did you give it him?"

She did not answer at once, but sighed deeply and heavily. "He would not let me go," she said, after a moment's silence, "and I was quite tired out, and so I went out into the passage and said to Simon: 'If he would only let me go, I am so tired.' And he said: 'We are also sick of him; we were thinking of giving him a sleeping draught; he will fall asleep, and then you can go.' So I said, 'All right.' I thought it was harmless, and he gave me the packet. I went in. He was lying behind the partition, and at once called for brandy. I took a bottle of liqueur brandy from the table, poured out two glasses, one for him and one for myself, and put the powder into his glass and gave it him. Had I known, how could I have given it to him?"

"Well, and how did the ring come into your possession?" asked the president.

"He himself gave it to me."

"When did he give it you?"

"That was when we came back to his lodgings. I wanted to go away, and he gave me a knock on the head and broke my comb. I got angry and said I'd go away, and he took the ring off his finger and gave it to me so that I should not go," she said.

Then the public prosecutor again slightly raised himself, and, putting on an air of simplicity, asked for permission to put a few questions. Having received it, he said, bending his head over his embroidered collar: —

"I should like to know how long the prisoner remained in the merchant Smelkov's room."

Maslova again seemed frightened; she again looked anxiously from the public prosecutor to the president, and said hurriedly: —

"I do not remember how long."

"Yes, but does the prisoner remember if she went anywhere else in the lodging-house after she left Smelkov?"

Maslova considered for a moment. "Yes, I did go into an empty room next to his."

"Yes, and why did you go there?" asked the public prosecutor, forgetting himself and addressing her direct.

"I went in to rest a bit, and to wait while an *izvozchik* was called."

"And was Kartinkin in the room with the prisoner, or not?"

"He came in."

"Why did he come in?"

"There was some of the merchant's brandy left, and we finished it together."

"Oh, finished it together! Very well! And did the prisoner talk to Kartinkin, and, if so, what about?"

Maslova suddenly frowned, blushed very red, and said hurriedly:—

"What about? I did not talk about anything, and that's all I know. Do what you like with me; I am not guilty, and that's all."

"I have nothing more to ask," said the prosecutor, and, drawing up his shoulders in an unnatural manner, he began writing among the notes for his speech, that, on the prisoner's own evidence, she had been in the empty room with Kartinkin.

There was a short silence.

"You have nothing more to say?"

"I have told everything," she said with a sigh, and sat down.

Then the president noted down something, and having listened to a whisper from the member on his left he announced a ten minutes' adjournment, rose hurriedly, and left the Court. The communication he had received from the tall bearded member with the kindly eyes was that the member, having felt a slight stomach derangement, wished to do a little massage and take some drops. And this was why the proceedings were interrupted.

When the judges had risen, the advocates, the jury, and the witnesses also rose, and, with the pleasant feeling that part of the business was finished, began moving in different directions.

Nekhlyudov went into the jurymen's room, and sat down by the window.

Chapter XII

"YES, THIS was Katusha!"

The relations between Nekhlyudov and Katusha had been the following:—

When Nekhlyudov first saw Katusha he was a student in his third year at the university, and was preparing an essay on land tenure during the summer vacation, which he passed with his aunts. Up to then he had always spent the summer with his mother and sister on his mother's large estate near Moscow. But that year his sister had married and his mother had gone abroad to a watering-place, and he, having his essay to write, resolved to spend the summer with his aunts. It was very quiet on their secluded estate, and there was nothing to distract his mind; his aunts loved their nephew and heir very tenderly, and he, too, was fond of them and of their simple, old-fashioned life.

During that summer on his aunts' estate, Nekhlyudov passed through that blissful state of his existence when a young man himself, without guidance from any one outside, realises for the first time all the beauty and significance of life and the importance of the task allotted in it to man, and, grasping the possibility of unlimited advance towards perfection for one's self and for all the world, gives himself to his task, not only hopefully but with full conviction of attaining to the perfection he imagines. In that year, while still at the university, he had read Spencer's *Social Statics*, and Spencer's views on landholding especially impressed him, he himself being heir to large estates. His father had not been rich, but his mother had received ten thousand acres of land for her dowry. At that time he fully realised all the cruelty and injustice of private property in land, and being one of those to whom a sacrifice to the demands of conscience gives the highest spiritual enjoyment, he decided that he would not retain property rights, but would let the peasant labourers have the land he had inherited from his father. It was on this land question he was writing his essay.

He arranged his life on his aunts' estate in the following manner. He got up very early—sometimes at three o'clock—and before sunrise went through the morning mists to bathe in the river below the hill. He returned while the dew still lay on the grass and flowers. Sometimes, having finished his coffee, he sat down with his books of reference and his papers to work at his essay; but very often, instead of reading or writing, he left home again and wandered through the fields and woods. Before dinner he lay down and slept somewhere in the garden. At dinner he amused and entertained his aunts with his bright spirits, then rode on horseback, or went for a row on the river, and in the evening sat reading or playing "patience" with his aunts.

Many a night, especially a moonlight night, he could not sleep, simply because he was so filled with emotional joy of life; and instead of sleeping he wandered about the garden with his dreams and thoughts, sometimes till daybreak.

And so, peacefully and happily, he lived through the first month of his stay with his aunts, taking no particular notice of their half-ward, half-servant, the black-eyed, quick-footed Katusha. Then—at the age of nineteen—Nekhlyudov, brought up under his mother's wing, was still quite pure. If a woman figured in his dreams at all it was only as a wife.

All the other women, whom, according to his ideas, he could not marry, were not women for him but human beings.

But on Ascension Day that summer, a neighbour of his aunts' and her family—two young daughters and a schoolboy—together with a young artist of peasant origin who was staying with them, came to spend the day. After tea they all went for a game in the meadow in front of the house, where the grass had already been mown. They played at the game of widow, and Katusha joined them. Running about and changing partners several times, Nekhlyudov caught Katusha and she became his partner. Up to this time he had liked Katusha's looks, but the possibility of any nearer relations with her had never entered his mind.

"Impossible to catch those two unless they should stumble," said the merry young artist, whose turn it was to catch, and who could run very fast with his short, bandy, but strong peasant legs.

"You! . . . and not catch us?" said Katusha.

"One, two, three," and the artist clapped his hands.

Katusha, hardly restraining her laughter, changed places with Nekhlyudov behind the artist's back, and after pressing his large hand with her little rough one, ran to the left, rustling with her starched petticoat. Nekhlyudov ran fast to the right, trying to escape from the artist, but when he looked round he saw the artist running after Katusha, who kept well ahead, her firm young legs moving rapidly. There was a lilac bush in front of them, and Katusha made a sign with her head to Nekhlyudov to join her behind it; for if they once clasped hands again they were safe from their pursuer—that is a rule of the game. He understood the sign and ran behind the bush, but he did not know that there was a small ditch there overgrown with nettles. He stumbled and fell into the nettles already wet with dew, stinging his hands, but rose immediately, laughing at his mishap.

Katusha, her eyes black as sloes and her face radiant with joy, was flying towards him, and they caught hold of each other's hand.

"Got stung, I dare say?" she said, arranging her hair with her free hand, breathing hard and looking straight up at him with a pleasant smile.

"I didn't know there was a ditch here," he answered, smiling also, and keeping her hand in his. She drew nearer to him, and he himself, not knowing how it happened, stooped towards her. She did not move away, and he pressed her hand tight and kissed her on the lips.

"There! you've done it!" she said; and freeing her hand with a swift movement she ran away from him.

Breaking two branches of white lilac from which the blossoms were already falling, she began fanning her burning face with them; then, with her head turned looking back at him, she walked away, swaying her arms briskly in front of her, and joined the other players.

After this there grew up between Nekhlyudov and Katusha those peculiar relations which often exist between a pure young man and girl who are attracted to one another.

When Katusha came into the room, or even when he saw her white apron from afar, everything brightened up in Nekhlyudov's eyes; as when the sun appears everything becomes more interesting, more joyful, more important. The whole of life seemed full of gladness. And she felt the same. But it was not only Katusha's presence that had this effect on Nekhlyudov. The mere thought that Katusha existed (and for her the mere thought that Nekhlyudov existed) had the same effect.

Whether he received an unpleasant letter from his mother, or could not get on with his essay, or felt the unreasoning sadness often experienced by young people, he had only to remember Katusha and that he should see her, and it all vanished.

Katusha had much work to do in the house, but she managed to get a little leisure for reading, and Nekhlyudov gave her Dostoyevsky and Turgenev (whom he had just read himself) to read. She liked Turgenev's A Quiet Nook best. They had talks at moments snatched when meeting in the passage, on the verandah, or in the yard, and occasionally in the room of his aunts' old servant, Matrena Pavlovna, with whom he sometimes used to drink tea, and where Katusha worked. These talks in Matrena Pavlovna's presence were the pleasantest. When they were alone it was worse. Their eyes at once began to say something very different and far more important than what their mouths uttered. Their lips puckered and they felt a kind of dread of something that made them part quickly.

These relations between Nekhlyudov and Katusha continued during the whole of the remainder of his first visit to his aunts. They noticed it and became frightened, and even wrote to Princess Helena Ivanovna, Nekhlyudov's mother. His aunt Mary Ivanovna feared Dmitry would form an illicit intimacy with Katusha; but her fears were groundless, for Nekhlyudov, himself hardly conscious of it, loved Katusha, loved her as the pure love, and therein lay his safety—his and hers. He not only did not feel any desire to possess her physically, but the very thought of it filled him with horror. The fears of the more poetical Sophia Ivanovna, that Dmitry, with his thorough-going, resolute character, having fallen in love with a girl, might make up his mind to marry her without considering either her birth or her station, had more foundation.

Had Nekhlyudov at that time been conscious of his love for Katusha, and especially had he been told that he must on no account join his life with that of a girl in her position, it might easily have happened that with his usual straightforwardness he would have come to the conclusion that there could be no possible reason for him not to marry any girl whatever if only he loved her. But his aunts did not mention their fears to him, and when he went away he was still unconscious of his love for Katusha. He was sure that what he felt for her was only one of the manifestations of the joy of life that filled his whole being, and that this sweet, merry lassie shared this joy with him. Yet when he was going away and Katusha stood with his aunts in the porch, and watched him with her dark, slightly squinting eyes filled with tears, he felt that, after all, he was leaving something beautiful, precious, something which would never recur. And he grew very sad.

"Good-bye, Katusha," he said, looking across Sophia Ivanovna's cap as he was getting into the carriage; "thank you for everything."

"Good-bye, Dmitry Ivanich," she said, with her pleasant, tender voice, keeping back the tears that filled her eyes; and she ran away into the hall, where she could cry in peace.

Chapter XIII

AFTER THAT, Nekhlyudov did not see Katusha for more than two years. When he saw her again he had just been promoted to the rank of officer and was going to join his regiment. On the way he came to spend a few days with his aunts, but he was now a very different young man from him who had spent the summer with them three years before. He had then been an honest, unselfish lad, ready to sacrifice himself for any good cause; now he was a depraved, refined egotist, caring only for his own enjoyment. Then God's world seemed a mystery which he tried enthusiastically and joyfully to solve; now everything in life seemed clear and simple, defined by the conditions of the life he was leading. Then he had felt the importance and necessity of communion with nature, and with those who had lived and thought and felt before him—philosophers and poets. What he now considered necessary and important were human institutions and intercourse with his comrades. Then women seemed mysterious and charming—charming by the very mystery that enveloped them; now the purpose of women, all women except those of his own family and the wives of his friends, was a very definite one: women were the best means towards an already experienced enjoyment. Then money was not needed, for he did not require even one-third of what his mother allowed him, and it was possible to refuse the property inherited from his father and give it to the peasants.

But now his allowance of fifteen hundred rubles a month did not suffice, and he had already had some unpleasant talks about it with his mother.

Then he had looked on his spirit as his *I*; now it was his healthy strong animal *I* that he looked upon as himself.

And all this terrible change had come about because he had ceased to believe himself and had taken to believing others. This he had done because it was too difficult to live believing one's self: believing one's self, one had to decide every question, not in favour of one's animal *I*, which is always seeking for easy gratification, but in almost every case against it. Believing others, there was nothing to decide; everything had been decided already, and always in favour of the animal *I* and against the spiritual. Nor was this all. Believing in his own self, he was always exposing himself to the censure of those around him; believing others, he had their approval. Thus, when Nekhlyudov thought and spoke of the serious matters of life — God, truth, riches, poverty — all around him thought it out of place and even rather ridiculous, and his mother and aunts called him, with kindly sarcasm, *notre cher philosophe*. But when he read novels, told improper anecdotes, went to see funny vaudevilles in French theatre and gaily repeated the jokes, everybody admired and encouraged him. When he considered it right to limit his needs, wearing an old overcoat, taking no wine — everybody thought it odd and considered it posing; but when he spent large sums on hunting, or on furnishing a special and luxurious study for himself, everybody admired his taste and gave him expensive presents to encourage his hobby. While he kept pure and meant to remain so till he married, his friends feared for his health, and even his mother was not grieved but rather pleased when she found out that he had become a "real" man, and had gained over some French woman from his friend. (As to the episode with Katusha, the Princess could not without horror think that he might have come to marry her.) In the same way, when Nekhlyudov came of age and, because he considered the holding of private property in land wrong, gave to the peasants the small estate inherited from his father, this step filled his mother and family with dismay, and served all his relatives as an excuse for making fun of him. He was continually told that these peasants were no richer after having received the land, but, on the contrary, poorer, having started three public-houses and left off doing any work. But when Nekhlyudov entered the Guards and spent and gambled away so much with his aristocratic companions that Helena Ivanovna, his mother, had to draw on her capital, she was hardly pained, considering it quite natural and even good that wild oats should be sown at an early age and in good society, as her son was doing. At first Nekhlyudov struggled: all he had considered good while he had faith in himself was considered bad, and what he had considered evil was looked upon as good, by those among whom he lived, but the struggle grew too hard. And at last Nekhlyudov gave in, that is, he left off believing his own self and began believing others. At first this giving up of faith in himself was unpleasant, but it did not long continue so. At that time he acquired the habits of smoking and drinking, and soon got over this unpleasant feeling and even felt great relief.

Nekhlyudov, with his passionate nature, gave himself unreservedly to the new way of life so approved of by all around him, and he quite stifled the inner voice which demanded something different. This began after he moved to Petersburg, and it reached its climax when he entered the army.

Military life in general depraves men. It places them in conditions of complete idleness, that is, absence of all rational and useful work; frees them from their common human duties, which it replaces by merely conventional duties to the honour of the regiment, the uniform, the flag; and, while giving them on the one hand absolute power over other men, also puts them into conditions of servile obedience to those of higher rank than themselves.

But when, to the general depravity caused by military service, with its honours, uniforms, flags, its permitted violence and murder, there is added the depravity caused by riches and near intercourse with members of the Imperial family (as is the case in the select regiment of the Guards in which all the officers are rich and of good family), then this depravity develops into a perfect mania of selfishness. And this mania of selfishness attacked Nekhlyudov from the moment he entered the army and began living as his companions did. He had no occupation whatever, except, dressed in a uniform splendidly made and well brushed by other people, and with weapons also made and cleaned and handed to him by others, to ride to parade on a fine horse which had been bred, broken in, and fed by others. There, with other men like himself, he had to flourish a sword, to fire off guns, and teach others to do the same. He had no other work, and the highly placed persons, young and old, the Tsar and those near him, not only sanctioned this occupation but praised and thanked him for it.

What was considered good and important besides this, was to eat, and particularly to drink, in officers' clubs and the best restaurants, squandering large sums of money, which came from some invisible source; then theatres, balls, women; then again riding on horseback, flourishing swords and jumping, and again the squandering of money—wine, cards, and women.

This kind of life depraves military men even more than others, because if any other than a military man leads such a life he cannot help being ashamed of it in the depth of his heart. A military man is, on the contrary, proud of a life of this kind, especially in war time, and Nekhlyudov had entered the army just after war with the Turks had been declared. "We are prepared to sacrifice our lives at the war, and therefore a gay, reckless life is not only pardonable, but absolutely necessary for us—and so we lead it."

Such were Nekhlyudov's confused thoughts at this period of his existence, and he felt all the time the delight of being free from the moral restraints he had formerly set himself. And the state he lived in was that of a chronic mania of selfishness.

He was in this state when, after an absence of about three years, he came again to visit his aunts.

Chapter XIV

NEKHLYUDOV WENT to visit his aunts because their estate lay near the road he had to travel in order to join his regiment (which had already gone to the front), because they had very warmly asked him to come, and especially because he wanted to see Katusha. Perhaps in his inmost heart he had already formed those evil designs against Katusha which his now uncontrolled animal self suggested to him; but he was not conscious of this, wishing only to revisit the spot where he had been so happy, to see his rather funny, but dear, kind-hearted old aunts, who always, without his noticing it, surrounded him with an atmosphere of love and admiration, and to see sweet Katusha, of whom he had retained so pleasant a memory.

He arrived at the end of March, on Good Friday, after the thaw had set in. It was pouring with rain, so that he had not a dry thread on him, and he was feeling very cold, but yet vigorous and full of spirits as always at that time. "Is she still with them?" he thought, as he drove into the familiar, old-fashioned courtyard surrounded by a low brick wall, and now filled with snow off the roofs.

He expected she would come out when she heard the sledge bells, but she did not. Two bare-footed women with pails and tucked-up skirts, who had evidently been scrubbing the floors, came out of the side door. She was not at the front door either, and only Tikhon, the man-servant, with his apron on, evidently also busy cleaning, came out into the porch. His aunt Sophia Ivanovna alone met him in the anteroom; she was wearing a silk dress and a cap.

"Well, this is nice of you to come," said Sophia Ivanovna, kissing him. "Mary is not well: she got tired in church; we have been to communion."

"I congratulate you, Aunt Sophia,"[1] said Nekhlyudov, kissing Sophia Ivanovna's hand. "Oh, I beg your pardon, I have made you wet."

"Go to your room—why, you are soaking wet. Dear me, you have got a moustache! . . . Katusha! Katusha! Get him some coffee; be quick."

"In a minute," came the sound of a well-known, pleasant voice from the passage; and Nekhlyudov's heart cried out, "She's here!" and it was as if the sun had come out from behind the clouds.

Nekhlyudov, followed by Tikhon, went gaily to his old room to change his things. He felt inclined to ask Tikhon about Katusha: how she was, what she was doing, was she not going to be married? But Tikhon was so respectful and at the same time so severe, insisted so firmly on pouring the water out of the jug for him, that Nekhlyudov could not make up his mind to ask him about Katusha, but only inquired about Tikhon's grandsons, about the old so-called "brother's horse," and about the dog Polkan. All were alive except Polkan, who had gone mad the summer before.

When he had taken off all his wet things and just begun to dress again, Nekhlyudov heard quick, familiar footsteps and a knock at the door. Nekhlyudov knew the steps and also the knock. No one but she walked and knocked like that.

Having thrown his wet greatcoat over his shoulders, he opened the door.

"Come in." It was she, Katusha, the same, only sweeter than before. The slightly-squinting naïve black eyes looked up in the remembered way. Now, as then, she had on a white apron. She brought him from his aunts a piece of scented soap, with the wrapper just taken off, and two towels, one a long Russian embroidered one, the other a bath towel. The unused soap with the stamped inscription, the towels, and her own self—all were equally clean, fresh, undefiled, and pleasant. The irrepressible smile of joy at the sight of him made the sweet firm lips pucker up as of old.

"How do you do, Dmitry Ivanich?" she uttered with difficulty, her face suffused with a rosy blush.

"Good morning? How do you do?" he said, also blushing; "alive and well?"

"Yes, the Lord be thanked. And here is your favourite pink soap, and towels from your aunts," she said, putting the soap on the table and hanging the towels over the back of a chair.

"There is everything here," said Tikhon, in defence of the visitor's

---

[1] It is usual in Russia to congratulate those who have received communion.

self-dependence, and pointed to Nekhlyudov's open dressing-case filled with brushes, perfume, fixatoire, a great many bottles with silver lids, and all sorts of toilet appliances.

"Thank my aunts, please. Oh, how glad I am to be here!" said Nekhlyudov, his heart filling with light and tenderness as of old.

She only smiled in answer to these words, and went out.

The aunts, who had always loved Nekhlyudov, welcomed him this time more warmly than ever. Dmitry was going to the war, where he might be wounded or killed, and this touched the old ladies.

Nekhlyudov had arranged to stay only a day and night with his aunts, but when he had seen Katusha he agreed to stay over Easter with them, and telegraphed to his friend Schonbock, whom he was to have joined at Odessa, to come and meet him at his aunt's instead.

As soon as he had seen Katusha, Nekhlyudov's former feelings for her awoke again. Again, just as then, he could not see her white apron without emotion; he could not listen to her steps, her voice, her laugh, without a feeling of joy; he could not look at her eyes, black as sloes, without a feeling of tenderness, especially when she smiled; and, above all, he could not notice without confusion how she blushed when they met. He felt he was in love, but not as before when this love was a kind of mystery to him and he would not own, even to himself, that he loved, and when he was persuaded that one could love only once; now he knew he was in love and was glad of it, and knew vaguely, though he sought to conceal it even from himself, what this love was and what it might lead to. In Nekhlyudov, as in every man, there were two beings; one the spiritual, seeking only that kind of happiness for himself which tends towards the happiness of all; the other, the animal man, seeking only his own happiness, and ready to sacrifice to it the happiness of the rest of the world. At this period of his mania of self-love, brought on by life in Petersburg and in the army, this animal man ruled supreme and completely crushed the spiritual man in him.

But when he saw Katusha and experienced the same feelings as he had had three years before, the spiritual man in him raised its head once more and began to assert its rights. And up to Easter, during two whole days, an unacknowledged, ceaseless struggle went on within him.

He knew in the depths of his soul that he ought to go away, that there was no real reason for staying on at his aunts', knew that no good could come of it; and yet it was so pleasant, so delightful, that he did not honestly acknowledge the facts to himself, and stayed.

On Easter Eve, the priest and the deacon who came to the house to take the service had had (so they said) the greatest difficulty in getting over the three miles that lay between the church and the old ladies' house, coming across the puddles and the bare earth in a sledge.

Nekhlyudov attended the service with his aunts and the servants, and kept looking at Katusha, who was near the door and brought in the censers for the priests. Then, having given the priests and his aunts the Easter kiss, though it was not midnight and therefore not Easter yet, he was already going to bed when he heard the old servant Matrena Pavlovna preparing to go to the church to have the *koulitches*[2] and *paskas*[3] blest after the midnight service. "I shall go too," he thought.

The road to the church was impassable either in a sledge or on wheels, so Nekhlyudov, who behaved in his aunts' house just as if he were at home, ordered the old horse, "the brother's horse," to be saddled; and instead of going to bed he put on his gay uniform, a pair of tight-fitting riding breeches, and his overcoat, and mounting the old, over-fed, and heavy horse, which neighed continually all the way, he rode in darkness through the puddles and snow to the church.

Chapter XV

FOR NEKHLYUDOV this early mass remained for ever after one of the brightest and most vivid memories of his life. When he rode out of the darkness, broken only here and there by patches of white snow, into the churchyard illuminated by a row of lamps around the church, the service had already begun.

The peasants, recognising Mary Ivanovna's nephew, led his horse, which was pricking up its ears at the sight of the lights, to a dry place for dismounting, put it up for him, and showed him into the church, which was full of people. On the right stood the peasants: the old men in homespun coats, clean white linen bands[1] wrapped round their legs; the young men in new cloth coats, bright-coloured belts round their waists, and top-boots.

On the left stood the younger women, with red silk kerchiefs on their heads, black velveteen sleeveless jackets, bright red shirt sleeves, gay-coloured skirts—green, blue, and red—and thick leather boots. The

---

[2] Easter cakes.
[3] A kind of sweetened cream cheese.

---

[1] Long strips of linen are worn by the peasants instead of stockings.

old women, dressed more quietly, stood behind them, with white kerchiefs, home-spun coats, old-fashioned skirts of dark homespun material, and wearing shoes. Gaily dressed children, their hair well oiled,
went in and out among them.

The men, making the sign of the cross, bowed down and raised their
heads again, shaking back their hair.

The women, especially the old ones, fixed their eyes on an icon surrounded with candles and made the sign of the cross, firmly pressing
their folded fingers to the kerchief on their foreheads, to their shoulders, and to their stomachs, and, whispering something, stooped or
knelt down. The children, imitating the grown-up people, prayed
earnestly when they knew that they were being observed. The gilt cases
containing the icons glittered brightly, illuminated on all sides by tall
candles ornamented with golden spirals. The candelabra were filled
with tapers, and from the choir sounded most merry tunes sung by
amateur choristers, with bellowing bass and shrill boys' voices among
them.

Nekhlyudov passed up to the front. In the middle of the church
stood the aristocracy of the place: a landed proprietor with his wife and
son (the latter dressed in a sailor suit), the police officer, the telegraph
clerk, a tradesman in top-boots, and the village elder with a medal on
his breast; and to the right of the ambo, just behind the landed proprietor's wife, stood Matrena Pavlovna in a short lilac dress and fringed
white shawl, and Katusha in a white dress with a tucked bodice and
blue sash, and a red bow in her black hair.

Everything seemed festive, solemn, bright and beautiful: the priest
in his silver cloth vestments with gold crosses; the deacon; the clerk and
chanters in their silver and gold surplices; the amateur choristers in
their best clothes, with their well-oiled hair; the merry tunes of the holiday hymns that sounded like dance-music; and the continual blessing
of the people by the priest, who held a thick candle decorated with
flowers; and the again and again repeated cry of "Christ is risen! Christ
is risen!" All was beautiful; but, above all, Katusha, in her white dress,
blue sash, and the red bow on her black head, her eyes beaming with
rapture.

Nekhlyudov knew that she felt his presence without looking at him.
He noticed this as he passed her, walking up to the altar. He had nothing to tell her, but he invented something, and whispered as he passed
her: "Aunt told me that she would break her fast after the mass."

The young blood rushed up to Katusha's sweet face, as it always did
when she looked at him. The black eyes, laughing and full of joy, gazed
naïvely up and remained fixed on Nekhlyudov.

"I know," she said, with a smile.

At this moment the clerk was going out with a copper coffee-pot[2] of holy water in his hand, and, not noticing Katusha, brushed her with his surplice. Evidently he brushed against Katusha through wishing to pass Nekhlyudov at a respectful distance, and Nekhlyudov was surprised that he, the clerk, did not understand that everything here, yes and in all the world, only existed for Katusha, and that everything else might remain unheeded, but not she, because she was the centre of all. For her the gold glittered round the icons; for her all these candles in candelabra and candlesticks were alight; for her were sung these joyful hymns, *Behold the Passover of the Lord! Rejoice, O ye people!* All—all that was good in the world was for her. And it seemed to him that Katusha knew that it was all for her, when he looked at her well-shaped figure, the tucked white dress, and the rapt, joyous expression of her face, by which he knew that just exactly what was singing in his own soul was singing in hers also.

In the interval between the early and the late service Nekhlyudov left the church. The people stood aside to let him pass, and bowed. Some knew him; others asked who he was.

He stopped on the steps. The beggars standing there came clamouring around him; and he gave them all the change he had in his purse and descended the steps. Dawn was breaking, but the sun had not yet risen. The people grouped themselves among the graves in the churchyard. Katusha had remained inside, and Nekhlyudov stood waiting for her.

The people were still coming out, clattering with their nailed boots on the stone steps, and dispersing over the churchyard.

A very old man with shaking head, his aunts' cook, stopped Nekhlyudov in order to give him the Easter kiss; his wife, an old woman with a wrinkled face, took an egg, dyed yellow, out of her handkerchief and gave it to Nekhlyudov; and a smiling young peasant in a new coat and green belt came up.

"Christ is risen," he said, with laughing eyes, and coming close to Nekhlyudov he enveloped him in his peculiar but pleasant peasant smell, and, tickling him with his curly beard, kissed him three times straight on the mouth with his firm fresh lips.

While the peasant was kissing Nekhlyudov and giving him a dark brown egg, the lilac dress of Matrena Pavlovna and the dear black head with the red bow appeared.

Katusha caught sight of him over the heads of those in front of her, and he saw how her face brightened up.

She had come out with Matrena Pavlovna on to the porch, and

---

[2] Coffee-pots are often used in Russia for holding holy water.

stopped there distributing alms to the beggars. A beggar with a red scab in place of a nose came up to her. She gave him something, drew nearer him, and evincing no sign of disgust but her eyes still shining with joy, kissed him three times. And while she was doing this her eyes met Nekhlyudov's with a look as if she were asking, "Am I doing right?" "Yes, dear, yes, it is right; everything is right, everything is beautiful. I love!"

They came down the steps of the porch, and he came up to them. He did not mean to give them the Easter kiss, but only to be nearer to her.

Matrena Pavlovna bowed her head, and said with a smile, "Christ is risen!" and her tone implied, "To-day we are all equal." She wiped her mouth with her handkerchief rolled into a ball, and extended her lips towards him.

"He is, indeed," answered Nekhlyudov, kissing her. Then he looked at Katusha; she blushed, and drew nearer. "Christ is risen, Dmitry Ivanich." "He is risen, indeed," answered Nekhlyudov, and they kissed twice, then paused as if considering whether a third kiss were necessary, and, having decided that it was, kissed a third time and smiled.

"Aren't you going to the priest's?" asked Nekhlyudov.

"No, we shall sit out here for a bit, Dmitry Ivanich," said Katusha with effort, as if she had accomplished some joyous task, and, her whole chest heaving with a deep sigh, she looked straight in his face with a look of devotion, virgin purity, and love, in her very slightly squinting eyes.

In the love between a man and a woman there always comes a moment when this love has reached its zenith—a moment when it is unconscious, unreasoning, and with nothing sensual about it. Such a moment had come for Nekhlyudov on that Easter night. When he now recalled Katusha, that moment veiled all else: the smooth glossy black head, the white tucked dress closely fitting her graceful maidenly form, her as yet undeveloped bosom, the blushing cheeks, the tender shining black eyes, and her whole being stamped with those two marked characteristics, purity and chaste love—love not only for him (he knew that) but for everybody and everything, not for the good alone but for all that is in the world, even for that beggar whom she had kissed.

He knew she had that love in her, because that night and morning he was conscious of it in himself, and conscious that in this love he became one with her. Ah! if it had all stopped there, at the point it had reached that night! "Yes, all that horrible business had not yet happened on Easter night!" he thought, as he sat by the window of the juryman's room.

Chapter XVI

WHEN HE returned from church Nekhlyudov broke the fast with his aunts and took a glass of spirits and some wine, having got into the habit of drinking while with his regiment, and on reaching his room he fell asleep at once, dressed as he was. He was awakened by a knock at the door. He knew it was her knock, and got up, rubbing his eyes and stretching himself.

"Katusha, is it you? Come in," he said.

She opened the door.

"Dinner is ready," she said. She still had on the same white dress, but not the bow in her hair. She looked at him with a smile, as if she had communicated some very good news to him.

"I am coming," he answered, as he rose, taking his comb to arrange his hair.

She stood still for a minute, and he, noticing it, threw down his comb and made a step towards her, but at that very moment she turned suddenly and went with quick light steps along the strip of carpet in the middle of the passage.

"Dear me, what a fool I am," thought Nekhlyudov. "Why did I not stop her?" And he ran and overtook her.

What he wanted her for he did not know himself, but he felt that when she came into his room something should have been done, something that is generally done on such occasions, and that he had omitted to do it.

"Katusha, wait," he said.

"What do you want?" she said, stopping.

"Nothing, only——" and, with an effort, remembering how men in his position generally behave, he put his arm round her waist.

She stood still and looked into his eyes.

"Don't, Dmitry Ivanich, you must not," she said, blushing to tears and pushing away his arm with her strong hard hand. Nekhlyudov let her go, and for a moment he felt not only confused and ashamed but disgusted with himself. He should now have believed himself, and he would have known that this confusion and shame were caused by the best feelings of his soul demanding to be set free; but he thought it was only his stupidity, and that he ought to behave as every one else did. He overtook her again and kissed her on the neck.

This kiss was very different from that first thoughtless kiss behind the lilac bush, and very different from the kiss this morning in the church-yard. This was a dreadful kiss, and she felt it so.

"Oh, what are you doing?" she cried, in a tone as if he had irreparably broken something of priceless value, and ran quickly away.

He came into the dining-room. His aunts, elegantly dressed, their family doctor, and a neighbour were already there. Everything seemed very ordinary, but in Nekhlyudov a storm was raging. He understood nothing of what was being said, and answered at random, thinking only of Katusha. He kept recalling the sensation of that last kiss when he had caught her up in the passage, and he could think of nothing else. When she came into the room he, without looking round, felt her presence with his whole being and had to force himself not to look at her.

After dinner he went at once to his room, and for a long time walked up and down in great excitement, listening to every sound in the house and expecting to hear her steps. The animal man in him had now not only lifted his head, but had succeeded in trampling under foot the spiritual man of the days of his first visit and even of that very morning. That dreadful animal man in him now ruled supreme.

Though he was watching for her all day he could not manage to meet her alone. She was probably trying to avoid him. In the evening, however, she was obliged to go into the room next to his. The doctor had been asked to stay the night, and she had to make his bed. When he heard her go in Nekhlyudov followed her, treading softly and holding his breath as though he were going to commit a crime.

She was putting a clean pillow-case on the pillow, holding it by two of its corners with her arms inside the pillow-case. She turned round and smiled; not a happy, joyful smile as before, but in a frightened, piteous way. The smile seemed to tell him that what he was doing was wrong. He stopped for a moment. There was still the possibility of a struggle. Though feebly, the voice of his real love for her was still speaking of her, her feelings, her life. Another voice was saying, "Take care! don't let opportunity for your own happiness, your own enjoyment, slip by!" And this second voice completely stifled the first. He went up to her determinedly, and a terrible, ungovernable animal passion took possession of him.

With his arm round her he made her sit down on the bed; and feeling that there was something more to be done, he sat down beside her.

"Dmitry Ivanich, dear! please, let me go," she said in a piteous tone. "Matrena Pavlovna is coming," she cried, tearing herself away. Some one was really coming to the door.

"Well, then, I'll come to you in the night," he whispered. "You'll be alone?"

"What are you thinking of? On no account. No, no!" she said, but only with her lips; the tremulous confusion of her whole being said something very different.

It was Matrena Pavlovna who had come to the door. She came in with a blanket over her arm, looked reproachfully at Nekhlyudov, and began angrily scolding Katusha for having taken the wrong blanket.

Nekhlyudov went out in silence, but did not even feel ashamed. He could see by Matrena Pavlovna's face that she was blaming him, he knew she was blaming him with reason, and felt he was doing wrong, but this novel, low, animal excitement, having freed itself from all the old feelings of real love for Katusha, ruled supreme, leaving room for nothing else. He now knew what he had to do in order to gratify this feeling, and was considering how to find an opportunity of doing it.

He went about as if demented all the evening, now into his aunts' room, then back into his own, then out into the porch, thinking all the time how he could meet her alone; but she avoided him, and Matrena Pavlovna watched her closely.

Chapter XVII

AND SO the evening passed and night came. The doctor went to bed. Nekhlyudov's aunts had also retired; and he knew that Matrena Pavlovna was now with them in their bedroom, so that Katusha was sure to be alone in the maids' sitting-room. He again went out into the porch. It was dark, damp, and warm out of doors, and that white spring mist which drives away the last snow, or is caused by the thawing of the last snow, filled the air. From the river below the hill, about a hundred paces from the front door, came a strange sound. It was the ice breaking up. Nekhlyudov descended the steps and went to the window of the maids' room, stepping over the puddles on the patches of glazed snow. His heart was beating so fiercely in his breast that he seemed to hear it; his laboured breath came and went in a burst of long-drawn sighs. In the maids' room a small lamp was burning, and Katusha sat alone by the table looking thoughtfully in front of her. Nekhlyudov stood a long time without moving, and waited to see what she, not knowing that she was observed, would do. For a minute or two she did not move; then she lifted her eyes, smiled and shook her head as if chiding herself, then changed her pose and dropped both her arms on the table and again began gazing down before her. He stood and looked at her, involuntarily listening to the beating of his own heart and the strange sounds from the river. There on the river, beneath the white mist, the unceasing labour went on, and sounds as of something sobbing, cracking, dropping, being shattered to pieces, mingled with the tinkling of the thin bits of ice as they broke against each other like glass.

There he stood, looking at Katusha's serious, suffering face, which betrayed the inner struggle of her soul, and he felt pity for her; but, strange though it may seem, this pity only increased his desire. Desire had taken entire possession of him.

He knocked at the window. She started as if she had received an electric shock, her whole body trembled, and a look of terror came into her face. Then she jumped up, approached the window, and brought her face close to the pane. The look of terror did not leave her face even when, holding her hands up to her eyes like blinkers and peering through the glass, she recognised him. Her face was unusually grave; he had never seen it so before. She returned his smile, but only in submission to him; there was no smile in her soul, only fear. He beckoned her with his hand to come out into the yard to him. But she shook her head and remained at the window. He brought his face close to the pane, and was going to call out to her, but at that moment she turned to the door. Evidently some one inside had called her. Nekhlyudov moved away from the window. The mist was so dense that five steps from the house the windows could not be seen, but the light from the lamp shone red and huge out of a shapeless black mass. And on the river the same strange sounds went on, sobbing and rustling and crackling and tinkling. Somewhere in the mist not far off, a cock crowed; another answered, and then others far in the village took up the cry, till the sound of the crowing blent into one, while around was silent excepting the river. It was the second time the cocks crowed that night.

Nekhlyudov walked up and down behind the corner of the house, and once or twice stepped into a puddle. Then he again came up to the window. The lamp was still burning, and she was again sitting alone by the table as if uncertain what to do. He had hardly approached the window when she looked up. He tapped. Without looking who it was she at once ran out of the room, and he heard the outside door open with a snap. He waited for her near the side porch, and put his arms round her without saying a word. She clung to him, put up her face, and met his kiss with her lips. They were standing behind the corner of the side porch, on a place where the snow had all melted, and he was filled with tormenting, ungratified desire. Then the door again gave the same sort of snap and opened, and the voice of Matrena Pavlovna called out angrily "Katusha!"

She tore herself away from him and returned to the maids' room. He heard the latch click and then all was quiet. The red light disappeared and only the mist remained, and the bustle on the river went on. Nekhlyudov went up to the window, nobody was to be seen; he tapped but got no answer. He went back into the house by the front door, but could not sleep. He got up and went with bare feet along the passage to her door, next Matrena Pavlovna's room. He heard Matrena Pavlovna snoring quietly, and was about to go on when she coughed and turned on her creaking bed, and his heart stopped, and he stood immovable for about five minutes. When all was quiet and she began to snore peacefully again, he went on, trying to step on the boards that did not creak, and came to Katusha's door. No sound was to be heard. She was probably awake, or else he would have heard her breathing. But as soon as he whispered "Katusha!" she jumped up and began to persuade him, as if angrily, to go away.

"What do you mean by it? What are you doing? Your aunts will hear." These were her words, but all her being was saying, "I am all thine." And it was this only that Nekhlyudov understood.

"Open! Let me in just for a moment! I implore you!" He hardly knew what he was saying.

She was silent; then he heard her hand feeling for the latch. The latch clicked, and he entered the room. He caught hold of her just as she was—in her coarse, stiff chemise, with her bare arms—lifted her, and carried her out.

"Oh, dear! What are you doing?" she whispered; but he, paying no heed to her words, carried her into his room.

"Oh don't; you mustn't! Let me go!" she said, clinging closer to him.

.   .   .   .

When she left him, trembling and silent, giving no answer to his words, he again went out into the porch and stood trying to understand the meaning of what had happened.

It was getting lighter. From the river below, the creaking and tinkling and sobbing of the breaking ice came still louder, and a gurgling sound could now also be heard. The mist had begun to sink, and from above it the waning moon dimly lit up something black and weird.

"What is the meaning of it all? Is it a great joy, or a great misfortune, that has befallen me?" he asked himself.

"It happens to everybody—everybody does it," he said to himself, and went to bed and to sleep.

Chapter XVIII

THE FOLLOWING day the gay, handsome, and brilliant Schonbock joined Nekhlyudov at his aunt's house, and quite won their hearts by his refined and amiable manner, his high spirits, his generosity, and his affection for Dmitry.

But though the old ladies admired his generosity it rather perplexed them, for it seemed exaggerated. He gave a ruble to some blind beggars who came to the gate, gave fifteen rubles in tips to the servants, and when Sophia Ivanovna's pet dog hurt his paw and it bled, he tore into strips his hem-stitched cambric handkerchief (which Sophia Ivanovna knew cost at least fifteen rubles a dozen) and bandaged the dog's foot with it. The old ladies had never met people of this kind, and did not know that Schonbock owed two hundred thousand rubles which he was never going to pay, and that therefore twenty-five rubles more or less did not matter a bit to him.

Schonbock stayed only one day, and he and Nekhlyudov both left that night. They could not be away from their regiment any longer, for their leave was fully up.

On this last day with his aunts, while the previous night was still fresh in his memory, two feelings kept struggling in Nekhlyudov's breast. One was the burning, sensual recollection of animal love (though it had far from fulfilled his expectations) mixed with a certain satisfaction at having gained his end; and the other was the consciousness of having done something very wrong, which had to be put right not for her sake but for his own.

At the stage which Nekhlyudov's selfish mania had now reached he could think of nothing but himself. He was wondering whether his conduct, if found out, would be blamed much, or at all; but he did not consider what Katusha was now going through, and what was going to happen to her.

He saw that Schonbock guessed his relations to her, and this flattered his vanity.

"Ah, I see how it is you have taken such a sudden fancy to your aunts that you have been living with them nearly a week," Schonbock remarked when he had seen Katusha. "Well, I don't wonder—I should have done the same. She's charming."

Nekhlyudov was also thinking that though it was a pity to go away before having fully gratified the cravings of his love for her, yet the absolute necessity of parting had its advantages, because it put a sudden stop to relations it would be very difficult for him to continue. Then he thought that he ought to give her some money, not for her, not because she might need it, but because it was the thing to do and he would be considered dishonourable if he did not pay her after having made use of her.

So he gave her what seemed to him a liberal amount considering his and her station. On the day of his departure, after dinner, he went out and waited for her at the side entrance. She flushed up when she saw him and wished to pass by, directing by a look his attention to the open door of the maids' room, but he stopped her.

"I have come to say good-bye," he said, crumpling in his hand an envelope with a hundred-ruble note inside. "There, I——"

She guessed what he meant, knit her brows, and shaking her head pushed his hand away.

"Take it; oh, you must!" he stammered, and thrust the envelope into the bib of her apron, and ran back to his room, groaning and frowning as if he had hurt himself. And for a long time he strode up and down writhing as in pain, and even stamping and groaning aloud as he thought of this last scene. "But what else could I have done? Is it not what happens to every one? To Schonbock, with that governess he was telling me about; to Uncle Grisha; and to my father who, when he was living in the country, had by a peasant woman that illegitimate son Mitinka, who is still living. And if every one does the same . . . well, I suppose it can't be helped." In this way he tried to get peace of mind, but in vain. The recollection of what had passed burnt his conscience.

In his soul—in the very depths of his soul—he knew that he had acted in a base, cruel, cowardly manner, and that the knowledge of this act of his must prevent him, not only from finding fault with any one else, but even from looking straight into other people's eyes, not to mention the impossibility of considering himself a splendid, noble, high-minded fellow, as he did and had to do to go on living his life boldly and merrily. There was only one solution of the problem—not to think about it. He succeeded in doing so. The life he was now entering upon, the new surroundings, new friends, the war, all helped him to forget. And the longer he lived the less he thought about it, until at last he forgot it completely.

Once only, when, after the war, he went to see his aunts in hopes of meeting Katusha, and heard that after his last visit she had left, and that his aunts had heard she had been confined somewhere or other and had gone quite to the bad, his heart ached. Judging by the time of her confinement, the child might or might not have been his. His aunts blamed her and said she inherited her mother's depraved nature, and he was pleased to hear this opinion of theirs. It seemed to acquit him. At first he thought of trying to find her and her child, but then, just because in the depths of his soul he felt so ashamed and pained when thinking about her, he did not make the necessary effort to find her, but tried again to forget his sin, ceasing to think about it.

And now this strange coincidence brought it all back to his memory, and demanded from him the acknowledgment of the heartless, cruel cowardice which had made it possible for him to live these ten years with such a sin on his conscience. But he was still far from such acknowledgment, and his only fear was that everything might now be found out, and that she or her advocate might recount it all and put him to shame before every one present.

Chapter XIX

IN THIS state of mind Nekhlyudov left the Court and went into the jurymen's room. He sat by the window listening to what was being said around him, and smoked all the time.

The merry merchant seemed with all his heart to sympathise with Smelkov's way of spending his time.

"There, old fellow, that was something like! Real Siberian fashion! He knew what he was about, no fear! That's the sort of wench for me."

The foreman was stating his conviction that in some way or other the expert's conclusions were the important thing. Peter Gerasimovich was joking about something with the Jewish clerk, and they burst out laughing. Nekhlyudov answered all the questions addressed to him in monosyllables and only longed to be left in peace.

When the usher, with his sideways gait, called the jury back to the Court, Nekhlyudov was seized with fear, as if he were going not to judge but to be judged. In the depth of his soul he felt he was a scoundrel, who ought to be ashamed to look people in the face, yet, by sheer force of habit, he stepped on to the platform in his usual self-possessed manner, and sat down, crossing his legs and playing with his pince-nez.

The prisoners had also been led out, and were now brought in again. There were some new faces in Court—witnesses—and Nekhlyudov noticed that Maslova could not take her eyes off a very fat woman who sat in the row in front of the grating, very showily dressed in silk and velvet, a high hat with a large bow on her head, and an elegant little reticule on her arm, which was bare to the elbow. This was, as he subsequently found out, one of the witnesses, the mistress of the establishment to which Maslova had belonged.

The examination of the witnesses commenced; they were asked their names, religion, etc. Then, after some question as to whether the witnesses were to be examined on oath or not, the old priest came in again, dragging his legs with difficulty, and, again fingering the golden cross on his breast, swore the witnesses and the expert in the same quiet manner, and with the same assurance that he was doing something useful and important.

The witnesses having been sworn, all but Kitaeva, the keeper of the brothel, were led out again. She was asked what she knew about this affair. Kitaeva nodded her head and the big hat at every sentence, and smiled affectedly. She gave a very full and intelligent account, speaking with a strong German accent. First of all, the hotel servant Simon, whom she knew, came to her establishment to get a girl for a rich Siberian merchant, and she sent Lubov. After a time Lubov returned with the merchant. The merchant was already a bit "elevated"—she smiled as she said this—and went on drinking and treating the girls. He ran short of money and sent this same Lubov to his lodgings. He had taken a "predilection" to her. She looked at the prisoner as she said this.

Nekhlyudov thought he saw Maslova smile here, and this seemed disgusting to him. A strange, indefinite feeling of loathing, mingled with suffering, arose in him.

"And what was your opinion of Maslova?" asked the blushing and confused applicant for a judicial post, appointed to act as Maslova's advocate.

"Zee ferry pest," answered Kitaeva. "Zee yoong voman is etucated and elecant. She vas prought up in a coot family and can reat French. She tid have a trop too moch sometimes, put nefer forcot herself. A ferry coot girl."

Katusha looked at the woman, then suddenly turned her eyes on the jury and fixed them on Nekhlyudov, and her face grew serious and even severe. One of her serious eyes squinted, and those two strange eyes for some time gazed at Nekhlyudov, who, in spite of the terrors that seized him, could not take his look off these squinting eyes, with their bright, clear whites.

He thought of that dreadful night, with its mist and the ice breaking on the river below, and especially of the waning moon with upturned horns that had risen towards morning, lighting up something black and weird. These two black eyes now looking at him reminded him of this weird, black something.

"She has recognised me," he thought, and he shrank back as if expecting a blow. But she had not recognised him. She sighed quietly, and again looked at the president. Nekhlyudov also sighed. "Oh, if it would only get on quicker," he thought.

He now felt the same loathing and pity and vexation as when, out shooting, he was obliged to kill a wounded bird. The wounded bird struggles in the game bag. One is disgusted and yet feels pity, and one is in a hurry to kill the bird and forget about it.

Such mixed feelings filled Nekhlyudov's breast as he sat listening to the examination of the witnesses.

Chapter XX

BUT, AS if to spite him, the case dragged out to a great length. After each witness had been examined separately, and the expert last of all, and a great number of useless questions had been put by the public prosecutor and by both advocates with the usual air of importance, the president invited the jury to examine the objects offered as material evidence. They included an enormous ring with a small rosette of diamonds, which had evidently been worn on the first finger, and a test tube in which the poison had been analysed. These things had seals and labels attached to them.

Just as the witnesses were about to look at these things, the public prosecutor rose and demanded that before they did this the results of the doctor's examination of the body should be read. The president, who was hurrying the business through as fast as he could in order to get to his Swiss girl, though he knew that the reading of the paper could have no other effect than that of producing weariness and putting off the dinner-hour, and that the public prosecutor only wanted it read because he knew he had the right to demand it, had no option but to express his consent.

The secretary got out the doctor's report and again began to read in his lisping voice, making no distinction between the *r*'s and *l*'s.

The external examination proved that:—

"(1) Therapont Smelkov's height was six feet five inches."

"Not so bad, that. A very good size," whispered the merchant, with interest, into Nekhlyudov's ear.

"(2) He looked about forty years of age.

"(3) The body was of a swollen appearance.

"(4) The flesh was of a greenish colour, with dark spots in several places.

"(5) The skin was raised in blisters of different sizes and in places had come off in large pieces.

"(6) The hair was chestnut; it was thick, and separated easily from the skin when touched.

"(7) The eyeballs protruded from their sockets, and the cornea had grown dim.

"(8) Out of the nostrils, both ears, and the mouth, oozed serous liquid; the mouth was half open.

"(9) The neck was almost hidden by the swelling of the face and chest."

And so on, and so on.

Four pages were covered with the twenty-seven paragraphs describing all the details of the external examination of the enormous, fat, swollen, and decomposing body of the merchant who had been making merry in the town. The indefinite loathing that Nekhlyudov felt was increased by the description of the corpse. Katusha's life, the serous liquid oozing from the nostrils of the corpse, the eyes protruding from their sockets, and his own treatment of Katusha, all seemed to belong to the same order of things, and he felt surrounded and wholly engulfed by things of a like nature.

When the reading of the report of the external examination was ended, the president heaved a sigh and raised his head hoping it was finished; but the secretary at once went on to the description of the internal examination. The president again dropped his head on to his hand and shut his eyes. The merchant next to Nekhlyudov could hardly keep awake, and now and then his body swayed to and fro. The prisoners and the gendarmes sat perfectly quiet.

The internal examination showed that:—

"(1) The skin was easily detachable from the bones of the skull, and there was no coagulated blood.

"(2) The bones of the skull were of average thickness and in sound condition.

"(3) On the membrane of the brain there were two discoloured spots about four inches long, the membrane itself being of a dull white."

And so on for thirteen paragraphs more.

Then followed the names and signatures of the assistants, and the doctor's conclusion showing that the changes observed in the stomach, and to a lesser degree in the bowels and kidneys, at the post-mortem examination, and described in the official report, gave *great probability* to the conclusion that Smelkov's death was caused by poison which had entered his stomach mixed with alcohol. To decide from the state of the stomach what poison had been introduced was difficult; but it was necessary to suppose that the poison entered the stomach mixed with alcohol, since a great quantity of the latter was found in Smelkov's stomach.

"He could drink, and no mistake," whispered the merchant again, having just woken up.

The reading of this report had taken a full hour, but it had not satisfied the public prosecutor, for, when it had been read through and the president turned to him, saying: "I suppose it is superfluous to read the report of the examination of the internal organs?" he answered in a severe tone, without looking at the president: "I shall ask to have it read."

He raised himself a little, and showed by his manner that he had a right to have this report read and would claim this right; and that if that were not granted it would serve as a cause of appeal.

The member of the Court with the big beard, who suffered from catarrh of the stomach, feeling quite done up, turned to the president:— "What is the use of reading all this? It is only dragging it out. These new brooms do not sweep clean; they only take a long while doing it."

The member with the gold spectacles said nothing, but only looked gloomily in front of him, expecting nothing good, either from his wife or from life in general. The reading of the report commenced:—

In the year 188—, on February 15, I, the undersigned, commissioned by the medical department, made an examination, No. 638"— the secretary began again with firmness, raising the pitch of his voice as if to dispel the sleepiness that had overtaken all present—"in the presence of the assistant medical inspector, of the internal organs:—

"(1) The right lung and the heart (contained in a 6-lb. glass jar).

"(2) The contents of the stomach (in a 6-lb. glass jar).

"(3) The stomach itself (in a 6-lb. glass jar).

"(4) The liver, the spleen, and the kidneys (in a 9-lb. glass jar).

"(5) The intestines (in a 9-lb. earthenware jar)."

The president here whispered to one of the members, then stooped to the other, and having received their consent, he said: "The Court considers the reading of this report superfluous." The secretary stopped reading and folded the paper, and the public prosecutor angrily began to write down something.

"The gentlemen of the jury may now examine the articles of material evidence," said the president. The foreman and several of the others rose and went to the table, not quite knowing what to do with their hands. They looked in turn at the ring, the glass vessels, and the test tube. The merchant even tried on the ring.

"Ah! that was a finger," he said, returning to his place; "like a cucumber," he added. Evidently the image he had formed in his mind of the gigantic merchant amused him.

Chapter XXI

WHEN THE examination of the articles of material evidence was finished, the president announced that the investigation was now concluded, and immediately called on the prosecutor to proceed, hoping that as the latter was also a man, he, too, might feel inclined to smoke or dine, and show some mercy to others. But the public prosecutor showed mercy neither to himself nor to any one else. He was very stupid by nature, but besides this, he had had the misfortune of finishing school with a gold medal and of receiving a reward for his essay on *Servitude* when studying Roman Law at the university, and was therefore self-confident and self-satisfied in the highest degree (his success with the ladies also conducing to this), and his stupidity had become extraordinary.

When called on to speak, he rose slowly, showing the whole of his graceful figure in his embroidered uniform. Putting his hand on the desk he looked round the room, slightly bowing his head, and, avoiding the eyes of the prisoners, he proceeded to deliver the speech he had prepared while the reports were being read.

"Gentlemen of the jury! The case that now lies before you is, if I may so express myself, very characteristic."

According to his view, the speech of a public prosecutor should always have a public importance, like the celebrated speeches made by advocates who have become distinguished. True, the audience consisted of three women—a sempstress, a cook, and Simon's sister—and a coachman; but this did not matter. The celebrities had also begun in that way. To be always at the height of his position, that is, to penetrate into the depths of the psychological significance of crime and lay bare the wounds of society, was one of the prosecutor's principles.

"You see before you, gentlemen of the jury, a crime characteristic, if I may so express myself, of the end of our century; bearing, so to say, the specific features of that very painful phenomenon, the corruption to which those elements of our present-day society—which are, if I may say so, particularly exposed to the scorching rays of this process—are subject."

The public prosecutor spoke at great length, trying not to forget any of the notions he had formed in his mind, and, on the other hand, never to hesitate but to let his speech flow on for an hour and a quarter without a break.

Only once he stopped, and for some time stood swallowing his saliva, but he soon mastered himself and made up for the interruption by heightened eloquence. He spoke, now with a tender, insinuating accent, stepping from foot to foot and looking at the jury; now in quiet businesslike tones, glancing into his notebook; now with a loud accusing accent, looking from the audience to the advocates. But he avoided looking at the prisoners, who were all three gazing fixedly at him. Every new craze then in vogue among his set was alluded to in his speech;

everything that then was, and some things that still are, considered to be the last words of scientific wisdom: heredity and congenital crime, Lombroso and Tarde, evolution and the struggle for existence, hypnotism and hypnotic influence, Charcot and decadence.

According to his definition, the merchant Smelkov was a type of the genuine, sturdy Russian, who, having fallen into the hands of deeply degraded individuals, had perished in consequence of his generous, trusting nature.

Simon Kartinkin was the atavistic production of serfdom, a stupefied, ignorant, unprincipled man, who had not even any religion. Euphemia was his mistress, and a victim of heredity; all the signs of degeneration were observable in her. The chief wirepuller in the affair was Maslova, presenting the phenomenon of decadence in its lowest form. "This woman," he said, looking at her, "has, as we have to-day heard from her mistress in this Court, received an education, and can not merely read and write, but knows French. She is an orphan, and in all likelihood carries in her the germs of criminality. She was educated in an enlightened, noble family, and might have lived by honest work, but, deserting her benefactress, she gave herself up to her passions, for the gratification of which she entered a brothel, where she was distinguished from her companions by her education, and chiefly, gentlemen of the jury, as you have heard from her mistress, by her power of acting on the visitors by means of that mysterious capacity lately investigated by science, especially by the school of Charcot, known by the name of hypnotic influence. By these means she gets hold of this Russian, this kind-hearted Sadko,[1] the rich guest, and uses his trust in order first to rob and then pitilessly to murder him."

"Well, he is piling it on now, isn't he?" said the president, with a smile, bending towards the serious member.

"A fearful blockhead!" said the serious member.

Meanwhile the public prosecutor went on with his speech.

"Gentlemen of the jury," gracefully swaying his body; "in your hands rests not only the fate of these persons, but also, to some extent, the fate of society, which will be influenced by your verdict. Grasp the full significance of this crime, the danger that menaces society from those whom I may be permitted to term pathological individuals, such as Maslova. Guard it from infection; guard the innocent and strong elements of society from contagion and even from destruction."

And as if himself overcome by the importance of the expected verdict, the public prosecutor sank into his chair, evidently highly delighted with his speech.

---

[1] Sadko, the hero of a legend.

The sense of the speech, when divested of all its flowers of rhetoric, was that Maslova, having gained the merchant's confidence, hypnotised him and went to his lodgings with his key meaning to take all the money herself, but having been caught in the act by Simon and Euphemia, had had to share it with them. Then, in order to hide the traces of the crime, she had returned to the lodgings with the merchant and there poisoned him.

After the prosecutor had spoken, a middle-aged man, in swallow-tail coat and low-cut waistcoat showing a large half-circle of starched white shirt, rose from the advocates' bench and made a speech in defence of Kartinkin and Bochkova. This was an advocate engaged by them for three hundred rubles. He declared them both innocent, and put all the blame on Maslova. He denied the truth of Maslova's statements that Bochkova and Kartinkin were with her when she took the money, laying great stress on the point that her evidence could not be accepted, she being charged with poisoning. The one thousand eight hundred rubles, the advocate said, could have been easily earned by two honest and industrious persons getting from three to five rubles a day in tips from the lodgers. The merchant's money was stolen by Maslova and given over to some one, or even lost, as she was not in a normal state. The poisoning was committed by Maslova alone.

He therefore begged the jury to acquit Kartinkin and Bochkova of stealing the money; or, if they could not acquit them of the theft, at least to admit that it was done without any participation in the poisoning.

With a thrust at the public prosecutor, the advocate remarked, in concluding, that the brilliant observations of his learned friend on heredity, while explaining scientific facts concerning heredity, were inapplicable in this case, as Bochkova was of unknown parentage. The public prosecutor noted something down with an angry look, and shrugged his shoulders in contemptuous surprise.

Then Maslova's advocate rose, and timidly and hesitatingly began his speech in her defence. Without denying that she had taken part in the stealing of the money, he insisted on the fact that she had no intention of poisoning Smelkov, but had given him the powder only to make him fall asleep. He tried to indulge in a little eloquence by describing how Maslova was led into a life of debauchery by a man who had remained unpunished, while she had to bear all the burden of her fall; but this excursion into the domain of psychology was so unsuccessful that it made everybody feel uncomfortable. When he muttered something about men's cruelty and women's helplessness, the president tried to help him by asking him to keep to the facts of the case.

When he had finished, the public prosecutor got up to reply. He defended his position against the first advocate by saying that even if Bochkova were of unknown parentage the truth of the doctrine of heredity was thereby in no way invalidated, since the laws of heredity were so far proved by science that we can not only deduce the crime from heredity, but heredity from the crime. As to the statement made in defence of Maslova, that she was debauched by an imaginary (he laid a particularly venomous stress on the word "imaginary") seducer, he could only say that from the evidence before them it appeared much more likely that she had played the part of temptress to many and many a victim who had fallen into her hands. Having said this he sat down in triumph.

Then the prisoners were offered permission to speak in their own defence.

Euphemia Bochkova repeated once more that she knew nothing about it and had taken part in nothing, and firmly laid the whole blame on Maslova. Simon Kartinkin only repeated several times: "It's your business, but I am innocent; it's unjust." Maslova said nothing in her defence. When the president told her she might do so, she only lifted her eyes to him, cast a look round the room like a hunted animal, and, dropping her head, began to cry, sobbing aloud.

"What's the matter?" the merchant asked Nekhlyudov, hearing him utter a strange sound. This was a forcibly suppressed sob. Nekhlyudov had not yet understood the significance of his present position, and attributed the sobs he could hardly keep back and the tears that filled his eyes to the weakness of his nerves. He put on his pince-nez in order to hide the tears, then got out his handkerchief and began blowing his nose.

Fear of the disgrace that would befall him if every one in the Court knew of his conduct stifled the inner working of his soul. This fear was, during this first period, stronger than all else.

Chapter XXII

AFTER THE last words of the prisoners had been heard, the form in which the questions were to be put to the jury was settled, which also took some time. At last the questions were formulated, and the president began the summing-up.

Before putting the case to the jury, he spoke for some time in a pleasant, homely manner, explaining to them that burglary was burglary and theft was theft, that stealing from a place which was under lock and key was stealing from a place under lock and key, and that stealing from a place not under lock and key was stealing from a place not under lock and key. While explaining this, he looked several times at Nekhlyudov as if wishing to impress upon him these important truths in hopes that, having comprehended them, Nekhlyudov would make his fellow-jurymen also understand them. When he considered that the jury were sufficiently imbued with these truths, he proceeded to enunciate another—namely, that a murder is an action which has, as its consequence, the death of a human being, and that poisoning could therefore also be termed murder. When, in his opinion, this truth had also been received by the jury, he went on to explain that if theft and murder were committed at the same time the combination of the crimes was theft with murder.

Although he was himself anxious to finish as soon as possible, although he knew that his Swiss girl would be waiting for him, he had grown so used to his occupation that, having begun to speak, he could not stop himself, and went on to impress on the jury with much detail that if they found the prisoners guilty they would have the right to give a verdict of guilty; and if they found them not guilty, to give a verdict of not guilty; and if they found them guilty of one of the crimes and not of the other, they might give a verdict of guilty on the one count and of not guilty on the other. Then he explained that though this right was given them they should use it with reason. He was going to add that if they gave an affirmative answer to any question that was put to them, they would thereby affirm everything included in the question; so that if they did not wish to affirm the whole of the question they should mention the part of the question they wished to be expected. But, glancing at the clock, and seeing it was already five minutes to three, he resolved to trust to their being intelligent enough to understand this without further comment.

"The facts of this case are the following," began the president, and repeated all that had already been said several times by the advocates, the public prosecutor, and the witnesses.

The president spoke, and the members beside him listened with deeply attentive expressions, but looked from time to time at the clock, for they considered the speech too long, though very good—that is, such as it ought to be. The public prosecutor, the lawyers, and, in fact, every one in the Court, shared the same impression. The president finished the summing-up.

It seemed as if everything had been said; but no, the president could not as yet forgo his right of speaking. So pleasant was it to hear the impressive tones of his own voice, that he found it necessary to say a few words more about the importance of the rights given to the jury: how carefully they should use those rights and how they ought not to abuse them, about their being on their oath, that they were the conscience of society, that the secrecy of the debating-room should be considered sacred, and so forth.

From the time the president commenced his speech, Maslova, as if fearful of losing a single word, did not take her eyes off him; so that Nekhlyudov was not afraid of meeting her eyes, and kept looking at her all the time. And his mind passed through those phases in which a face we have not seen for many years first strikes us with the external changes wrought during the time of separation, and then gradually becomes more and more like its old self, when the changes made by time seem to disappear, and before our spiritual eyes rises only the principal expression of one exceptional, unique, spiritual individuality.

Yes, in spite of the prison cloak, in spite of the developed figure, the fullness of the bosom and of the lower part of the face, in spite of a few wrinkles on the forehead and temples, and the swollen eyes, this was certainly the same Katusha who, on that Easter night, had so innocently looked up to him whom she loved, her fond, laughing eyes full of joy and life.

"What a surprising coincidence that after all these years, during which I never saw her, this case should have come up to-day when I am on the jury, and that it is in the prisoner's dock I see her again! And how will it end? Oh, if they would only get on quicker!"

Still he would not give in to the feelings of repentance which began to arise within him. He tried to consider it all as a chance incident, which would pass without affecting his manner of life. He felt himself in the position of a puppy, when its master, taking it by the scruff of its neck, rubs its nose in the mess it has made. The puppy whines, draws back and wants to get away as far as possible from the effects of its misdeed, but the pitiless master does not let go.

And so Nekhlyudov, feeling all the repulsiveness of what he had done, felt also the powerful hand of the Master, but he did not yet understand the whole significance of his action and would not recognise the Master's hand. He did not wish to believe that it was the effect of his deed that lay before him, but the pitiless hand of the Master held him, and he had a foreboding that he should not escape. He was still keeping up his courage and sat on his chair in the first row in his usual self-possessed pose, one leg carelessly thrown over the other, and playing with his pince-nez. Yet all the while, in the depths of his soul, he felt the cruelty, cowardice, and baseness, not only of this particular action of his but of his whole self-willed, depraved, cruel, idle life; and that dreadful veil which had in some unaccountable manner hidden from him this sin of his, and the whole of his subsequent life for ten years, was beginning to shake, and he caught glimpses of what was covered by that veil.

Chapter XXIII

AT LAST the president finished his speech, and lifting the list of questions with a graceful movement of his arm, he handed it to the foreman, who came up to take it. The jury, glad to be able to get away into the debating-room, got up, one after another, and left the Court, looking as if ashamed of something, and again not knowing what to do with their hands. As soon as the door was closed behind them a gendarme came up to it, pulled his sword out of the scabbard, and, holding it up to his shoulder, stood at the door The judges got up and went away. The prisoners were also led out. When the jury came into the debating-room the first thing they did was to take out their cigarettes, as before, and begin smoking. The sense of the unnaturalness and falseness of their position, which all of them had experienced while sitting in their places in the Court, passed when they entered the debating-room and started smoking, and they settled down with a feeling of relief and at once began an animated conversation.

"'Tisn't the girl's fault. She's got mixed up in it," said the kindly merchant. "We must recommend her to mercy."

"That's just what we have to consider," said the foreman. "We must not give way to our personal impressions."

"The president's summing-up was good," remarked the colonel.

"Good? Why, it nearly sent me to sleep!"

"The chief point is that the servants could have known nothing about the money if Maslova had not been in league with them," said the clerk of Jewish extraction.

"Well, do you think that it was she who stole it?" asked one of the jury.

"I will never believe it," cried the kindly merchant; "it was all that red-eyed hag's doing."

"They are a nice lot, all of them," said the colonel.

"But she says she never went into the room."

"Oh, believe her, by all means!"

"I should not believe that jade, not for the world."

"Whether you believe her or not does not settle the question," said the clerk.

"The girl had the key," said the colonel.

"What if she had?" retorted the merchant.

"And the ring?"

"But didn't she tell all about it?" again cried the merchant. "The fellow had a temper of his own, and had had a drop too much besides, and gave the girl a knock; what could be simpler? Well then, he's sorry—quite naturally. 'There, never mind,' says he; 'take this.' Why, I heard them say he was six foot five high; I should think he must have weighed twenty stone."

"That's not the point," said Peter Gerasimovich. "The question is, whether it was she who invented and instigated this affair, or the servants."

"It was not possible for the servants to do it alone; she had the key."

This kind of random talk went on for a considerable time. At last the foreman said: "I beg your pardon, gentlemen, but had we not better take our places at the table and discuss the matter? Come, please." And he took the chair.

"But they're up to anything, these wenches," said the clerk; and as a confirmation of his opinion that Maslova was the chief culprit, he related how a comrade of his had had his watch stolen on the boulevard by a loose woman.

À *propos* of this the colonel narrated a still more striking case: the theft of a silver samovar.

"Gentlemen, I beg you to attend to the questions," said the foreman, tapping the table with his pencil.

All were silent.

The questions were expressed in the following terms:—

"(1) Is the peasant of the village Borki, Krapivensky District, Simon Petrov Kartinkin, thirty-three years of age, guilty of having, in agreement with other persons, given the merchant Smelkov, on the 17th January 188—, in the town of ——, with intent to deprive him of life for the purpose of robbing him, poisoned brandy which caused Smelkov's death, and of having stolen from him about two thousand six hundred rubles in money and a diamond ring?

"(2) Is Euphemia Ivanovna Bochkova, forty-three years of age, guilty of the crimes described above?

"(3) Is Katerina Mikhaylovna Maslova, twenty-eight years of age, guilty of the crimes described in the first question?

"(4) If the prisoner Euphemia Bochkova is not guilty on the first question, is she guilty of having, on the 17th January 188—, in the town of ——, while in service at the Hotel Mauritania, stolen from a locked portmanteau belonging to the merchant Smelkov, a lodger in that hotel, and which was in the room occupied by him, two thousand six hundred rubles, for which object she unlocked the portmanteau with a key she brought and fitted to the lock?"

The foreman read the first question.

"Well, gentlemen, what do you think?"

This question was quickly answered. All agreed to say "Guilty," as if convinced that Kartinkin had taken part both in the poisoning and the robbery. An old *artelshik*,[1] whose answers were all in favour of acquittal, was the only exception.

The foreman thought he did not understand, and began to point out to him that everything pointed to Kartinkin's guilt. The old man answered that he did understand, but still thought it better to have pity on him. "We are not saints ourselves," he said, and kept to his opinion.

The answer to the second question concerning Bochkova was, after much dispute and many exclamations, answered by the words, "Not guilty," there being no clear proofs of her having taken part in the poisoning—a fact her advocate had strongly insisted on. The merchant, anxious to acquit Maslova, insisted that Bochkova was the chief instigator of it all. Many of the jury shared this view, but the foreman, wishing to be in strict accord with the law, declared they had no grounds to consider Bochkova as an accomplice in the poisoning. After much disputing, the foreman's opinion triumphed.

To the fourth question, concerning Bochkova, the answer was "Guilty." But on the *artelshik's* insistence she was recommended to mercy.

The third question, concerning Maslova, raised a fierce dispute. The foreman maintained she was guilty both of the poisoning and the theft, to which the merchant would not agree. The colonel, the clerk, and the old *artelshik* sided with the merchant, the rest seemed shaky, and the opinion of the foreman began to gain ground, chiefly because all the jurymen were getting tired, and preferred to take up the view that would bring them sooner to a decision and thus liberate them.

From all that had passed, and from his former knowledge of Maslova, Nekhlyudov was certain that she was innocent of both the theft and the poisoning; and he felt sure that all the others would come to the same conclusion. When he saw that the merchant's awkward defence (evidently based on his physical admiration for her, which he did not even try to hide), and the foreman's insistence, and especially everybody's weariness, were all tending to her condemnation, he longed to express his opinion, but feared to do so lest his relations with Maslova should be discovered. Yet he felt he could not allow things to

---

[1] Member of an *artel*, an association of workmen, in which the members share profits and liabilities.

go on in that way; and, blushing and growing pale again, he was about to speak, when Peter Gerasimovich, irritated by the authoritative manner of the foreman, began to raise his objections, and said the very thing Nekhlyudov was about to say.

"Allow me for one moment," he said. "You seem to think that her having the key proves she is guilty of the theft; but what could be easier than for the servants to open the portmanteau with a false key after she was gone?"

"Of course, of course," said the merchant.

"She could not have taken the money, because in her position she would hardly know what to do with it."

"That's just what I say," remarked the merchant.

"But it is very likely that her coming put the idea into the servants' heads, and that they grasped the opportunity, and threw all the blame on her."

Peter Gerasimovich spoke so irritably that the foreman became irritated too, and went on obstinately defending the opposite views; but Peter Gerasimovich spoke so convincingly that the majority agreed with him, and decided that Maslova was not guilty of stealing the money, and that the ring was given her.

But when the question of her having taken part in the poisoning was raised, her zealous defender, the merchant, declared that she must be acquitted, because she could have had no motive for the poisoning. The foreman, however, said that it was impossible to acquit her, because she herself pleaded guilty to having given the powder.

"Yes, but thinking it was opium," said the merchant.

"Opium can also deprive one of life," said the colonel, who was fond of wandering from the subject; and he began telling how his brother-in-law's wife would have died of an overdose of opium if there had not been a doctor at hand so that steps could be taken at once. The colonel told his story so impressively, with such self-possession and dignity, that no one had the courage to interrupt him. Only the clerk, infected by his example, decided to break in with a story of his own: "There are some who get so used to it that they can take forty drops. I have a relative——" but the colonel would not allow himself to be interrupted, and went on to relate the effects of the opium on his brother-in-law's wife.

"But, gentlemen, do you know it is getting on towards five o'clock?" said one of the jury.

"Well, gentlemen, what are we to say, then?" inquired the foreman. "Shall we say she is guilty, but without intent to rob? And without stealing any property? Will that do?"

Peter Gerasimovich, pleased with his victory, agreed.

"But she must be recommended to mercy," said the merchant.

All agreed; only the old *artelshik* insisted that they should say "Not guilty."

"It comes to the same thing," explained the foreman; "without intent to rob, and without stealing any property. Therefore, not guilty—that's evident."

"All right; that'll do. And we recommended her to mercy," said the merchant gaily.

They were all so tired, and so confused by the discussions, that nobody thought of adding that she was guilty of giving the powder, but without intent to take life. Nekhlyudov was so excited that he did not notice this omission, and so the answers were written down in the form agreed upon and taken to the Court.

Rabelais tells of a lawyer who in conducting a case quoted all sorts of laws, read twenty pages of senseless judicial Latin, and then proposed to the judges to throw dice, and if the numbers proved odd the defendant would be right, if even, the plaintiff.

It was much the same in this case. The resolution was taken not because everybody agreed upon it, but because the president, who had been summing-up at such length, omitted to say what he always said on such occasions, that the answer might be, "Yes, guilty, but without the intent of taking life"; because the colonel had related the story of his brother-in-law's wife at such great length; because Nekhlyudov was too excited to notice that the proviso "without intent to take life" had been omitted, and thought that the words "without intent" nullified the conviction; because Peter Gerasimovich had retired from the room while the questions and answers were being read, and chiefly because, being tired, and wishing to get away as soon as possible, all were ready to agree to the decision which would soonest bring matters to an end.

The jurymen rang the bell. The gendarme who stood outside the door with his sword drawn put the sword back into the scabbard, and stepped aside. The judges took their seats and the jury came out one by one.

The foreman brought in the paper with an air of solemnity, and handed it to the president, who looked at it, and, spreading out his hands in astonishment, turned to consult his companions. The president was surprised that the jury, having put in one proviso—without intent to rob—did not put in a second proviso—without intent to take life. From the decision of the jury it followed that Maslova had not stolen nor robbed, and had yet poisoned a man without any apparent reason.

"Just see what an absurd decision they have come to," he whispered to the member on his left. "This means penal servitude in Siberia, and she is innocent."

"Surely you do not mean to say she is innocent?" answered the serious member.

"Yes she is, positively innocent. I think this is a case for putting Article 817 into practice." (Article 817 states that if the Court considers the decision of the jury unjust it may set it aside.)

"What do you think?" said the president, turning to the other member. The kindly member did not answer at once. He looked at the number on a paper before him and added up the figures; the sum would not divide by three. He had settled in his mind that if it did divide by three he would agree to the president's proposal, but though the sum would not so divide, his kindness made him agree all the same.

"I, too, think it should be done," he said.

"And you?" asked the president, turning to the serious member.

"On no account," he answered firmly. "As it is, the papers accuse the juries of acquitting prisoners. What will they say if the judges do it? I shall not agree to that on any account."

The president looked at his watch. "It is a pity, but what's to be done?" and he handed the questions to the foreman to read out. All got up, and the foreman, stepping from foot to foot, coughed, and read the questions and the answers. All the Court—secretary, advocates, and even the public prosecutor—expressed surprise. The prisoners sat impassive, evidently not understanding the meaning of the answers. Everybody sat down again, and the president asked the prosecutor what punishments the prisoners should be subjected to.

The prosecutor, glad of his unexpected success in getting Maslova convicted, and attributing it entirely to his own eloquence, looked up the necessary information, rose and said:—

"With Simon Kartinkin I should deal according to Article 1452, and paragraph 4 of Article 1453. Euphemia Bochkova according to Article 1659. Katerina Maslova according to Article 1454."

All three punishments were the heaviest that could be inflicted.

"The Court will adjourn to consider the sentence," said the president, rising. Everybody rose after him and, with the pleasant feeling of a task well done, began to leave the room or move about in it.

"D' you know, sirs, we have made a shameful hash of it?" said Peter Gerasimovich, approaching Nekhlyudov, to whom the foreman was relating something. "Why, we've got her to Siberia."

"What do you say?" exclaimed Nekhlyudov. This time he did not notice the teacher's familiarity.

"Why! we did not put in our answer 'Guilty, but without intent to cause death.' The secretary just told me that the public prosecutor is for condemning her to fifteen years' penal servitude."

"Well, but it was decided that way," said the foreman.

Peter Gerasimovich began to dispute this, saying that since she did not take the money it followed naturally that she could not have had any intention of committing murder.

"But I read the answer before going out," said the foreman, defending himself, "and nobody objected."

"I had just then gone out of the room," said Peter Gerasimovich, turning to Nekhlyudov, "and your thoughts must have been wool-gathering to let the thing pass."

"I never thought——" said Nekhlyudov.

"Oh, you didn't?"

"But we can get it put right," said Nekhlyudov.

"Oh dear, no; it's finished."

Nekhlyudov looked at the prisoners. They whose fate was being decided still sat motionless behind the railing in front of the soldiers. Maslova was smiling. An evil feeling stirred in Nekhlyudov's soul. Up to now, expecting her acquittal and thinking she would remain in the town, he was uncertain how to act towards her. Any kind of relation with her would be so very difficult. But Siberia and penal servitude at once cut off every possibility of any kind of relation with her. The wounded bird would stop struggling in the game-bag, and would remind him of its existence no longer.

Chapter XXIV

PETER GERASIMOVICH'S assumption was correct.

The president came back from the consulting-room with a paper, and read as follows:—

"April 28, 188—. By His Imperial Majesty's ukase, the M—— Criminal Court, on the strength of the decision of the jury, in accordance with Section 3 of Article 771, and Section 3 of Articles 776 and 777, decrees that the peasant, Simon Kartinkin, thirty-three years of age, and the *meshchanka* Katerina Maslova, twenty-eight years of age, shall be deprived of all property rights and be sent to penal servitude in Siberia, Kartinkin for eight, Maslova for four years, with the consequences stated in Article 25 of the code. The *meshchanka*, Bochkova, forty-three years of age, shall be deprived of all special personal and acquired rights, and be imprisoned for three years with consequences in accord with Article 48 of the code. The costs of the case to be borne equally by the prisoners; in case of their being without sufficient property, the costs to be transferred to the Treasury. Articles of material evidence to be sold, the ring to be returned, the glass vessels destroyed."

Kartinkin stood holding his arms close to his sides and moving his lips. Bochkova seemed perfectly calm. Maslova, when she heard the sentence, blushed scarlet. "I'm not guilty, not guilty!" she suddenly cried, so that it resounded through the room. "It is a sin! I am not guilty! I never wished—I never thought! It is the truth I am saying—the truth!" and sinking on the bench she burst into tears and sobbed aloud. When Kartinkin and Bochkova went out she still sat crying, so that a gendarme had to touch the sleeve of her cloak.

"No; it is impossible to leave it so," said Nekhlyudov to himself, utterly forgetting his evil thoughts. He hurried out into the corridor after her. Without knowing why, he wished to look at her once more. There was quite a crowd at the door. The advocates and jury were going out, pleased to have finished the business, so he was obliged to wait a few seconds, and when he at last got out into the corridor she was far in front. He hurried along the corridor after her, regardless of the attention he was attracting, caught her up, passed her, and stopped. She had ceased crying and only sobbed, wiping her red discoloured face with the end of her kerchief. She passed without noticing him. Then he hurried back to see the president. The latter had already left the Court, and Nekhlyudov following him into the lobby, went up to him just as he had put on his light grey overcoat and was taking his silver-mounted walking-stick from an attendant.

"Sir, may I have a few words with you concerning the case that has just been tried?" said Nekhlyudov. "I am one of the jury."

"Oh, certainly, Prince Nekhlyudov. I shall be delighted. I think we have met before," said the president, pressing Nekhlyudov's hand and recalling with pleasure the evening when he first met Nekhlyudov, and had danced so gaily, better than all the young people. "What can I do for you?"

"There was a mistake in the answer concerning Maslova. She is not guilty of the poisoning, and yet she is condemned to penal servitude," said Nekhlyudov, with a preoccupied and gloomy air.

"The Court passed sentence in accordance with the answers you yourselves gave," said the president, moving towards the front entrance, "though they seemed not to be quite consistent." And he remembered that he had been going to explain to the jury that a verdict of "guilty" meant guilty of intentional murder unless the words "without intent to take life" were added, but had, in his hurry to get the business over, omitted to do so.

"Yes, but could not the mistake be rectified?"

"A reason for an appeal can always be found. You will have to speak to an advocate," said the president, putting on his hat a little to one side and continuing to move towards the door.

"But this is terrible."

"Well, you see, there were two possibilities before Maslova," said the president, evidently wishing to be as polite and pleasant to Nekhlyudov as he could. Then, having arranged his whiskers over his coat-collar, he put his hand lightly under Nekhlyudov's elbow, and, still directing his steps towards the front entrance, he said, "You are going too?"

"Yes," said Nekhlyudov, quickly putting on his coat, and following him.

They stepped out into the bright, merry sunlight, and had to raise their voices on account of the rattling of wheels in the street.

"The situation is a curious one, you see," said the president; "what lay before this Maslova was one of two things: either to be almost acquitted and only imprisoned for a short time—or, taking the preliminary confinement into consideration, perhaps not at all—or Siberia. There is nothing between. Had you but added the words, 'without intent to cause death,' she would have been acquitted."

"Yes, it was inexcusable of me to omit that," said Nekhlyudov.

"That's where the whole matter lies," said the president, with a smile, and looked at his watch. He had only three-quarters of an hour left before the time appointed by his Clara would elapse.

"Now, if you like, speak to the advocates. You'll have to find a reason for an appeal, but that can be easily done." Then, turning to an *izvozchik*, he called out, "To the Dvoryanskaya, thirty kopeyks; I never give more."

"All right, your honour; I'll take you."

"Good afternoon. If I can be of any use, my address is House Dvornikov, on the Dvoryanskaya; it's easy to remember." And bowing in a friendly manner he got into the trap and drove off.

Chapter XXV

HIS conversation with the president, and the fresh air, quieted Nekhlyudov a little. He now thought that the feelings he had experienced had been exaggerated by the unusual surroundings in which he had spent the whole of the morning.

"Of course it's a strange and striking coincidence, and it is absolutely necessary to do all in my power to lighten her fate, and to do it as soon as possible. Yes, at once! I must find out here in the Court where Fanarin or Mikishin lives," he said, recalling the names of two well-known advocates. He returned to the Court, took off his overcoat, and went upstairs. In the first corridor he met Fanarin himself. He stopped him, and told him that he was just going to look him up on a matter of business.

Fanarin knew Nekhlyudov by sight and name, and said he would be very glad to be of service to him.

"Though I am rather tired, still, if your business will not take very long, perhaps you might tell me what it is now. Will you step in here?" And he led Nekhlyudov into a room, probably some judge's cabinet. They sat down by the table.

"Well, and what is your business?"

"First of all, I must ask you to keep the business private. I do not want it known that I take an interest in the affair."

"Oh, that of course. Well?"

"I was on the jury to-day, and we have condemned a woman to Siberia, an innocent woman. This troubles me very much." Nekhlyudov, to his own surprise, blushed and became confused. Fanarin glanced at him rapidly, and looked down again, listening.

"Well?" said he.

"We have condemned a woman, and I should like to appeal to a higher Court."

"To the Senate, you mean," said Fanarin, correcting him.

"Yes, and I should like to ask you to take the case in hand." Nekhlyudov wanted to get the most difficult part over, and added: "I will take the costs of the case on myself, whatever they may be."

"Oh, we shall settle all that," said the advocate, smiling with condescension at Nekhlyudov's inexperience in these matters. "What is the case?"

Nekhlyudov stated what had happened.

"All right. I'll set to work and look through the case to-morrow. Then come the day after—no—better on Thursday. Come to me after six and I will give you an answer. Well, and now let us go; I have a few inquiries to make here."

Nekhlyudov took leave of him and went out.

The talk with the advocate, and the fact that he had taken measures for Maslova's defence, quieted him still more. He went out into the street. The weather was beautiful, and he was glad to draw in a long breath of spring air. He was at once surrounded by *izvozchiks* offering their services, but went on foot. At once a whole swarm of pictures and memories of Katusha and his conduct to her began whirling in his brain, and he felt depressed and everything seemed gloomy. "No, I

shall consider all this later on; I must now get rid of all these disagreeable impressions," he thought to himself.

He remembered the Korchagins' dinner and looked at his watch. It
was not yet too late to get there in time. He heard the ringing of a passing tramcar, ran to catch it, and jumped on. He jumped off again when
they got to the market-place, took a good *izvozchik*, and ten minutes
later he was at the entrance of the Korchagins' big house.

Chapter XXVI

"PLEASE to walk in, your excellency," said the friendly, fat doorkeeper
of the Korchagins' big house, opening the door, which moved noiselessly on its patent English hinges; "you are expected. They are at dinner, but the orders are to admit you." The doorkeeper went as far as the
staircase and rang.

"Are there any strangers?" asked Nekhlyudov, taking off his overcoat.

"Only M. Kolsosov and Michael Sergeyevich besides the family."

A very handsome footman, in a swallow-tail coat and white gloves,
looked down from the landing.

"Please to walk up, your excellency," he said. "You are expected."

Nekhlyudov went up and passed through the splendid large dancing-
room, which he knew so well, into the dining-room. There the whole
Korchagin family—except the mother Sophia Vasilyevna, who never
left her boudoir—were sitting round the table. At the head of the table
sat old Korchagin; on his left, the doctor, and on his right, a visitor, Ivan
Ivanich Kolosov, a former *Maréchal de noblesse*, now a bank director,
Korchagin's friend and a Liberal. Next on the left side sat Miss Rayner,
the governess of Missy's little sister, and the four-year-old girl herself.
Opposite them, Missy's brother, Petya, the only son of the Korchagins,
a public-school boy in the Sixth Class. It was because of his examinations that the whole family were still in town. Next to him sat a university student who was coaching him, and Missy's cousin, Michael
Sergeyevich Telegin, generally called Misha; opposite him, Catherine
Alexeyevna, a forty-year-old maiden lady, a Slavophil; and at the foot of
the table sat Missy herself, with an empty place by her side.

"Ah! that's right! Sit down. We are still at the fish," said old
Korchagin with difficulty, chewing carefully with his false teeth, and
lifting his bloodshot eyes (which had no visible lids to open them) to
Nekhlyudov.

"Stephen," he said, with his mouth full, addressing the stout, dignified butler and pointing with his eyes to the empty place. Though Nekhlyudov knew Korchagin very well, and had often seen him at dinner, to-day this red face with the sensual, smacking lips, the fat neck above the napkin stuck into his waistcoat, and the whole overfed military figure, struck him very disagreeably. Nekhlyudov involuntarily remembered what he knew of the cruelty of this man, who, when in command, used to have men flogged, and even hanged, without rhyme or reason, simply because he was rich and had no need to curry favour.

"Immediately, your excellency," said Stephen, getting a large soup-ladle out of the sideboard, which was decorated with a number of silver vases. And he made a sign with his head to the handsome footman, who began at once to arrange the untouched knives and forks and the napkin, elaborately folded with the embroidered family crest uppermost, in front of the empty place next to Missy. Nekhlyudov went round shaking hands with every one, and all, except old Korchagin and the ladies, rose when he approached. And this walk round the table, this shaking the hands of people, with many of whom he never talked, seemed unpleasant and odd. He excused himself for being late, and was about to sit down between Missy and Catherine Alexeyevna, but old Korchagin insisted that if he would not take a glass of vodka he at least must whet his appetite with a bit of something at the side-table, on which stood small dishes of lobster, caviar, cheese, and salt herring. Nekhlyudov did not realise how hungry he was until he began to eat, and then, having taken some bread and cheese, he went on eating with zest.

"Well, have you succeeded in undermining the bases of society?" asked Kolosov, ironically quoting an expression used by a reactionary newspaper in attacking trial by jury. "Acquitted the culprits and condemned the innocent, eh?"

"Undermining the bases—undermining the bases," repeated Prince Korchagin, laughing. He had a firm faith in the wisdom and learning of his chosen friend and companion.

At the risk of seeming rude, Nekhlyudov left Kolosov's question unanswered, and, sitting down to his steaming soup, went on eating.

"Do let him eat," said Missy, with a smile. She used the pronoun as a reminder of her intimacy with Nekhlyudov. Kolosov went on in a loud voice and lively manner to give the contents of the article against trial by jury which had aroused his indignation. Missy's cousin, Michael Sergeyevich, endorsed all his statements, and related the contents of another article in the same paper. Missy looked, as usual, very distinguée, and well, unobtrusively well, dressed.

"You must be terribly tried and hungry," she said, after waiting until Nekhlyudov had swallowed what was in his mouth.

"Not particularly. And you? Have you been to look at the pictures?" he asked.

"No, we put that off. We have been playing tennis at the Salamatovs. It is quite true, Mr. Crooks plays remarkably well."

Nekhlyudov had come here in order to distract his thoughts, for he used to like being in this house, both because its refined luxury had a pleasant effect on him and because of the atmosphere of tender flattery that unobtrusively surrounded him. But, strange to say, to-day everything in the house was repulsive to him—everything: beginning with the door-keeper, the broad staircase, the flowers, the footman, the table decorations, up to Missy herself, who to-day seemed unattractive and affected. Kolosov's self-assured, trivial tone of Liberalism was unpleasant; as was also the sensual, self-satisfied, bull-like appearance of old Korchagin, and the French phrases of Catherine Alexeyevna, the Slavophil. The constrained looks of the governess and the student were unpleasant too, but the most unpleasant of all was the pronoun "him" that Missy had used. Nekhlyudov had long been wavering between two ways of regarding Missy; sometimes he looked at her as if by moonlight and could see in her nothing but what was beautiful; then suddenly, as if the bright sun shone on her, he saw her defects and could not help seeing them. This was such a day for him. To-day he saw all the wrinkles of her face, saw the way her hair was crimped, the sharpness of her elbows, and, especially, how large her thumb-nail was and how like her father's.

"Tennis is a dull game," said Kolosov; "we used to play *laptá*[1] when we were children. That was much more amusing."

"Oh no, you have never tried it; it's awfully interesting," said Missy, laying, it seemed to Nekhlyudov, a very affected stress on the word "awfully." Then a discussion arose in which Michael Sergeyevich, Catherine Alexeyevna, and all took part, except the governess, the student, and the children, who sat silent and wearied.

"Oh, these everlasting disputes!" said old Korchagin, laughing, and he pulled the napkin out of his waistcoat, noisily pushed back his chair (which the footman instantly caught hold of) and left the table.

Everybody rose after him, and went up to another table on which, in bowls, stood glasses of warm scented water. They rinsed their mouths; then resumed the conversation, interesting to no one.

"Don't you think so?" said Missy to Nekhlyudov, calling for a confirmation of the statement that nothing shows up a man's character like a game. She noticed that preoccupied and, as it seemed to her, dissatisfied look which she feared, and she wanted to find out what had caused it.

"Really I can't say; I have never thought about it," Nekhlyudov answered.

---

[1] [Lapta is a game similar to baseball, but using a flat bat rather than a cylindrical one.]

"Will you come to mamma?" asked Missy.

"Yes, yes," he said, in a tone which plainly showed that he did not want to go, and took out a cigarette.

She looked at him in silence questioningly, and he felt ashamed. "To come into a house, and give the people the dumps," he thought about himself; then, trying to be amiable, said that he would go with pleasure if the Princess would admit him.

"Oh yes! Mamma will be pleased. You may smoke there; Ivan Ivanich is also there."

The mistress of the house, Princess Sophia Vasilyevna, was a recumbent lady. It was the eighth year that, when visitors were present, she lay dressed in lace and ribbons, surrounded with velvet, gilding, ivory, bronze, lacquer, and flowers, never going out, and only receiving, as she put it, intimate friends, namely, those who according to her idea stood out from the common herd.

Nekhlyudov was admitted into the number of these friends because he was considered clever, because his mother had been an intimate friend of the family, and because it was desirable that Missy should marry him.

Sophia Vasilyevna's room lay beyond the large and the small drawing-rooms. In the large drawing-room, Missy, who was in front of Nekhlyudov, stopped resolutely, and taking hold of the back of a small gilt chair, faced him.

Missy was very anxious to get married, and as he was a suitable match and she also liked him, she had accustomed herself to the thought that he should be hers (not she his). She pursued her aim with that unconscious yet obstinate cunning often observable in the mentally diseased, and now began talking to him in order to get him to explain his intentions.

"I see something has happened," she said. "Tell me, what is the matter with you?"

He remembered the meeting in the Law Courts, and frowned and blushed.

"Yes, something has happened," he said, wishing to be truthful; "a very unusual and serious event."

"What is it, then? Can you not tell me what it is?"

"Not now. Please do not ask me to tell you. I have not yet had time fully to consider it," and he blushed still more.

"And so you will not tell me?" A muscle twitched in her face and she pushed back the chair she was holding.

"No, I cannot," he answered, feeling that these words were also an answer to himself acknowledging that, in reality, something very important had happened to him.

"Well, then, come!" She shook her head as if to expel useless thoughts, and went on in front of him with a quicker step than usual.

He fancied that her mouth was unnaturally compressed in order to keep back tears. He was ashamed of having hurt her, and yet he knew that the least weakness on his part would mean disaster, that is, would bind him to her. And to-day he feared this more than anything, and he followed her silently to the Princess's boudoir.

Chapter XXVII

PRINCESS SOPHIA VASILYEVNA, Missy's mother, had finished her very elaborate and nourishing dinner. (She always had it alone, so that no one should see her performing this unpoetical function.) By her couch stood a small table with her coffee, and she was smoking a *pachitos*. Princess Sophia Vasilyevna was a long, thin woman, with dark hair, large black eyes, and long teeth, and still pretended to be young.

Her intimacy with the doctor was getting talked about. Nekhlyudov had known of that for some time; but when she saw the doctor sitting by her couch, his oily, glistening beard parted in the middle, he not only remembered the rumours about them, but felt greatly disgusted. By the table, on a low, soft, easy chair next to Sophia Vasilyevna, sat Kolosov stirring his coffee. A glass of liqueur stood on the table. Missy came in with Nekhlyudov, but did not stay.

"When mamma gets tired of you and drives you away, then come to me," she said, turning to Kolosov and Nekhlyudov, and speaking as if nothing had occurred; and she went away, smiling merrily and stepping noiselessly on the thick carpet.

"How do you do, dear friend? Sit down and talk," said Princess Sophia Vasilyevna, with her artificial and insincere-looking but very natural smile, showing her fine, long teeth—a splendid imitation of what her own had once been. "I hear that you have come from the Law Courts very much depressed. I think it must be very trying to a person with a heart," she added in French.

"Yes, that is so," said Nekhlyudov. "One often feels one's own de . . . ; one feels one has no right to judge."

"*Comme c' est vrai*," she cried, as if struck by the truth of this remark. She was in the habit of artfully flattering all those with whom she conversed. "Well, and what of your picture? It does interest me so. If I were not such a sad invalid, I should have been to see it long ago," she said.

"I have quite given it up," Nekhlyudov replied dryly. The falseness of her flattery seemed as evident to him to-day as her age, which she was trying to conceal, and he could not put himself into the right state to behave politely.

"Oh, that *is* a pity! . . . Why, he has a real talent for art; I have it from Repin's own lips," she added, turning to Kolosov.

"Why is it she is not ashamed of lying so?" Nekhlyudov thought, and frowned.

When she had convinced herself that Nekhlyudov was in a bad temper and that one could not entice him into an agreeable and clever conversation, Sophia Vasilyevna turned to Kolosov, asking his opinion of a new play. She asked it in a tone as if Kolosov's opinion would decide all doubts, and each word of this opinion be worthy of being immortalised. Kolosov found fault both with the play and its author, and that led him to express his views on art. Princess Sophia Vasilyevna, while trying to defend the play, seemed at the same time impressed by the truth of his arguments, either giving in at once, or at least modifying her opinion. Nekhlyudov looked and listened, but neither saw nor heard what was going on before him.

Listening now to Sophia Vasilyevna, now to Kolosov, Nekhlyudov noticed that neither he nor she cared anything about the play or each other, and that if they talked it was only to gratify the physical desire to move the muscles of the throat and tongue after having eaten; and that Kolosov, having drunk vodka, wine, and liqueur, was a little tipsy—not tipsy like the peasants, who drink seldom, but like people to whom drinking wine has become a habit. He did not reel about or talk nonsense, but he was in a state that was not normal: excited and self-satisfied. Nekhlyudov also noticed that during the conversation Princess Sophia Vasilyevna kept glancing uneasily at the window, through which a slanting ray of sunshine, which might vividly light up her aged face, was beginning to creep towards her.

"How true," she said, in reference to some remark of Kolosov's, touching the button of an electric bell by the side of her couch. The doctor rose, and, like one who is at home, left the room without saying anything. Sophia Vasilyevna followed him with her eyes, and continued the conversation.

"Please, Philip, draw these curtains," she said, pointing to the window, when the handsome footman came in answer to the bell.

"No; whatever you may say, there is some mysticism in him; without mysticism there can be no poetry," she said, one of her black eyes angrily following the footman's movements as he was drawing the curtains.

"Without poetry, mysticism is superstition; without mysticism, poetry is—prose," she pursued, with a sorrowful smile, still not losing sight of the footman and the curtains. "Philip, not that curtain; the one at the large window," she exclaimed in a suffering tone. Sophia Vasilyevna was evidently pitying herself for having to make the effort of saying these words; and, to soothe her feelings, she raised to her lips, with her jewel-bedecked fingers, the scented, smoking *pachitos*.

The broad-chested, muscular, handsome Philips bowed slightly, as if begging pardon; and stepping lightly across the carpet with his broad-calved, strong legs, obediently and silently went to the other window, and, looking at the Princess, began carefully to arrange the curtain so that not a single ray should dare fall on her. But again he did not satisfy her, and again she had to interrupt the conversation about mysticism, and correct in a martyred tone the unintelligent Philip, who was tormenting her so pitilessly. For a moment a light flashed in Philip's eyes.

"The devil take you! What do you want?" was probably what he said to himself, thought Nekhlyudov, who had been observing the whole scene. But the strong, handsome Philip at once managed to conceal the signs of his impatience, and quietly went on carrying out the orders of the worn, weak, false Sophia Vasilyevna.

"Of course, there is a good deal of truth in Darwin's teaching," said Kolosov, lolling back in the low chair and looking at Sophia Vasilyevna with sleepy eyes; "but he overstepped the mark. Oh yes."

"And you? Do you believe in heredity?" asked Sophia Vasilyevna, turning to Nekhlyudov, whose silence annoyed her.

"In heredity?" he asked. "No, I don't." At this moment his whole mind was occupied by strange images that in some unaccountable way rose in his imagination. By the side of the strong and handsome Philip he seemed at this minute to see the nude figure of Kolosov as an artist's model; with his stomach like a melon, his bald head, and his arms without muscle, like pestles. In the same dim way the limbs of Sophia Vasilyevna, now covered with silks and velvets, rose up in his mind as they must be in reality; but this mental picture was too horrid and he tried to drive it away.

Sophia Vasilyevna measured him with her eyes.

"Well, but you know Missy is waiting for you," she said. "Go and find her. She wants to play you a new piece by Grieg; it is most interesting."

"She does not mean to play anything; the woman is simply lying, for some reason or other," thought Nekhlyudov, rising and pressing Sophia Vasilyevna's transparent and bony, ringed hand.

Catherine Alexeyevna met him in the drawing-room, and at once began, in French as usual:—

"I see the duties of a juryman act depressingly upon you."

"Yes; pardon me, I am in low spirits to-day, and have no right to weary others by my presence," said Nekhlyudov.

"Why are you in low spirits?"

"Allow me not to speak of that," he said, looking round for his hat.

"Don't you remember how you used to say that we must always tell the truth? And what cruel truths you used to tell us all! Why do you not wish to speak out now? . . . Don't you remember, Missy?" she said, turning to Missy, who had just come in.

"We were playing a game then," said Nekhlyudov seriously; "one may tell the truth in a game, but in reality we are so bad . . . I mean I am so bad, that I, at least, cannot tell the truth."

"Oh, do not correct yourself, bur rather tell us why we are so bad," said Catherine Alexeyevna, playing with her words and pretending not to notice how serious Nekhlyudov was.

"Nothing is worse than to confess to being in low spirits," said Missy. "I never do it, and therefore am always in good spirits. Well, are you coming? We'll try to disperse your *mauvaise humeur.*"

Nekhlyudov felt as a horse must feel when it is being caressed to make it submit to having the bit put in its mouth and be harnessed, and to-day he felt less than ever inclined to pull.

He excused himself, saying he had to be at home, and began taking leave. Missy kept his hand longer than usual.

"Remember that what is important to you is important to your friends," she said. "Are you coming to-morrow?"

"Probably not," said Nekhlyudov; and feeling ashamed, without knowing whether for her or for himself, he blushed and went away.

"What is it? *Comme cela m'intrigue,*"[1] said Catherine Alexeyevna. "I must find out all about it. I suppose it is some *affaire d' amour propre; il est très susceptible, notre cher* Mitya!"[2]

"*Plutôt une affaire d'amour sale,*"[3] Missy was going to say, but stopped and looked down with a face from which all the light had gone—a very different face from the one with which she had looked at him. Even to Catherine Alexeyevna she would not make so vulgar a pun, but only said: "We all have our good and our bad days."

"Is it possible that he, too, will deceive?" she thought; "after all that has happened it would be very bad of him."

If Missy had had to explain what she meant by "after all that has happened" she could have said nothing definite, and yet she knew that he had not only excited her hopes but had almost given her a promise. No definite words had passed between them—only looks and smiles and

---

[1] How it excites my curiosity.

[2] Some affair of wounded self-love (or clean love); he is very touchy, our dear Mitya!

[3] Rather, an affair of dirty love.

hints; but still she considered him as her own, and to lose him would be very hard.

Chapter XXVIII

"SHAMEFUL AND stupid, horrid and shameful!" Nekhlyudov kept saying to himself, as he walked home along the familiar streets. The depression he had felt whilst speaking to Missy would not leave him. He felt that, looking at it externally as it were, he was in the right, for he had never said anything to her that could be considered binding, never made her an offer; but he knew that in reality he had bound himself to her, had promised to be hers. And yet to-day he felt with his whole being that he could not marry her.

"Shameful and horrid, horrid and shameful!" he repeated to himself, not only about his relations with Missy, but about everything. "Everything is horrid and shameful," he muttered, as he stepped into the porch of his house. "I am not going to have any supper," he said to his man-servant Korney, who followed him into the dining-room, where the cloth was laid for supper and tea. "You may go."

"Yes, sir," said Korney, yet he did not go, but began clearing the supper off the table. Nekhlyudov looked at Korney with a feeling of ill-will. He wished to be left alone, and it seemed to him that everybody was bothering him in order to spite him. When Korney had gone away with the supper things Nekhlyudov went up to the samovar and was going to make himself some tea, but, hearing Agrafena Petrovna's footsteps, he went hurriedly into the drawing-room so as not to be seen by her, and shut the door after him. It was in this room his mother had died three months before. On entering the room, in which two lamps with reflectors were burning, one lighting up his father's portrait and the other his mother's, he remembered what his last relations with his mother had been. And they also seemed unnatural and disgusting. And this was also shameful and horrid. He remembered how, during the latter period of her illness, he had simply wished her to die. He had said to himself that he wished it for her sake, that she might be released from her suffering, but in reality he wished for his own sake to be released from the sight of her sufferings.

Trying to recall a pleasant recollection of her, he went up to look at her portrait, painted by a celebrated artist for five thousand rubles. She was depicted in a low-necked black velvet dress, and the artist had evidently painted with particular care the outlines of the breasts, the space between them, the dazzlingly beautiful shoulders and the neck. This was quite revolting and horrid. There was something very revolting and blasphemous in this representation of his mother as a half-nude beauty. It was all the more disgusting because three months ago, in this very room, lay this same woman, dried up to a mummy, yet filling not only this room, but the whole of the house, with an unbearably disagreeable smell which nothing would overcome. He seemed to smell it even now. And he remembered how a few days before her death she had clasped his hand with her bony, discoloured fingers, looked into his eyes, and said, "Do not judge me, Mitya, if I have not done what I should," and how the tears came into her eyes, grown pale with suffering.

"Ah, how horrid!" he said to himself, looking up once more at the half-naked woman, with the splendid marble shoulders and arms, and the triumphant smile on her lips. The half-bared bosom of the portrait reminded him of another young woman whom he had seen exposed in the same way a few days before. It was Missy, who had devised an excuse for calling him into her room just as she was ready to go to a ball, so that he might see her in her ball dress. It was with disgust that he remembered her fine shoulders and arms. "And that coarse, animal father of hers, with his doubtful past and his cruelties, and the *bel esprit* her mother, with her doubtful reputation!" All this disgusted him, and also made him feel ashamed. "Shameful and horrid; horrid and shameful!"

"No, no," he thought; "freedom I must have: freedom from all these false relations with the Korchagins and Mary Vasilyevna and from the inheritance and all the rest. Oh, to breathe freely!—to go abroad, to Rome, and work at my picture." He remembered his doubts as to his talent for art. "Well, never mind; only just to breathe freely. First Constantinople, then Rome. Only to get through with this jury business, and to arrange with the advocate first."

Then suddenly there arose in his mind an extremely vivid picture of the prisoner with black slightly-squinting eyes, and how she began to cry when the prisoners' last words had been heard; and he hurriedly put out his cigarette, pressing it into the ash-tray, lit another, and began pacing up and down the room. One after another the scenes he had lived through with her rose in his mind. He recalled that last meeting with her, the animal passion that had seized him, and the disappointment after it had been gratified. He remembered the white dress and blue sash, the early mass. "Why, I loved her, really loved her with a good, pure love that night; I loved her even before; yes, I loved her when I stayed with my aunts the first time and was writing my composition." And he remembered himself as he had then been. A breath of that freshness, youth and fulness of life seemed to touch him, and he grew painfully sad.

The difference between what he had been then and what he now was, was enormous: just as great, if not greater, than the difference between Katusha in church that night, and the prostitute who had been carousing with the merchant and whom they had condemned this morning. Then he was free and fearless, and innumerable possibilities lay ready to open before him; now he felt himself caught in the meshes of a stupid, empty, valueless, frivolous life, out of which he saw no means of extricating himself even if he wished to, which he hardly did. He remembered how proud he was at one time of his straightforward-ness, how he had made a rule of always speaking the truth, and really had been truthful; and how he was now sunk deep in lies, the most dreadful of lies—lies considered as truth by all who surrounded him. And, as far as he could see, there was no way out of these lies. He had sunk in the mire, got used to it, wallowed in it.

How was he to break off his relations with Mary Vasilyevna and her husband in such a way as to be able to look him and his children in the eyes? How disentangle himself from Missy? How escape the contradic-tion of his recognition that holding land was unjust and his retention of the land inherited from his mother? How atone for his sin against Katusha? This last, at any rate, could not be left as it was. He could not abandon a woman he had loved, and satisfy himself by paying money to an advocate to save her from hard labour in Siberia. She had not even deserved hard labour. Atone for a fault by paying money? Had he not then, when he gave her the money, thought he was atoning for his fault?

And he clearly recalled to mind that moment when, having stopped her in the passage, he thrust the money into her apron-bib and ran away. "Oh, that money!" he thought, with the same horror and disgust he had then felt. "Oh, dear! oh, dear! how disgusting," he cried out aloud, as he had done then. "Only a scoundrel, a knave, could do such a thing. And I–I am that knave, that scoundrel!" he went aloud. "But is it possible?"—he stopped and stood still—"is it possible that I am really a scoundrel?—Well, who but I?" he answered himself. "And then, is this the only thing?" he went on convicting himself. "Was not my con-duct towards Mary Vasilyevna and her husband base and disgusting? And my attitude towards money? To use riches, considered by me unlawful, on the plea that they were supplied to me by my mother? And the whole of my idle, detestable life? And my conduct towards Katusha to crown all? Knave and scoundrel! Let them judge me as they like; I could deceive them, but myself I cannot deceive."

And, suddenly, he understood that the aversion he had lately, and particularly to-day, felt for everybody—the Prince, and Sophia Vasilyevna, and Korney, and Missy—was an aversion for himself. And strange to say, in this acknowledgment of his baseness there was something though painful yet joyful and quieting.

More than once in Nekhlyudov's life there had been what he called a "cleansing of the soul." By cleansing of the soul he meant a state of mind in which, after a long period of sluggish inner life, a total cessation of its activity, he began to clear out all the rubbish that had accumulated in his soul and caused the cessation of true life. After such an awakening, Nekhlyudov always made some rules for himself which he meant to follow for ever after, wrote his diary, and began afresh a life which he hoped never to change again. "Turning over a new leaf," he called it to himself in English. But each time the temptations of the world entrapped him, and without noticing it he fell again, often lower than before.

He had thus several times in his life raised and cleansed himself. The first time this happened was during the summer he spent with his aunts; this was his most vital and rapturous awakening, and its effects had lasted some time. Another awakening was when he left the Civil Service and joined the army at war-time, ready to sacrifice his life. But here the choking-up process was soon accomplished. Then an awakening came when he left the army and went abroad, devoting himself to art.

From that time until now a long period had elapsed without any cleansing, and therefore the discord between the demands of his conscience and the life he was leading was greater than it had ever been before. He was horror-struck when he saw how great the divergence was. It was so great, and the defilement was so complete, that he despaired of the possibility of being cleansed. "Have you not tried before to perfect yourself and become better, and nothing has come of it?" whispered the voice of the tempter within. "What is the use of trying any more? Are you the only one?—all are alike, such is life," whispered the voice. But the free spiritual being, which alone is true, alone powerful, alone eternal, had already awakened in Nekhlyudov, and he could not but believe in it. Enormous though the distance was between what he wished to be and what he was, nothing appeared insurmountable to the newly awakened spiritual being.

"At any cost I will break this lie that binds me; will tell everybody the truth, and act the truth," he said resolutely, aloud. "I shall tell Missy the truth; tell her I am a profligate and cannot marry her, and have only uselessly upset her. I shall tell Mary Vasilyevna. . . . Oh, there is nothing to tell her. I shall tell her husband that I, scoundrel that I am, have been deceiving him. I shall dispose of the inheritance in such a way as to acknowledge the truth. I shall tell her, Katusha, that I am a scoundrel and have sinned against her, and will do all I can to ease her lot. Yes, I will see her, and ask her to forgive me. . . .

"Yes, I will beg her pardon, as children do." . . . He stopped—"will marry her if necessary." He stopped again, folded his hands in front of his breast as he used to do when a little child, lifted his eyes, and said, addressing some one: "Lord, help me, teach me, come, enter within me, and purify me of all this abomination."

He prayed, asking God to help him, to enter into him and cleanse him; and what he was praying for had happened already: the God within him had awakened in his consciousness. He felt himself one with Him, and therefore felt not only the freedom, fulness and joy of life, but all the power of righteousness. All, all the best that a man can do, he felt capable of doing. His eyes filled with tears as he was saying all this to himself; good and bad tears: good because they were tears of joy at the awakening of the spiritual being within him, the being that had been asleep all these years, and bad tears because they were also tears of tenderness to himself at his own goodness.

He felt hot, and went to the window and opened it. The window faced the garden. It was a moonlit, quiet, fresh night; something rattled past, and then all was still. The shadow of a tall poplar fell on the ground just opposite the window, and all the intricate pattern of its bare branches was clearly defined on the clean-swept gravel. To the left the roof of a coach-house shone white in the moonlight—in front the black shadow of the garden wall was visible through the tangled branches of the trees. Nekhlyudov gazed at the roof, the moonlit garden, and the shadows of the poplar, and drank in the fresh, invigorating air.

"How delightful, how delightful; oh God, how delightful!" he said, meaning that which was going on in his soul.

Chapter XXIX

MASLOVA ONLY reached her cell at six in the evening, tired and foot-sore, having, unaccustomed as she was to walking, gone ten miles on the stony road that day. She was crushed by the unexpectedly severe sentence and tormented by hunger. During the first interval of the trial, when the soldiers were eating bread and hard-boiled eggs near her, her mouth watered and she realised she was hungry, but considered it beneath her dignity to beg of them. Three hours later the desire to eat had passed, and she only felt weak. It was then she received the unexpected sentence. At first she thought she had misunderstood: she could not imagine herself as a convict in Siberia, and could not believe what she heard. But seeing the quiet, business-like faces of judges and jury, who heard this news as if it were perfectly natural and expected, she grew indignant, and proclaimed loudly to the whole Court that she was not guilty. Seeing that her scream was also taken as something natural and expected, which could not alter matters, she began to cry in despair, feeling that she must submit to the cruel and surprising injustice that had been done her. What astonished her most was that young men—or, at any rate, not old men—the same men who always looked so approvingly at her (one of them, the public prosecutor, she had seen in quite a different humour) had condemned her. While she was sitting in the prisoners' room before the trial and during the intervals, she saw these men look in at the open door, pretending they had to pass there on some business, or enter the room and gaze on her with approval. And then, for some unknown reason, these same men had condemned her to hard labour, though she was innocent of the charge laid against her. At first she cried, but then quieted down and sat perfectly stunned in the prisoners' room, waiting to be led back. She wanted only one thing now—to smoke. She was in this state when Bochkova and Kartinkin were led into the same room after being sentenced. Bochkova began at once to scold her, and to call her a "convict."

"Well! What have you gained? Justified yourself, have you? you slut! What you have deserved, that you've got. Out in Siberia you'll give up your finery, no fear!"

Maslova sat motionless with her hands inside her sleeves, hanging her head and looking in front of her at the dirty floor. She only said: "I don't bother you, so don't you bother me. . . . I don't bother you, do I?" she repeated several times, and was silent again. She brightened up a little when Bochkova and Kartinkin were led away and an attendant brought her three rubles.

"Are you Maslova?" he asked. "Here you are; a lady sent it you," he said, giving her the money.

"A lady—what lady?"

"You just take it. I'm not going to talk to you."

This money was sent by Kitaeva, the brothel-keeper. As she was leaving the Court she turned to the usher with the question whether she might give Maslova a little money. The usher said she might. Having got permission, she removed the three-buttoned suède kid glove from her plump white hand, brought out of the back folds of her silk skirt an elegant purse, and took out of it a bundle of coupons[1] just cut from

---

[1] In Russia coupons cut off interest-bearing papers are often used as money.

interest-bearing papers she had earned in her establishment, chose one worth two rubles and fifty kopeyks, and added two twenty and one ten kopeyk coins, and gave all this to the usher. The usher called an attendant, and in the presence of the donor handed the money to him.

"Blease to giff it accurately," said Caroline Albertovna Kitaeva.

The attendant was hurt by her want of confidence, and that was why he treated Maslova so brusquely.

Maslova was glad of the money, because it could give her the only thing she now desired. 'If I could but get cigarettes and take a whiff!' she said to herself, and all her thoughts centered on the one desire to smoke. She so longed for it that she greedily breathed in the air when the fumes of tobacco reached her from the door of a room that opened into the corridor. But she had long to wait, for the secretary, who should have given the order for her to go, forgot about the prisoners while talking and even disputing with one of the advocates about the article forbidden by the censor.

At last, about five o'clock, she was allowed to go, and was led away through the back door by her escort, the Nizhny man and the Chuvash. Then, still within the entrance to the Law Courts, she gave them twenty kopeyks, asking them to get her two rolls and some cigarettes. The Chuvash laughed, took the money, and said: "All right; I'll get 'em," and did indeed get her the rolls and the cigarettes and honestly return the change. She was not allowed to smoke on the way, and with her craving unsatisfied she continued her walk to the prison. When she was brought to the gate of the prison, a hundred convicts who had arrived by rail were being led in. The convicts—bearded, clean shaven, old, young, Russians, foreigners, some with their heads shaved, and rattling the chains on their legs—filled the ante-room with dust, noise, and an acid smell of perspiration. Passing Maslova, all the convicts looked at her, and some came up to her and brushed against her in passing.

"Ay, here's a wench—a fine one," said one.

"My respects to you, miss," said another, winking at her.

One dark man with a moustache, the rest of his face and the nape of his neck clean shaven, rattling his chains and catching his feet in them, sprang up to her and embraced her.

"What! don't you know your chum? Come, come; don't give yourself airs," shouted he, showing his teeth, and his eyes glittering when she pushed him away.

"You rascal! what are you up to?" shouted the inspector's assistant, coming up from behind. The convict shrank back and jumped away. The assistant turned on Maslova.

"What are you here for?"

Maslova was going to say she had been brought back from the Law Courts, but she was so tired that she did not care to speak.

"She has returned from the Law Courts, sir," said one of the soldiers, coming forward with his fingers to his cap.

"Well, hand her over to the chief warder. I won't have this sort of thing."

"Yes, sir."

"Sokolov, take her in!" shouted the assistant inspector.

The chief warder came up, gave Maslova an angry push on the shoulder, and making a sign with his head for her to follow, led her into the corridor of the women's ward. There she was searched, and as nothing prohibited was found on her (she had hidden her box of cigarettes inside a roll) she was led into the same cell she had left in the morning.

Chapter XXX

THE CELL in which Maslova was imprisoned was a long room twenty-one feet long and sixteen feet broad; it had two windows and a large, dilapidated stove. Two-thirds of the space was taken up by plank-beds. The planks they were made of had warped and shrunk. Opposite the door hung a dark-coloured icon with a wax candle sticking to it and a bunch of immortelles hanging down from it. To the left, on a blackened part of the floor behind the door, stood a stinking tub. The inspection had taken place, and the women were locked in for the night.

The occupants of this room were fifteen persons, including three children. It was still quite light. Only two of the women were lying down: a consumptive woman imprisoned for theft, and an idiot arrested because she had no passport, who spent most of her time in sleep. The consumptive woman was not asleep, but lay with wide-open eyes, her cloak folded under her head, trying to keep back the phlegm that irritated her throat, so as not to cough.

Some of the other women, most of whom had nothing on but coarse brown holland chemises, stood looking out of the window at the convicts down in the yard, and three sat sewing. Among these latter was that same old woman who had seen Maslova off in the morning—Korableva, a tall, powerful, austere-looking woman, with knit brows, a flabby double chin, a short plait of fair hair, turning grey on the temples, and a hairy wart on her cheek. She was sentenced to hard labour in Siberia for killing her husband with an axe because he made up to her daughter. She was at the head of the women in the cell, and found means of carrying on a trade in spirits with them. Beside her sat another woman, who was sewing a coarse canvas sack. This was the wife of a railway watchman,[1] imprisoned for three months because she did not come out with the flags to meet a train that was passing, and an accident occurred in consequence. She was a short, snub-nosed woman, with small black eyes; kind and talkative. The third of the women who were sewing was Theodosia, quite a young girl, white and rosy, very pretty, with bright child's eyes, and long, fair plaits, which she wore twisted round her head. She was kept in prison for attempting to poison her husband. She had done this immediately after her wedding (she had been given in marriage without her consent at the age of sixteen). But in the eight months during which she had been let out on bail, she had not only made it up with her husband but had come to love him, so that when her trial came on they were heart and soul to one another. Although her husband, her father-in-law, and especially her mother-in-law, who had grown very fond of her, did all they could to get her acquitted, she was sentenced to hard labour in Siberia. The kind, merry, ever-smiling Theodosia had her plank-bed next to Maslova's, and had grown so fond of her that she took it upon herself as a duty to attend and wait on her. Two other women were sitting without any work on the plank-beds. One was a woman of about forty, with a pale, thin face, who had probably once been very handsome. She sat with her baby at her thin, white breast. The crime she had committed was that when a conscript was (according to the peasants' view) unlawfully taken from their village, and the people stopped the police officer and released the conscript, she (an aunt of the lad unlawfully taken) was the first to catch hold of the bridle of the horse on which he was being carried off. The other woman who sat doing nothing was a kindly, grey-haired old woman with a bent back. She sat on the bed behind the stove, and pretended to catch a fat four-year-old boy who ran backwards and forwards in front of her, laughing gaily. This boy had only a little shirt on and his hair was cut short. As he ran past the old woman he kept repeating, "There, haven't caught me!"

This old woman and her son were accused of incendiarism. She bore her imprisonment with perfect cheerfulness, but was concerned about her son, and chiefly about her "old man," who she feared would get into a terrible state with no one to wash for him.

Besides these seven women there were four standing at one of the open windows, holding on to the iron bars. They were making signs

---

[1] There are small watchmen's cottages at distances of about one mile from each other along the Russian railways, and the watchmen or their wives have to meet every train.

and shouting to the convicts whom Maslova had met on returning to the prison, and who were now passing through the yard. One of these women was big and heavy, with a flabby body, red hair, and freckles on her pale yellow face, her hands, and her fat neck, which protruded from her unbuttoned collar. She shouted something indecent in a loud, raucous voice, and laughed hoarsely. This woman was serving her terms for theft. Beside her stood an awkward, dark little woman, no bigger than a child of ten, with a long waist and very short legs, a red blotchy face, eyes too far apart, and thick lips which did not hide her long teeth. She broke by fits and starts into screeching laughter at what was going on in the yard. She was to be tried for stealing and incendiarism. They nicknamed her Horoshavka[2] because of her love for finery. Behind her, in a very dirty, grey chemise, stood a thin, miserable-looking, pregnant woman who was to be tried for concealment of theft. This woman stood silent, but kept smiling with pleasure and approval at what was going on below. With these stood a short, thick-set peasant woman with prominent eyes and an amiable face, the mother of the boy who was playing with the old woman, and of a seven-year-old girl. These were in prison with her because she had no one to leave them with. She was serving her term of imprisonment for illicit sale of spirits. She stood a little farther from the window knitting a stocking, and though she listened to the other prisoners' words she shook her head disapprovingly, frowned, and closed her eyes. But her seven-year-old daughter, in her little chemise, with loose flaxen hair, her blue eyes fixed, stood holding the red-haired woman by the skirt, and attentively listened to the words of abuse that the women and the convicts flung at each other, repeating them softly, as if learning them by heart. The twelfth prisoner, who paid no attention to what was going on, was a deacon's daughter, a very tall, stately girl, who had drowned her baby in a well. She went about barefoot, wearing only a dirty chemise. The thick short plait of her fair hair had come undone and hung down untidily. Looking at no one, she paced up and down the free space of the cell, turning abruptly every time she came up to the wall.

Chapter XXXI

WHEN THE padlock rattled and the door opened to let Maslova into the cell, all turned towards her. Even the deacon's daughter stopped for a

---

[2] A made-up word from *horosha*, good-looking.

moment and looked at Maslova with lifted brows, but, without saying a word, resumed her energetic striding up and down.

Korableva stuck her needle into the brown sacking and looked questioningly at Maslova through her spectacles.

"Lor' gracious! back again? and I felt sure they'd acquit you. So you've got it?" she said in her hoarse bass, almost like a man's. She took off her spectacles and put her work down beside her on the plank-bed.

"And here have old Aunty and I been saying, 'Why, it may well be they'll let her go free at once.' That also happens, they say. Some get a heap of money even, it all depends on one's luck," the watchman's wife began, singing her words. "And just see how it's turned out. It seems our guessing was all wrong. The Lord willed otherwise, ducky," she went on in her pleasant tones.

"Is it possible? Have they sentenced you?" asked Theodosia, with tender concern, looking at Maslova with her light-blue, childlike eyes; and her bright young face changed as if she were going to cry.

Maslova did not answer, but went on to her place, the second from the end, and sat down beside Korableva.

"Have you had anything to eat?" said Theodosia, rising and coming up to Maslova.

Maslova gave no reply, but, putting the rolls on the bedstead, took off her dusty cloak, and the kerchief off her curly black head. The old woman who had been playing with the boy came up and stood in front of Maslova. "Tz, tz, tz," she clicked with her tongue, shaking her head pityingly. The boy also came up with her, and, putting out his upper lip, stared with wide-open eyes at the rolls Maslova had brought. When, after all that had happened to her that day, Maslova saw all these sympathetic faces, her lips trembled and she felt inclined to cry, but she succeeded in restraining herself until the old woman and the boy came up. When she heard the kind, pitying clicking of the old woman's tongue, and met the boy's serious eyes turned from the rolls to her face, she could bear it no longer; her face quivered, and she burst out sobbing.

"Didn't I tell you to insist on having a proper advocate?" said Korableva. "Well, what is it? Exile?"

Maslova could not answer, but took from inside a roll the box of cigarettes, on which was a picture of a pink-faced lady with hair done up very high and a dress cut low in front, and passed it to Korableva. Korableva looked at it and shook her head, chiefly because she did not approve of Maslova putting her money to such bad use, but she took out a cigarette nevertheless, lit it at the lamp, took a puff, and almost forced it into Maslova's hand. Maslova, still crying, began greedily to inhale the tobacco smoke. "Penal servitude," she muttered, blowing out the smoke, and sobbing.

"Don't they fear the Lord, the cursed soul-slayers?" muttered Korableva, "sentencing the lass for nothing." At this moment the sound of loud, coarse laughter came from the women who were still at the window. The little girl also laughed, and her childish treble mingled with the hoarse and screeching laughter of the others. One of the convicts outside had done something that produced this effect on the onlookers.

"Lawks! see the shaved hound, what he's doing," said the red-haired woman, her whole fat body shaking with laughter; and leaning against the grating she shouted meaningless obscene words.

"Ugh, the fat fright's cackling. What is she laughing at?" said Korableva, and again turned to Maslova: "How many years?" she asked.

"Four," said Maslova, and the tears ran down her cheeks in such profusion that one fell on the cigarette. She crumpled it up angrily and took another.

Though the watchman's wife did not smoke, she picked up the cigarette Maslova had thrown away and began straightening it out, talking unceasingly.

"There, now, ducky, so it's true," she said, "Truth's gone to the dogs and they do what they please, and here we were guessing that you'd go free. Korableva says: 'She'll go free.' 'No,' says I. 'No, dear, my heart tells me they'll give it her,' says I. And so it's turned out," she went on, evidently listening with pleasure to her own voice.

The woman who had been standing by the window now also came up to Maslova, the convicts who had amused them having gone away. The first to come up were the woman imprisoned for illicit trade in spirits, and her little girl. "Why such a hard sentence?" asked the woman, sitting down by Maslova and knitting fast.

"Why so hard? Because there's no money. That's why! Had there been money, and a good lawyer been hired that's up to their tricks, they'd have acquitted her, no fear," said Korableva. "There's what's-his-name—that hairy one with the long nose. He'd bring you out clean from pitch, mum, he would. Ah, if we'd only had him!"

"Him, indeed," said Horoshavka, grinning and sitting down near them. "Why, he wouldn't spit at you for less than a thousand rubles."

"Seems you've also been born under an unlucky star," interrupted the old woman imprisoned for incendiarism. "Only think: to entice the lad's wife, and to lock him up to feed vermin, and me too, in my old days——" she began to re-tell her story for the hundredth time. "If it isn't the beggar's staff, it's the prison. Yes, the beggar's staff and the prison don't wait for an invitation."

"Ah, it seems that's the way with all of them," said the spirit-trader; and looking at her little girl's head she put down her knitting, drew the child between her knees, and began to search her head with deft fingers. "'Why do you sell spirits?' indeed," she went on. "Why?—but what's one to feed the children on?"

These words brought to Maslova's mind a craving for drink.

"A little vodka," she said to Korableva, drying her tears with her sleeve and sobbing less frequently.

"All right, fork out," said Korableva.

Chapter XXXII

MASLOVA GOT out the money, which she had also hidden in a roll, and passed the coupon to Korableva. Korableva, though she could not read, accepted it, trusting to Horoshavka, who knew everything, and who said that the slip of paper was worth two rubles fifty kopeyks, and then climbed up to the ventilator, where she had hidden a small flask of vodka. Seeing this, the women whose places were farther off went away. Meanwhile Maslova shook the dust out of her cloak and kerchief, got up on the bedstead, and began eating a roll.

"I kept your tea for you," said Theodosia, getting down from a shelf a mug and a tin teapot wrapped in a rag, "but I'm afraid it's quite cold." The liquid was quite cold, and tasted more of tin than of tea, yet Maslova filled the mug and began drinking it with her roll. "Finashka, here you are," she said, breaking off a bit of the roll and giving it to the boy, who stood looking at her mouth.

Meanwhile Korableva handed the flask of vodka and a mug to Maslova, who offered some to her and to Horoshavka. These prisoners were considered the aristocracy of the cell because they had some money, and they shared what they possessed with others. In a few minutes Maslova brightened up and related with vivacity what had happened at the Court, mimicking the public prosecutor, and describing what had struck her most, namely, how all the men had followed her about. In the Court they all looked at her, she said, and kept coming into the prisoners' room while she was there.

"One of the guard even says: 'It's all to look at you that they come.' One would come in, 'Where is such a paper?' or something; but I see it is not the paper he wants, he just devours me with his eyes," she said, shaking her head. "Regular artists."

"Yes, that's so," flowed the musical tones of the watchman's wife: "they're like flies after sugar. They can do without anything else, but the likes of them will go without bread sooner than miss that!"

"And here, too," Maslova interrupted her, "the same thing. Hardly had they brought me back when in comes a gang from the railway. They pestered me so, I did not know how to rid myself of them. Thanks to the assistant—he turned them off. One bothered so, I hardly got away."

"What's he like?" asked Horoshavka.

"Dark, with moustaches."

"It must be him."

"Him—who?"

"Why, Shcheglov; him as has just gone by."

"Who is Shcheglov?"

"What, she don't know Shcheglov! Why, he ran away twice from Siberia. Now they've got him, but he'll run away again. The warders themselves are afraid of him," said Horoshavka, who managed to exchange notes with the male prisoners and knew all that went on in the prison. "He'll run away, that's flat."

"Well, if he does get away he won't take us with him," said Korableva, turning to Maslova. "But you'd better tell us now what the advocate says about petitioning. Now's the time to hand it in."

Maslova replied that she knew nothing about it.

At that moment the red-haired woman came up to the "aristocracy" with both freckled hands in her thick hair, scratching her head with her nails.

"I'll tell you all about it, Katerina," she began. "First and foremost, you'll have to write down you're dissatisfied with the sentence, then give notice to the *Procureur*."

"What do you want here?" said Korableva angrily; "smell the vodka, do you? Your chatter's not wanted. We know what to do without your advice."

"No one's speaking to you; what do you stick your nose in for?"

"It's vodka you want, that's why you come wriggling yourself in here."

"Well, give her some," said Maslova, always ready to share anything she possessed with anybody.

"I'll give her something!"

"Come on, then," said the red-haired one, advancing towards Korableva. "Think I'm afraid of the likes of you?"

"Convict fright."

"That's her as says it."

"Slut!"

"I? A slut? Convict! Murderess!" screamed the red-haired one.

"Go away, I tell you," said Korableva gloomily, but the red-haired one came nearer, and Korableva struck her in the chest. The red-haired woman seemed only to have waited for this, and with a sudden movement caught hold of Korableva's hair with one hand and with the other struck her in the face. Korableva seized this hand, and Maslova and Horoshavka caught the red-haired woman by her arms, trying to pull her away, but she let go the old woman's hair for an instant only to twist it round her fist again. Korableva, with her head bent to one side, dealt out blows with one arm and tried to catch the red-haired woman's hand with her teeth, while the rest of the women crowded round screaming and trying to separate the fighters; even the consumptive one came up and stood coughing and watching the fight. The children cried and huddled together. The noise brought the woman warder and a jailer. The fighting women were separated, and Korableva, taking out the bits of torn hair from her head, and the red-haired one, holding her torn chemise together over her yellow breast, began to complain loudly.

"I know, it's all the vodka. Wait a bit: I'll tell the inspector to-morrow: he'll give it you. Can't I smell it? Mind, get it all out of the way, or it'll be the worse for you," said the warder. "We've no time to settle your disputes. Get to your places and be quiet."

But quiet was not soon re-established. For a long time the women went on disputing and explaining to one another whose fault it all was. At last the warder and the jailer left the cell, the women grew quieter and began going to bed, and the old woman went to the icon and commenced praying.

"The two jail-birds have met," the red-haired woman suddenly called out in a hoarse voice from the plank-beds at the other end of the room, accompanying every word with frightfully vile abuse.

"Mind you don't get it again," Korableva replied, also adding words of abuse, and both were quiet again.

"If I'd not been stopped I'd have pulled your damned eyes out," again began the red-haired one, and an answer of the same kind did not fail to follow from Korableva. Then again a short interval and more abuse. But the intervals became longer and longer, as when a thundercloud is passing, and at last all is quiet.

All the rest were in bed, and some began to snore; but the old woman, who always prayed a long time, went on bowing before the icon, and the deacon's daughter, who had got up after the warder left, was pacing up and down the room again. Maslova kept thinking that she was now a convict condemned to hard labour, and that she had twice been reminded of this—once by Bochkova and once by the red-haired woman—and she could not reconcile herself to the thought. Korableva, who was next to her, turned over on her bed.

"There, now," said Maslova, in a low voice; "who would have thought it? See what others do and get nothing for it."

"Never mind, lass. People manage to live in Siberia. As for you, you'll not be lost there either," Korableva said, trying to comfort her.

"I know I'll not be lost; still it is hard. It's not the fate I want—I, who am used to a comfortable life."

"Ah, one can't go against God," said Korableva, with a sigh. "One can't, my dear."

"I know, granny. Still, it's hard."

They were silent for a while.

"Do you hear that baggage?" whispered Korableva, drawing Maslova's attention to a strange sound proceeding from the other end of the room.

It was the smothered sobbing of the red-haired woman. The red-haired woman was crying because she had been abused and had not got any of the vodka she wanted so badly; also because she remembered how all her life she had been abused, mocked at, offended, and beaten. Trying to comfort herself she brought back to mind her love for the factory workman, Fedka Molodenkov, her first love, but then she remembered too how that love had ended. This Molodenkov, being drunk one day, for fun smeared her with vitriol on a tender part, and while she writhed in pain he and his companions roared with laughter. Remembering this she pitied herself, and, thinking no one heard her, began to cry as children cry, sniffing with her nose and swallowing the salt tears.

"I'm sorry for her," said Maslova.

"Of course, one's sorry," said Korableva, "but she shouldn't come bothering."

Chapter XXXIII

THE NEXT morning Nekhlyudov awoke conscious that something had happened to him, and even before he remembered what it was, he knew it to be something important and good.

"Katusha—the trial!" Yes, he must stop lying and tell the whole truth.

By a strange coincidence, on that very morning he received the long-expected letter from Mary Vasilyevna, the wife of the *Maréchal de noblesse*—the very letter he particularly needed. She gave him full freedom, and wished him happiness in his intended marriage.

"Marriage!" he repeated, with irony. "How far I am from all that at present."

And he remembered the intentions he had formed the day before: to tell the husband everything, to make a clean breast of it, and express his readiness to give him any kind of satisfaction. But to-day all this did not seem so easy as on the day before. And then, too, why make a man unhappy by telling him what he does not know? Yes, if he came and asked he would tell him all, but to go purposely and tell—no! that was unnecessary.

And telling the whole truth to Missy seemed just as difficult this morning. Again he could not begin to speak without offence. As in many worldly affairs, something had to remain unexpressed. Only one thing he was firm on: not to visit there, and to tell the truth if asked.

But in connection with Katusha nothing was to remain unspoken. "I will go to the prison, and will tell her everything and ask her to forgive me. And if need be . . . yes, if need be, I will marry her," he thought.

This idea that, on moral grounds, he was ready to sacrifice all and marry her, again made him feel very tender towards himself. Concerning money matters, he resolved to arrange them in accord with his conviction that the holding of landed property was unlawful. Even if he should not be strong enough to give up everything, he would still do what he could, not deceiving himself or others.

It was long since he had met the coming day with so much energy. When Agrafena Petrovna came in, he told her, with more firmness than he thought himself capable of, that he no longer needed this house or her services. There had been a tacit understanding that he was keeping up so large and expensive an establishment because he was thinking of getting married. The giving up of the house had, therefore, a special significance. Agrafena Petrovna looked at him in surprise.

"I thank you very much, Agrafena Petrovna, for all your care of me, but I no longer require so large a house nor so many servants. If you wish to help me, be so good as to see to the things, put them away as used to be done during my mother's lifetime, and when Natasha comes she will arrange about everything." Natasha was Nekhlyudov's sister.

Agrafena Petrovna shook her head. "See to the things? Why, they'll be required again," she said.

"No, they won't, Agrafena Petrovna; I assure you they won't be required," said Nekhlyudov, in answer to what the shaking of her head expressed. "Please, also, tell Korney that I will pay him two months' wages, but shall have no further need of him."

"It is a pity, Dmitry Ivanich, that you should think of doing this," she said. "Supposing you do go abroad, you'll still require a place of residence again."

"You are mistaken in your thoughts, Agrafena Petrovna; I am not going abroad. If I go anywhere it will be in quite another direction." He suddenly blushed very red. "Yes, I must tell her," he thought; "no hiding; everybody must be told."

"A very strange and important thing happened to me yesterday. Do you remember my Aunt Mary Ivanovna's Katusha?"

"Oh yes. Why, I taught her to sew."

"Well, yesterday this Katusha was tried in the Court, and I was on the jury."

"Oh Lord! What a pity!" cried Agrafena Petrovna. "What was she being tried for?"

"Murder; and it is all my doing."

"Well, this is strange; how could it be all your doing?" said Agrafena Petrovna, with a flash in her old eyes.

She knew of the affair with Katusha.

"Yes, I am the cause of it all; and it is this that has altered all my plans."

"What difference can it make to you?" said Agrafena Petrovna, repressing a smile.

"This difference; that I, being the cause of her getting on that path, must do all I can to help her."

"That is just according to your own good pleasure; you are not particularly in fault there. It happens to every one, and if one's reasonable, it all gets smoothed over and forgotten," she said seriously and severely. "Why should you place it to your account? There's no need. I had heard she had strayed from the right path. Well, whose fault is it?"

"Mine! That's why I want to put it right."

"It is hard to put right."

"That is my business. But if you are thinking about yourself, then I will tell you that, as my mother expressed the wish——"

"I am not thinking about myself. I have been so bountifully treated by the dear defunct that I desire nothing. Lisenka" (her married niece) "has been inviting me, and I shall go to her when I am not wanted any longer. Only it is a pity you should take this so to heart; it happens to everybody."

"Well, I do not think so. And I still beg that you will help me to let this house and will put away the things. And please do not be angry with me. I am very, very grateful to you for all you have done."

And strangely enough, from the moment Nekhlyudov recognised that it was he who was so bad and disgusting, others were no longer disgusting to him; on the contrary, he felt a kindly respect for Agrafena Petrovna and for Korney.

He would have liked to go and confess to Korney also, but Korney's manner was so insinuatingly deferential that he had not the resolution to do it.

On the way to the Law Courts, passing along the same streets with the same *izvozchik* as the day before, he was surprised to feel himself so different a being. The marriage with Missy, which only yesterday seemed so probable, appeared quite impossible now. The day before, he felt it was for him to choose and he had no doubts of her being happy to marry him; to-day he felt himself unworthy not only of marrying but even of being on intimate terms with her. "If she only knew what I am, nothing would induce her to receive me. And only yesterday I was finding fault with her for her flirtation with that fellow. But no, even if she would have me, how could I be at peace, not to say happy, knowing that the other is in prison and to-day or to-morrow may be transported to Siberia. That woman, ruined by me, will be on her way to penal servitude, while I receive congratulations and pay calls with my young wife; or, with the *Maréchal de noblesse,*—whom I have shamefully deceived—count votes at the meetings for and against the proposals of the local school inspection, etc.; or continue to work at my picture, which will certainly never get finished, for I have no business to waste time on such things. I can do nothing of the kind now," he continued, rejoicing at the change he felt within himself. "The first thing now is to see the advocate and find out his decision, and then . . . then go and see her, the convict of yesterday, and tell her everything."

And when he pictured to himself how he would see her and tell her all, confess his sin to her, and tell her that he would do all in his power to atone for it and would marry her, a special feeling of elation seized him, and tears came into his eyes.

Chapter XXXIV

ON COMING into the Law Courts, Nekhlyudov met the usher of yesterday in the corridor, and asked him where the prisoners who had been sentenced were kept, and to whom one had to apply for permission to visit them. The usher told him that the condemned prisoners were kept in different places, and that, until they received their sentence in its final form, permission to visit them depended on the *Procureur.*

"I'll come and call you myself after the sitting, and take you to the

Procureur. He is not even here at present. After the sitting! And now please come in; we are about to commence."

Nekhlyudov thanked the usher (who to-day seemed to him much to be pitied) for his kindness, and went to the jurymen's room. As he approached the room the other jurymen were just leaving it to go into the Court. The merchant had again partaken of a little refreshment and was as merry as on the day before, and greeted Nekhlyudov like an old friend. And to-day Peter Gerasimovich did not arouse any unpleasant feelings in Nekhlyudov by his familiarity and loud laughter.

Nekhlyudov would have liked to tell all the jurymen about his relations to yesterday's prisoner. "By rights," he thought, "I ought to have got up yesterday during the trial and disclosed my guilt." But when he entered the Court with the other jurymen, and witnessed the same procedure as on the day before: "The Court is coming," again proclaimed, again three men with embroidered collars ascending the platform, the same settling of the jury on their high-backed chairs, the same gendarmes, the same portrait, the same priest: Nekhlyudov felt that though it ought to have been done, he would have been as unable yesterday as to-day to interrupt all this solemnity.

The preparations for the trials were just the same as on the day before, excepting that the swearing-in of the jury and the president's address to them were omitted.

The case before the Court this day was one of burglary. The prisoner, guarded by two gendarmes with naked swords, was a thin, narrow-chested lad of twenty, with a bloodless, sallow face, and dressed in a grey cloak. He sat alone in the prisoners' dock and gazed with lowering brows at every one who entered the Court. This lad was accused of having, together with a companion, broken the lock of a shed and stolen several old mats valued at three rubles and sixty-seven kopeyks. According to the indictment, a policeman had stopped this lad as he was passing with his companion, who was carrying the mats on his shoulder. They confessed at once and were both locked up. The lad's companion, a locksmith, died in prison, so the lad was being tried alone. The old mats were lying on the table as objects of material evidence.

The business was conducted just in the same manner as the day before, with the whole armoury of evidence, proofs, witnesses, swearing-in, questions, experts, and cross-examinations. In answer to every question put to him by the president, the prosecutor, or the advocate, the policeman (one of the witnesses) invariably ejected the words: "Just so," or "Can't say." In spite of his being stupefied and rendered a mere machine by discipline, his reluctance to speak about the arrest of this prisoner was evident. Another witness, an old house-proprietor and the owner of the mats, evidently a splenetic old man, when asked whether the mats were his, reluctantly identified them as such. When the public prosecutor asked him what he meant to do with these mats, what use they were to him, he got angry, and answered: "The devil take those mats; I don't want them at all. Had I known there would be all this bother about them I should not have gone looking for them, but would rather have added a ten-ruble note or two to them, only not to be dragged here and pestered with questions. I have spent something like five rubles on *izvozchiks*. Besides I am not well. I am suffering from rupture and rheumatism."

This is what the witnesses said. The accused himself confessed everything, and looking round stupidly, like a trapped animal, related in a halting voice how it had all happened. The case was clear, but the public prosecutor, drawing up his shoulders as he had done the day before, asked subtle questions calculated to entrap a wily criminal.

In his speech he proved the theft to have been committed in a dwelling-place and a lock broken: and argued that the lad therefore must be severely punished. The defending advocate appointed by the Court maintained that the theft was not committed in a dwelling-place, and that, therefore, while the crime could not be denied, the prisoner was not so dangerous to society as the prosecutor asserted. The president assumed the same rôle of absolute neutrality and justice as on the previous day, and explained and impressed on the jury facts which they all knew and could not help knowing. As on the day before, adjournments took place, again they smoked, again the usher shouted "The Court is coming," and again, trying not to fall asleep, the two gendarmes guarded the prisoner with their naked weapons.

The proceedings showed that this lad was apprenticed at a tobacco factory by his father, and remained there five years. This year he had been discharged by the owner after a strike, and, having lost his place, had wandered about the town without any work, drinking away all he had. In a *traktir*[1] he met another like himself, who had lost his place before the prisoner had, a locksmith by trade, and a drunkard. One night these two, both drunk, broke the lock of a shed and took the first thing they happened to lay hands on. They confessed all and were put in prison, where the locksmith died while awaiting the trial. The lad was now being tried as a dangerous creature, from whom society must be protected.

"Just as dangerous a creature as yesterday's culprit," thought Nekhlyudov, listening to all that was going on before him. "They are dangerous; and we who judge them are not dangerous? I—a rake, a

---

[1] A cheap restaurant.

deceiver—and we all, all those who know me for what I am, and not only do not despise me but even respect me? . . .

"It is clear that he is not an exceptional evil-doer but a very ordinary lad—every one see its—and that he has become what he is simply because he got into circumstances that create such characters. Therefore, to prevent such boys from going wrong, the circumstances that create these unfortunate beings must be done away with. Had some one chanced to take pity on him and given him some help at the time when poverty made them send him to town, it might have been sufficient," Nekhlyudov thought, looking at the lad's sickly and frightened face. "Or even later, when after twelve hours' work at the factory he was going to the public-house, led away by his companions, had some one then come and said, 'Don't go, Vanya; it is not right,' he would not have gone, nor got into bad ways, and would not have done wrong.

"But no; no one who would take pity on him came across this apprentice in the years he lived in town like a poor little animal, and, with his hair cut close so as not to breed vermin, ran errands for the workmen. On the contrary, all he heard and saw from the older workmen and his companions since he came to live in town, was that he who cheats, drinks, swears, who gives another a thrashing, who goes on the loose, is a fine fellow.

"Ill, his constitution undermined by unhealthy labour, drink, and debauchery—knocking aimlessly about town, bewildered as in a dream, he gets into some sort of a shed, and takes some old mats which nobody needs; and here we, instead of considering how to destroy the causes which have brought this lad to his present condition, think to mend matters by punishing him!

"Terrible!"

Nekhlyudov thought all this, no longer listening to what was going on, and he was horror-struck by what was being revealed to him. He could not understand why he had not been able to see all this before, and why others were unable to see it.

Chapter XXXV

DURING AN adjournment Nekhlyudov got up and went out into the corridor, with the intention of not returning to the Court. Let them do what they liked with him, he could take part no more in this awful and horrid tomfoolery.

Having inquired for the cabinet of the *Procureur*, he went straight to him. The attendant did not wish to let him in, saying that the *Procureur* was busy, but Nekhlyudov paid no heed and went to the door, where he was met by an official. He asked to be announced to the *Procureur*, saying he was on the jury and had a very important communication to make.

His title and good clothes were of assistance to him. The official announced him to the *Procureur*, and Nekhlyudov was admitted. The *Procureur* met him standing, evidently annoyed at the persistence with which Nekhlyudov demanded admittance.

"What is it you want?" the *Procureur* asked severely.

"I am on the jury, my name is Nekhlyudov, and it is absolutely necessary for me to see the prisoner Maslova," Nekhlyudov said quickly and resolutely, blushing, and feeling that he was taking a step which would have a decisive influence on his life.

The *Procureur* was a short, dark man, with short, grizzly hair, quick, sparkling eyes, and a thick, close-cropped beard on his projecting lower jaw.

"Maslova? Yes, of course, I know. Accused of poisoning," the *Procureur* said quietly. "But why do you want to see her?" And then, as if wishing to tone down his question, he added: "I cannot give you the permission without knowing why you require it."

"I require it for a particularly important reason," Nekhlyudov began, flushing up.

"Yes?" said the *Procureur*, lifting his eyes and looking attentively at Nekhlyudov. "Has her case been heard or not?"

"She was tried yesterday and unjustly sentenced to four years' hard labour: she is innocent."

"Yes? If she was sentenced only yesterday," went on the *Procureur*, paying no attention to Nekhlyudov's statement concerning Maslova's innocence, "she must still be in the preliminary detention prison—until the sentence is delivered in its final form. Visiting is allowed there only on certain days; I should advise you to inquire there."

"But I must see her as soon as possible," Nekhlyudov said, his jaw trembling as he felt that decisive moment approaching.

"Why must you?" said the *Procureur*, lifting his brows with some impatience.

"Because she is innocently condemned to penal servitude, and it is my fault," said Nekhlyudov in a trembling voice, feeling he was saying what need not be said.

"In what way?" asked the *Procureur*.

"Because I seduced her and brought her to her present position. If she were not what I have helped to make her, she would not have been exposed to such an accusation."

"All the same, I cannot see what that has to do with visiting her."

"This: that I want to follow her, and . . . marry her," stammered Nekhlyudov, touched to tears by his own conduct.

"Really! Dear me!" said the *Procureur*. "This is certainly a very exceptional case. I believe you are a member of the Krasnopersk rural administration?" he asked, as if he remembered having heard before of this Nekhlyudov who was now making so strange a declaration.

"I beg your pardon, but I do not think that has anything to do with my request," answered Nekhlyudov, flushing angrily.

"Certainly not," said the *Procureur*, with a scarcely perceptible smile and not in the least abashed; "only your wish is so extraordinary and so out of the common."

"Well; but can I have a permit?"

"The permit? Yes, I will give you an order of admittance at once. Take a seat."

He went up to the table, sat down, and began to write.

"Please sit down."

Nekhlyudov continued to stand.

Having written an order of admittance and handed it to Nekhlyudov, the *Procureur* looked curiously at him.

"I must also state that I can no longer take part in the sessions."

"Then you will have to lay valid reasons before the Court, as of course you know."

"My reasons are that I consider all judging not only useless but immoral."

"Yes," said the *Procureur*, with the same scarcely perceptible smile, as if to show that this kind of declaration was well known to him and was a subject for amusement. "Yes, but you will certainly understand that I, as *Procureur*, cannot agree with you on this point. Therefore I should advise you to apply to the Court, which will consider your declaration and find it valid or invalid, and in the latter case will impose a fine. Apply, then, to the Court."

"I have made my declaration, and shall apply nowhere else," Nekhlyudov said angrily.

"Well then, good afternoon," said the *Procureur*, bowing his head, evidently anxious to be rid of this strange visitor.

"Who was that you had here?" asked one of the members of the Court as he entered, just after Nekhlyudov left the room.

"Nekhlyudov; you know, the same that used to make all sorts of strange statements at the Krasnopersk rural meetings. Just fancy! He is on the jury, and among the prisoners there is a woman or girl sentenced to penal servitude whom he says he seduced, and now he wants to marry her."

"You don't mean to say so."

"That's what he told me. And in such a strange state of excitement."

"There is something abnormal in the young men of to-day."

"Oh, but he is not so very young."

"No. But how tiresome your famous Ivashenko was. He carries the day by wearying one out. He talked and talked without end."

"Oh, such people should be simply stopped, or they become real obstructionists."

Chapter XXXVI

FROM THE *Procureur* Nekhlyudov went straight to the preliminary detention prison. However, no Maslova was to be found there, and the inspector explained to Nekhlyudov that she would probably be in the old temporary prison.

The distance between the two prisons was very great, and Nekhlyudov only reached the old prison towards evening. He was going up to the door of the large, gloomy building, but the sentry stopped him and rang. A jailer came in answer to the bell. Nekhlyudov showed him his order of admittance, but the jailer said he could not let him in without the inspector's permission. Nekhlyudov went to see the inspector. As he was going up the stairs he heard distant sounds of some complicated bravura played on the piano. When a cross servant-girl, with a bandaged eye, opened the door to him, these sounds seemed to escape from the room and to strike his ear. It was a rhapsody of Liszt's that everybody was tired of, splendidly played, but only up to a certain point. When that was reached the same thing was repeated. Nekhlyudov asked the bandaged maid whether the inspector was in. She answered that he was not.

"Will he be back soon?"

The rhapsody again stopped, but recommenced and was again repeated loudly and brilliantly up to the same magic point.

"I will go and ask," and the servant went away.

The rhapsody had just got into full swing, but suddenly, before reaching the magic point, broke off, and instead came the sound of a voice:—

"Tell him he is not in and won't be to-day; he is out visiting. What do they come bothering for?" said a woman's voice from behind the door; and again the rhapsody rattled on and stopped, and the sound of a chair pushed back was heard. It was plain that the irritated pianist meant to rebuke the tiresome visitor who had come at such an untimely hour.

"Papa is not in," said, crossly, a pale, sickly-looking girl with crimped hair and rings round her dull eyes, as she came out into the ante-room; but seeing a young man in a good coat she softened.

"Come in, please. . . . What is it you want?"

"I want to see a prisoner in this prison."

"A political one, I suppose?"

"No, not a political one. I have a permit from the *Procureur*."

"Well, I don't know, and papa is out; but come in, please," she said again, "or else speak to the assistant. He is in the office at present; you might apply there. What name, please?"

"Thank you," said Nekhlyudov, without answering her question, and went out.

The door had not yet closed behind him when the same lively tones recommenced, tones so unsuitable to the place, and to the appearance of the sickly girl who was resolutely practising them. In a courtyard Nekhlyudov met an officer with bristly moustaches and asked for the assistant inspector. It was the assistant himself. He looked at the order of admittance, but said that he could not admit him on a pass for the preliminary prison. Besides, it was too late. "Please to come again to-morrow. To-morrow, at ten, everybody is allowed in. Come then, and the inspector himself will be at home. Then you can have the interview either in the common room, or, if the inspector allows it, in the office."

And so Nekhlyudov did not succeed in getting an interview that day, and returned home. Excited at the idea of meeting Maslova, he no longer thought about the Law Courts as he went along the streets, but recalled his conversations with the *Procureur* and with the inspector's assistant.

The fact that he had been seeking an interview with her, and had told the *Procureur*, and had been to two prisons in order to see her, so excited him that it was long before he could calm down. When he got home he at once brought out his diary, which had long remained untouched, read a few sentences out of it, and then wrote as follows:—

"For two years I have not written anything in my diary and thought I never should return to such childishness. Yet it is not childishness, but converse with my own self, with this real divine self which lives in every man. All this time that this self slept there was no one for me to converse with. I was awakened by an extraordinary event on the 28th of April, in the Law Court, when I was on the jury. I saw her in the prisoners' dock, the Katusha seduced by me, in a prisoner's cloak. Through a strange mistake and my own fault she was condemned to penal servitude. I have just been to the *Procureur* and to the prison, but I was not admitted. But I have resolved to do all I can to see her, to confess to her, and to atone for my sin—even by marriage. God help me! My soul is at peace, and I am full of joy."

Chapter XXXVII

THAT NIGHT Maslova lay long awake with her eyes open; and gazing at the door, before which the deacon's daughter kept pacing, she pondered. She was thinking that nothing would induce her to marry a convict at Sakhalin, but that she would arrange matters somehow with one of the prison officials, a clerk, a warder, or even a warder's assistant. "Aren't they all given that way? Only I must not get thin or else I am lost."

She remembered how her advocate had looked at her, and also the president and the men she met, and those who came in on purpose at the Court. She remembered how her companion Bertha, who came to see her in prison, had told her about the student whom she had "loved" while she was at Kitaeva's, and who had inquired about her and pitied her very much. She recalled the fight with the red-haired woman and felt sorry for her. She recalled the baker, who had sent her out an extra roll. She recalled many to mind, only not Nekhlyudov. She never brought back to mind the days of her childhood and youth and her love for Nekhlyudov. That would have been too painful. Those memories lay untouched somewhere deep in her soul; she had forgotten him and never recalled or even dreamt of him. To-day, in the Court, she did not recognise him; not only because when she last saw him he was in uniform, without a beard, and had only a small moustache and thick, curly, though short hair, and now was bald and bearded, but because she never thought about him. She had buried his memory on that terrible dark night when he, returning from the army, had passed by on the railway without stopping to see his aunts. Katusha then knew she was pregnant. As long as she hoped he would come, she did not consider the child that lay beneath her heart a burden, and was often surprised and touched when she felt its soft and sudden movements within herself. But on that night everything changed, and the child became nothing but a weight.

His aunts had expected Nekhlyudov, and had asked him to come and see them in passing; but he had telegraphed that he could not come, having to be in Petersburg at an appointed time. When Katusha heard this she made up her mind to go to the station and see him. The train was to pass by at two o'clock in the night. Katusha having helped the old ladies to bed and persuaded a little girl, the cook's daughter, Mashka, to come with her, put on a pair of old boots, threw a shawl over her head, gathered up her dress, and ran to the station.

It was a warm, rainy, windy autumn night. The rain now pelted down in warm, heavy drops, now stopped again. She could hardly see the path across the field, and in the wood it was pitch-black, so that, although Katusha knew the way well, she lost the path and reached the little station where the train stopped for three minutes, not before it, as she had hoped, but after the second bell had been rung. Hurrying up the platform Katusha saw him at once at the window of a first-class carriage. This carriage was brightly lit up. Two officers sat opposite each other on the velvet-covered seats, playing cards, and on the table between the seats stood two thick, dripping candles. In close-fitting breeches and a white shirt, he sat on the arm of the seat, leaning against the back, and was laughing at something. As soon as she recognised him she knocked at the carriage window with her benumbed hand. But at that very moment the last bell rang, and after a backward jerk the carriages gradually began to move forward one after the other. One of the players rose with the cards in his hand and looked out. She knocked again and pressed her face to the window, but the carriage moved on and she walked by it looking in. The officer tried to lower the window, but could not. Nekhlyudov pushed him aside, and began lowering it himself. The train went faster so that she had to walk quickly. The train went on still faster and the window was lowered. But just then the guard pushed her aside, and jumped in. Katusha ran on along the wet boards of the platform, and when she came to the end she could hardly save herself from falling as she ran down the steps. She was now running by the side of the railway, though the first-class carriage had long passed her and the second-class carriages were gliding by faster, and at last the third-class carriages—still faster. But she ran on, and when the last carriage with the lamps at the back had gone by, she had already reached the tank which fed the engines, and was unsheltered from the wind, which was blowing her shawl about and making her skirt cling round her legs. The shawl flew off her head, but she still ran on.

"Katerina Mikhaylovna, you've lost your shawl!" screamed the little girl, who was trying to keep up with her.

Katusha stopped, threw back her head, and catching hold of it with both hands sobbed aloud.

"Gone!" she screamed.

"He is sitting in a velvet armchair and joking and drinking in a brightly-lit carriage and I, out here in the mud, in the darkness, in the wind and the rain, am standing and weeping," she thought to herself; and sat down on the ground, sobbing so loud that the little girl was frightened and put her arms round her, wet as she was.

"Come home, dear," she said.

"When a train passes—then under a carriage, and there will be an end," Katusha was thinking, without heeding the girl.

And she made up her mind to do it, when, as always happens when a moment of quiet follows great excitement, he, the child within her—his child—suddenly shuddered, gave a push, slowly stretched himself, and again pushed with something thin, delicate, and sharp. Suddenly all that a moment before had been tormenting her so that it had seemed impossible to live: all her bitterness towards him, and the wish to revenge herself, even by dying, passed away. She grew quieter, got up, put the shawl on her head and went home.

Wet, muddy and quite exhausted, she returned, and from that day the change which brought her where she now was began to operate in her soul. Beginning from that dreadful night she ceased to believe in God and in goodness. She had herself believed in God, and believed that other people also believed in Him; but after that night she became convinced that no one believed, and that all that was said about God and His laws was deception and untruth. He whom she loved and who had loved her—yes, she knew that—had thrown her away after having enjoyed her; had abused her love. Yet he was the best of all the people she knew. All the rest were still worse. All that afterwards happened strengthened her in this belief at every step. His aunts, the pious old ladies, turned her away when she could no longer serve them as she used to. And of all those she met, the women used her as a means of getting money, and the men, from the old police officer down to the warders of the prison, considered her as an object for pleasure. And no one in the world cared for aught but pleasure. In this belief the old author with whom she had lived in the second year of her life of independence had strengthened her. He had told her outright that it was this that constitutes the happiness of life, and he called it poetic and aesthetic.

Everybody lived for himself alone, for his pleasure, and all the talk about God and righteousness was deception. And if sometimes doubts arose in her mind, and she wondered why everything was so badly arranged in the world that all hurt each other and made every one suffer, she thought it best not to dwell on it; and if she felt melancholy she could smoke or drink, or, best of all, have a love-affair with some man, and it would pass.

Chapter XXXVIII

ON SUNDAY morning at five o'clock, when a whistle sounded in the corridor of the women's ward of the prison, Korableva, who was already awake, roused Maslova.

"Oh, dear! a convict!" thought Maslova with horror, involuntarily breathing in the air that had become terribly noisome towards morning. She wished to fall asleep again, to re-enter the region of oblivion, but the habit of fear overcame sleepiness and she sat up and looked round, drawing her feet under her. The women had all got up; only the elder children were still asleep. The woman imprisoned for trading in spirits was drawing a cloak from under the children carefully, so as not to wake them. The watchman's wife was hanging up to dry the rags that served the baby as swaddling clothes, while the baby was screaming desperately in the arms of the blue-eyed Theodosia, who was hushing it with a gentle voice. The consumptive woman was coughing, her hands pressed to her chest, the blood rushing to her face, and she sighed loudly, almost screaming, in the intervals of coughing. The fat, red-haired woman was lying on her back with her knees drawn up, loudly and gaily relating a dream. The old woman accused of incendiarism was standing in front of the icon, crossing herself and bowing, and repeating the same words over and over again. The deacon's daughter sat on the bedstead, looking before her with a dull, sleepy look. Horoshavka was twisting her black, oily, coarse hair round her fingers. The sound of slipshod feet was heard in the passage, and the door opened to let in two convicts, dressed in jackets and grey trousers that did not reach to their ankles. With serious cross faces they lifted the stinking tub and carried it out of the cell. The women went out to the taps in the corridor to wash. There again the red-haired woman began a quarrel with a woman from another cell. Again abuse, screams, and complaints.

"Is it the solitary cell you want?" shouted an old jailer, slapping the red-haired woman on her bare, fat back, so that it resounded through the corridor. "Don't let me hear any more of it!"

"Lawks! the old one's playful," said the woman, taking his action for a caress.

"Now then, hurry up; get ready for mass."

Maslova had hardly time to dress and do her hair when the inspector came with his assistants.

"Come out for inspection," cried a jailer.

Other prisoners came out of other cells and all stood in two rows along the corridor, each woman having to place her hand on the shoulder of the woman in front of her. They were all counted.

After the inspection the woman warder led the prisoners to church. Maslova and Theodosia were in the middle of a column of over a hundred women from the different cells. All were dressed in white skirts and white jackets and wore white kerchiefs on their heads, except a few who had their own coloured clothes on. The latter were wives who, with their children, were following their convict husbands to Siberia. The whole flight of stairs was filled with the procession. The patter of softly-shod feet mingled with the voices and even an occasional laugh. When turning on the landing Maslova saw her enemy, Bochkova, in front, and pointed out her angry face to Theodosia. As they descended the stairs the women ceased talking, and crossing themselves and bowing they entered the as yet empty church, which glistened with gilding. Their places were on the right, and they crowded in, jostling and pushing one another.

After the women came the men in their grey cloaks: those condemned to banishment, those serving their term in the prison, and those exiled by their communes; and, coughing loudly, they took their stand, crowding the left side and the middle of the church.

On one side of the gallery above stood men sentenced to penal servitude in Siberia, who had been led into the church before the others. Each of them had half his head shaven, and their presence was indicated by the clanking of the chains on their feet. On the other side of the gallery stood those in preliminary confinement, without chains, their heads not shaven.

The prison church had been rebuilt and ornamented by a rich merchant, who spent several tens of thousands of rubles on the building, and it glittered with gay colours and gold.

For a time there was silence in the church, and only coughing, blowing of noses, crying of babies, and now and then the rattling of chains, was heard. But at last the convicts who stood in the middle moved and pressed against each other, till they made a passage in the centre of the church, down which the prison inspector passed to take his place in the nave in front of every one.

Chapter XXXIX

THE service began.

It consisted of the following. The priest, having dressed himself up in a strange and very inconvenient garb of gold cloth, cut and arranged little bits of bread on a saucer and then put most of them into a cup with wine, repeating at the same time different names and prayers. Meanwhile the deacon first read Slavonic prayers, difficult to understand in themselves and rendered still more incomprehensible by being read very fast, and then sang them in turn with the convicts. The prayers chiefly expressed desire for the welfare of the Emperor and his family. These petitions were repeated many times, separately and together with other prayers, the people kneeling. Besides this, several verses from the Acts of the Apostles were read by the deacon in a peculiarly strained voice, which made it impossible to understand what he read, and then the priest himself read very distinctly a part of St. Mark's Gospel, in which it is told how Christ, having risen from the dead, before flying up to heaven to sit down at His Father's right hand, first showed himself to Mary Magdalene, out of whom he had driven seven devils, and then to eleven of His disciples, and how He ordered them to preach the Gospel to the whole world, declaring that he who did not believe should perish, but he who believed and was baptized should be saved, and should, besides, drive out devils and cure people by laying hands on them, should talk in strange tongues, should handle serpents, and if he drank poison should not die but remain well.

The essence of the service consisted in the supposition that the bits of bread cut up by the priest and put into the wine, when manipulated and prayed over in a certain way, turned into the flesh and blood of God.

These manipulations consisted in the priest, hampered by the gold cloth sack he had on, regularly lifting and holding up his arms, and then sinking to his knees and kissing the table and all that was on it; but chiefly in his taking a cloth by two of its corners and waving it rhythmically and softly over the silver saucer and the golden cup. It was supposed that at this point the bread and the wine turned into flesh and blood; therefore this part of the service was performed with the utmost solemnity.

"Now, to the blessed, most pure, and most holy Mother of God," the priest cried from behind the golden partition which divided part of the church from the rest. And the choir began solemnly to sing that it was very right to glorify the Virgin Mary, who had borne Christ without losing her virginity, and was therefore worthy of greater honour than some kind of cherubim and greater glory than some kind of seraphim. After this, the transformation was considered accomplished, and the priest, having taken the napkin off the saucer, cut the middle piece of bread in four, and put it first into the wine and then into his mouth. He was supposed to have eaten a piece of God's flesh and swallowed a little of His blood. Then the priest drew a curtain, opened the middle door in the partition, and taking the gold cup in his hands came out of the door, inviting those who wished to do so also to come and have some of God's flesh and blood contained in the cup. A few children appeared to wish to.

After having asked the children their names, the priest carefully took a bit of bread soaked in wine out of the cup with a spoon and pushed it deep into the mouth of a child. This he did to each child in turn; and the deacon, while wiping the children's mouths, sang in a merry voice that the children were eating God's flesh and drinking God's blood. After this the priest carried the cup back behind the partition and there drank all the remaining blood and ate up the remaining pieces of God's flesh, and after having carefully sucked his moustaches and wiped his mouth and the cup, he stepped briskly from behind the partition, the thin soles of his calfskin boots creaking. The principal part of this Christian service was now finished, but the priest, wishing to comfort the unfortunate prisoners, added to the ordinary service another. This consisted in his going up to the gilt hammered-out image (with black face and hands), illuminated by a dozen wax candles, supposed to represent the very God he had been eating, and, proceeding, in a strange, discordant voice, to hum or sing the following words:—

"Jesu sweetest, glorified of the Apostles, Jesu, lauded by the martyrs, Almighty Monarch: save me, Jesu my Saviour. Jesu most beautiful, have mercy on him who cries to Thee, Saviour Jesu. Born of prayer Jesu, save all Thy Saints, all Thy prophets, and find them worthy of the joys of heaven. Jesu, lover of men."

Then he stopped, drew breath, crossed himself and bowed to the ground, and every one—the inspector, the warders, the prisoners—did the same, and the clinking of the chains sounded more continuously from above. Then he continued: "Creator of angels, and Lord of powers, Jesu most wonderful, the angels' amazement, Jesu most powerful, the Redeemer of our forefathers. Jesu sweetest, the praise of patriarchs. Jesu most glorious, the strength of kings. Jesu most good, the fulfilment of prophets. Jesu most amazing, the strength of martyrs. Jesu most humble, the joy of monks. Jesu most merciful, the sweetness of priests. Jesu most charitable, the continence of the fasting. Jesu most sweet, the joy of the just. Jesu most pure, chastity of the celibates. Jesu before all ages, the salvation of sinners. Jesu, Son of God, have mercy on me."

Every time he repeated the word "Jesu" his voice became more and more wheezy. At last he came to a stop, and holding up his silk-lined cassock and kneeling down on one knee he stooped to the ground. The choir then began to sing, repeating the words, "Jesu, Son of God, have mercy on me," and the convicts stooped down and rose again, shaking back the hair that was left on their heads, and rattling the chains that were bruising their thin ankles.

This continued for a long time. First came the glorification, which ended with the words, "Have mercy on me." Then more glorifications, ending with "Alleluia!" And the convicts made the sign of the cross, and bowed, first at each sentence, then after every two, and then after three; and all were very glad when the glorification ended and the priest shut the book with a sigh of relief and retired behind the partition. One last act remained. The priest took from a table a large gilt cross with enamel medallions at the ends, and came out into the centre of the church with it. First the inspector came up and kissed the cross, then the jailers, and then the convicts, pushing and jostling, and abusing each other in whispers. The priest, talking to the inspector, pushed the cross and his hand now against the mouths and now against the noses of the convicts, who were trying to kiss both the cross and the hand of the priest. And thus ended the Christian service, intended for the comfort and the edification of these brothers who had gone astray.

Chapter XL

AND NONE of those present, from the inspector down to Maslova, seemed conscious of the fact that this Jesus, whose name the priest repeated such a great number of times, whom he praised with all these curious expressions, had forbidden the very things that were being done there: that he had not only prohibited this meaningless much-speaking and the blasphemous incantation over the bread and wine, but had also, in the clearest words, forbidden men to call other men their master or to pray in temples; had taught that every one should pray in solitude; had forbidden to erect temples, saying that he had come to destroy them and that one should worship, not in a temple, but in spirit and in truth; and, above all, that not only had he forbidden to judge, to imprison, to torment, to execute men, as was done here, but had even prohibited any kind of violence, saying that he had come to give freedom to the captives.

No one present seemed conscious that all that was going on here was the greatest blasphemy, and a mockery of that same Christ in whose name it was being done. No one seemed to realise that the gilt cross with the enamel medallions at the ends, which the priest held out to the people to be kissed, was nothing but the emblem of that gallows on which Christ had been executed for denouncing just what was going on here. That these priests, who imagined they were eating and drinking the body and blood of Christ in the form of bread and wine, were in reality guilty, not of eating and drinking His flesh and His blood, in the form of wine and bits of bread, but of ensnaring "these little ones" with whom he identified himself, of depriving them of the greatest blessings and submitting them to most cruel torments, and of hiding from men the tidings of great joy which he had brought—that thought did not enter the mind of any one present.

The priest did his part with a quiet conscience because he had been brought up from childhood to consider that this was the one true faith, which had been held by all the holy men of olden time, and was still held by the Church and demanded by the State authorities. He did not believe that the bread turned into flesh, that to repeat so many words was useful for the soul, or that he had actually swallowed a bit of God. No one could believe this; but he believed that one ought to believe it. What strengthened him most in this faith was the fact that, by fulfilling its demands, he had for the last eighteen years been able to draw an income which enabled him to support his family, and send his son to a high school, and his daughter to a school for the daughters of the clergy. The deacon believed in the same way and even more firmly than the priest, for he had forgotten the substance of the dogmas of this faith, and knew only that the prayers for the dead, the masses, with and without the acathistus, all had a definite price, which real Christians readily paid; and therefore he called out his "have mercy, have mercy" very willingly, and read and said what was appointed with the same quiet certainty of its being necessary with which other men sell faggots, flour, or potatoes. The prison inspector and the warders, though they had never understood, or considered, the meaning of these dogmas and of all that went on in church, believed that they must believe because the higher authorities and the Tsar himself believed. Besides, though dimly (and themselves unable to explain why), they felt that this faith supported their cruel occupations. But for this faith it would have been more difficult, perhaps impossible, for them with a quiet conscience to use all their powers to torment people, as they were now doing. The inspector was such a kind-hearted man that if unsupported by this faith he could not have lived as he was now living. Therefore he stood motionless, bowed and crossed himself zealously, tried to feel touched when the song about the cherubims was being sung, and when the children received communion he lifted one of them and held him up to the priest.

The great majority of the prisoners believed that in these gilt images, these vestments, candles, cups, crosses, in this repetition of incomprehensible words—"Jesu sweetest" and "have mercy"—there lay a mystic power through which much convenience in this life and in that to come might be obtained. Only a few saw clearly the deception practised on those who adhered to this faith, and laughed at it in their hearts; but the majority, having made several attempts—by means of prayers, masses, and candles—to get the conveniences they desired, and not having got them (their prayers remaining unanswered), were each of them convinced that their want of success was accidental, and that this organisation, approved by the educated and by the archbishops, is very important and necessary, if not for this life, at any rate for that hereafter.

Maslova also believed in this way. She felt, like the rest, a mixed sensation of piety and dulness. She stood at first in the crowd behind a railing, so that she could see no one but her companions; but when those to receive communion moved on, she and Theodosia stepped to the front, and they saw the inspector, and, behind him, standing among the jailers, a little peasant with a very light beard and fair hair. This was Theodosia's husband, and he was gazing with fixed eyes at his wife. During the acathistus Maslova occupied herself in scrutinising him and talking to Theodosia in whispers, and bowed and made the sign of the cross only when every one else did.

Chapter XLI

NEKHLYUDOV LEFT home early. A peasant from the country was driving along the side street and calling out in a voice peculiar to his trade, "Milk! milk! milk!"

The first warm spring rain had fallen the day before, and now wherever the ground was not paved the grass shone green. The birch trees in the gardens looked as if strewn with green fluff, the wild cherry and the poplars unfolded their long fragrant leaves, and in shops and dwelling-houses the double window-frames were being removed and the windows cleaned.

In the Tolkutchy[1] market, which Nekhlyudov had to pass on his way, a dense crowd was surging along the row of booths, and tattered men walked about selling topboots, which they carried under their arms, and renovated trousers and waistcoats, which hung over their shoulders.

Men in clean coats and shining boots, liberated from the factories, it being Sunday, and women with bright silk kerchiefs on their heads and cloth jackets trimmed with jet, were already thronging at the doors of

---

[1] Literally "jostling market," where second-hand clothes and all sorts of cheap goods are sold.

the *traktirs*. Policemen, with yellow cords to their uniforms, and carrying pistols, were on duty, looking out for some disorder which might
distract the ennui that oppressed them. On the paths of the boulevards
and on the newly revived grass children and dogs ran about playing,
and nurses sat merrily chattering on the benches. Along the streets, still
fresh and damp on the shady side but dry in the middle, heavy carts
rumbled unceasingly, cabs rattled, and tramcars passed ringing by. The
air vibrated with the pealing and clanging of church bells, calling the
people to attend a service like that which was now being conducted in
the prison. And the people, dressed in their Sunday best, were passing
on their way to their different parish churches.

The *izvozchik* did not drive Nekhlyudov up to the prison itself, but
to the last turning that led to the prison.

Several persons—men and women—most of them carrying small
bundles, stood at this turning, about a hundred steps from the prison.
To the right there were several low wooden buildings; to the left a two-
storied house with a signboard. The huge brick building, the prison
proper, was just in front, but the visitors were not allowed to approach
it. A sentry was pacing up and down in front, and shouted at any one
who tried to pass him.

At the gate of the wooden buildings to the right, opposite the sentry,
sat a jailer on a bench, dressed in a uniform with gold cords, a notebook
in his hands. The visitors came up to him and named the persons they
wanted to see, and he put the names down. Nekhlyudov also went up,
and gave the name of Katerina Maslova. The jailer wrote down the
name.

"Why don't they admit us?" asked Nekhlyudov.

"The service is going on. When the mass is over you'll be admitted."

Nekhlyudov stepped aside from the waiting crowd. A barefooted
man in tattered clothes, crumpled hat, and with red streaks all over his
face, detached himself from the crowd and moved towards the prison.

"Now then, where are you going?" shouted the sentry with the rifle.

"You hold your row," answered the tramp, not in the least abashed by
the sentry's words, but turning back nevertheless. "Well, if you'll not let
me in, I can wait. But, no! Must needs shout, as if he were a general."

The crowd laughed approvingly. The visitors were for the most part
badly dressed people, some were even ragged, but there were also some
respectable-looking men and women. Next to Nekhlyudov stood a
clean-shaven, stout, and red-cheeked man, holding a bundle
appaerntly containing underclothing. Nekhlyudov asked him if this
was his first visit there. The man replied that he came every Sunday,
and they began a conversation. He was the doorkeeper at a bank; he
had come to see his brother, who had been arrested for forgery. The

good-natured fellow told Nekhlyudov the whole story of his life, and was going to question him in turn when their attention was attracted by a student and a veiled lady, who drove up in a trap with rubber tyres drawn by a big thoroughbred horse. The student was carrying a large bundle. He came up to Nekhlyudov, and asked if, and how, he could give the prisoners the rolls he had brought. His fiancée (the lady with him) wished it, and her parents had advised them to take some rolls to the prisoners.

"I myself am here for the first time," said Nekhlyudov, "and don't know; but I think you had better ask that man," and he pointed to the jailer with the gold cords and the book, sitting on the right.

As they were speaking, the large iron door with a window in it opened, and an officer in uniform, followed by another jailer, stepped out. The jailer with the notebook proclaimed that the admittance of visitors would now commence. The sentry stepped aside, and all the visitors rushed to the door as if afraid of being too late. At the door there stood a jailer who counted aloud as the visitors came in—sixteen, seventeen, and so on. Another jailer stood inside the building and also counted the visitors, touching each one with his hand as they entered a second door, so that when they went away again not one visitor should be able to remain inside the prison and not one prisoner get out. The jailer, without looking whom he was touching, slapped Nekhlyudov on the back, and Nekhlyudov felt hurt by the touch of the jailer's hand; but remembering what he had come about he felt ashamed of feeling annoyed and of taking offence.

The first apartment behind the entrance doors was a large vaulted room with iron bars to the small windows. In this room, which was called the meeting-room, Nekhlyudov was startled by the sight of a large picture of the Crucifixion.

"What's that here for?" he thought, his mind involuntarily connecting the subject of the picture with liberation and not with imprisonment.

He went on slowly, letting the hurrying visitors pass before, and experienced a mingled feeling of horror at the evil-doers locked up in this building; compassion for those who, like Katusha, and the boy they tried the day before, were here though guiltless; and shyness and tender emotion at the thought of the interview before him. The jailer at the other end of the meeting-room said something as they passed, but Nekhlyudov, absorbed in his own thoughts, paid no attention to him, and, continuing to follow the main current of visitors, got into the men's part of the prison instead of the women's.

Letting those more eager pass before him, he was the last to enter the visiting-room. As soon as Nekhlyudov opened the door of this room he was struck by the deafening roar of a hundred voices shouting at once, the reason of which he did not at once understand. But when he came nearer to the people he saw that they were all pressing against nets dividing the room in two, like flies settling on sugar, and he understood what it meant. The two halves of the room, the windows of which were opposite the door he had come in by, were separated, not by one, but by two nets reaching from the floor to the ceiling. The wire nets were stretched seven feet apart, and soldiers were walking up and down the space between them. On the farther side of the nets were the prisoners; on the nearer, the visitors. Between them was the double row of nets and the seven foot space so that they could not hand anything to one another, and any one who was short-sighted could not even distinguish the faces on the other side. It was also difficult to talk; one had to scream in order to be heard.

On both sides were faces pressed close to the nets—faces of wives, husbands, fathers, mothers, children, trying to see each other's features, and to say what was necessary in such a way as to be understood.

But as each one tried to be heard by the one he was talking to, and his neighbour tried to do the same, they did their best to drown each other's voices, and from this resulted the row interrupted by cries which struck Nekhlyudov when he first came in. It was impossible to hear, and it was only by the faces that one could guess what was being said, and the relations between the speakers. Next Nekhlyudov an old woman with a kerchief on her head stood pressed to the net, her chin trembling, shouting something to a pale young fellow, half of whose head was shaved, who listened attentively with raised brows. By the side of the old woman was a young man in a peasant's coat, who listened, shaking his head with dissatisfaction, to a lad very like himself. Next stood a man in rags, who shouted, waving his arms and laughing. Next to him a woman, with a good woollen shawl on her shoulders, sat on the floor holding a baby in her lap and crying bitterly. This was apaprently the first time she had seen the grey-headed man on the other side in prison clothes and with his head shaved. Beyond her was the doorkeeper who had spoken to Nekhlyudov outside; he was shouting with all his might to a grey-haired convict on the other side.

When Nekhlyudov understood that he would have to speak under such conditions, a feeling of indignation against those who were able to make and enforce such conditions arose in him; he was surprised that, placed in such a dreadful position, no one seemed offended at this outrage on human feelings. The soldiers, the inspector, and the prisoners themselves, acted as if they acknowledged all this to be necessary.

Nekhlyudov remained in this room for about five minutes, feeling strangely depressed, conscious of how powerless he was, and how much at variance with all the world. He was seized with a curious moral nausea, comparable to the physical sensations of sea-sickness.

Chapter XLII

"WELL, but I must do what I came here for," he said, trying to pluck up courage. "What is to be done now?" He looked round for an official, and seeing a thin little man in the uniform of an officer pacing up and down behind the people, he approached him.

"Can you tell me, sir," he said with exceedingly strained politeness of manner, "where the women are kept, and where one is allowed to interview them?"

"Is it the women's side you want to go to?"

"Yes, I should like to see one of the women prisoners," Nekhlyudov said, with the same strained politeness.

"You should have said so when you were in the hall. Who is it, then, that you want to see?"

"I want to see a prisoner called Katerina Maslova."

"Is she a political one?"

"No, she is simply——"

"Yes, and is she sentenced?"

"Yes, sentenced the day before yesterday," Nekhlyudov answered meekly, fearing to spoil the good-humour of the inspector, who seemed favourably disposed towards him.

"If you want to go to the women's side please to step this way," said the officer, having decided from Nekhlyudov's appearance that he was worthy of attention. "Siderov, conduct the gentleman to the women's side," he said, turning to a moustached corporal with medals on his breast.

"Yes, sir."

At this moment heartrending sobs were heard coming from some one near the net.

Everything here seemed strange to Nekhlyudov; but strangest of all was that he should have to thank and feel himself under an obligation to the inspector and the chief jailers—the very men who were performing the cruel deeds that were done in this building.

The corporal showed Nekhlyudov out of the men's room into the corridor, and straight across, through a door on the opposite side, into the women's visiting-room.

This room, like that of the men, was divided by two wire nets; but it was much smaller. There were both fewer visitors and fewer prisoners, but the noise and the shouting were the same as in the men's room. Authority walked between the nets in the same way, but here authority was represented by a woman warder, dressed in a blue-edged uniform jacket with gold cord on the sleeves, and with a blue belt. Here also, as in the men's room, the people were pressing close to the wire netting on both sides: on the nearer side the townspeople in varied attire, on the farther side the prisoners, some in white prison clothes, others in their own coloured dresses. The whole length of the net was taken up by the people standing close to it. Some rose on tiptoe to be heard across the heads of others; some talked sitting on the floor.

The most remarkable of the prisoners, both by her piercing screams and her appearance, was a thin, dishevelled gipsy. Her kerchief had slipped off her curly hair, and she stood near a post in the middle of the prisoners' division shouting something, accompanied by quick gestures, to a gipsy man in a blue coat girdled tightly below the waist. Next to the gipsy man a soldier sat on the ground talking to a prisoner; next to the soldier, pressing close to the net, stood a young peasant with a fair beard and a flushed face, keeping back his tears with difficulty. A pretty, fair-haired prisoner, with bright blue eyes, was speaking to him. These two were Theodosia and her husband. Next to them was a tramp, talking to a broad-faced woman; then two women, then a man, then again a woman, and in front of each a prisoner. Maslova was not among them. But some one stood by the window behind the prisoners, and Nekhlyudov knew it was she. His heart began to beat faster and his breath stopped. The decisive moment was approaching. He went up to the net and recognized her. She stood behind the blue-eyed Theodosia, and smiled, listening to what Theodosia was saying. She was not in a prison cloak now, but wore a white dress, tightly drawn in at the waist by a belt and very full in the bosom. From under her kerchief appeared the black curls of her fringe, just as in the Court.

"In a moment now it will be decided," he thought. "How shall I call her? Or will she come herself?"

She was expecting Bertha; that this man had come to see her never entered her head.

"Whom do you want?" said the warder who was walking between the nets, coming up to Nekhlyudov.

"Katerina Maslova," Nekhlyudov uttered, with difficulty.

"Katerina Maslova, some one to see you," cried the warder.

Maslova looked round, and, with head thrown back and expanded chest, she came up to the net with that expression of readiness which he so well knew, pushed in between two prisoners, and gazed at Nekhlyudov with a surprised and questioning look. But concluding from his clothing that he was a rich man, she smiled.

"Is it me you want?" she asked, bringing her smiling face, with the slightly squinting eyes, nearer the net.

"I . . . I . . . I wished to see . . . I wished to see you . . . I . . ." He was not speaking louder than usual.

"No nonsense, I tell you!" shouted the tramp who stood next to him. "Have you taken it or not?"

"Very weak; dying," some one else was screaming from the other side.

Maslova could not hear what Nekhlyudov was saying, but the expression of his face as he was speaking reminded her of something she did not wish to recall. The smile vanished from her face and a deep line of suffering appeared on her brow.

"I cannot hear what you are saying," she called out, wrinkling her brow and frowning more and more.

"I have come . . ." said Nekhlyudov.

"Yes, I am doing my duty—I am confessing," thought he; and at this thought the tears came to his eyes, he felt a choking sensation in his throat, and holding on with both hands to the net he made efforts to keep from bursting into tears.

"Had she been well I'd not have come," some one shouted at one side of him.

"God is my witness, I know nothing," screamed a prisoner from the other side.

Maslova noticed his excitement and recognised him.

"You're like . . . but no, I don't remember," she shouted without looking at him, and her flushed face grew still more gloomy.

"I have come to ask you to forgive me," he said in a loud but monotonous voice, like a lesson learnt by heart.

Having said these words he became confused and looked round; but immediately came the thought that if he felt ashamed it was all the better—he had to bear this shame; and he continued in a loud voice:—

"Forgive me; I have wronged you terribly."

She stood motionless, not taking her squinting eyes off him.

He could not go on speaking, and stepping away from the net he tried to suppress the sobs that were choking him.

The inspector, the officer who had directed Nekhlyudov to the women's side and whose interest he seemed to have aroused, came into the room, and seeing Nekhlyudov not at the net asked him why he was not talking to the woman he wanted to see. Nekhlyudov blew his nose, gave himself a shake, and, trying to appear calm, said:—

"It's so inconvenient through these nets; nothing can be heard."

Again the inspector considered for a moment. "Ah well, she can be brought out here for a while. . . . Mary Karlovna," turning to the warder, "lead Maslova out."

Chapter XLIII

A MINUTE later Maslova came out by the side door. Stepping softly, she came up close to Nekhlyudov, stopped, and looked up at him from under her brows. Her black hair was arranged in curls over her forehead in the same way as it had been two days ago; her face, though unhealthy and puffy, was attractive and quite calm, but the glittering black eyes glanced strangely from under the swollen lids.

"You may talk here," said the inspector, and stepped aside. Nekhlyudov moved towards a seat by the wall.

Maslova cast a questioning look at the inspector, and then, shrugging her shoulders in surprise, followed Nekhlyudov to the bench, and having arranged her skirt sat down beside him.

"I know it is hard for you to forgive me," he began, but stopped. His tears were choking him. "But though I can't undo the past, I will now do what is in my power. Tell me——"

"How have you managed to find me?" she said, without answering his question, neither looking away from him nor quite at him with her squinting eyes.

"Oh God, help me! Teach me what to do," Nekhlyudov thought, looking at her changed and now no longer pleasant face. "I was on the jury the day before yesterday," he said. "You did not recognise me?"

"No, I did not; there was not time for recognitions. I did not even look," she said.

"There was a child, was there not?" he asked, and felt himself blushing.

"Thank God he died at once," she answered, abruptly and resentfully, turning away from him.

"What do you mean? Why?"

"I was so ill myself I nearly died," she said, without raising her eyes.

"How could my aunts have let you go?"

"Who keeps a servant that has a baby? They sent me off as soon as they noticed. But what's the use of talking? I remember nothing. That's all finished."

"No, it is not finished; I wish to redeem my sin."

"There's nothing to redeem. What's been has been and is past," she said; and, which he never expected, she looked at him and smiled in an unpleasantly luring, yet piteous, way.

Maslova had never expected to see him again, and certainly not here and not now; therefore when she first recognised him she could not keep back the memories which she had never wished to revive. In the first moment she recalled confusedly that new wonderful world of feeling and of thought which had been opened to her by the charming young man who loved her and whom she loved, and then she remembered his incomprehensible cruelty and the whole string of humiliations and sufferings which flowed from and followed that magic joy. She felt sick at heart. But, unable to understand it, she did now what she was always in the habit of doing: she rid herself of these memories by enveloping them in the mist of a depraved life. In the first moment she associated the man now sitting beside her with the lad she had loved; but feeling that this gave her pain she dissociated them again. Now this well-dressed, carefully-got-up gentleman with perfumed beard was no longer the Nekhlyudov whom she had loved, but only one of the people who make use of creatures like herself when they need them, and whom creatures like herself had to make use of in their turn as profitably as they could: and that is why she looked at him now with an alluring smile. She was silent, considering how she could best make use of him.

"That's all at an end," she said. "Now I'm condemned to Siberia," and her lip trembled as she said this dreadful word.

"I knew, I was certain, you were not guilty," said Nekhlyudov.

"Guilty! Of course not; as if I could be a thief or a robber. They say here that all depends on the advocate," she continued. "A petition should be handed in, only they say it's expensive."

"Yes, most certainly," said Nekhlyudov. "I have already spoken to an advocate."

"No money ought to be spared; he should be a good one," she said.

"I will do all that is possible."

They were silent, and then she smiled again in the same way.

"And I should like to ask you . . . a little money if you can . . . not much . . . ten rubles," she said suddenly.

"Yes, yes," Nekhlyudov said, with a sense of confusion, and felt for his pocket-book.

She looked rapidly at the inspector, who was walking up and down the room.

"Don't give it in front of him; he'd take it away."

Nekhlyudov took out his pocket-book as soon as the inspector had turned his back, but had no time to hand her the note before the inspector faced them again, so he crushed it up in his hand.

"This woman is dead," Nekhlyudov thought, looking at the once sweet face, now defiled and puffy and lit up by an evil glitter in the black, squinting eyes, which were now glancing at the hand in which he held the note, now following the inspector's movements; and for a moment he hesitated. The tempter that had been speaking to him in the night again raised his voice, trying to lead him out of the realm of his inner life into the realm of his outer life, away from the question of what he should do, to the question of what the consequences would be and what would be practical.

"You can do nothing with this woman," said the voice; "you will only tie a stone round your neck, which will drown you, and prevent you from being useful to others. Is it not better to give her all the money you have here, say good-bye, and finish with her for ever?" whispered the voice.

And yet he felt that now, at this very moment, something most important was taking place in his soul—that his inner life was, as it were, wavering in the balance, so that the slightest effort would sink it to one side or the other. And he made this effort by calling to his assistance that God whose presence he had felt in his soul the day before, and that God instantly responded. He resolved to tell her everything now—at once.

"Katusha, I have come to ask you to forgive me and you have given me no answer. Have you forgiven me? Will you ever forgive me?" he asked.

She did not listen to him, but looked at his hand and at the inspector. When the latter turned she hastily stretched out her hand, grasped the note, and hid it under her belt.

"That's odd; what you are saying," she said with a smile of disdain, as it seemed to him.

Nekhlyudov felt that there was in her soul one who was hostile to him, and who was supporting her, as she now was, preventing him from getting at her heart. But, strange to say, this did not repel him, but drew him nearer to her by some fresh, peculiar power. He knew that he must awaken her soul, that this would be terribly difficult; but the very difficulty attracted him. He now felt towards her as he had never before felt towards her or any one else. There was nothing personal in his feeling—he wanted nothing from her for himself—he only wished that she might not remain as she now was, that she might awaken again and become what she had been.

"Katusha, why do you speak like that? I know you, I remember you—and the old days in Panovo."

"What's the use of recalling what's past?" she remarked dryly.

"I am recalling it in order to put it right, to atone for my sin, Katusha," and he was going to say that he would marry her, but, meeting her eyes, he read in them something so dreadful, so coarse, so repellent, that he could not go on.

At this moment the visitors began to go. The inspector came up to Nekhlyudov and said that the time was up.

"Good-bye; I have still much to say to you, but you see it is impossible to do so now," said Nekhlyudov, and held out his hand. "I will come again."

Maslova rose meekly, waiting to be dismissed.

"I think you have said all."

She took his hand but did not press it.

"No; I shall try to see you again, somewhere where we can talk, and then I shall tell you what I have to say—something very important."

"Well then, come; why not?" she answered, and smiled the smile she gave to the men whom she wished to please.

"You are more than a sister to me," said Nekhlyudov.

"That's odd," she said again, shaking her head, and went behind the netting.

Chapter XLIV

BEFORE THIS interview Nekhlyudov thought that when she saw him and knew of his intention to serve her, Katusha would be pleased and touched and would be Katusha again; but, to his horror, he found that Katusha existed no more, and that in her place was Maslova. This astonished and horrified him.

What astonished him most was that Katusha was not ashamed of her position,—not the position of a prisoner (she was ashamed of that), but her position as a prostitute—she seemed satisfied and even proud of it. And yet it could not be otherwise. Everybody, in order to be able to act, has to consider his occupation important and good. Therefore, in whatever position a person is, he is certain to form such a view of the life of men in general as will make his occupation seem important and good.

It is usually imagined that a thief, a murderer, a spy, a prostitute, acknowledging his or her profession to be evil, is ashamed of it. But the contrary is true. People whom fate and their sin-mistakes have placed in a certain position, however false that position may be, form a view of life in general which makes their position seem good and admissible. In order to keep up their view of life, these people instinctively keep to the circle of those who share their views of life and of their own place in it. This surprises us where the persons concerned are thieves bragging about their dexterity, prostitutes vaunting their depravity, or murderers boasting of their cruelty. But it surprises us only because the circle, the atmosphere, in which these people live, is limited, and chiefly because we are outside it. Can we not observe the same phenomenon when the rich boast of their wealth—robbery; when commanders of armies pride themselves on their victories—murder; and when those in high places vaunt their power—violence? That we do not see the perversion in the views of life held by these people, is only because the circle formed by them is larger and we ourselves belong to it.

It was in this manner that Maslova had formed her views of life and of her own position. She was a prostitute condemned to Siberia, and yet she had a conception of life which made it possible for her to be satisfied with herself, and even to pride herself on her position.

According to this conception the highest good for all men—old, young, schoolboys, generals, educated and uneducated—was sexual intercourse with attractive women; therefore, all men, even when they pretended to be occupied with other things, in reality desired nothing else. She was an attractive woman, and it lay in her power to satisfy, or not to satisfy, this desire, and she was therefore an important and necessary person. The whole of her former and present life was a confirmation of the correctness of this conception.

During the last ten years of her life, wherever she found herself, she saw that all men—from Nekhlyudov and the old police officer down to the jailers in the prison—needed her; for she did not observe and she took no notice of those men who had no need of her. Therefore all the world seemed to her a collection of people agitated by lust, who were trying to get possession of her by all possible means—deception, violence, purchase, or cunning. This, then, was how Maslova understood life; and on such a view of life she was by no means the lowest but a very important person. And Maslova prized this view more than anything else; she could not but prize it, for if she lost this view of life, she would lose the importance it accorded her. And in order not to lose the meaning of her life, she instinctively clung to the set that looked at life in the same way that she did. Feeling that Nekhlyudov wanted to lead her out into another world, she resisted him, foreseeing that she would have to lose her place in life, with the self-possession and self-respect it gave her. For this reason she drove from her the recollections of her early youth and of her first relations with Nekhlyudov. These recollections did not correspond with her present conception of the world, and were therefore quite struck out of her memory, or, rather, lay somewhere buried and untouched, closed up and plastered over so that they should not escape; as bees, in order to protect the results of their labour, sometimes plaster up a nest of wax-worms. Therefore, the present Nekhlyudov was not the man she had once loved with a pure love, but only a rich gentleman whom she could and must make use of, and with whom she could have only the same relations as with men in general.

"No, I could not tell her the chief thing," thought Nekhlyudov, moving towards the exit with the rest of the visitors. "I did not tell her that I would marry her; I did not tell her so, but I will," he thought.

The two jailers at the door let the visitors out again, counting them again and touching each one with their hands, so that no extra person should go out and none remain within. The slap on his shoulder did not offend Nekhlyudov this time; he did not even notice it.

Chapter XLV

NEKHLYUDOV MEANT to rearrange the whole of his external life: to send away his servants, let his large house, and move into lodgings; but Agrafena Petrovna pointed out that it was useless to change anything before the winter. No one would rent a town house for the summer; and anyhow he would have to live and keep his things somewhere. And so all his efforts to change his manner of life (he meant to live more simply, as the students live) led to nothing. Not only did everything remain as it was, but the house was suddenly filled with new activity. Everything made of wool or fur was taken out to be aired and beaten. The gatekeeper, the boy, the cook, and Korney himself, took part in this activity. All sorts of strange furs which no one ever used, and various uniforms, were taken out and hung on a line; then the carpets and furniture were brought out, and the gatekeeper and the boy rolled their sleeves up their muscular arms and stood beating these things, keeping strict time, while the rooms were filled with the smell of naphthaline.

When Nekhlyudov crossed the yard or looked out of the window and saw all this going on, he was surprised at the great number of things there were, all quite useless. Their only use, Nekhlyudov thought, was to provide exercise for Agrafena Petrovna, Korney, the gatekeeper, the boy, and the cook.

"But it's not worth while altering my manner of life now," he thought, "while Maslova's case is not decided. Besides, it is too difficult. It will alter of itself when she is set free, or is exiled and I follow her."

On the appointed day Nekhlyudov drove up to the advocate Fanarin's splendid house, which was decorated with huge palms and other plants, and wonderful curtains: in fact, with all the expensive luxury that indicates the possession of much idle money (money acquired without labour), and which only those display who grow rich suddenly. In the waiting-room, just as at a doctor's, he found many dejected-looking people sitting at tables on which lay illustrated papers meant to amuse them, and awaiting their turns to be admitted to the advocate. The advocate's assistant sat in the room at a high desk, and, recognising Nekhlyudov, came up to say he would announce him at once. But the assistant had not reached the door when it opened, and the sounds of loud, animated voices were heard: the voice of a middle-aged, sturdy merchant, with a red face and thick moustaches, and dressed in very new clothes, and the voice of Fanarin himself. Both faces bore the expression generally seen on the faces of those who have just concluded a profitable but not quite honest transaction.

"Your own fault, you know, my dear sir," Fanarin said, smiling.

"We'd all be in 'eaven were it not for hour sins."

"Oh yes, yes; we all know that," and both laughed unnaturally.

"Oh, Prince Nekhlyudov! Please to step in," said Fanarin, seeing him, and nodding once more to the merchant he led Nekhlyudov into his consulting room, which was furnished in a severely correct style.

"Won't you smoke?" said the advocate, sitting down opposite Nekhlyudov and trying to repress a smile, apparently still excited by the success of the transaction just concluded.

"Thanks; I have come about Maslova's case."

"Yes, yes; directly! But, oh, what rogues these fat money-bags are!" he said. "You saw that fellow here. Why, he has about twelve million rubles, and he says 'eaven' and 'hour sins'; and if he can squeeze a twenty-fiver out of you he'll have it, if he has to wrench it out with his teeth."

"He says 'eaven' and 'hour,' and you say 'squeeze out a twenty-fiver,'" Nekhlyudov thought, with an insurmountable feeling of aversion towards this man, who wished to show by his free and easy manner that he and Nekhlyudov belonged to one and the same camp while his other clients belonged to another.

"He has worried me to death—a fearful scoundrel. I felt I must relieve my feelings," said the advocate, as if to excuse his speaking about things that had no reference to the business in hand. "Well, now about your case. I have read it attentively, and 'disapprove of the contents thereof,' as Turgenev says. I mean that greenhorn of an advocate has left no valid reason for an appeal."

"Well then, what can be done?"

"One moment. Tell him," he said to his assistant, who had just come in, "that I keep to what I have said. If he can, it's all right; if not, no matter."

"But he won't agree."

"Well then, no matter," and his face from cheery and serene turned sullen and angry.

"There now!—and it is said that we advocates get our money for nothing," he remarked after a pause, putting the former pleasant amiability into his expression. "Having freed one insolvent debtor from a totally false charge, they all flock to me now. Yet every such case costs enormous labour. Do not we, too, 'leave bits of flesh in the inkstand'? as some writer or other has said.[1]

"Well, as to your case, or, rather, the case you are taking an interest in. It has been conducted abominably. There is no valid reason for appealing. Still," he continued, "we can but try to get the sentence quashed. This is what I have noted." He took up several sheets of paper covered with writing, and began to read rapidly, slurring over the uninteresting legal terms and laying particular stress on some sentences. "'To the Court of Appeal, Criminal Department, etc., etc. According to the decisions, etc., the verdict, etc., So-and-so Maslova pronounced guilty of having caused the death through poison of the merchant Smelkov, and has, according to Article 1454 of the Penal Code, been sentenced to Siberia,' etc., etc." He stopped. Evidently, in spite of being so used to it, he still felt pleasure in listening to his own productions. "'This sentence is the direct result of the most obvious judicial infringements and errors,'" he continued impressively, "'and there are grounds for its revocation. Firstly, the reading of the medical report of the examination of Smelkov's intestines was interrupted by the president at the very beginning.' That is point one."

"But it was the prosecuting side that demanded this reading," Nekhlyudov said, with surprise.

"That does not matter. There might have been reasons for the defence to demand this reading too."

"Oh, but there could have been no reason whatever for it."

"It is a ground for appeal, though. To continue, 'Secondly,'" he went on reading, "'when Maslova's advocate, in his speech for the defence, wishing to characterise Maslova's personality, referred to the causes of her fall, he was interrupted by the president calling him to order for alleged deviation from the direct subject. Yet, as has been repeatedly pointed out by the Senate, the elucidation of the criminal's characteristics, and of his or her moral standpoint in general, has a significance of the first importance in criminal cases, even if only as a guide in set-

---

[1] [The writer mentioned is Tolstoy himself, who wrote: "One ought to write only when one leaves a piece of one's flesh in the inkpot each time one dips one's pen."]

tling the question of responsibility.' That's point two," he said, with a look at Nekhlyudov.

"But he spoke so badly that no one could make anything of it," Nekhlyudov said, still more astonished.

"The fellow's quite a fool, and of course could not be expected to say anything sensible," Fanarin said, laughing; "but, all the same, it will do as a reason for appeal. 'Thirdly, the president in his summing-up, contrary to the direct meaning of Section I, Article 801 of the Criminal Code, omitted to inform the jury what the judicial points are that constitute guilt; and did not mention that the fact of Maslova having administered the poison to Smelkov being admitted, the jury had a right not to impute the guilt of murder to her, since the proofs of wilful intent to deprive Smelkov of life were absent, and to pronounce her guilty only of carelessness, resulting in the death of the merchant, which she did not desire.' This is the chief point."

"Yes; but we ought to have known that ourselves. It was our mistake."

"And now the fourth point," the advocate continued. "'The form of the answer given by the jury contained an evident contradiction. Maslova is accused of wilfully poisoning Smelkov under the influence of cupidity, that being the only motive she could have had for the murder. The jury in their verdict acquit her of the intent to rob, and of participation in stealing the valuables; from which it follows that they intended also to acquit her of the intent to murder, and only through a misunderstanding, which arose from the incompleteness of the president's summing-up, omitted to express this in due form in their answer. Therefore an answer of this kind by the jury absolutely demanded the application of Articles 817 and 898 of the Criminal Code of procedure, *i.e.* an explanation by the president to the jury of their mistake, and another debate and verdict on the question of the prisoner's guilt.'"

"Then why did the president not do it?"

"I, too, should like to know why," Fanarin said, laughing.

"Then the Senate will, of course, correct this error?"

"That will all depend on who presides there at the time. Well now, there it is. I have further said," he continued rapidly, "a verdict of this kind gave the Court no right to condemn Maslova to be punished as a criminal, and to apply Section 3, Article 771 of the Penal Code to her case. This is a decided and gross violation of the basic principles of our criminal law. On the grounds stated, I have the honour of appealing to you, etc., etc., for the annulment according to Articles 909, 910 Section 2, 912 and 928 of the Criminal Code, etc., etc. . . . and to remit this case to another department of the same Court for a further examination.' There! all that can be done is done, but, to be frank, I have little hope of success, though, of course, it all depends on what members are present in the Senate. If you have any influence there you can but try."

"I do know some of them."

"All right; only be quick about it. Else they'll all go off to cure their piles; and then you may have to wait three months before they return. Then, in case of failure, we have still the possibility of appealing to his Majesty. That also depends on some manœuvring behind the scenes. And in that case, too, I am at your service—I mean in wording the petition, not behind the scenes."

"Thank you. Now as to your fees?"

"My assistant will hand you the petition and tell you."

"One thing more. The *Procureur* gave me a pass to visit this person in prison, but they tell me that in order to get an interview at another time and in another room than the usual ones, I must get a permission from the governor. Is this necessary?"

"Yes, I think so. But the governor is away at present; a vice-governor is in his place. And he is such a dense fool that you'll scarcely be able to do anything with him."

"Is it Maslennikov?"

"Yes."

"I know him," said Nekhlyudov, and got up to go. At this moment a horribly ugly, bony, snub-nosed, yellow-faced little woman flew into the room. It was the advocate's wife, who did not seem to be in the least bit troubled by her ugliness.

She was attired in the most original manner: she seemed enveloped in something made of velvet and silk, something yellow and green, and her thin hair was crimped. She stepped triumphantly into the room, followed by a tall, smiling man with a greenish complexion, dressed in a coat with silk facings, and with a white tie. This was an author. Nekhlyudov knew him by sight.

"Anatole," she said, opening the door of another room, "you must come to me. Here is Simon Ivanich, who promises to read his poem, and you must absolutely come and talk about Garshin."

Nekhlyudov noticed that she whispered something to her husband, and, thinking it concerned him, wished to go away, but she caught him up and said: "I beg your pardon, Prince, I know you, and so I think an introduction is not necessary, and I beg you will stay and take part in our literary matinée. It will be most interesting. Anatole speaks admirably."

"You see what a lot I have to do," said Fanarin, spreading out his hands and smilingly pointing to his wife, as if to show how impossible it was to resist so charming a creature.

Nekhlyudov, with a sad and solemn look, thanked the advocate's wife with extreme politeness for the honour she did him in inviting him, but refused the invitation and left the room.

"What an affected fellow!" said the advocate's wife, when he was gone.

In the waiting-room the assistant handed him the written petition, and said that the fees would come to one thousand roubles, and explained that Mr Fanarin did not usually undertake this kind of business, but did it only to oblige Nekhlyudov.

"And about this petition. Who is to sign it?"

"The prisoner may do it herself, or if that is inconvenient Mr. Fanarin can, if he gets a power of attorney from her."

"Oh, no. I will take the petition to her and get her to sign it," said Nekhlyudov, glad of an excuse for seeing her before the regular day.

Chapter XLVI

AT THE usual hour the jailer's whistle sounded in the corridors of the prison, the iron doors of the cells rattled, bare feet pattered, heels clattered, and the prisoners who acted as scavengers passed along the corridors filling the air with disgusting smells. The prisoners washed, dressed, and came out for inspection, and then went to get boiling water for their tea.

The conversation at breakfast in all the cells was very lively. It was about two prisoners who were to be flogged that day. One, Vasilyev, was a young man of some education, a clerk, who had killed his mistress in a fit of jealousy. His fellow-prisoners liked him because he was merry and generous, and firm in his behaviour with the prison authorities. He knew the regulations and insisted on their being carried out. Therefore he was disliked by the authorities.

Three weeks before, a jailer struck one of the scavengers because he had spilt some soup over his new uniform. Vasilyev took the part of the scavenger, saying that it was against the law to strike a prisoner.

"I'll teach you the law," said the jailer, and angrily abused Vasilyev. Vasilyev replied in like manner, and the jailer was going to hit him, but Vasilyev seized the jailer's hands, held them fast for two or three moments, then giving them a twist pushed the jailer out of the door. The jailer complained to the inspector, who ordered Vasilyev to be put into a solitary cell.

The solitary cells were a row of dark closets locked from outside, and there were neither beds nor chairs nor tables in them, so that the inmates had to sit or lie on the dirty floor, while the rats, of which there were a great many in those cells, ran over them. The rats were so bold that they stole bread from the prisoners, and even attacked them if they stopped moving. Vasilyev said he would not go into the solitary cell because he had done nothing wrong; but they used force. Then he began struggling, and two other prisoners helped him to free himself from the jailers. All the jailers assembled, and among them was one named Petrov, who was distinguished for his strength. The prisoners were thrown down and pushed into the solitary cells. The governor was immediately informed that something very like a mutiny had taken place, and he sent back an order to flog the two chief offenders, Vasilyev and the tramp Nepomnyashchy, each to have thirty strokes with a birch rod. The flogging was to take place in the women's visiting-room.

This had been well known in the prison since the evening, and it was being talked about with animation in all the cells.

Korableva, Horoshavka, Theodosia, and Maslova sat together in their corner drinking tea, all of them flushed and animated by the vodka they had drunk, for Maslova, who now had a constant supply, treated her companions freely.

"He's not been a-rioting or anything," Korableva said, referring to Vasilyev, as she bit tiny pieces off a lump of sugar with her strong teeth. "He only stuck up for a chum, becos it's not lawful to strike prisoners nowadays."

"And he's a fine fellow, I've heard say," said Theodosia, who, bareheaded, with her long plaits round her head, sat on a log of wood opposite the plank-bedstead on which the teapot stood.

"There now, if you were to ask him," the watchman's wife said to Maslova (by "him" she meant Nekhlyudov).

"I shall tell him. He'll do anything for me," Maslova said, tossing her head and smiling.

"Yes, but when is he coming? And they've already gone to fetch them," said Theodosia. "It is terrible," she added, with a sigh.

"I once saw how they flogged a peasant in the village. Father-in-law, he sent me once to the village elder. Well, I went, and there . . ." The watchman's wife began her long story, which was interrupted by the sound of voices and steps in the corridor above them.

The women were silent, and sat listening.

"There they are, hauling him along, the devils!" Horoshavka said. "They'll do him to death, they will. The jailers are so mad with him because he never would give in to them."

All was quiet again upstairs, and the watchman's wife finished her story of how she was that frightened when she went into the barn and saw them flogging a peasant her inside turned at the sight, and so on. Horoshavka related how Shcheglov had been flogged and never uttered a sound. Then Theodosia put away the tea-things, and Korableva and the watchman's wife took up their sewing. Maslova sat down on the bedstead with her arms round her knees, dull and depressed. She was about to lie down and try to sleep when the woman warder called her to come to the office to see a visitor.

"Now, mind and don't forget to tell him about us," the old woman (Menshova) said, while Maslova was arranging the kerchief on her head before the dim looking-glass. "We did not set fire to the house, but he did it himself, the fiend; his workman saw him do it, and will not damn his soul by denying it. You just tell him to ask to see my Mitry. Mitry will tell him all about it, as plain as can be. Just think of our being locked up in prison when we never dreamt of any ill, while he, the fiend, is enjoying himself at the pub with another man's wife."

"That's not the law," remarked Korableva.

"I'll tell him—I'll tell him," answered Maslova. "Suppose I have another drop, just to keep up my courage," she added, with a wink; and Korableva poured out half a cup of vodka, which Maslova drank. Then, having wiped her mouth, and repeating the words "Just to keep up my courage," she followed the warder along the corridor, tossing her head and smiling gaily.

Chapter XLVII

NEKHLYUDOV HAD been waiting in the hall a long time.

When he arrived at the prison he rang at the entrance door and handed the permit from the *Procureur* to the jailer on duty who met him.

"Whom do you want to see?"

"The prisoner Maslova."

"You can't at present: the inspector is engaged."

"Is he in the office?" asked Nekhlyudov.

"No, here in the visiting-room," said the jailer, who appeared confused.

"Why, is it a visiting day?"

"No, it's special business."

"I should like to see him. What should I do?" said Nekhlyudov.

"When the inspector comes out you'll tell him—wait a bit," said the jailer.

At this moment a sergeant-major, with a smooth, shiny face, and moustache impregnated with tobacco smoke, came out of a side door, the gold cords of his uniform glistening, and addressed the jailer in a severe tone.

"What do you mean by letting any one in here? The office——"

"I was told the inspector was here," said Nekhlyudov, surprised at the agitation he noticed in the sergeant-major's manner.

At this moment the inner door opened and Petrov came out, heated and perspiring.

"He'll remember it," he muttered, turning to the sergeant-major. The latter indicated Nekhlyudov by a look, and Petrov with knitted brows went out through a door at the back.

"Who will remember it? Why do they all seem so confused? Why did the sergeant-major make a sign to him?" Nekhlyudov thought.

The sergeant-major, again addressing Nekhlyudov, said: "You cannot meet here; please step across to the office."

Nekhlyudov was about to comply when the inspector came out of the door at the back, looking even more confused than his subordinates and sighing continually. When he saw Nekhlyudov he turned to the jailer.

"Fedotov, have Maslova, cell 5, women's ward, taken to the office."

"Will you come this way, please?" he said, turning to Nekhlyudov. They ascended a steep staircase and entered a small one-windowed room. The inspector sat down.

"Mine are heavy, heavy duties," he remarked, again addressing Nekhlyudov, as he took out a cigarette.

"You are tired, evidently," said Nekhlyudov.

"Tired of the whole of the service—the duties are very trying. One tries to lighten their lot and only makes it worse; my only thought is how to get away. Heavy, heavy duties!"

Nekhlyudov did not know what the inspector's special difficulties were, but he saw that to-day he was in a particularly dejected and hopeless condition, calling for pity.

"Yes, I should think the duties are very heavy," he said. "Why do you serve in this capacity?"

"I have a family, and no means."

"But, if it is so hard——"

"Well, still, you know, it is possible to be of some use; I soften things down as much as I can. Another in my place would conduct things quite differently. Why, we have more than two thousand people here. And what people! One must know how to manage them. It is easier said than done, you know. After all, they are human beings; one cannot help pitying them." And the inspector began telling Nekhlyudov of a fight that had lately taken place among the convicts, which had ended in one man being killed.

The story was interrupted by the entrance of Maslova accompanied by a jailer.

Nekhlyudov saw her through the doorway before she had noticed the inspector. Her face was flushed and she was following the warder briskly, smiling and tossing her head. When she saw the inspector she suddenly changed, and gazed at him with a frightened look; but quickly recovering she addressed Nekhlyudov boldly and gaily.

"How d' you do?" she said, drawling out her words, and smilingly took his hand and shook it vigorously, not as she had done the first time.

"Here, I've brought you a petition to sign," said Nekhlyudov, rather surprised by the boldness with which she greeted him to-day. "The advocate has written out a petition which you will have to sign, and then we will send it to Petersburg."

"All right! That can be done. Anything you like," she said, with a wink and a smile.

Nekhlyudov drew a folded paper from his pocket, and went up to the table.

"May she sign it here?" asked Nekhlyudov, turning to the inspector.

"Yes, sit down. Here's a pen; can you write?" said the inspector.

"I could at one time," she said; and, after arranging her skirt and the sleeves of her jacket, she sat down at the table, smiling, took the pen awkwardly in her small, energetic hand, and glanced at Nekhlyudov with a laugh.

Nekhlyudov told her what to write, and pointed out where she was to sign.

Sighing deeply as she dipped her pen into the ink, and carefully shaking off some drops, she wrote her name.

"Is that all?" she asked, looking from Nekhlyudov to the inspector, and putting the pen now on the inkstand, now on the papers.

"I have a few words to say to you," Nekhlyudov said, taking the pen from her.

"All right; tell me," she said. And suddenly, as if remembering something or feeling sleepy, she grew serious.

The inspector rose and left the room, leaving Nekhlyudov with her.

Chapter XLVIII

THE JAILER who had brought Maslova in sat on a window-sill at some distance from them.

The decisive moment had come for Nekhlyudov. He had been

incessantly blaming himself for not having told her the principal thing at the first interview, and was now determined to tell her that he would marry her. She was sitting at the farther side of the table. Nekhlyudov sat down opposite her. It was light in the room, and Nekhlyudov for the first time saw her face quite near. He distinctly saw the crow's-feet round her eyes, the wrinkles round her mouth, and the swollen eyelids. He pitied her more than ever. Leaning over the table so as not to be heard by the jailer—a man of Jewish type with grizzly whiskers— Nekhlyudov said:—

"Should this petition come to nothing we will appeal to the Emperor. All that is possible shall be done."

"There now, if we had had a proper advocate from the first," she interrupted. "My counsel was quite a silly. He did nothing but pay me compliments," she said, and laughed. "If it had been known then that I was acquainted with you it would have been another matter. They think every one's a thief."

"How strange she is to-day," Nekhlyudov thought, and was just going to say what he had on his mind when she began again:—

"There's something I want to say. We have here an old woman; such a fine one, d'you know, she just surprises every one. She is imprisoned for nothing, and her son too, and everybody knows they are innocent, though they are accused of having set fire to a house. D'you know, hearing I was acquainted with you, she says: 'Tell him to ask to see my son; he'll tell him all about it.'" As Maslova spoke she turned her head from side to side, and glanced at Nekhlyudov. "Their name's Menshov. Well, will you do it? Such a fine old thing, you know; you can see at once she's innocent. You'll do it, there's a dear," and she smiled, glanced up at him, and then cast down her eyes.

"All right. I'll find out about them," Nekhlyudov said, more and more astonished by her free-and-easy manner. "But I was going to speak to you about myself. Do you remember what I told you last time?"

"You said a lot last time. What was it you told me?" she said, continuing to smile and to turn her head from side to side.

"I said I had come to ask you to forgive me . . ." he began.

"What's the use of that? Forgive, forgive, where's the good of . . . You'd better . . ."

"To atone for my sin, not by mere words, but in deed. I have made up my mind to marry you."

An expression of fear suddenly came over her face. Her squinting eyes remained fixed on him and yet seemed not to be looking at him.

"What's that for?" she said, with an angry frown.

"I feel that it is my duty before God to do it."

"What God have you found now? You are not talking sense. God, indeed! What God? You ought to have remembered God then," she said, and stopped with her mouth open. It was only now that Nekhlyudov noticed that her breath smelt of spirits; and he understood the cause of her excitement.

"Try and be calm," he said.

"Why should I be calm? You think I'm tipsy? I am tipsy, yet I know what I'm saying," she began quickly, flushing scarlet. "I am a convict, a whore, and you are a gentleman and a prince. There's no need for you to soil yourself by touching me. You go to your princesses: my price is a ten ruble note."

"However cruelly you may speak, you cannot express what I myself am feeling," he said, trembling all over; "you cannot imagine to what extent I feel myself guilty towards you."

"Feel yourself guilty!" she said angrily, mimicking him. "You did not feel so then, but threw me a hundred rubles. That . . . is your price!"

"I know, I know; but what is to be done now?" said Nekhlyudov. "I have decided not to leave you, and I shall do what I have said."

"And I say you shan't," she said, and laughed aloud.

"Katusha!" he began, touching her hand.

"You go away. I am a convict and you a prince, and you've no business here," she cried, her whole appearance transformed by her anger, and pulling away her hand.

"You want to save yourself through me," she continued, hurrying to express what had risen in her soul. "You've got pleasure out of me in this life, and want to save yourself through me in the life to come. You are disgusting to me—your spectacles and the whole of your dirty fat mug. Go, go!" she screamed, starting to her feet.

The jailer came up to them.

"What are you kicking up this row for? That won't——"

"Let her alone, please," said Nekhlyudov.

"She must not forget herself," said the jailer.

"Please wait a little," said Nekhlyudov, and the jailer returned to the window.

Maslova sat down again, dropping her eyes and firmly clasping her small hands. Nekhlyudov stooped over her, not knowing what to do.

"You do not believe me?" he said.

"That you mean to marry me? It will never be. I'd rather hang myself. So there!"

"Well, still I shall go on serving you."

"That's your affair, only I don't want anything from you. That's the plain truth," she said.

"Oh, why did I not die then?" she added, and began to cry piteously. Nekhlyudov could not speak; her tears infected him. She lifted her eyes, looked at him in surprise, and began to wipe her tears with her kerchief.

The jailer came up again and reminded them that it was time to part. Maslova rose.

"You are excited. If possible I will come again to-morrow—you must think it over," said Nekhlyudov.

She gave him no answer, and, without looking up, followed the jailer out of the room.

"Well, lass, you'll have rare times now," Korableva said when Maslova returned to the cell. "Seems he's mighty sweet on you; make the most of it while he's after you. He'll help you out. Rich people can do anything."

"Yes, that's so," remarked the watchman's wife, with her musical voice. "When a poor man thinks of getting married there's many a slip 'twixt the cup and the lip; but a rich man need only make up his mind and it's done. We knew a toff like that, duckie. What d'you think he did?"

"Well, have you spoken about my affairs?" the old woman asked.

But Maslova gave her fellow-prisoners no answer; she lay down on the plank-bedstead, her squinting eyes fixed on a corner of the room, and remained there until the evening.

A painful struggle went on in her soul. What Nekhlyudov had said brought back to her memory that world in which she had suffered, and which she had left without having understood, hating it. She was now awakened from the trance in which she had been living; but to live with a clear memory of what had been was impossible: it would have been too great a torment. So in the evening she again bought some vodka and drank with her companions.

Chapter XLIX

"So THIS is what it means—this," thought Nekhlyudov as he left the prison, only now fully understanding his crime. Had he not tried to expiate his guilt he would never have found out how great his crime was. Nor was this all; she, too, would never have felt the whole horror of what had been done to her. Only now he saw what he had done to the soul of this woman; only now she saw and understood what had been done to her. Up to this time Nekhlyudov had played with a sensation of self-admiration, had admired his own remorse; now he was simply filled with horror. He knew he could not abandon her now, and yet he could not imagine what would come of their relations to one another.

Just as he was going out, a jailer with a disagreeably insinuating countenance, and with a cross and medals on his breast, came up with an air of mystery and handed him a note.

"Here is a note from a certain person, your excellency," he said to Nekhlyudov, as he gave him the envelope.

"What person?"

"You will know when you read it. A political prisoner. I am in that ward, so she asked me; and though it is against the rules, still, feelings of humanity . . ." The jailer spoke in an unnatural manner.

Nekhlyudov was surprised that a jailer of the ward where political prisoners were kept should pass notes inside the very prison walls and almost within sight of every one; he did not then know that this was both a jailer and a spy. However, he took the note, and read it on coming out of the prison.

It was written in a bold hand, and ran as follows: "Having heard that you visit the prison and are interested in the case of a criminal prisoner, the desire to see you arose in me. Ask for a permit to see me. It will be given you, and I can tell you much that concerns your protégée, as well as our group.—Yours gratefully, Vera Dukhova."

Vera Dukhova had been a school-mistress in an out-of-the-way village of the Novgorod Government, where Nekhlyudov and some friends of his had once stayed while bear-hunting. She had applied to Nekhlyudov for some money to enable her to enter for a course of study. Nekhlyudov gave her the money and forgot about her, and it now appeared that this lady was a political convict and in prison (where she had probably heard his story); and was offering her services.

How simple and easy everything had then been, and how hard and complicated it all was now!

Nekhlyudov gladly and vividly recalled those times, and his acquaintance with Dukhova. It was just before Lent, at a spot forty miles from the railway. The sport had been successful—two bears had been killed—and the company were having dinner before starting on their return journey, when the owner of the shooting-hut where they were putting up came in to say that the deacon's daughter wanted to speak to Prince Nekhlyudov.

"Is she pretty?" some one asked.

"None of that, please," Nekhlyudov said, and rose with a serious look on his face. Wiping his mouth, and wondering what the deacon's daughter could want with him, he went into the host's private hut.

There he found a girl in a felt hat and a warm cloak—a sinewy, ugly girl; only her eyes with their arched brows were beautiful.

"Here, miss, speak to him," said the old housewife; "this is the Prince himself. I shall go out meanwhile."

"In what way can I be of service to you?" Nekhlyudov asked.

"I . . . I . . . I see you are rich, and throw away your money on such nonsense—on sport," began the girl, in great confusion. "I know . . . I only want one thing . . . to be of use to the people, and I can do nothing because I know nothing." Her eyes were so truthful, so kind, and her resolute and yet shy expression was so touching, that Nekhlyudov, as often happened to him, suddenly felt himself in her position— understood and sympathised.

"What can I do for you?"

"I am a teacher, but I should like to take the university course, and am not not allowed to do so. That is, not that I am not allowed to; they'd allow me to, but I have not the means. Give them to me, and when I have finished the course I will repay you. I've been thinking that the rich kill bears and give the peasants drink; and all this is bad. Why should they not do good? I only want eighty rubles. . . . But if you don't wish to, never mind," she added crossly.

"On the contrary, I am very grateful to you for this opportunity. I will bring the money at once," said Nekhlyudov.

He went out into the passage, and there met one of his companions, who had been listening to his conversation. Paying no heed to his chaffing, Nekhlyudov took the money out of his purse and gave it to her.

"Oh, please, do not thank me; it is I who should thank you," he said.

It was pleasant to remember all this now: pleasant to remember how he had nearly had a quarrel with an officer who tried to make an objectionable joke of it; how another of his friends had taken his part, and how that led to a closer friendship between them. How successful the whole of that hunting expedition had been, and how happy he had felt when returning to the railway station that night. . . .

The line of sledges—the horses driven tandem—glide quickly along the narrow road through the forest; now between high trees, now between low firs weighted down by the snow caked in heavy lumps on their branches. A red light flashes in the dark; some one lights a fragrant cigarette. Joseph, a bear-driver, changes over from sledge to sledge, up to his knees in snow, and while putting things to rights he speaks of the elk now going about on the deep snow and gnawing the bark off the aspen trees, of the bears that are lying asleep in their deep hidden dens, from whence their breath puffs warm through their breathing holes.

All this comes back to Nekhlyudov's mind, but, above all, the joyous sense of health, strength, and freedom from care: the lungs breathing in the frosty air so deeply that the fur cloak is drawn tightly on his chest; the fine snow dropping from the low branches on to his face; his body warm, his face fresh, and his soul free from care, self-reproach, fear, or desire. . . . How beautiful it was. And now, O God! what torment, what trouble!

Evidently Vera Dukhova was a revolutionist and imprisoned as such. He must see her, especially as she promised to advise him about Maslova.

Chapter L

WAKING EARLY next morning, Nekhlyudov remembered what he had done the day before, and was seized with fear.

But, in spite of this fear, he was more determined than ever to continue what he had begun.

Conscious of a sense of duty, he left home and went to see Maslennikov, in order to obtain from him permission to visit Maslova in prison, and also the Menshovs—mother and son—about whom Maslova had spoken to him. Besides this, he wished to ask permission to see Dukhova, who might be of use to Maslova.

Nekhlyudov had known this Maslennikov a long time: they had been in the regiment together. At that time Maslennikov had been treasurer to the regiment. He was a kind-hearted and zealous officer, knowing and wishing to know nothing beyond the regiment and the imperial family. Now Nekhlyudov saw him as an official who had exchanged the regiment for an administrative post. He was married to a rich and energetic woman, who had forced him to make this exchange. She made fun of him and caressed him, as if he were a pet animal of hers. Nekhlyudov had been to see them once during the winter, but the couple were so uninteresting to him that he had not gone again.

At the sight of Nekhlyudov Maslennikov's face beamed all over. He had the same fat, red face, and was as corpulent and as well dressed as in his military days. Then he used always to be dressed in a well-brushed uniform made according to the latest fashion, tightly fitting his chest and shoulders; now it was a civil service uniform he wore, but that, too, tightly fitted his well-fed body and showed off his broad chest, and was cut according to the latest fashion. In spite of the difference in age (Maslennikov was forty), the two men were very familiar with one another.

"Hallo, old fellow! How good of you to come! Let us go and see my wife. I have just ten minutes to spare before the meeting. My chief is away, you know, so I am at the head of the Government administration," he said, unable to disguise his satisfaction.

"I have come on business."

"What is it?" asked Maslennikov in an anxious and severe tone, putting himself at once on his guard.

"There is a person, whom I am very much interested in, in prison" (at the word "prison" Maslennikov's face grew stern); "and I should like to have an interview, not in the common visiting-room, but in the office, and not only at the usual visiting hours. I am told it depends on you."

"Certainly, *mon cher*, I'll do anything for you," said Maslennikov, putting both hands on Nekhlyudov's knees, as if to tone down his grandeur; "but remember, I am monarch only for an hour."

"Then you will give me an order that will enable me to see her?"

"It's a woman?"

"Yes."

"What is she there for?"

"Poisoning, but she had been unjustly condemned."

"Yes, there you have it, your just jury system, *ils n'en font point d'autres*,"[1] he said, in French for some unknown reason. "I know you do not agree with me, but it can't be. helped, *c'est mon opinion bien arrêtée*,"[2] he added, giving utterance to an opinion he had been reading for the last twelve months in a reactionary Conservative paper. "I know you are a Liberal."

"I don't know whether I am a Liberal or not," Nekhlyudov said, smiling. It always surprised him to find himself ranked with a political party and called a Liberal, when he maintained that a man should be heard before he was judged; that before being condemned all men were equal; that nobody at all ought to be ill-treated and beaten, but especially not those who had not yet been tried by law. "I don't know whether I am a Liberal or not; but I do know that however bad the present jury system is, it is better than the old tribunals."

"And whom have you for an advocate?"

"I have spoken to Fanarin"

"Dear me, Fanarin!" said Maslennikov, with a grimace, recollecting how this Fanarin had examined him as a witness at a trial the year before, and had, in the politest manner, held him up to ridicule for half an hour.

---

[1] They can't do otherwise.
[2] It is my very decided opinion.

"I should advise you not to have anything to do with him. Fanarin *est un homme taré.*"[3]

"I have one more request to make," said Nekhlyudov, without replying. "There's a young woman whom I knew long ago, a teacher—a very pitiable little thing—she is now also imprisoned, and wants to see me. Could you give me a permit to visit her?"

Maslennikov bent his head on one side and considered.

"She's a political one?"

"Yes, I have been told so."

"Well, you see, only relations get permission to visit political prisoners. Still, I'll give you an open order. *Je sais que vous n'abuserez pas.*[4] What's the name of your protégée? Dukhova? *Elle est jolie?*"[5]

"*Hideuse.*"

Maslennikov shook his head disapprovingly, went up to the table, and wrote on a sheet of paper with a printed heading:—

"The bearer, Prince Dmitry Ivanich Nekhlyudov, is to be allowed to interview in the prison office the prisoner, Masvlova, and also the medical assistant, Dukhova," and he finished with an elaborate flourish.

"Now you'll be able to see what order we maintain there. And it is very difficult to keep order, it is so crowded, especially with people condemned to exile; but I watch strictly, and love the work. You will see they are very comfortable and contented. But one must know how to deal with them. Only a few days ago we had a little trouble—insubordination; another would have called it mutiny, and would have made many miserable, but with us it all passed quietly. We must have solicitude on the one hand, firmness and power on the other," and he clenched his fat, white, turquoise-ringed fist, which issued out of the starched cuff of his shirt-sleeve, fastened with a gold stud. "Solicitude and firm power."

"Well, I don't know about that," said Nekhlyudov. "I went there twice, and felt very much depressed."

"Do you know, you ought to get acquainted with the Countess Passek," continued Maslennikov, warming to the conversation. "She has given herself up entirely to this sort of work. *Elle fait beaucoup de bien.*[6] Thanks to her—and, perhaps I may add without false modesty, to me—everything has been changed, changed in such a way that the former horrors no longer exist, and they are really quite comfortable there. Well, you'll see. As to Fanarin, I do not know him personally—

---

[3] A very bad man.

[4] I know you will not abuse it.

[5] Is she pretty?

[6] She does much good.

besides, my social position keeps our ways apart—but he is positively a bad man; and then he takes the liberty of saying such things in the Court—such things!"

"Well, thank you," Nekhlyudov said, taking the paper, and without listening further he bid good-day to his former fellow-officer.

"But won't you go in and see my wife?"

"Please excuse me; I have no time now."

"Dear me, she will never forgive me," said Maslennikov, accompanying his old acquaintance down to the first landing, as he was in the habit of doing to persons of not the greatest, but the second greatest importance, with whom he classed Nekhlyudov, "now do go in, if only for a moment."

But Nekhlyudov remained firm; and while the footman and the doorkeeper rushed to give him his stick and overcoat, and opened the door, outside of which stood a policeman, Nekhlyudov repeated that he really could not stay.

"Well then, on Thursday please. It is her 'at home.' I will tell her you are coming," called Maslennikov from the stairs.

Chapter LI

NEKHLYUDOV drove straight from Maslennikov's to the prison and went to the inspector's lodging, which he now knew. He was again struck by the sounds of the same piano of inferior quality; but this time it was not a rhapsody that was being played, but exercises by Clementi, again with the same vigour, distinctness, and rapidity. The servant with the bandaged eye said the inspector was in, and showed Nekhlyudov into a small drawing-room where there was a sofa and, on a table in front of it, a large lamp, standing on a piece of crochet-work, and having a pink paper shade which was burnt on one side. The inspector entered, with his usual sad and weary look.

"Take a seat, please. What can I do for you?" he said, buttoning the middle button of his uniform.

"I have just been to the vice-governor's, and have this order from him. I should like to see the prisoner Maslova."

"Markova?" asked the inspector, unable to hear distinctly because of the music.

"Maslova!"

"Oh, yes!" The inspector got up and went to the door whence proceeded Clementi's roulades.

"Mary, can't you stop just a minute!" he said, in a voice that showed that this music was the bane of his life. "One can't hear a word."

The piano was silent; but one could hear the sound of reluctant steps, and some one looked in at the door.

The inspector seemed to feel eased by the interval of silence, lit a thick cigarette of mild tobacco, and offered one to Nekhlyudov.

Nekhlyudov declined.

"It is Maslova that I want to see."

"Maslova! It's not very convenient to see Maslova to-day," said the inspector.

"How's that?"

"Well, you know, it's all your own fault," said the inspector, with a slight smile. "Prince, give no money into her hands. If you like, give it me: I will keep it for her. You see, you must have given her some money yesterday; she got some spirits (it's an evil we cannot manage to root out), and to-day she is quite tipsy, even violent."

"Is it possible?"

"Oh yes, it is. I have even been obliged to have recourse to severe measures, and to put her into a separate cell. She is a quiet woman in an ordinary way. But please do not give her any money. These people are so . . ."

What had happened the day before came vividly back to Nekhlyudov's mind, and again he was seized with fear.

"And Dukhova, a political prisoner; might I see her?"

"Yes, if you like," said the inspector. "Now then, what do you want?" he said, addressing a little girl of five or six, who came into the room and walked up to her father with her head turned towards Nekhlyudov and her eyes fixed on him. "There now, you'll be toppling," said the inspector, smiling, as the little girl ran up to him, and, not looking where she was going, caught her foot in a rug.

"Well then, if I may, I will go."

The inspector embraced the little girl, who was still gazing at Nekhlyudov, got up, and tenderly motioning the child aside, went into the ante-room. Hardly had he put on the overcoat, into which the maid helped him, when, before he had reached the door, the distinct sounds of Clemnti's roulades again began.

"She was at the Conservatoire, but there is such disorder there. She has a great gift," said the inspector, as they went down the stairs. "She means to play at concerts."

The inspector and Nekhlyudov arrived at the prison. The gates were instantly opened when they appeared. The jailers, with their fingers lifted to their caps, followed the inspector with their eyes. Four men, with their heads half shaved, who were carrying tubs filled with something, cringed when they saw him. One of them frowned angrily, his black eyes glaring.

"Of course, a talent like that must be developed, it would not do to bury it, but in small apartments, you know, it is rather tiresome." The inspector went on with the conversation, taking no notice of these prisoners, and dragging his feet he followed Nekhlyudov into the hall with weary steps.

"Who is it you want to see?"

"Dukhova."

"Oh, she's in the tower. You'll have to wait a little," he said.

"Might I not meanwhile see the prisoners Menshov, mother and son, who are accused of incendiarism?"

"Oh yes, cell No. 21. Yes, they can be sent for."

"But might I not see Menshov in his cell?"

"Oh, you'll find the meeting-room pleasanter."

"No. I should prefer the cell. It is more interesting."

"Well, you have found something to be interested in!" Here the assistant, a smartly dressed officer, entered by the side door.

"Here, see the Prince into Menshov's cell, No. 21," said the inspector to his assistant; "and then take him to the office. And I'll go and call—what's her name?"

"Vera Dukhova."

The inspector's assistant was a fair young man, with dyed moustache, who diffused a smell of eau-de-cologne. "This way, please," he said to Nekhlyudov, with a pleasant smile. "Our establishment interests you?"

"Yes, it does interest me; and besides, I look upon it as a duty to help a man who, as I am told, is confined here, though innocent."

The assistant shrugged his shoulders. "Yes, that does happen," he said quietly, politely stepping aside to let the visitor enter the stinking corridor first. "But it also happens that they lie. This way, please."

The doors of the cells were open, and some of the prisoners were in the corridor. The assistant nodded slightly to the jailers, and cast a side glance at the prisoners, who, keeping close to the wall, crept back to their cells, or stood like soldiers, with their arms at their sides, following the official with their eyes. After passing through one corridor, the assistant showed Nekhlyudov into another on the left, separated from the first by an iron door.

This corridor was narrower and darker, and smelt even worse than the first. The corridor had doors on both sides, with little holes in them about an inch in diameter. There was only an old jailer, with a sad, wrinkled face, in this corridor.

"Where is Menshov?" asked the inspector's assistant.

"The eighth cell to the left."

"And these? Are they occupied?" asked Nekhlyudov.

"Yes, all but one."

Chapter LII

"MAY I look in?" asked Nekhlyudov.

"Oh, certainly," answered the assistant, smiling, and turned to the jailer with some question. Nekhlyudov looked into one of the little holes, and saw a tall young man with a small black beard pacing up and down the cell in his underclothing. Hearing some one at the door he looked up with a frown, but continued to pace the cell.

Nekhlyudov looked into another hole. His eye met another, a big, frightened eye, looking out of the hole at him, and he quickly stepped aside. In the third cell he saw a very small man asleep on the bed, covered, head and all, with his prison cloak. In the fourth a pale, broad-faced man was sitting with his elbows on his knees and his head bent low down. At the sound of footsteps this man raised his head and glanced up. His face, especially his large eyes, bore an expression of hopeless dejection. One could see that it did not even interest him to know who was inspecting his cell. Whoever it might be, the prisoner evidently hoped for nothing good from him. Nekhlyudov was seized with dread, and went to Menshov's cell, No. 21, without stopping to peep through any more holes. The jailer unlocked the door and opened it. A young man, with long neck, well–developed muscles, a small head, and kind round eyes, stood by the bed, hastily putting on his cloak, and turned to the newcomers with a frightened face. Nekhlyudov was specially struck by the kind round eyes, that were throwing frightened and inquiring glances by turns at him, at the jailer, at the assistant, and back again.

"Here's a gentleman who wants to inquire into your affair."

"Thank you kindly."

"Yes, I was told about you," Nekhlyudov said, crossing the cell to the dirty grated window, "and I should like to hear all about your case from yourself."

Menshov also came up to the window, and at once began telling his story, at first looking shyly at the inspector's assistant, but gradually growing bolder. When the assistant left the cell and went into the corridor to give some orders, the man grew quite bold. The story was told with the accent and in the manner natural to a very ordinary, good

peasant lad. To hear it told by a prisoner dressed in this degrading clothing, and inside a prison, seemed very strange to Nekhlyudov.
Nekhlyudov listened, and continued at the same time to look around
him: at the low bedstead with its straw mattress, the window with thick
iron gratings, the dirty, damp wall, and at the piteous face and form of
this unfortunate disfigured peasant in his prison cloak and shoes; and
he felt sadder and sadder, would have liked not to believe what this
good-natured fellow was saying. It seemed too dreadful to think that
people could do such a thing as to take a man, without any reason
except that he himself had been injured, dress him in convict clothes,
and keep him in such a horrible place. And yet the thought that this
seemingly true story, told with such a good-natured expression on the
face, might be an invention and a lie, was still more dreadful. This was
the story. Soon after the marriage, the village innkeeper had enticed
the young fellow's wife. He tried everywhere to get justice. But everywhere the innkeeper managed to bribe the officials, and was acquitted.
Once he took his wife back by force, but she ran away next day. Then
he went to demand her back, but, though he saw her when he came in,
the innkeeper told him she was not there, and ordered him to go away.
He would not go, so the innkeeper and his servant beat him until they
drew blood. The next day a fire broke out in the inn, and the young
man and his mother were accused of having set the house on fire. He
had not set it on fire, but was visiting a friend at the time.

"And is it true that you did not set it on fire?"

"It never entered by head to do it, sir. It must be my enemy that did
it himself. I heard he had insured it just before. They said it was mother
and I that did it, and that we had threatened him. It is true I once went
for him—my heart couldn't stand it any longer—but as to setting the
house on fire, I didn't do it. He set it on fire himself and then accused
us. I was not there just when the fire broke out, but he purposely
arranged it so that it should happen when mother and I had been
there."

"Can this be true?"

"God is my witness it is true. Oh, sir, be so good . . ." and
Nekhlyudov had difficulty in preventing him from bowing down to the
ground. "Have pity . . . you see I am perishing without any reason." And
suddenly his face quivered, and he turned up the sleeves of his cloak
and began to cry, wiping the tears with the sleeve of his dirty shirt.

"Are you ready?" asked the assistant.

"Yes. . . . Well, cheer up. We will do what we can," said Nekhlyudov,
and went out. Menshov stood close to the door, so that the jailer
knocked him in shutting it, and while the jailer was locking it he
remained looking out through the little hole.

Chapter LIII

RETURNING along the broad corridor past the men dressed in light yellow cloaks, short wide trousers, and prison shoes, who looked eagerly at him (it was dinner-time, and the cell doors were open), Nekhlyudov felt a strange mixture of sympathy for them, and horror and perplexity at the conduct of those who put and kept them here; and besides, though he knew not why, he felt ashamed of himself for calmly examining it all.

In one of the corridors somebody clattering with his shoes ran in at the door of a cell. Several men came out from it and stood in Nekhlyudov's way, bowing to him.

"Please, your honour—we don't know what to call you—get our affair settled somehow."

"I am not an official. I know nothing about it."

"Well anyhow, you come from outside; tell somebody—one of the authorities if need be," said an indignant voice. "Show some pity on us, as a human being. Here we are suffering the second month for nothing."

"What do you mean? Why?" said Nekhlyudov.

"Why?" We ourselves don't know why, but we're here the second month now."

"Yes, it's quite true, and it is owing to an accident," said the assistant. "These people were taken up because they had no passports, and they ought to have been sent back to their native province; but the prison there is burnt, and the local authorities have written asking us not to send them on. So we have sent all the other passportless people to their different provinces, but are keeping these."

"What! For no other reason than that?" Nekhlyudov exclaimed, stopping at the door.

A crowd of about forty men, all dressed in prison clothes, surrounded him and the assistant, and several began talking at once. The assistant stopped them.

"Let some one of you speak."

A tall, good-looking peasant of about fifty, a stone-mason, stepped out from the rest. He told Nekhlyudov that all of them had been ordered back to their homes and were now being kept in prison for not having passports, yet they had passports which were only a fortnight in arrears. The same thing had happened every year—they had many times omitted to renew their passports till they were overdue, and nobody had ever said anything—but this year they had been taken up, and were being kept in prison two months, as if they were criminals.

"We are all masons, and belong to the same *artel*. We are told that the prison in our province is burnt, but that is not our fault. Do help us."

Nekhlyudov listened, but hardly understood what the good-looking old man was saying, his attention being riveted to a large, dark-grey, many-legged louse that was creeping along the man's cheek.

"How is that? Can it be, for such a reason?" Nekhlyudov said, turning to the assistant.

"Yes, they should have been sent off and taken back to their homes," calmly said the assistant, "but they seem to have been forgotten or something."

Before the assistant had finished speaking, a small, nervous man, also in prison dress, came out of the crowd, and strangely contorting his mouth began to say that they were being ill-used for nothing.

"Worse than dogs . . ." he was saying.

"Now, now; not too much of this. Hold your tongue or you know . . ."

"What do I know?" screamed the little man desperately. "What is our crime?"

"Silence!" shouted the assistant, and the little man was silent.

"But what is the meaning of all this?" Nekhlyudov thought to himself as he came out of the cell, while a hundred eyes were fixed upon him through the openings of the cell doors and by prisoners that met him, making him feel as if he were running the gauntlet.

"Is it really possible that perfectly innocent people are kept here?" Nekhlyudov exclaimed, when they left the corridor.

"What would you have us do? They lie so. To hear them talk they are all of them innocent," said the inspector's assistant. "But it does happen that some are really imprisoned for nothing."

"Well, these have done nothing."

"Yes, we must admit that. Still the people are fearfully spoilt. There are some types—desperate fellows, who have to be looked sharply after. Yesterday two of that sort had to be punished."

"Punished? How?"

"Flogged with a birch rod, by order."

"But corporal punishment is abolished."

"Not for such as are deprived of their rights. They are still liable to it."

Nekhlyudov thought of what he had seen the day before while waiting in the hall, and now understood that the punishment was then being inflicted; and the mixed feeling of curiosity, depression, perplexity, and moral nausea, that grew into physical nausea, took hold of him more strongly than ever.

Without listening to the inspector's assistant or looking round, he hurriedly left the corridor and went to the office. The inspector was in the office, occupied with other business, and had forgotten to send for Dukhova. He only remembered his promise to have her called when Nekhlyudov entered the room.

"Sit down, please. I'll send for her at once," said he.

Chapter LIV

THE OFFICE consisted of two rooms. The first room, with a large dilapidated stove and two dirty windows, had in one corner a black stand for measuring the prisoners, while in another hung a large icon of Christ, as is usual in places where people are tortured. In this room several jailers were standing. In the next room sat about twenty persons, men and women in groups and in pairs, talking in low voices. There was a writing-table by the window.

The inspector sat down by the table, and offered Nekhlyudov a chair beside him. Nekhlyudov sat down, and looked at the people in the room.

The first who drew his attention was a young man with a pleasant face, dressed in a short jacket, standing in front of a middle-aged woman with dark eyebrows, to whom he was eagerly telling something, gesticulating with his hands the while. Beside them sat an old man, with blue spectacles, holding the hand of a young woman in prisoner's clothes, who was telling him something. A schoolboy, with a fixed, frightened look on his face, was gazing at the old man. In one corner sat a pair of lovers. The girl was quite young and pretty, with short fair hair and an energetic expression, and was elegantly dressed; the young man had fine features and wavy hair, and he wore a rubber jacket. They sat in their corner whispering to one another, and seemed dazed by love. Nearest to the table sat a grey-haired woman dressed in black, evidently the mother of a young consumptive-looking fellow, also in a rubber jacket; her head lay on his shoulder. She was trying to say something, but her sobs prevented her; she began several times, but had to stop. The young man held a paper in his hand, and, apparently not knowing what to do, kept folding and pressing it with an angry look on his face. Besides them was a short-haired, stout, red-faced girl, with very prominent eyes, dressed in a grey dress and a cape. She sat beside the weeping mother, tenderly stroking her. Everything about this girl was beautiful: her large white hands, her short wavy hair, her firm nose and lips; but the chief charm of her face lay in her kind, truthful, hazel eyes. The beautiful eyes turned away from the mother for just a moment when Nekhlyudov

came in, and met his look. But she turned back at once and said something to the mother. Not far from the lovers a dark, dishevelled man,
with a gloomy face, sat talking angrily to a beardless visitor, who looked
as if he belonged to the sect of the Skotpsy.[1]

Nekhlyudov, sitting by the inspector's side, looked round with
strained curiosity. A little boy with cropped hair came up to him and
addressed him in a shrill voice.

"And whom are you waiting for?"

Nekhlyudov was surprised at the question, but looking at the boy,
and seeing the serious little face, with its bright attentive eyes fixed on
him, answered him seriously that he was waiting for a woman of his
acquaintance.

"Is she, then, your sister?" the boy asked.

"No, not my sister," Nekhlyudov answered in surprise. "And you,
with whom are you here?" he asked the boy.

"I?—with mamma; she's a political one," he replied.

"Mary Pavlovna, take Kolya!" said the inspector, evidently considering Nekhlyudov's conversation with the boy contrary to the rules.

Mary Pavlovna, the beautiful girl who had attracted Nekhlyudov's
attention, rose tall and erect, and with firm, almost manly steps,
approached Nekhlyudov and the boy.

"What is he asking you—who you are?" she inquired, with a slight
smile, looking straight into his face with a trustful look in her kind,
prominent eyes, and as simply as if there could be no doubt whatever
that she was and must be on sisterly terms with everybody.

"He likes to know everything," she said looking at the boy with so
sweet and kind a smile that both the boy and Nekhlyudov were obliged
to smile back.

"He was asking me whom I have come to see."

"Mary Pavlovna, it is against the rules to speak to strangers. You know
it is," said the inspector.

"All right, all right," she said, and went back to the consumptive lad's
mother, holding Kolya's little hand in her large white one, while he
continued gazing up into her face.

"Who is this little boy?" Nekhlyudov asked of the inspector.

"His mother is a political prisoner, and he was born in prison," said
the inspector in a pleased tone, as if glad to point out how exceptional
his establishment was.

"Is it possible?"

"Yes, and now he is going to Siberia with her."

"And that young girl?"

---

[1] The Skoptsy seek to attain purity by castration.

"I cannot answer your question," said the inspector, shrugging his shoulders. "Besides, here is Dukhova."

Chapter LV

THROUGH A door at the back of the room entered, with a wriggling gait, the thin, yellow Vera Dukhova, with her large kind eyes.

"Thanks for having come," she said, pressing Nekhlyudov's hand. "Do you remember me? Let us sit down."

"I did not expect to see you like this."

"Oh, I am very happy. It is so delightful, so delightful, that I desire nothing better," said Vera Dukhova, with her usual expression of fright in the large, kind, round eyes fixed on Nekhlyudov, and twisting the terribly thin, sinewy neck encircled by the shabby, crumpled, dirty collar of her bodice.

Nekhlyudov asked her how she came to be in prison.

In answer she began relating all about her affairs with great animation. Her speech was intermingled with many special words, such as propaganda, disorganisation, social groups, sections and sub-sections, about which she seemed to think everybody knew, but which Nekhlyudov had never heard of. She told him all the secrets of the Narodovolstvo,[1] evidently convinced that he was pleased to hear them. Nekhlyudov looked at her miserable little neck, her thin, unkempt hair, and wondered why she had been doing all these strange things, and why she was now telling all this to him. He pitied her, but not as he had pitied Menshov, the peasant, kept in this stinking prison for no fault of his own. She was pitiable because of the confusion that filled her mind. It was clear that she considered herself a heroine ready to lay down her life for the success of her cause; yet she could hardly have explained what that cause was, or in what its success consisted.

The business that Vera Dukhova wanted to see Nekhlyudov about was the following: a friend of hers, a girl named Shustova, who had not even belonged to their "sub-section," as she expressed it, had been arrested with her about five months before, and imprisoned in the Petropavlovsky fortress because some prohibited books and papers (which she was keeping for other people) had been found in her possession. Vera Dukhova felt herself in some measure to blame for her friend's arrest, and implored Nekhlyudov, as a man with connections among influential people, to do all he could to get this friend liberated.

---

[1] Literally, "People's Freedom," a revolutionary movement.

Besides this, Dukhova asked him to try to get permission for another friend of hers, Gurkevich (who was also imprisoned in the Petropavlovsky fortress), to see his mother, and to procure some scientific books which he required for his studies.

Nekhlyudov promised to do what he could when he went to Petersburg. As to her own story, this is what she said. Having finished a course of midwifery, she became connected with a group of adherents to the Narodovolstvo. At first all went on smoothly. They wrote proclamations and occupied themselves with propaganda work in the factories; then, an important member of their group having been arrested, their papers were seized and all concerned were arrested. "I was also arrested, and shall be exiled. But what does it matter? I feel perfectly happy." She concluded her story with a piteous smile.

Nekhlyudov made some inquiries concerning the girl with the prominent eyes. Vera Dukhova told him that this girl was the daughter of a General, had long been attached to the revolutionary party, and was imprisoned because she pleaded guilty to having shot a gendarme. She lived in a house with some conspirators, where they had a secret printing press. One night, when the police came to search this house, the occupiers resolved to defend themselves, put out the lights, and began destroying the things that might incriminate them. The police forced their way in, and one of the conspirators fired, mortally wounding a gendarme. When an inquiry was instituted, this girl said that it was she who had fired, though she had never had a revolver in her hands, and would not have hurt a fly. But she kept to her statement, and was now condemned to penal servitude in Siberia.

"An altruistic, fine character," said Vera Dukhova approvingly.

The third business Vera Dukhova wanted to speak about concerned Maslova. She knew—as everybody does know such things in prison— the story of Maslova's life and Nekhlyudov's connection with her, and advised him to take steps to get her removed, either into the political prisoners' ward, or into the hospital to help to nurse the sick, of whom there were very many at that time, so that extra nurses were needed.

Nekhlyudov thanked her for the advice, and said he would try to act upon it.

Chapter LVI

THEIR CONVERSATION was interrupted by the inspector, who rose and announced that the time was up, and that the prisoners and their friends must part. Nekhlyudov took leave of Vera Dukhova and went to the door, where he stopped, watching what was going on.

"Gentlemen, time's up, time's up!" said the inspector, now rising, now sitting down again.

The inspector's order only called forth heightened animation among the prisoners in the room, and no one left. Some rose and continued to talk standing, some went on talking without rising. A few began crying and taking leave of each other. The mother and her consumptive son were especially pathetic. The young fellow kept twisting his bit of paper, and his face seemed angry, so great were his efforts not to be infected by his mother's emotion. The mother, hearing that it was time to part, put her head on his shoulder and sobbed and sniffed loudly. The girl with the large, kind eyes—Nekhlyudov could not help watching her—was standing opposite the sobbing mother, and was saying something to her in a soothing tone. The old man with the blue spectacles stood holding his daughter's hand and nodding in answer to what she said. The young lovers rose, and, holding hands, looked silently into one another's eyes.

"Those are the only merry ones here," said a young man in a short coat, who stood by Nekhlyudov's side also looking at those who were about to part, and he pointed to the lovers.

Feeling Nekhlyudov's and the young man's eyes fixed on them, the lovers—the young man with the rubber coat and the pretty girl—stretched out their arms, and with their hands clasped in each other's danced round and round again.

"To-night they are going to be married here in prison, and she will follow him to Siberia," said the young man.

"What is he?"

"A convict, condemned to penal servitude. Let those two at least have a little joy; otherwise it is too painful," the young man added, listening to the sobs of the consumptive lad's mother.

"Now, my good people! Please, please do not oblige me to have recourse to severe measures," said the inspector, repeating the same words several times over. "Please!" he went on, in a weak, hesitating manner. "It is high time. What do you mean by it? This sort of thing is quite impossible. . . . I am now asking you for the last time," he repeated wearily, putting out his cigarette and lighting another.

It was evident that, artful, old, and common as are the devices enabling men to do evil to others without feeling responsible for it, the inspector could not but feel conscious that he was one of those guilty of causing the sorrow which was manifesting itself in this room. And it was apparent that this troubled him sorely.

At length the prisoners and their visitors began to separate—the one by the inner, the other by the outer, door. The men with the rubber jackets passed out, and the consumptive youth and the dishevelled man. Mary Pavlovna went out with the boy born in prison.

The visitors went out, too. The old man with the blue spectacles, stepping heavily, went out followed by Nekhlyudov.

"Yes, a strange state of things this," said the talkative young man, as if continuing an interrupted conversation, while descending the stairs side by side with Nekhlyudov. "Yet we have reason to be grateful to the inspector, who does not keep strictly to the rules, kind-hearted fellow. If they can get a talk it does relieve their hearts a bit after all."

While talking to the young man, who introduced himself as Medinstev, Nekhlyudov reached the hall. There the inspector came up to them with a weary step.

"If you wish to see Maslova," he said, apparently desiring to be polite to Nekhlyudov, "please come tomorrow."

"Very well," answered Nekhlyudov, and hurried away.

The sufferings of the evidently innocent Menshov seemed terrible; but not so much his physical suffering as the perplexity, the distrust in goodness and in God, which he could not help feeling, seeing the cruelty of the people who tormented him without any reason.

Terrible was the disgrace and suffering cast on those scores of guiltless people simply because something was not written on paper as it should have been. Terrible were the brutalised jailers, whose occupation is to torment their brothers, and who were certain that they were fulfilling an important and useful duty; but most terrible of all seemed this sickly, elderly, kind-hearted inspector, obliged to part mother and son, father and daughter, who were just such people as himself and his own children.

"What is it all for?" Nekhlyudov asked himself, but, more than ever, he felt that sensation of moral nausea turning into physical nausea which always overcame him when he visited the prison; and he could find no answer to his question.

Chapter LVII

THE NEXT day Nekhlyudov went to see the advocate, and spoke to him about the Menshovs' case, begging him to undertake their defence. The advocate promised to look into the case, and if it turned out to be as Nekhlyudov said, which was very probable, he would undertake their defence free of charge. Then Nekhlyudov told him of the hundred and thirty men who were kept in prison owing to a mistake. "On whom did it depend? Whose fault was it?"

The advocate was silent for a moment, evidently anxious to give a correct reply.

"Whose fault is it? No one's," he said decidedly. "Ask the *Procureur*, he'll say it is the governor's fault; ask the governor, he'll blame the *Procureur*. No one is at fault."

"I am just going to see the vice-governor. I will tell him."

"Oh! that's quite useless," said the advocate, with a smile. "He is such a—he is not a relation or friend of yours?—such a blockhead, if I may say so, and yet a crafty animal at the same time."

Nekhlyudov remembered what Maslennikov had said about the advocate, and did not answer, but took leave and went on to Maslennikov's. He had to ask him two things: about Maslova's removal to the prison hospital, and about the hundred and thirty passportless men innocently imprisoned. It was very hard to ask favours of a man whom he did not respect, but it was the only means of attaining his end, and he had to go through with it.

As he drove up to Maslennikov's house Nekhlyudov saw a number of carriages by the front door, and remembered that it was the vice-governor's wife's "at home" day, to which he had been invited. At the moment Nekhlyudov drove up a carriage stood in front of the door, and a footman in livery with a cockade in his hat, was helping a lady down the doorsteps. She was holding up her train, showing her thin ankles, black stockings, and slippered feet. Among the carriages was a closed landau, which he knew to be the Korchagins'. Their grey-haired, red-cheeked coachman took off his hat and bowed in a respectful yet friendly manner to Nekhlyudov, as to a gentleman he knew well. Nekhlyudov had not had time to inquire for Maslennikov when the latter appeared on the carpeted stairs, accompanying a very important guest not only to the first landing but to the bottom of the stairs. This very important visitor, a military man, was speaking French about a lottery for the benefit of some children's homes to be founded in the city, and was expressing the opinion that this was a good occupation for the ladies. "It amuses them, and the money comes. *Qu'elles s'amusent et que le bon Dieu les bénisse.*"[1]

"Ah, Nekhlyudov! How d'you do? How is it one never sees you nowadays?" he greeted Nekhlyudov. "*Allez presenter vos devoirs à Madame.*[2] And the Korchagins are here and Nadine Bukshevden. *Toutes les jolies femmes de la ville,*"[3] said the important guest, slightly raising his uni-

---

[1] Let them amuse themselves, and may God bless them.
[2] Go and pay your respects to Madame.
[3] All the pretty women of the town.

formed shoulders as he presented them to his own richly liveried servant to have his military overcoat put on. "*Au revoir, mon cher.*" And he pressed Maslennikov's hand.

"Now, come up; I am so glad," said Maslennikov excitedly, grasping Nekhlyudov's hand. In spite of his corpulence Maslennikov hurried quickly up the stairs. He was in particularly good spirits, owing to the attention paid him by the important personage. Every such attention gave him the sense of delight which is felt by an affectionate dog when its master pats it, strokes it, or scratches its ears. It wags its tail, cringes, jumps about, presses its ears down, and rushes madly round in a circle. Maslennikov was ready to do the same. He did not notice the serious expression on Nekhlyudov's face, paid no heed to his words, but dragged him irresistibly towards the drawing-room, so that Nekhlyudov could not but follow.

"Business afterwards. I will do whatever you want," said Maslennikov, as he drew Nekhlyudov through the dancing-hall. "Announce Prince Nekhlyudov," he said to a footman, without stopping. The footman started off at a trot and passed them.

"*Vous n'avez qu'a ordonner.*[4] But you must first see my wife. As it is, I got it for letting you go without seeing her last time."

By the time they reached the drawing-room the foot-man had already announced Nekhlyudov, and from between the bonnets and heads that surrounded it the smiling face of Anna Ignatyevna, the vice-governor's wife, beamed on Nekhlyudov. At the other end of the drawing-room several ladies were seated round the tea-table, and some military men and civilians stood near them. The clatter of male and female voices was unceasing.

"*Enfin!* we thought you had quite forgotten us. How have we offended?" With these words, intended to convey an idea of intimacy which had never existed between herself and Nekhlyudov, Anna Ignatyevna greeted the new-comer.

"You are acquainted?—Madame Tilyaevskaya, M. Chernov. Sit down a bit nearer. Missy, *venez donc à notre table; on vous apportera votre thé . . .*[5] And you," she said, to an officer who was talking to Missy, having evidently forgotten his name, "do come here . . . A cup of tea, Prince?"

"I shall never, never agree with you. It is quite simple: she did not love," a woman's voice was heard saying.

"But she loved tarts."

---

[4] You have only to command.
[5] Missy, do come to our table; your tea shall be brought to you.

"Oh, your eternal silly jokes!" laughingly put in another lady, respelendent in silks, gold, and jewels.

"*C'est excellent* these little biscuits, and so light. I think I'll take another."

"Well, are you leaving town soon?"

"Yes, this is our last day. That is why we have come."

"Yes, it must be lovely in the country; we are having a delightful spring."

Missy, with her hat on, and in some kind of dark-striped dress that fitted her like a skin, was looking very handsome. She blushed when she saw Nekhlyudov.

"Oh, I thought you had left," she said to him.

"I am on the point of leaving. Business is keeping me in town, and it is on business I have come here."

"Won't you come to see mamma? She would like to see you," she said, and knowing that what she was saying was not true, and that he too knew it, she blushed still more.

"I fear I shall scarcely have time," Nekhlyudov said gloomily, trying to appear as if he had not noticed her blush.

Missy frowned angrily, shrugged her shoulders and turned towards an elegant officer, who grasped the empty cup she was holding and, knocking his sword against the chairs, manfully carried the cup across to another table.

"You must really contribute towards the Home fund."

"I am not refusing, but only wish to keep my bounty fresh for the lottery. There I shall let it appear in all its glory."

"Well, look out for yourself," said a voice, followed by an evidently feigned laugh.

Anna Ignatyevna was in raptures; her "at home" was a brilliant success.

"Micky tells me you are busying yourself with prison work. I can understand you so well," she said to Nekhlyudov. "Micky" (she meant her fat husband, Maslennikov) "may have his faults, but you know how kind-hearted he is. All these miserable prisoners are his children. He does not regard them in any other light. *Il est d'une bonté . . .*"[6] and she stopped, finding no words to do justice to the *bonté* of her husband by whose orders men were flogged, and, smiling, she turned quickly to a shrivelled old woman covered with bows of lilac ribbon, who came in just then.

Having said as much as was absolutely necessary, and with as little

---

[6] [He has such kindness.]

meaning as conventionality required, Nekhlyudov rose and went up to Maslennkiov.

"Can you give me a few minutes, please?"

"Oh yes. Well, what was it? Let us come in here."

They entered a small Japanese sitting-room, and sat down by the window.

Chapter LVIII

"WELL, *je suis à vous.*[1] Will you smoke? But wait a bit; we must be careful and not make a mess here," said Maslennikov, and brought out an ash-tray. "Well?"

"There are two matters I wish to ask you about."

"Dear me!"

An expression of gloom and dejection came over Maslennikov's countenance, and every trace of the excitement of the dog whom its master has scratched behind the ears vanished completely. The sound of voices reached them from the drawing-room. A woman's voice was heard, saying, *"Jamais, jamais je ne croirai!"*[2] and, from the other side, a man's voice, relating something in which the names of the Comtesse Vorontsov and Victor Apraksin kept recurring. A hum of voices, mixed with laughter, came from another direction. Maslennikov tried at one and the same time to listen to what was going on in the drawing-room and to what Nekhlyudov was saying.

"I have come again about that same woman," said Nekhlyudov.

"Oh yes; I know. The one innocently condemned."

"I should like to ask for her to be appointed to serve in the prison hospital. I have been told that this could be arranged."

Maslennikov pursed up his lips and considered.

"That will be scarcely possible," he said. "However, I will see what can be done, and will wire you a reply to-morrow."

"I have been told there are many sick, and that help is needed."

"All right, all right. I will let you know in any case."

"Please do," said Nekhlyudov.

The sound of general and even natural laughter came from the drawing-room.

---

[1] [I'm at your service.]
[2] [I'll never, never believe it!]

"It's all that Victor. He is wonderfully smart when he is in the right vein," said Maslennikov.

"The next thing I wanted to tell you," said Nekhlyudov, "is that a hundred and thirty persons are imprisoned only because their passports are overdue. They have been kept here over a month." And he related the circumstances of the case.

"How have you come to know of this?" said Maslennikov, looking uneasy and dissatisfied.

"I went to see a prisoner, and these men came and surrounded me in the corridor, and asked——"

"What prisoner did you go to see?"

"A peasant who is kept in prison though innocent. I have put his case into the hands of a lawyer. But that is not the point. Is it possible that people who have done nothing wrong are imprisoned only because their passports are overdue? And——"

"That's the department of the *Procureur*," Maslennikov interrupted angrily. "There, now, you see what comes of what you call a prompt and just form of trial! It is the duty of the public prosecutor to visit the prison and find out if the prisoners are kept there lawfully. But that set play cards; that's all they do."

"Am I to understand that you can do nothing?" Nekhlyudov said despondingly, remembering that the advocate had foretold that vice-governor would put the blame on the *Procureur*.

"Oh yes, I can. I will see about it at once."

"So much the worse for her. *C'est un souffre-douleur*,"[3] came the voice of a woman, evidently indifferent to what she was saying, from the drawing-room.

"So much the better. I shall take it also," a man's voice was heard to say from the other side, followed by the playful laughter of a woman who was apparently trying to prevent the man from taking something away from her.

"No, no; not on any account," the woman's voice said.

"All right, then. I will do all this," Maslennikov repeated, and he put out the cigarette he held in his white, turquoise-ringed hand. "And now let us join the ladies."

"Just a moment," Nekhlyudov said, stopping at the door of the drawing-room. "I was told that some men received corporal punishment in the prison yesterday. Is this true?"

Maslennikov blushed.

"Oh, that's what you are after! No, *mon cher*, decidedly it won't do to let you in there! you want to get at everything. Come, come,—Anna is

---

[3] She is a laughing-stock.

calling us," he said, catching Nekhlyudov by the arm, and again becoming as excited as after the attention paid him by the important person; only now his excitement was not joyful, but anxious.

Nekhlyudov pulled his arm away, and without taking leave of any one or saying a word, he passed through the drawing-room with a dejected look and went down into the hall, past the footman, who sprang towards him, and out at the street door.

"What is the matter with him? What have you done to him?" asked Anna of her husband.

"This is à la française,"[4] remarked some one.

"À la française," indeed—it is à la zoulou."[5]

"Oh, but he's always been like that." Some one got up, some one else came in, and the clatter continued its course. The company used this episode of Nekhlyudov as a convenient topic of conversation for the rest of the "at home."

On the day following his visit to Maslennikov, Nekhlyudov received a letter from him written in a fine, firm hand on thick, glazed paper with a coat-of-arms, and sealed with sealing-wax. Maslennikov said that he had written to the doctor concerning Maslova's removal to the hospital, and hoped Nekhlyudov's wish would receive attention. The letter was signed, "Your affectionate elder comrade," and the signature ended with a large, firm, and artistic flourish. "Fool!" Nekhlyudov could not refrain from saying, especially because in the word "comrade" he felt Maslennikov's condescension towards him, that is, he felt that while Maslennikov was filling this position, morally most dirty and shameful, he still thought himself a very important man, and wished, if not exactly to flatter Nekhlyudov, at least to show that he was not too proud to call him comrade.

Chapter LIX

ONE OF the most widespread superstitions is that every man has his own special definite qualities: that he is kind, cruel, wise, stupid, energetic, apathetic, and so on. Men are not like that. We may say of a man that he is more often kind than cruel, more often wise than stupid, more often energetic than apathetic, or the reverse; but it would not be true to say of one man that he is kind and wise, of another that he is

---

[4] [The French way.]
[5] [The Zulu way.]

bad and stupid. And yet we always classify mankind in this way. And this is false. Men are like rivers: the water is the same in one and all; but every river is narrow here, more rapid there, here slower, there broader, now clear, now dull, now cold, now warm. It is the same with men. Every man bears in himself the germs of every human quality; but sometimes one quality manifests itself, sometimes another, and the man often becomes unlike himself, while still remaining the same man.

In some people these changes are very rapid, and Nekhlyudov was such a man. These changes in him were due both to physical and to spiritual causes. Such a change took place in him now.

The feeling of triumph and joy at the renewal of life, which he had experienced after the trial and after the first interview with Katusha, vanished completely, and after the last interview fear and revulsion replaced that joy. He was determined not to leave her, and not to change his decision of marrying her if she wished it; but it seemed very hard, and made him suffer.

On the day after his visit to Maslennikov, he again went to the prison to see her.

The inspector allowed him to speak to her, only not in the office nor in the advocate's room, but in the women's visiting-room.

In spite of his kindness, the inspector was more reserved with Nekhlyudov than previously. An order for greater caution had apparently been sent as a result of his conversation with Maslennikov. "You may see her," the inspector said; "but please remember what I said as regards money. And as to her removal to the hospital that his excellency wrote to me about, it could be done; the doctor would agree. Only she herself does not wish it. She says: 'Much need have I to carry out the slops for the scurvy beggars.' You don't know these people, Prince," he added.

Nekhlyudov did not reply, but asked to have the interview. The inspector called a jailer, and Nekhlyudov followed him into the women's visiting-room, where there was no one but Maslova waiting. She came from behind the netting, quiet and timid, close up to him, and said, without looking at him —

"Forgive me, Dmitry Ivanich, I said much that was wrong the day before yesterday."

"It is not for me to forgive," Nekhlyudov began.

"But all the same, you must leave me," she interrupted, and in the terribly squinting eyes with which she looked at him Nekhlyudov read the former strained, angry expression.

"Why should I leave you?"

"You must."

"But why?"

She again looked up, with, as it seemed to him, the same angry look.

"Well, that's how it is," she said. "You *must* leave me. It is true what I am saying—I cannot. You must just give it up altogether. Her lips trembled and she was silent for a moment. "It is true. I'd rather hang myself."

Nekhlyudov felt that in this refusal there was hatred and unforgiving resentment, but that there was also something besides, something good. This confirmation of her previous refusal—which she was making quite calmly—at once quenched all the doubts in Nekhlyudov's breast, and brought back the serious, triumphant emotion he had felt in relation to Katusha.

"Katusha, what I have said I will say again," he uttered, very seriously. "I ask you to marry me. If you do not wish to, and for as long as you do not wish to, I shall only continue to follow you, and will go where you are taken."

"That's your business. I shall not say anything more," she answered, and her lips bean to tremble again.

He, too, was silent, feeling unable to speak.

"I shall now go to the country, and then to Petersburg," he said, when he was quieter again. "I will do my utmost to get your . . . our case I mean, reconsidered, and, God willing, the sentence may be revoked."

"And if it is not revoked, never mind. I have deserved it, if not in this case, in other ways," she said, and he saw how difficult it was for her to keep back her tears.

"Well, have you seen Menshov?" she suddenly asked, to hide her emotion. "It's true they are innocent, isn't it?"

"Yes, I think so."

"Such a splendid old woman," she said.

And he told her all he had found out about Menshov, and asked her if she wanted anything.

She answered that she did not.

They were again silent.

"Well, and as to the hospital?" she suddenly said, looking at him with her squinting eyes. "If you like I will go, and I will not drink any more, either."

Nekhlyudov looked into her eyes. They were smiling.

"That is very good," was all he could say, and then he took leave of her.

"Yes, yes, she is quite a different being," Nekhlyudov thought. After all his former doubts, he now felt something he had never before experienced—the certainty that love is invincible.

·   ·   ·

When Maslova returned to her noisome cell after this interview, she took off her cloak, and with her hands folded on her lap sat down in her place on the plank-bedstead. In the cell were only the consumptive woman, the Vladimir woman and her baby, Menshov's old mother, and the watchman's wife. The deacon's daughter had been declared mentally deranged and removed to the hospital the day before. The rest of the women were away, washing clothes. The old woman was asleep, the cell door stood open, and the watchman's children were in the corridor outside. The Vladimir woman, with her baby in her arms, and the watchman's wife, with the stocking she was knitting with deft fingers, came up to Maslova.

"Well, have you had a chat?" they asked.

Maslova sat silent on the high bedstead, swinging her legs, which did not reach to the floor.

"What's the good of snivelling?" said the watchman's wife. "The chief thing's not to get into the dumps. Eh, Katusha, cheer up!" she went on, moving her fingers rapidly.

Maslova did not answer.

"And our women have all gone washing," said the Vladimir woman. "I heard them say much has been given in alms to-day. Quite a lot has been brought."

"Finashka," called out the watchman's wife. "Where's the little imp gone to?"

She took a knitting needle, stuck it through both the ball and the stocking, and went out into the corridor.

At this moment the sound of women's voices was heard from the corridor, and the inmates of the cell entered, in their prison shoes but with no stockings on their feet. Each was carrying a bread roll, some even two. Theodosia came up to Maslova at once.

"What's the matter; is anything wrong?" she asked, looking lovingly at Maslova with her clear blue eyes. "This is for our tea," and she put the rolls on a shelf.

"Why, surely he has not changed his mind about marrying?" asked Korableva.

"No, he has not, but I don't wish it," said Maslova, "and I told him so."

"More fool you!" muttered Korableva in her deep tones.

"If one's not to live together, what's the use of marrying?" said Theodosia.

"There's your husband—he's going with you," said the watchman's wife.

"Well, of course, we are already married," said Theodosia. "But why should he go through the ceremony if he is not to live with her?"

"Why, indeed! Don't be a fool! You know if he marries her she'll roll in wealth," said Korableva.

"He says, 'Wherever they take you, I'll follow,'" said Maslova. "If he does, it's well; if he does not, well also. I am not going to ask him to. Now he is going to try and arrange the matter in Petersburg. He is related to all the Ministers there. But all the same, I have no need of him," she continued.

"Of course not," suddenly agreed Korableva, evidently thinking about something else as she sat examining the contents of her bag. "Well, shall we have a drop?"

"You have some," replied Maslova. "I won't."

BOOK TWO

Chapter I

MASLOVA'S CASE was likely to come before the Senate in a fortnight, and Nekhlyudov meant to be in Petersburg then, and (as the advocate who drew up the petition advised) to petition the Emperor should the appeal to the Senate be disregarded. In that case—and according to the advocate it was best to be prepared for that, since the grounds for appeal were so slight—the party of convicts among whom Maslova was included might start early in June, and therefore, to be able to follow her to Siberia as he was firmly resolved to do, it was necessary for Nekhlyudov to visit his estates and and settle matters there. He first went to the nearest, Kusminsky, a large estate in the black-earth district from which he derived the bulk of his income.

Nekhlyudov had lived on that estate in his childhood and youth, and had been there twice since; and once, at his mother's request, he had taken a German steward there, and had verified the accounts with him. The state of things there, and the peasants' relations to the management (that is, to the proprietor) had therefore long been known to him. The relations of the peasants to the proprietor were those of utter dependence on his management. Nekhlyudov knew all this when, as a university student, he had confessed and preached the doctrines of Henry George and, on the basis of that teaching, had given to the peasants the land inherited from his father. It is true that after serving in the army, when he got into the habit of spending twenty thousand rubles a year, those former views ceased to be regarded as binding, and were forgotten, and he not only left off asking himself where the money his mother allowed him came from, but even avoided thinking about it. But his mother's death, the coming into the property, and the necessity of managing it, again raised the question of his position in relation to private property in land. A month before, Nekhlyudov would have answered that he had not the strength to alter the existing order of things; that it was not he who was managing the estate; and he would, one way or another, have eased his conscience, continuing to live far from his estates and having the money sent him. But now he decided that he could not allow things to go on as they were, but would have to alter them in a way unprofitable to himself, even though he had all these complicated and difficult relations with the prison world—for which a social position and especially money were necessary—as well as a probable journey to Siberia before him. Therefore he decided not to farm the land, but to let it to the peasants at a low rent, and so enable them to cultivate it without depending on a landlord. More than once, when comparing the position of a landowner with that of an owner of serfs, Nekhlyudov had compared the renting of land to the peasants instead of cultivating it with hired labour, to the old system by which serf proprietors used to exact a money payment from their serfs in lieu of labour. It was not a solution of the problem, but it was a step towards the solution; it was a movement towards a less rude form of slavery. And that was how he meant to act.

Nekhlyudov reached Kusminsky about noon. Trying to simplify his life in every way, he did not telegraph, but at the station hired a peasant trap with two horses. The driver was a young fellow in a nankeen coat, with a belt below his long waist. He was glad to talk to the gentleman, especially as while they were talking his broken-winded white horse and the emaciated spavined one could go at a foot-pace, which they always liked to do.

The driver spoke about the steward at Kusminsky without knowing that he was driving "the master." Nekhlyudov had purposely not told him who he was.

"That ostentatious German," said the driver (who had been to town and had read novels) as he sat sideways on the box, passing his hand from the top to the bottom of his long whip, and trying to show off his accomplishments—"that ostentatious German has procured three light bays, and when he drives out with his lady—oh, my! At Christmas he had a Christmas-tree in the big house. I drove some of the visitors there. It had 'lectric lights; you could not see the like of it in the whole of the province. He has cribbed a heap of money. It's awful! What's it to him! I heard say he has bought a fine estate."

Nekhlyudov had imagined that he was quite indifferent to the way the steward managed his estate, and to what advantages the steward derived from it. The words of the long-waisted driver, however, were not pleasant to hear.

He admired the beautiful day: the thick, darkening clouds which now and then covered the sun; the fields on which the peasants were everywhere hoeing the young oats; the thick, green meadows above which larks were soaring; the woods already all covered, except the late oaks, with fresh young green; the pastures speckled with grazing cattle and horses; the fields in the distance being ploughed—but every now and then he remembered there was something unpleasant, and, when he asked himself what it was, he remembered the driver's tale about how the German was managing Kusminsky. When he reached his estate and set to work, this unpleasant feeling passed.

An examination of the office books, and a talk with the steward, who naïvely pointed out the advantages to be derived from the facts that the peasants had very little land of their own and that what they had lay in the midst of the landlord's fields, made Nekhlyudov more than ever determined to give up farming and let his land to the peasants.

From the office books and his talk with the steward Nekhlyudov found that two-thirds of the best of the cultivated land was now being tilled with improved machinery by labourers receiving fixed wages, while the other third was tilled by the peasants, who received five rubles per desyatin.[1] That is, the peasants had to plough each desyatin three times, harrow it three times, sow and mow the corn, make it into sheaves, and deliver it on the threshing ground, for five rubles, while the same amount of work done by wage labour came to at least ten rubles. Everything the peasants got from the estate they paid for in labour at a very high price. They paid in labour for the use of the meadows, for wood, and for potato-tops; and nearly all of them were in debt to the office. Thus, for the land lying beyond the cultivated fields, and hired by the peasants, four times the price that its value would yield if invested at five per cent was taken from the peasants.

Nekhlyudov had known all this before, but he now saw it in a new light, and wondered how he and others in his position could help seeing how abnormal such conditions are. The steward's arguments that if the land were let to the peasants the agricultural implements would fetch next to nothing, as not even a quarter of their value could be got for them; that the peasants would spoil the land; and that Nekhlyudov would be a great loser, only strengthened Nekhlyudov's conviction that he was performing a good action in letting the land to the peasants and thus depriving himself of a large part of his income. He decided to settle this business now, at once, while he was there. The reaping and selling of the corn and the selling of the agricultural implements and useless buildings—all this could be left for the steward to manage in due season. But he asked for his steward now to call the peasants of the three neighbouring villages that lay in the midst of the Kusmisky estate

---

[1] About two and three-quarters acres.

to come to a meeting, at which he would tell them his intentions and arrange the terms on which they were to rent the land.

With a pleasant sense of the firmness he had shown in face of the steward's arguments, and of his readiness to make a sacrifice, Nekhlyudov left the office, and, thinking over the business before him, he strolled round the house, through the neglected flower-garden — this year the flowers were planted in front of the steward's house — over the tennis ground, now overgrown with dandelions, and along the lime-tree walk, where he used to go to smoke his cigar, and where he had flirted with the pretty Kirimova, his mother's visitor. Having briefly prepared in his mind the speech he was going to make to the peasants, he again had a talk with the steward, and after tea, having once more arranged his thoughts, he went into the room prepared for him in the big house, and formerly used as a spare bedroom.

In this clean little room, with pictures of Venice on the walls and a mirror between the two windows, there stood a clean bed with a spring mattress, and by the side of it a small table, with a decanter of water, matches, and an extinguisher. On a table by the looking-glass lay his open portmanteau, with his dressing-case and some books in it: a Russian book, *An Investigation of the Laws of Criminality*, and a German and an English book on the same subject, which he meant to read while travelling in the country. But it was too late for that to-day, and he prepared to go to bed so as to be able to get up early and be ready for the interview with the peasants.

An old-fashioned inlaid mahogany arm-chair stood in the corner of the room, and this chair, which Nekhlyudov remembered as standing in his mother's bedroom, suddenly raised a perfectly unexpected sensation in his soul. He was suddenly filled with regret at the thought of the house that would tumble to ruin, the garden that would run wild, the forest that would be cut down, and of all these farmyards, stables, sheds, machines, horses, cows, which he knew had cost so much effort, though not to himself, to acquire and to keep. It had seemed easy to give up all this, but now it was hard, not only to give this away, but even to let the land and lose half his income. And at once an argument to show that, after all, it was unreasonable to let the land to the peasants and thus destroy his property, came to his service. "I must not hold property in land. But if I possess no property in land, I cannot keep up the house and farm. . . . But then I am going to Siberia, and shall need neither the house nor the estate," said one voice. "All this is so," said another voice, "but you are not going to spend all your life in Siberia. You may marry, and have children, and must hand the estate on to them in as good condition as you received it. There is a duty to the land, too. To give it up, to destroy everything, is very easy; to acquire it, very difficult. Above all, you must consider your future life and what you will do with yourself, and you must dispose of your property accordingly. And then, are you really acting according to your conscience, or are you doing it in order to show off?" Nekhlyudov asked himself all this, and had to acknowledge that he was influenced by the thought of what people would say about him. And the more he thought about it the more questions arose, and the more unsolvable they seemed.

In hopes of ridding himself of these thoughts by falling asleep, and solving the problems with a fresh head in the morning, he lay down on his clean bed. But it was long before he could sleep. Together with the fresh air and the moonlight, the croaking of frogs entered the room, mingling with the trills of a couple of nightingales in the park and of one close to the window in a bush of lilacs in bloom. Listening to the nightingales and the frogs, Nekhlyudov remembered the music of the inspector's daughter, and the inspector himself. That reminded him of Maslova, and how her lips trembled, like the croaking of the frogs, when she said, "You must just give it up altogether." Then the German steward began going down to the frogs and had to be held back, but he not only went down but turned into Maslova, who began reproaching Nekhlyudov, saying, "You are a prince, and I am a convict." "No, I must not give in," thought Nekhlyudov, and he roused himself and asked himself, "Well, am I acting rightly or wrongly? I don't know and don't care. It's all the same: I must sleep." And he began himself to descend to where he had seen the inspector and Maslova climbing down, and there it all ended.

Chapter II

NEKHLYUDOV WOKE at nine o'clock in the morning. As soon as the young office clerk who attended on "the master" heard Nekhlyudov stirring, he brought him his boots, shining as they had never shone before, and some cold, beautifully clear spring water, and informed him that the peasants were already assembling. Nekhlyudov jumped out of bed and collected his thoughts. Not a trace remained of yesterday's regret at giving up his property and thus destroying it. He remembered this feeling of regret with surprise; looked forward with joy to the task before him, and was even involuntarily proud of it.

From the window he could see the old tennis ground overgrown with dandelions, on which the peasants were beginning to assemble. The frogs had not croaked in vain the night before: the day was dull. There was no wind; a soft warm rain had begun falling in the morning, and hung in drops on leaves, twigs, and grass. Besides the smell of the fresh vegetation, the smell of damp earth, asking for more rain, entered in at the window.

While dressing, Nekhlyudov several times looked out at the peasants gathered on the tennis ground. One by one they came, removed their caps, bowed to one another, and took their places in a circle, leaning on their sticks and conversing. The steward, a stout, muscular, strong young man, dressed in a short pea-jacket with a green stand-up collar and enormous buttons, came to say that all had assembled, but that they could wait until Nekhlyudov had had his breakfast—tea or coffee, whichever he pleased, both were ready.

"No, I think I had better go and see them at once," said Nekhlyudov, with an unexpected feeling of shyness and shame at the thought of the conversation he was about to have with the peasants. He was going to fulfil a wish of the peasants, for the fulfilment of which they had not even dared to hope: to let the land to them at a low price—that is, to confer a great boon; and yet he felt ashamed of something. When Nekhlyudov came up to the peasants, and the fair, the curly, the bald, the grey heads, were bared before him, he felt so confused that he could say nothing. The rain continued to come down in small drops, remaining on hair, beards, and the fluff of the men's rough coats. The peasants looked at "the master," waiting for him to speak, but he was so abashed that he could not. This awkward silence was broken by the sedate self-assured German steward, who considered himself a good judge of a Russian peasant, and who spoke Russian remarkably well. This stout, over-fed man, and Nekhlyudov himself, presented a striking contrast to the peasants, with their thin, wrinkled faces and the shoulder-blades protruding beneath their coarse coats.

"Here's the Prince wanting to do you a favour—to let the land to you; only you are not worthy of it," said the steward.

"How are we not worthy of it, Vasily Karlich? Don't we work for you? We were well satisfied with the deceased lady—God rest her soul!—and the young Prince will not forsake us now. Our thanks to him," said a red-haired, garrulous peasant.

"We have nothing against our master; all we complain of is want of land," said another broad-shouldered peasant. "Not enough to live on."

"Yes, that's why I have called you together. I should like to let you have all the land if you wish it."

The peasants said nothing, as if they either did not understand or did not believe it.

"Let's see. Let us have the land? How do you mean?" asked a middle-aged man.

"To let it to you, that you might have the use of it at a low rent."

"A very agreeable thing," said an old man.

"If only the rent is such as we can afford," said another.

"There's no reason why we should not rent the land."

"We are accustomed to live by tilling the ground."

"And it's quieter for you, too, that way. You'll have to do nothing but receive the rent. Only think of all the sin and worry now!" several voices were heard saying.

"The sin is all on your side," the German remarked. "If only you did your work, and were orderly——"

"That's impossible for the likes of us," said a sharp-nosed old man. "You say, 'Why did you let the horse get into the corn?' just as if I let it in. Why, I was swinging my scythe, or something of that sort, the live-long day, till the day seemed as long as a year, and so I fell asleep while watching the herd of horses at night, and it got into your oats, and now you're skinning me."

"Well, you should keep the rules."

"It's easy for you to talk about rules, but it's more than our strength can stand," answered a tall, dark, hairy, middle-aged man.

"Didn't I tell you to put up a fence?"

"Give us the wood to make it of then," said a short, plain-looking peasant. "I was going to put up a fence last year and cut down a sapling, and you put me to feed vermin in prison for three months. There was the end of that fence."

"What is he talking about?" asked Nekhlyudov, turning to the steward.

"*Der erste Dieb im Dorfe*,"[1] answered the steward in German. "He is caught stealing wood from the forest every year." Then turning to the peasant he added: "You must learn to respect other people's property."

"Well, don't we respect you?" said an old man. "We are obliged to respect you. Why, you can twist us into a rope; we are in your hands."

"Eh, my friend, it's impossible to do you. It's you who are always ready to do us," said the German.

"Do you, indeed. Didn't you smash my jaw for me, and I got nothing for it? No good going to law with the rich, it seems."

"You should obey the law yourself."

Evidently a tournament of words was going on without those who took part in it knowing exactly why; but it was noticeable that there was bitterness on one side, restricted by fear, and on the other a conscious-ness of importance and power. It was very trying to Nekhlyudov to lis-ten to all this, so he returned to the question of arranging the amount and the terms of the rent.

---

[1] The greatest thief in the village.

"Well now, how about the land? Do you wish to take it, and what price will you pay if I agree to let the whole of it to you?"

"The property is yours; it is for you to fix the price."

Nekhlyudov named the amount. Though it was far below that paid in the neighbourhood, the peasants declared it too high, and began bargaining, as is customary with them. Nekhlyudov thought his offer would be accepted with pleasure, but no signs of pleasure were visible. Only one thing showed Nekhlyudov that his offer was advantageous to the peasants. The question was put as to who would rent the land: the whole commune or a special society; and a violent dispute arose between those peasants who were in favour of excluding the weak and those not likely to pay the rent regularly, and the peasants who would have to be excluded on these grounds. At last, thanks to the steward, the amount and the terms of the rent were fixed; and the peasants went down the hill towards their villages talking noisily, while Nekhlyudov and the steward went into the office to draw up the agreement. Everything was settled in the way Nekhlyudov wished and expected it to be. The peasants had their land thirty per cent cheaper than they could have got it anywhere in the district. The revenue from the land was diminished by half, but was still more than sufficient for Nekhlyudov, especially as there would be money coming in for a forest he had sold, as well as for the agricultural implements, which would also be sold. Everything seemed excellently arranged, yet he felt ashamed of something. He could see that the peasants, though they spoke words of thanks, were not satisfied, but had expected more. So it turned out that he had deprived himself of a great deal, and yet had not fulfilled the hopes of the peasants.

The next day the agreement was signed, and, accompanied by several old peasants who had been chosen as deputies, Nekhlyudov, with the unpleasant feeling of something remaining undone, left the office, stepped into the steward's elegant equipage (as the driver from the station had called it), said good-bye to the peasants, who stood shaking their heads in a dissatisfied and disappointed manner, and drove off to the station. Nekhlyudov was dissatisfied with himself, and without knowing why, he felt all the time sad and ashamed of something.

Chapter III

FROM KUSMINSKY Nekhlyudov went to the estate he had inherited from his aunts; the one where he had first met Katusha. He meant to arrange about the land there just as he had done in Kusminsky. But besides this, he wished to find out all he could about Katusha and her and his baby; whether it was true that it had died, and how.

He got to Panovo early in the morning, and the first thing that struck him when he drove up, was the look of decay and dilapidation that all the buildings wore, especially the house itself. The iron roofs were red with rust, and a few sheets of iron were bent back, probably by a storm. The planks which covered the house were torn away in several places, where they could be easily abstracted by breaking the rusty nails that held them. Both porches, but especially the side porch he remembered so well, were rotten and broken; only the joists remained. Some of the windows were boarded up, and the building in which the bailiff lived, the kitchen, the stables—all were grey and decaying. Only the garden had not decayed, but had grown thicker and was in full bloom; cherry, apple, and plum trees in blossom, looking like white clouds, could be seen behind the fence. The lilac bushes that formed the hedge were in full bloom, as they had been when, twelve years ago, Nekhlyudov had played widdow with the sixteen-year-old Katusha, and had fallen and stung his hand in the nettles behind one of those same lilac bushes. The larch that his Aunt Sophia had planted near the house, and which was then only a short stick, had grown into a tree the trunk of which would have made a beam, and its branches were covered with soft yellow-green needles as with down. The river, now within its banks, rushed noisily over the mill dam. The meadow across the river was dotted over by the peasants' mixed herds.

The bailiff, a student who had left the seminary without finishing the course, met Nekhlyudov in the yard with a smile on his face. Still smiling, he asked him to come into the office, and, as if promising something exceptionally good by his smile, went behind the partition. For a moment some whispering was to be heard, and then the *izvozchik* who had driven Nekhlyudov from the station drove away with tinkling bells after receiving a tip, and all was silent. Then a barefooted girl in an embroidered peasant blouse, and with silk tassels for ear-rings, ran past the window, and a man walked by, clattering with his nailed boots on the trodden path.

Nekhlyudov sat down by the little casement, looked out into the garden and listened. A soft, fresh spring breeze, smelling of newly dug earth, blew in through the window, playing with the hair on his damp forehead and with the papers that lay on the window-sill, which was all cut about with a knife.

"Tra-pa-trop, tra-pa-trop," came a sound from the river, as the women who were washing clothes there beat them in regular measure with their wooden bats. The sound spread over the glittering surface of the mill-pond, the rhythm of the falling water came from the mill, and a frightened fly suddenly flew past his ear, buzzing loudly.

And all at once Nekhlyudov remembered how, long ago, when he was young and innocent, he had heard, above the rhythmical sound from the mill, the women's wooden bats beating the wet clothes, how in the same way the spring breeze had blown the hair about on his wet forehead and disturbed the papers on the window-sill which was all cut about with a knife, and how, just in the same way, a fly had buzzed loudly past his ear. It was not exactly that he remembered himself as a lad of nineteen; but he seemed to feel himself the same as he was then, with the same freshness and purity, full of the same grand and infinite possibilities for the future, and at the same time, as happens in a dream, he knew that all this could be no more, and he felt terribly sad.

"At what time would you like something to eat?" asked the bailiff with a smile.

"Whenever you like; I am not hungry. I shall take a walk through the village first."

"Would you not like to come into the house? Everything is in order inside. Have the goodness to look in, if the outside——"

"Not now, thank you; later on. Tell me, please, have you got a woman here called Matrena Harina?" (This was Katusha's aunt.)

"Oh yes; in the village, she keeps a secret pot-house. I know she does, and I accuse her of it and scold her; but as to taking her up, it would be a pity. An old woman, you know; she has grandchildren," said the foreman, continuing to smile as before, expressing both his wish to please "the master" and his conviction that Nekhlyudov looked upon these matters just as he did himself.

"Where does she live? I should like to go across and see her."

"At the end of the village; the farther side, the third from the end. To the left there is a brick cottage, and her hut is beyond that. But I'd better take you there," the bailiff said, with a graceful smile.

"No, thanks, I shall find it all right; and will you be so good as to call a meeting of the peasants, and tell them that I want to speak to them about the land?" said Nekhlyudov, intending to come to the same agreement with the peasants here as with those of Kusminsky, and, if possible, that very evening.

Chapter IV

COMING OUT of the gate, Nekhlyudov met the girl with the tassel ear-rings returning along the trodden path that lay across the pasture ground overgrown with dock and plantain. She had a long, brightly coloured apron on and was quickly swinging her left arm in front of her as she trotted briskly with her plump, bare feet. With her right arm she was pressing a fowl to her stomach. The fowl, his red comb shaking, seemed perfectly quiet; he only rolled up his eyes and stretched out and drew in one black leg, clawing the girl's apron. When the girl came nearer to "the master" she began to move more slowly, and her run came down to a walk. When she came up to him she stopped, and, after a backward jerk with her head, bowed to him; and only when he had passed did she recommence to run homeward with the fowl. As he went down towards the well, he met an old woman in a coarse, dirty blouse, carrying two pails full of water that hung on a yoke across her bent back. The old woman carefully put down the pails and bowed, with the same backward jerk of her head.

After passing the well, Nekhlyudov entered the village. It was a bright, hot day, and oppressive, though it was only ten o'clock. At intervals the sun was hidden by gathering clouds. A pungent but not unpleasant smell of dung filled the air in the street. It came from carts going up the hillside, but chiefly from the disturbed manure heaps in the yards of the huts, by the open gates of which Nekhlyudov had to pass. The peasants, bare-footed, their shirts and trousers soiled with manure, turned to look at the tall, stout gentleman with a glossy silk ribbon on his grey hat, who was walking up the village street, touching the ground every other step with a shiny, bright-knobbed walking-stick. The peasants returning from the fields at a trot and jolting in their empty carts, took off their hats, and in their surprise followed with their eyes the extraordinary man who was walking up their street. The women came out of the gates or stood in the porches of their huts, pointing him out to each other and gazing at him as he passed.

When Nekhlyudov was passing the fourth gate he was stopped by a cart coming out, its wheels creaking, loaded high with manure, which was pressed down and covered with a mat to sit on. A barefooted six-year-old boy, excited by the expectation of a ride, followed the cart. A young peasant, with shoes plaited of bark and making long strides, led the horse out of the yard. A long-legged, greyish colt jumped out of the gate; but, seeing Nekhlyudov, it pressed close to the cart, and, scraping its legs against the wheels, jumped forward past its excited, gently neighing mother, as she dragged the heavy load through the gateway. The next horse was led out by a barefooted old man, with protruding shoulder-blades, dressed in a dirty shirt and striped trousers. When the horses had reached the hard road, strewn over with bits of dry, grey manure, the old man returned to the gate and bowed to Nekhlyudov.

"You are our ladies' nephew, aren't you?"

"Yes, I am their nephew."

"You've kindly come to look us up, eh?" said the garrulous old man.

"Yes, I have. Well, how are you getting on?" asked Nekhlyudov, not knowing what to say.

"How do we get on? We get on very badly," the old man drawled, as if it gave him pleasure.

"Why so badly?" Nekhlyudov asked, stepping inside the gate.

"What is our life but the very worst life?" said the old man, following Nekhlyudov into that part of the yard which was roofed over. Nekhlyudov stopped under the roof.

"There they are—we are twelve in all," continued the old man, pointing to two women who, with forks in their hands, the kerchiefs tumbling off their heads, and with their skirts tucked up showing the calves of their dirty bare legs, stood perspiring on the remainder of the manure heap. "Not a month passes but I have to buy six puds[1] of rye, and where's the money to come from?"

"Don't you grow enough rye of your own?"

"My own?" repeated the old man, with a smile of contempt; "why I have only got land for three people, and last year we had not enough to last till Christmas."

"What do you do then?"

"What do we do? Why, I let one son go out as a labourer, and then I borrowed some money from your honour. We spent it all before Lent, and the tax is not paid yet."

"And how much is the tax?"

"Why, it's seventeen rubles for my household. Oh, Lord, such a life! One hardly knows one's self how one manages to live it."

"May I go into your hut?" asked Nekhlyudov, stepping across the yard over the yellow-brown layers of manure that had been raked up by the forks, and were giving off a strong smell.

"Why not? Come in!" said the old man, and stepping quickly with his bare feet over the manure, the liquid oozing between his toes, he passed Nekhlyudov and opened the door of the hut.

The women arranged the kerchiefs on their heads and let down their linen skirts, and stood looking with surprise at the clean gentleman with gold studs to his sleeves who was entering their house. Two little girls, with nothing on but coarse chemises, rushed out of the hut. Taking off his hat, and stooping to get through the low door, Nekhlyudov entered the passage, and then the dirty, narrow hut, that smelt of sour food, and where much space was taken up by two weav-

---

[1] Pud—thirty-six English lb.

ing looms. In the hut an old woman was standing by the stove, with the sleeves rolled up over her thin, sinewy, brown arms.

"Here is our master come to see us," said the old man.

"I'm sure he's very welcome," said the old woman kindly, pulling down her sleeves.

"I wanted to see how you live."

"Well, we live as you see. The hut is coming down, and might kill one any day; but my old man he says it's good enough, and so we live like kings," said the brisk old woman, nervously jerking her head. "I'm getting the dinner; going to feed the workers."

"And what are you going to have for dinner?"

"Our dinner? Our food is very good. First course, bread and *kvas*;[2] second course—*kvas* and bread," said the old woman, showing her teeth, which were half worn away.

"No, seriously, let me see what you are going to eat."

"To eat?" said the old man, laughing. "Ours is not a very cunning meal. You just show him, wife." The old woman shook her head.

"Want to see our peasant food? Well, you are an inquisitive gentleman, now I come to look at you. He wants to know everything. Did I not tell you bread and *kvas*? and then we'll have soup. A woman brought us some fish, and that's what the soup is made of, and after that, potatoes."

"Nothing more?"

"What more do you want? We'll also have a little milk," said the old woman, looking laughingly towards the door. The door stood open and the passage outside was full of people—boys, girls, women with babies—thronged together to look at the strange gentleman who wanted to see the peasants' food. The old woman seemed to pride herself on the way she behaved with a gentleman.

"Yes, it's a miserable life ours; that goes without saying, sir," said the old man. "What are you doing there?" he shouted to those in the passage.

"Well, good-bye," said Nekhlyudov, feeling ashamed and uneasy, though unable to account for the feeling.

"Thank you kindly for having looked us up," said the old man.

The people in the passage pressed closer together to let Nekhlyudov pass, and he went out and continued his way up the street. Two barefooted boys followed him out of the passage—the elder in a shirt that had once been white, the other in a worn and faded pink one. Nekhlyudov looked back at them.

---

[2] *Kvas*, a sour, non-intoxicant drink made of rye.

"And where are you going now?" asked the boy with the white shirt. Nekhlyudov answered—

"To Matrena Harina. Do you know her?"

The boy with the pink shirt began laughing at something; but the elder asked seriously:—

"Which Matrena is that? Is she old?"

"Yes, she is old."

"O—oh," he drawled; "that one; she's at the other end of the village—we'll show you. Yes, Fedka, we'll go with him, shall we?"

"Yes, but the horses?"

"They'll be all right, I dare say."

Fedka agreed, and all three went up the street.

Chapter V

NEKHLYUDOV FELT more at ease with the boys than with the grown-up people, and he began talking to them as they went along. The little one in the pink shirt ceased laughing, and spoke as sensibly and as exactly as the elder one.

"Can you tell me who are the poorest people you have got here?" asked Nekhlyudov.

"The poorest? Michael is poor, Simon Makarov and Martha—Martha is very poor."

"And Anisya, she is still poorer; she's not even got a cow. They go begging," said little Fedka.

"She's not got a cow, but there are only three of them, and Martha's family are five," objected the elder boy.

"But the other's a widow," the pink boy said, standing up for Anisya.

"You say Anisya is a widow, but Martha is just the same as a widow," said the elder boy; "just the same—she's also no husband."

"Where is her husband then?" Nekhlyudov asked.

"Feeding vermin in prison," said the elder boy, using the expression common among the peasants.

"A year ago he cut down two birch trees in the landlord's forest," the little pink boy hurried to explain, "so he was locked up; now he's been there six months, and the wife goes begging. There are three children and a sick grandmother," he went on circumstantially.

"And where does she live?" Nekhlyudov asked.

"In this very house," answered the boy, pointing to a hut, in front of which, on the footpath along which Nekhlyudov was walking, a tiny, flaxen-headed infant stood balancing himself with difficulty on his rickety legs.

"Vaska! Where's the little scamp got to?" shouted a woman in a dirty grey blouse as she ran out of the house. She rushed forward with a frightened look, seized the baby before Nekhlyudov came up to it, and carried it in, just as if she were afraid that Nekhlyudov would hurt her child.

This was the woman whose husband was imprisoned for Nekhlyudov's birch trees.

"Well, and this Matrena, is she also poor?" Nekhlyudov asked, as they came up to Matrena's house.

"She poor? No. Why, she sells spirits," the thin, pink little boy answered decidedly.

When they reached the house, Nekhlyudov left the boys outside and went through the passage into the hut. The hut was fourteen feet long. The bed that stood behind the big stove was not long enough for a tall person to stretch out on. "And on this very bed," Nekhlyudov thought, "Katusha bore her baby and lay ill afterwards." The greater part of the hut was taken up by a loom, on which the old woman and her eldest granddaughter were arranging the warp when Nekhlyudov entered, striking his forehead against the low doorway. Two other grandchildren came rushing in after Nekhlyudov, and stopped, holding on to the lintels of the door.

"Whom do you want?" asked the old woman crossly. She was in a bad temper because she could not manage to get the warp right, and besides, carrying on an illicit trade in spirits, she was always afraid when any stranger came in.

"I am the owner of the neighbouring estates, and should like to speak to you."

The old woman was silent, regarding him intently, and her face suddenly changed.

"Dear me, why it's you, my honey! and I, fool, thought it was just some passer-by. Forgive me, for heaven's sake!" said the old woman, with simulated tenderness in her voice.

"I should like to speak to you alone," said Nekhlyudov, with a glance towards the door, where behind the children stood a woman holding a wasted, pale baby with a sickly smile, and wearing a little patchwork cap.

"What are you staring at? I'll give it you. Just hand me my crutch," shouted the old woman to those at the door. "Shut the door, will you!"

The children went away, and the woman with the child closed the door.

"And I was thinking 'who's that?' and it's the master himself, my jewel, my treasure. Just think," said the old woman, "where he has deigned to come. Sit down here, your honour," she said, wiping the seat with her apron. "And I was thinking 'what devil is it coming in?' and it's your honour, the master himself, the good gentleman, our benefactor. Forgive me, old fool that I am; I'm getting blind."

Nekhlyudov sat down, and the old woman stood in front of him, leaning her cheek on her right hand, while the left held up the sharp elbow of her right arm.

She began in a singing voice.

"Dear me, you have grown old, your honour. You used to be as fresh as a daisy. And now! Cares also, I expect?"

"This is what I have come about. Do you remember Katusha Maslova?"

"Katerina; I should think so. Why, she is my niece. How could I help remembering? and the tears I have shed because of her. I know all about it. Eh, sir, who has not sinned before God? who has not offended against the Tsar? We know what youth is. You used to be drinking tea and coffee, so the devil got hold of you. He is strong at times. What's to be done? Now, if you had chucked her; but no, just see how you rewarded her, gave her a hundred rubles. And she? What has she done? She wouldn't be reasonable. Had she but listened to me she might have lived all right. I must say the truth, though she is my niece: that girl's no good. What a good place I found her! She would not submit, but abused her master. Is it for the likes of us to scold gentlefolk? Well, she was sent away. And then at the forester's. She might have lived there; but, no, she would not."

"I want to know about the child. She was confined at your house, was she not? Where is the child?"

"As to the child, I considered that well at the time. She was so bad I never thought she would get up again. Well, so I christened the baby quite properly, and we sent it to the Foundlings'. Why should one let an innocent soul languish when the mother is dying? Others do like this: they just leave the baby, don't feed it, and it wastes away. But, thinks I, no; I'd rather take some trouble and send it to the Foundlings'. There was money enough, so I sent it off."

"Did you get its registration number from the Foundling Hospital?"[1]

"Yes, there was a number, but the baby died," she said. "It died as soon as she took it there."

"Who is *she*?"

"That same woman who used to live in Skorodno. She made a business of it. Her name was Malanya. She's dead now. She was a wise woman. How do you think she used to do? They'd bring her a baby,

---

[1] There is a very large Foundling Hospital in Moscow, where eight or nine out of every ten children admitted die.

and she'd keep it and feed it until she had enough of them to take to the Foundlings'. When she had three or four, she'd take them all at once. She had such a clever arrangement, a sort of big cradle—a double one—and she could put them in one way or the other. It had a handle. So she'd put four of them in, feet to feet and the heads apart so that they should not knock against each other. And so she took four at once. She'd give 'em some pap in a rag to keep 'em quiet, the pets."

"Well, go on."

"Well, she took Katerina's baby in the same way, after keeping it a fortnight, I believe. It was in her house it began to sicken."

"And was it a fine baby?" Nekhlyudov asked.

"Such a baby, that if you wanted a finer you could not find one. Your very image," the old woman added, with a wink.

"Why did it sicken? Was the food bad?"

"Eh, what food? Only just a pretence of food. Naturally, when it's not one's own child. Only enough to get it there alive. She said she just managed to get it to Moscow and there it died. She brought a certificate—all in order. She was such a wise woman."

And this was all Nekhlyudov could find out about his child.

Chapter VI

AGAIN STRIKING his head against the tops of both doors, Nekhlyudov went out into the street, where the white and pink boys were waiting for him. A few new-comers were standing with them. Among the women, several of whom had babies in their arms, was the thin woman with the baby in the patchwork cap. The bloodless infant, held lightly in her arms, was smiling strangely all over its wizened little face, and continually moved its crooked thumb.

Nekhlyudov knew the smile to be one of suffering. He asked who the woman was.

"It is that very Anisya I told you about," said the elder boy.

Nekhlyudov turned to Anisya.

"How do you live?" he asked. "What do you do for a living?"

"How do I live—I go begging," said Anisya, and began to cry.

The wizened infant smiled all over its face and wriggled his legs, hardly thicker than worms.

Nekhlyudov took out his pocket-book, and gave the woman a ten-ruble note. Before he had gone two steps another woman with a baby caught him up, then an old woman, then another young one. All of them spoke of their poverty, and asked for help. Nekhlyudov gave them the sixty rubles—all in small notes—which he had with him, and terribly sick at heart turned back to the bailiff's house.

The bailiff met Nekhlyudov with a smile, and informed him that the peasants would gather for the meeting in the evening. Nekhlyudov thanked him, and went straight into the garden to stroll along the paths strewn with the petals of apple blossom and overgrown with weeds, and to think over all he had seen.

At first all was quiet, but soon Nekhlyudov heard from behind the bailiff's house two angry women's voices interrupting each other, and now and then the voice of the ever-smiling bailiff. Nekhlyudov listened.

"My strength's at an end. What are you doing, dragging the very cross[1] off my neck?" said an angry woman's voice.

"But she only got in for a moment," said another voice. "Give her back, I tell you. What do you want to torment the beast for; and the children, too, who want their milk?"

"Pay, then, or work it off," said the bailiff's voice.

Nekhlyudov left the garden and entered the porch, near which stood two dishevelled women—one of them pregnant and evidently near her time. On one of the steps of the porch, with his hands in the pockets of his holland coat, stood the bailiff. When they saw "the master" the women were silent and began arranging the kerchiefs on their heads, and the bailiff took his hands out of his pockets and began to smile.

This is what had happened. From what the bailiff said, it seemed that the peasants were in the habit of letting their calves and even their cows into the meadow belonging to the estate. Two cows belonging to the families of these two women had been found in the meadow, and driven into the yard. The bailiff demanded from the women thirty kopeyks for each cow or two days' work. The women, however, maintained that the cows had got into the meadow of their own accord; said that they had no money, and asked that the cows, which had stood without food in the blazing sun since morning, piteously lowing, should be returned to them, even if it had to be on the understanding that the money should be worked off later on.

"How often have I not begged of you," said the smiling bailiff, looking back at Nekhlyudov as if calling upon him to be a witness, "when you drive your cattle home at noon, to keep an eye on them?"

"I only ran to my little one for a bit, and they got away."

---

[1] Those baptized in the Russo-Greek Church always wear a cross round their necks; it is almost the last thing most of them will part with.

"Then don't run away when you have undertaken to watch the cows."

"And who's to feed the little one? You'd not give him the breast, I suppose?" said the other woman. "Now, if they had really damaged the meadow one would not take it so much to heart; but they only strayed in for a moment."

"All the meadows are damaged," the bailiff said, turning to Nekhlyudov. "If I exact no penalty there will be no hay."

"There now, don't go sinning like that; my cows have never been caught there before," shouted the pregnant woman.

"Now that one has been caught, pay up or work it off."

"All right, I'll work it off; only let me have the cow now, don't torture her with hunger," she cried angrily. "As it is, I have no rest day or night. Mother-in-law ill, husband in drink; I'm all alone to do all the work, and my strength's at an end. I wish you'd choke, you and your working it off."

Nekhlyudov asked the bailiff to let the women take the cows, and went back into the garden to go on thinking out his problem; but there was nothing more to think about.

Everything seemed so clear to him now, that he could not stop wondering how it was that everybody did not see it, and that he himself had been so long in perceiving what was so clearly evident. The people were dying out; had got used to the dying-out process, and so had formed habits of life adapted to it: there was the great mortality among the children, the over-working of the women, and the under-feeding, especially of the aged. And so gradually had the people come to this condition that they did not realise the full horror of it, and did not complain, and we therefore considered their condition natural and proper. Now it seemed as clear as daylight that the chief cause of the people's deep poverty was one that they themselves knew and always pointed out, namely, that the land which alone could feed them had been taken from them by the landlords.

And how evident it was that the children and the aged died because they had no milk, and that they had no milk because there was no pasture land, and no land to grow corn or make hay on. It was quite evident that all the misery of the people, or at least the greatest and directest cause of it, lay in the fact that the land which should feed them was not in their hands, but in the hands of those who, profiting by the ownership of the land, live by the work of these people. The land, so needful to men that they die when deprived of it, was tilled by these people on the verge of starvation, to the end that the corn might be sold abroad and the owners of the land might buy themselves hats and canes, and carriages and bronzes, etc. Nekhlyudov now understood this as clearly as he understood that horses when they have eaten all the grass in the enclosure where they are kept, must of necessity grow thin and starve unless they are put where they can get food off other land.

This was terrible, and must not go on. Means must be found to alter it, or at least not to take part in it. "And I will find them," he thought, as he walked up and down the path under the birch trees. "In scientific circles, Government institutions, and in the papers, we talk about the causes of poverty among the people and the means of ameliorating their condition; but we do not talk of the only sure means which would certainly lighten their condition, namely, giving back to them the land they need so much."

Henry George's fundamental position recurred vividly to Nekhlyudov's mind. He remembered how he had once been carried away by it, and he was surprised that he could have forgotten it. "The earth cannot be any one's property; it cannot be bought or sold any more than water, air, or sunshine. All have an equal right to the advantages it gives to men. And now he knew why he felt ashamed to remember the transaction at Kusminsky. He had been deceiving himself. Knowing that no man could have the right to own land, he had yet accepted this right as his, and had given the peasants a part of something to which, in the depth of his heart, he knew he had no right whatever. Now he would not act in this way, and would alter the arrangement in Kusminsky also. And he formed a project in his mind to let the land to the peasants, and to acknowledge the rent they paid for it to be their property, to be kept for the taxes and for communal uses. This, of course, was not the single-tax system, still it was as near an approach to it as could be made in the existing circumstances. His chief consideration, however, was that in this way he would no longer profit the possession of landed property.

When Nekhlyudov returned to the house, the bailiff, with a specially pleasant smile, asked him if he would not have his dinner now, expressing fear that the feast his wife was preparing, with the help of the girl with the earrings, might be overdone.

The table was covered with a coarse unbleached cloth, and an embroidered towel was laid on it in lieu of a napkin. A *vieux-saxe* soup tureen with a broken handle stood on the table full of potato soup, the stock being made of the fowl which had put out and drawn in his black leg, and who was now cut, or rather chopped, in pieces, which were here and there covered with hairs. After the soup more of the same hairy fowl was served roasted, and then curd pasties, very greasy and with a great deal of sugar. Little appetising as all this was, Nekhlyudov hardly noticed what he was eating; he was occupied with the thought that had in a moment dispersed the sadness with which he had returned from the village.

The bailiff's wife kept looking in at the door while the frightened girl with the earrings brought in the dishes; and the bailiff smiled more and more joyously, priding himself on his wife's culinary skill. After dinner, Nekhlyudov succeeded, with some trouble, in getting the bailiff to sit down. In order to revise his own thoughts, and to express them to some one, he explained his project of letting the land to the peasants, and asked the bailiff for his opinion. The bailiff, smiling as if he had thought all this himself long ago, and was very pleased to hear it, did not really understand it at all. This was not because Nekhlyudov did not express himself clearly, but because according to this project it turned out that Nekhlyudov was giving up his own profit for the profit of others; and the thought that every one is concerned only for his own profit, to the harm of others, was so deeply rooted in the bailiff's conceptions that he imagined he did not understand something when Nekhlyudov said that all the income from the land should go to form the communal capital of the peasants.

"Oh, I see; then you, of course, will receive the percentages from that capital," said the bailiff, brightening up.

"Dear me, no! Don't you see, I'm giving up the land altogether."

"But then you will not receive any income," said the bailiff, smiling no longer.

"No, I am going to give it up."

The bailiff sighed heavily, but then began smiling again. Now he understood. Nekhlyudov was evidently not quite normal; and at once he began to consider how he himself could profit by Nekhlyudov's project of giving up the land, trying to see this project in an aspect that promised advantage to himself. But when he saw that this, too, was impossible, he grew sorrowful: the project ceased to interest him; and he continued to smile only to please "the master."

Seeing that the bailiff did not understand him, Nekhlyudov let him go, and sat down by the window-sill that was all cut about and inked over, and began to put his project on paper.

The sun went down behind the limes, which were covered with fresh green, and the mosquitoes swarmed in, stinging Nekhlyudov. Just as he finished his notes he heard the lowing of cattle and the creaking of opening gates from the village, and the voices of the peasants gathering together for the meeting. He had told the bailiff not to call the peasants up to the office, as he meant to go into the village and meet the men where they assembled. Having hurriedly drunk a cup of tea offered him by the bailiff, Nekhlyudov went to the village.

Chapter VII

FROM THE crowd assembled in front of the house of the village elder came the sound of voices; but as soon as Nekhlyudov came up the talking ceased, and all the peasants took off their caps just as those in Kusminsky had done. The peasants here were of a much poorer class than those in Kusmínsky. The men wore bark shoes and homespun shirts and coats. Some were barefooted and in their shirts just as they had come from their work.

Nekhlyudov made an effort, and began his speech by telling the peasants of his intention to give up his land to them altogether. The peasants were silent, and the expression in their faces underwent no change.

"Because I hold and believe," said Nekhlyudov, blushing, "that every one has a right to the use of the land."

"That's certain. That's so, exactly," uttered several voices.

Nekhlyudov went on to say that the revenue from the land ought to be divided among all, and that he therefore suggested, in offering them the land, that they should rent the land at a price fixed by themselves, the rent to form a communal fund for their own use. Words of approval and agreement were still to be heard, but the serious faces of the peasants grew still more serious, and the eyes that had been fixed on the gentleman dropped, as if they were unwilling to put him to shame by letting him see that every one understood his trick, and would not be deceived by him.

Nekhlyudov spoke clearly, and the peasants were intelligent, but they did not and could not understand him, for the same reason that the bailiff had so long been unable to understand him.

They were fully convinced that it is natural for every man to consider his own interest. The experience of many generations had proved to them that the landlords always considered their own interest to the detriment of the peasants. Therefore, if a landlord called them to a meeting and made them some kind of a new offer, it could evidently only be in order to swindle them more cunningly than before.

"Well, then, what rent will you fix for the land?" asked Nekhlyudov.

"How can we fix a price? We cannot do it. The land is yours, and the power is in your hands," answered some voices from among the crowd.

"Oh, not at all. You will have the use of the money yourselves for communal purposes."

"We cannot do it; the commune is one thing, and this is another."

"Don't you understand," said the bailiff, with a smile (he had followed Nekhlyudov to the meeting), "the Prince is letting the land to you for money, and is giving you the money back to form a capital for the commune."

"We understand very well," said a cross, toothless old man, without raising his eyes. "Something like a bank; we should have to pay at a fixed time. We do not wish it; it is hard enough as it is, and that would ruin us altogether."

"That's no go. We prefer to go on the old way," began several dissatisfied and even rude voices.

The refusals grew very vehement when Nekhlyudov mentioned that he would draw up an agreement which he and they would sign.

"Why sign? We will go on working as we have done all along. What is all this for? We are ignorant men."

"We can't agree, because it's so strange to us. As it has been, so let it continue. Only the seeds we should like to withdraw."

This meant that under the present arrangement the seeds had to be provided by the peasants, and they would like the landlord to provide them.

"Then am I to understand that you refuse to take the land?" Nekhlyudov asked, addressing a middle-aged, bare-footed peasant, with a bright look on his face. He was dressed in a tattered coat, and held his worn cap in his left hand in the peculiarly straight position in which soldiers hold theirs when commanded to take them off.

"Just so," said this peasant, who had evidently not yet rid himself of the military hypnotism he had been subjected to while serving his time.

"Do you mean that you have sufficient land?" said Nekhlyudov.

"No, sir, we have not," said the ex-soldier, with an artificially pleased look, carefully holding his tattered cap in front of him, as if offering it to any one who liked to make use of it.

"Well, anyhow, you'd better think over what I have said."

Nekhlyudov spoke with surprise, and again repeated his offer.

"We have no need to think about it; as we have said, so it will be," angrily muttered the morose, toothless old man.

'I shall be staying here over to-morrow, and if you change your minds, send to let me know."

The peasants gave no answer.

So Nekhlyudov did not succeed in arriving at any result from this interview.

"If I might make a remark, Prince," said the bailiff, when they got home, "you will never come to any agreement with them; they are so obstinate. At a meeting these people just stick in one place, and there is no moving them. It is because they are frightened of everything. Why, those very peasants—say that white-haired one, or the dark one—

who were refusing, are intelligent men. When one of them comes to the office and one gets him to sit down to a cup of tea it's like being in the Palace of Wisdom—he is quite a diplomatist," said the bailiff, smiling; "he will consider everything rightly. At a meeting he's a different man—he keeps repeating one and the same——"

"Well, could not some of the more intelligent men be asked to come here?" said Nekhlyudov; "I would explain it carefully to them."

"That can be done," said the smiling bailiff.

"Yes, call them to-morrow, please."

"Oh, certainly I will," said the bailiff, and smiled still more joyfully. "I'll call them for to-morrow."

. . . .

"Just hear him; he's not artful, not he," said a black-haired peasant with an unkempt beard, as he sat jolting from side to side on a well-fed mare, addressing an old man in a torn coat who rode by his side. The two men were driving a herd of peasants' horses to graze in the night alongside the high road and, secretly, in the landlord's forest.

"Give you the land for nothing, you need only sign—haven't they done the likes of us often enough? No, my friend, none of your humbug. Nowadays we have a little sense," he added, and began calling a colt that had strayed.

He stopped his horse and looked round; but the colt had not remained behind, it had gone into the meadow by the roadside.

"Bother that son of a Turk; he's taken to getting into the landowner's meadows," said the dark peasant with the unkempt beard, hearing the crackling of the sorrel stalks over which the neighing colt was galloping in the scented meadow to which he had betaken himself.

"Do you hear that crackling? We'll have to send the women folk to weed the meadow when there's a holiday," said the thin peasant with the torn coat, "or else we'll blunt our scythes."

"'Sign,' he says," the unkempt man continued, giving his opinion of the landlord's speech. "'Sign,' indeed, and let him swallow you alive."

"That's certain," answered the old man. And then they were silent, and the only sound was that of the tramping hoof the horses along the high road.

Chapter VIII

WHEN NEKHLYUDOV returned he found that the office had been arranged as a bedroom for him. A high bedstead with a feather bed and two large pillows had been placed in the room. The bed was covered with a large dark-red silk quilt, elaborately and finely quilted, and very stiff. It evidently belonged to the trousseau of the bailiff's wife. The bailiff offered Nekhlyudov the remains of the dinner, but Nekhlyudov declined, and the bailiff, excusing himself for the poorness of the fare and accommodation, left Nekhlyudov to himself.

The peasants' refusal did not at all trouble Nekhlyudov. On the contrary, though at Kusminsky his offer had been accepted and he had even been thanked for it, and here he was met with suspicion and even enmity, he felt contented and joyful.

It was close in the not very clean office. Nekhlyudov went out into the yard, and was going into the garden, but he remembered that night: the window of the maidservants' room, the side porch—and he felt uncomfortable, and did not like to pass the spot defiled by guilty memories. He sat down on the doorstep, and breathing in the warm air, fragrant with the strong scent of young birch leaves, he remained for a long time looking into the dark garden and listening to the mill, the nightingales, and some bird that whistled monotonously in the bush close by. The light disappeared from the bailiff's window; in the east, behind the barn, appeared the light of the rising moon, and sheet lightning more and more frequently revealed the dilapidated house and the blooming, over-grown garden. It began to thunder in the distance, and a black cloud overspread a third of the sky. The nightingales and the other birds were silent. Above the murmur of the water from the mill came the cackling of geese, and then in the village and in the bailiff's yard the first cock-crowing began earlier than usual, as happens on warm, thundery nights. There is a saying that if the cocks crow early the night will be a merry one. For Nekhlyudov the night was more than merry: it was a happy, joyful night. Imagination renewed the impressions of the happy summer he had spent here as an innocent lad, and he felt himself as he had been, not only then but at all the best moments of his life. He not only remembered, but felt as he had felt when, at the age of fourteen, he prayed that God would show him the truth; or when as a child he had wept on his mother's lap when parting from her, promising to be always good and never to give her pain; he felt as he did when he and Nikolenka Irtenyev resolved always to support each other in living a good life and to try to make everybody happy.

He remembered how he had been tempted in Kusminsky, so that he had begun to regret the house and the forest and the farm and the land, and he asked himself if he regretted them now; and it even seemed strange to think that he could regret them. He remembered all he had seen to-day; the woman with the children whose husband was in prison for having cut down trees in his (Nekhlyudov's) forest; the terrible

Matrena, who considered, or at least talked as if she considered, that
women of her position must yield themselves to the gentlefolk; he
remembered her attitude towards babies, the way in which they were
taken to the Foundling Hospital, the unfortunate, smiling, wizened
baby with the patchwork cap, dying of starvation, and the weak pregnant woman obliged to work for himself because, overworked as she
was, she had neglected to look after her hungry cow. And then he suddenly remembered the prison, the shaven heads, the cells, the disgusting smells, the chains, and, by the side of it all, the madly lavish city life
of the rich, himself included.

The bright moon, now almost full, rose above the barn. Dark shadows fell across the yard, and he iron roof of the ruined house shone
bright. As if reluctant to waste this light, the nightingales again began
their trills.

Nekhlyudov called to mind how he had begun to consider his life in
the garden of Kusminsky when deciding what he was going to do, and
remembered how confused he had become, how he could not arrive at
any decision, how many difficulties each question had presented. He
asked himself these questions now, and was surprised how simple it all
was. It was simple because he was thinking now, not of what would be
the results for himself, but only of what he ought to do. And, strange to
say, what he ought to do for himself he could not decide, but what he
ought to do for others he knew indubitably. He knew for certain that
he must not leave Katusha, but go on helping her, and redeem his sin
towards her. He knew for certain that he must study, investigate, clear
up, understand, all this business concerning judgment and punishment, which he felt he saw differently from other people. What would
result from it all he did not know, but he knew for certain that he must
do it. And this firm assurance gave him joy.

The black cloud had spread over the whole sky; the lightning flashed
vividly, showing the yard and the old house with its tumble-down
porches; the thunder growled overhead. All the birds were silent, but
the leaves rustled and the wind reached the step where Nekhlyudov sat,
and played with his hair. One drop came down, then another, then
they came drumming on the dock-leaves and on the iron of the roof,
and all the air was filled by a bright flash; and before Nekhlyudov could
count three a fearful crash sounded overhead and spread pealing
through the heavens.

Nekhlyudov went in.

"Yes, yes," he thought. "The work that our life accomplishes, the
whole of this work, the meaning of it, is not, nor can be, intelligible to
me. What were my aunts for? Why did Nikolenka Irtenyev die?—while
I am still living? What was Katusha for? And my madness? Why that

war? Why my subsequent lawless life? To understand it, to understand
the whole of the Master's will, is not in my power. But to do His will
that is written in my conscience, is in my power—and what it is I know
for certain. And when I am fulfilling it I have sureness and peace."

The rain came down in torrents and rushed gurgling from the roof
into a tub beneath; the lightning lit up the house and yard less frequently. Nekhlyudov went into his room, undressed, and lay down, not
without fear of bugs, whose presence the dirty, torn wallpaper made
him suspect.

"Yes, to feel oneself not the master but a servant," he thought, and
rejoiced at the thought.

His fears were not groundless. Hardly had he put out his candle
when the vermin attacked and bit him.

"To give up the land and go to Siberia—fleas, bugs, dirt! Well, what
of it? If it must be, I will bear it." but in spite of the best intentions he
could not bear it, and sat down by the open window and gazed with
admiration at the retreating clouds and the reappearing moon.

Chapter IX

It was morning before Nekhlyudov could fall asleep, and therefore he
woke late. At noon seven men, chosen from among the peasants and
invited by the bailiff, came into the orchard, where, under the apple
trees, the bailiff had arranged a table and benches by driving posts into
the ground and fixing boards on top of them. It was some time before
the peasants could be persuaded to put on their caps and sit down on
the benches. Especially firm was the ex-soldier, who to-day had bark
shoes on. He stood erect, holding his cap according to the military regulation for funerals. When one of the peasants, a respectable-looking
broad-shouldered old man, with ringlets in his grizzly beard like
Michael Angelo's Moses, and grey hair that curled round his brown
bald forehead, put on his big cap, and, wrapping his coat round him,
got in behind the table and sat down, the rest followed his example.
When all had taken their places Nekhlyudov sat down opposite them,
and leaning on the table over the paper on which he had drawn up his
project he began his explanation.

Whether it was that there were fewer present, or that he was occupied with the business in hand and not with himself—whatever it was,
this time Nekhlyudov felt no confusion. He involuntarily addressed the
broad-shouldered old man with white ringlets in his grizzly beard,

expecting approbation or objections from him. But Nekhlyudov's conjecture was wrong. The respectable looking old patriarch, though he nodded his handsome head approvingly, and shook it and frowned when the others raised an objection, evidently understood with great difficulty, and only when the others repeated in their own words what Nekhlyudov had said. A little old fellow, almost beardless, blind of one eye, in a patched nankeen coat and old boots, who sat by the side of the patriarch, and who, as Nekhlyudov found out later, was an ovenbuilder, understood much better. This man moved his eyebrows rapidly, attended to Nekhlyudov's remarks carefully, and at once repeated them in his own words. An old, thick-set man, with a white beard and intelligent eyes, understood as quickly, and took every opportunity to make an ironical joke, clearly wishing to show off. The ex-soldier seemed also to understand matters, but got mixed, being used to senseless soldiers' talk. Most seriously interested of all was a tall man with a small beard, a long nose, and a bass voice, who wore clean home-made clothes and new bark-plaited shoes. This man understood everything and spoke only when there was need to. The other two old men, that same toothless one who, at the meeting the day before, had shouted a distinct refusal to every proposal of Nekhlyudov's, and a tall, white, lame old man with a kind face, his thin legs tightly wrapped round with strips of linen, said little, though they listened attentively.

Nekhlyudov first of all explained his views in regard to personal property in land.

"The land, according to my view, can neither be bought nor sold, because if it could be, a man with money enough could buy up all the land, and exact anything he liked for the use of it from those who have none."

"That's true," said the long-nosed man in his deep bass.

"Just so," said the ex-soldier.

"A woman takes a little grass for her cow; she's caught and imprisoned," said the white-bearded man.

"Our own land is five versts away, and as to renting any it's impossible; the price is raised so high that it won't pay," added the cross, toothless old man. "They twist us into ropes: it's worse than serfdom."

"I think as you do, and count it a sin to possess land, so I wish to give it away," said Nekhlyudov.

"Well, that's a good thing," said the old man with curls like Angelo's Moses, evidently thinking that Nekhlyudov meant to let the land.

"I have come here because I no longer wish to possess any land, and now we must consider the best way of dividing it."

"Just give it to the peasants, that's all," said the cross, toothless old man.

Nekhlyudov was abashed for a moment, feeling that these words implied doubt as to the honesty of his intentions, but he instantly recovered, and made use of the remark in reply to express that was in his mind.

"I should be glad to give it them," he said, "but to whom, and how? To which peasants? Why to your commune and not to that of Deminsk?" (The name of a neighbouring village with very little land.)

All were silent. Then the ex-soldier said, "Just so."

"Well, then, tell me, how would you divide the land among the peasants if you had to do it?" said Nekhlyudov.

"We should divide it up equally, so much for every man," said the oven-builder, quickly raising and lowering his brows.

"How else? Of course, so much per man," said the good-natured lame man with the white strips of linen round his legs.

All confirmed this statement, considering it satisfactory.

"So much per man? Then are the servants attached to the house also to have a share?" Nekhlyudov asked.

"Oh no," said the ex-soldier, trying to appear bold and merry. But the tall, reasonable man did not agree with him.

"If one is to divide, all must share alike," he said, in his deep bass, after a little consideration.

"It can't be done," said Nekhlyudov, who had already prepared his reply. "If all are to share alike, then those who do not work it themselves—do not plough—will sell their shares to the rich. And again the land will get into the hands of the rich. Those who live by working the land will multiply, and land will again be scarce. Then the rich will once more get those who need land into their power."

"Just so," ejaculated the ex-soldier.

"Forbid to sell the land; let only him who ploughs it have it," angrily interrupted the oven-builder.

To this Nekhlyudov replied that it was impossible to know who was ploughing for himself and who for another.

The tall, reasonable man proposed that an arrangement be made so that they should all plough in common, those who ploughed sharing the produce and those who did not getting nothing.

To this communistic project Nekhlyudov had also an answer ready. He said that for such an arrangement it would be necessary that all should have ploughs, and that all the horses should be equal, so that none should be left behind; that ploughs and horses, threshing machines and all other implements should be held in common, and that to have this it would be necessary for every one to agree to it.

"Our people could not be made to agree in a lifetime," said the cross old man.

"We should have regular fights," said the old man with the laughing eyes.

"And how about the quality of the land?" said Nekhlyudov. "Why should one have rich soil and another clay and sand?"

"Then it should be divided into small lots and every one receive an equal share," said the oven-builder.

To that Nekhlyudov replied that they were not considering only a division in one commune, but a general division of land in different governments. If the land were to be given to the peasants free, why should some have good soil and others bad? They would all want good soil.

"Just so," said the ex-soldier.

The others were silent.

"So that the thing is not as simple as it seems," said Nekhlyudov. "But not only we but many have been thinking about this. There is an American, Henry George; this is what he has thought out, and I agree with him. . . ."

"Why, you are the master, and you can give it away as you like. What is to hinder you? The power is yours," said the cross old man.

This confused Nekhlyudov, but he was pleased to see that not he alone was dissatisfied with the interruption.

"You wait a bit, Uncle Simon; let him tell us about it," said the reasonable man, in his imposing bass.

Nekhlyudov was encouraged by this, and began to explain Henry George's single-tax system.

"The earth is no man's; it is God's," he began.

"Just so; that it is," several voices replied.

"The land is common to all. All have the same right to it. But there is good land and bad land, and every one would like to take the good land. How is one to do in order to get it justly divided? In this way: he who uses the good land must pay the value of it to those who have got none," Nekhlyudov went on, answering his own question. "As it would be difficult to say who should pay to whom, and as money is needed for communal use, it should be arranged that he who uses the good land should pay the value of that land to the commune for its needs. Then every one would share equally. If you want to use land, pay for it— more for the good land, less for the bad land. If you do not wish to use land, don't pay anything, and those who use the land will pay the taxes and the communal expenses for you."

"That's correct," said the oven-builder, moving his eyebrows. "He who has good land must pay more."

"Well, he had a head, that George!" said the imposing patriarch with the ringlets.

"If only the payment is according to our strength," said the tall man with the bass voice, evidently seeing what the plan led to.

"The payment should be not too high and not too low. If it is too high, it will not be paid and there will be a loss; and if it is too low, possession of land will be bought and sold. There would be a trading in land," replied Nekhlyudov. "Well, that is what I wished to arrange among you here," he went on.

"That is just, that is right; yes, that would do," said the peasants encouragingly, fully understanding.

"He had a head, this George," said the broad-shouldered old man with the curls. "See what he has invented."

"Well then, suppose I wanted to take some land?" said the smiling bailiff.

"If there is an allotment to spare, take it and work it," said Nekhlyudov.

"What for? You have sufficient as it is," said the old man with the laughing eyes.

With this the conference ended.

Nekhlyudov repeated his offer, not requiring an immediate answer but advising the men to talk it over with the rest of the commune and to let him know the result.

The peasants said they would talk it over and bring an answer, and left in a state of great excitement. Their loud talk could be heard as they went along the road, and late into the night the sound of voices came along the river from the village.

The peasants did not go to work next day, but spent it considering the landlord's offer. The commune was divided into two parties—one which regarded the offer as a profitable one and saw no danger in accepting it, and another which suspected and feared an offer it did not understand. On the third day, however, all were agreed, and some were sent to Nekhlyudov to accept his offer. They were influenced in their decision by the explanation an old woman gave of the landlord's conduct, which did away with all fear of deceit. The explanation was that "the master" had begun to think of his soul, and acted in this way in the hope of salvation. This was confirmed by the large sums of money which Nekhlyudov had given in charity in Panovo. The fact that Nekhlyudov had never before been face to face with such great poverty and so bare a life as the peasants had come to in this place, and was appalled by it, made him give away money in charity, though he knew that this was not reasonable. He could not help giving money, of which he now had a great deal, having received a large sum for a forest he had sold the year before, and also some earnest-money on the sale of the stock and implements at Kusminsky. As soon as it was known that "the master" was giving away money in charity, crowds of people, chiefly women, came asking him for help. He did not in the least know how to give: how to decide how much, and to whom to give it. He felt that to refuse to give money, of which he had so much, to people in great poverty was impossible, yet to give casually to those who asked was not wise.

The last day he spent in Panovo Nekhlyudov looked over the things left in his aunts' house; and in the drawer at the bottom of the mahogany wardrobe, with the brass lions' heads with rings through them, he found many letters, and among them a photograph of a group, consisting of his aunts Sophia Ivanovna and Mary Ivanovna, himself as a student, and Katusha, pure, lovely, and full of the joy of living. Of all the things in the house he took only the letters and the photograph. The rest he left to the miller, who, at the ever smiling bailiff's recommendation, had bought the house and all it contained—to be taken down and carted away—for a tenth of its real value.

Recalling the feeling of regret he had felt in Kusminsky, at the loss of his property, Nekhlyudov was surprised how he could have felt it. Now he felt nothing but unceasing joy at the deliverance, and a sensation of newness, something like a traveller must experience when discovering new lands.

Chapter X

THE TOWN struck Nekhlyudov in a new and peculiar light on his return. He came back in the evening, after the lamps were lit, and drove from the railway station to his house, where the rooms still smelt of naphthaline. Agrafena Petrovna and Korney were both feeling tired and dissatisfied, and had even had a quarrel over those things that seemed made only to be hung out, aired, and packed away. Nekhlyudov's room was empty, but not in order, and the way to it was blocked up with boxes; so that his arrival evidently hindered the business which, by a curious kind of inertia, was going on in this house. After the impressions the misery of the life of the peasants had made on him, the evident folly of these proceedings, in which he had once taken part, was so distasteful to Nekhlyudov that he decided to go to a lodging the next day, leaving Agrafena Petrovna to put away the things as she thought fit until his sister should come and finally dispose of everything in the house.

Nekhlyudov left home early and chose a couple of rooms in a very modest and not particularly clean lodging-house within easy reach of the prison, and, having given orders for some of his things to be sent there, he went to see the advocate. It was cold out of doors. After some rainy and stormy weather it had turned to cold, as it often does in spring. It was so cold, and the wind was so keen, that Nekhlyudov felt quite chilly in his light overcoat, and he walked fast, hoping to get warmer. His mind was filled with thoughts of the peasants—the women, children, old men—and all the poverty and weariness which he had seen as if for the first time, especially the strangely smiling, old-faced infant writhing its calfless little legs; and he could not but contrast with it what was going on in the town. Passing by the butchers', fishmongers', and clothiers' shops, he was struck again, as if he had seen it for the first time, by the great number and well-fed appearance of the clean and fat shop-keepers, like whom you could not find one peasant in the country. These men were apparently convinced that the pains they took to deceive people who did not know much about their goods was not a useless but rather an important business. The coachmen with their broad hips and rows of buttons down their sides, the doorkeepers with gold cords on their caps, the servant girls with their aprons and curly fringes, and especially the swell *izvozchiks* with the napes of their necks clean-shaven, who sat lolling back in their traps examining the passers-by with dissolute and contemptuous air—all looked well fed. In all these people Nekhlyudov could not now help seeing some of those very peasants who had been driven into the town by the lack of land. Some of them had found means of profiting by the conditions of town life, and had become like their masters and were pleased with their position; others were in a worse condition than they had been in the country, and were more to be pitied than even the country people.

Such seemed the bootmakers Nekhlyudov saw in basement lodgings; the pale, dishevelled washerwomen with their thin bare arms, ironing at open windows out of which streamed soapy stream; such the two house-painters with their aprons and stockingless feet all bespattered and smeared with paint, whom Nekhlyudov met—their weak brown arms bared to above the elbows—carrying a pailful of paint and quarrelling with each other. Their faces looked haggard and cross. The dark faces of the carters jolting along in their carts wore the same expression, as did also those of the tattered men and women who stood begging at the street corners. The same kinds of aces were to be seen at the open windows of the eating-houses which Nekhlyudov passed. At the dirty tables, on which stood tea-things and bottles, and between which waiters dressed in white shirts were rushing hither and thither, red perspiring men with stupefied faces sat shouting and singing. One sat by the window with lifted brows, pouting lips and fixed eyes, as if trying to remember something.

"And why are they all gathered here?" Nekhlyudov asked himself, breathing in, together with the dust carried along by the cold wind, the smell of rancid oil and fresh paint.

In one street he caught up a row of carts loaded with some kind of iron, which so rattled on the uneven roadway that it made his ears and head ache. He began to walk still faster in order to pass the row of carts, when suddenly above the clatter he heard himself called by name. He stopped, and saw an officer with sharp-pointed, waxed moustaches and shining face, sitting in the trap of a swell *izvozchik* and waving his hand in a friendly manner, his smile disclosing unusually white teeth.

"Nekhlyudov! Can it be you?"

Nekhlyudov's first feeling was one of pleasure.

"Ah, Schonbock!" he exclaimed joyfully; but he knew the next moment there was nothing to be joyful about.

This was that same Schonbock who had been in the house of Nekhlyudov's aunts that day. Nekhlyudov had quite lost sight of him, but had heard that in spite of his debts he had somehow managed to remain in the cavalry, and by some means or other still kept his place among the rich. His gay, contented appearance corroborated this report.

"What a good thing I have caught you: there is no one in town. Ah, old fellow, you have grown old," he said, getting out of the trap and stretching his shoulders. "I only knew you by your walk. Look here, we must dine together. Is there any place where they feed one decently?"

"I'm afraid I can't spare the time," Nekhlyudov answered, thinking only how he could best get rid of his companion without hurting his feelings. "And what has brought you here?" he asked.

"Business, old chap. Guardianship business. I am a guardian now. I am managing Samanov's affairs—the millionaire, you know. He has softening of the brain, and he's got fifty-four thousand desyatins of land," he said, with peculiar pride, as if he had himself made all these desyatins. "His affairs were terribly neglected. All the land was let to the peasants, who paid nothing, and there were more than eighty thousand rubles of debts. I changed it all in one year, and have got seventy per cent more out of it. What do you think of that?" he asked proudly.

Nekhlyudov remembered having heard that, just because he had spent all his fortune and piled up debts, this Schonbock had, by some special influence, been appointed guardian to a rich old man who was squandering his property; and Schonbock was now evidently living by this guardianship. "How am I to get rid of him without offending him?" thought Nekhlyudov, looking at his full, shiny face with the waxed moustache, and listening to his friendly, good-humoured chatter about where one gets fed best, and his bragging about his doings as a guardian.

"Well then, where shall we dine?"

"Really I have no time," said Nekhlyudov, glancing at his watch.

"Well, look here. Will you be at the races to-night?"

"No, I shall not be there."

"Do come. I have none of my own now, but I back Grisha's horses. You remember; he has a fine stud. You'll come, won't you? And we'll have supper together."

"No, I shall not be able to have supper with you either," said Nekhlyudov, with a smile.

"Well, that's too bad! Where are you off to now? Shall I give you a lift?"

"I am going to see an advocate, close here—round the corner."

"Oh yes, of course. You have got something to do with the prisons—have turned into a prisoners' mediator, I hear," said Schonbock, laughing. "The Korchagins told me. They have left town already. What does it all mean? Tell me."

"Yes, yes, it is quite true," Nekhlyudov answered; "but I cannot tell you about it in the street."

"Of course, of course; you always were a crank. But you will come to the races?"

"No, I can't, and really I don't want to. Please do not be angry with me."

"Angry? Dear me, no! Where do you live?" And suddenly his face grew serious, his eyes became fixed, and he wrinkled up his brows. He seemed to be trying to remember something, and Nekhlyudov noticed in him the same dull expression as in the man with the raised brows and pouting lips whom he had seen at the window of the eating-house.

"How cold it is, eh?"

"Yes, yes."

"Have you got the parcels?" said Schonbock, turning to the *izvozchik*. "Well then, good-bye. I am very glad indeed to have met you," and pressing Nekhlyudov's hand warmly, he jumped into the trap and waved his white-gloved hand in front of his shiny face, with his usual smile showing his exceptionally white teeth.

"Can I also have been like that?" Nekhlyudov thought as he continued his way to the advocate's. . . . "Yes, I wished to be like that, though I was not quite like it. And I thought of living my life in that way."

Chapter XI

NEKHLYUDOV WAS admitted before his turn by the advocate, who at once began to talk about the Menshovs' case, which he had read with indignation at the inconsistency of the charge.

"This case is perfectly revolting," he said. "It is quite likely that the owner himself set fire to the building in order to get the insurance money, but the chief thing is that the Menshovs' guilt was not proved at all. There is no evidence whatever. It is all owing to the carelessness of the examining magistrate and the special zeal of the prosecutor. If they are tried here, and not in a provincial Court, I guarantee that they will be acquitted, and I shall charge nothing. Now then, the next case—Theodosia Birukova. The appeal to the Emperor is written. If you go to Petersburg you'd better take it with you and hand it in yourself, with a request of your own, or else they will only make a few inquiries, and nothing will come of it. You must try and get at some of the influential members of the Appeal Committee. I think that is all?"

"No; here I have a letter——"

"I see you have turned into a pipe—a spout through which all the complaints of the prison are poured," said the advocate with a smile. "It is too much; you'll not be able to manage it."

"No, but this is a striking case," said Nekhlyudov, and gave a brief outline of the case of a peasant in a village, who began to read and discuss the Gospels with his friends. The priests regarded this as a crime and informed the authorities. The magistrate examined him, the public prosecutor drew up an indictment, and the justices committed him for trial.

"This is really too terrible," Nekhlyudov said. "Can it be true?"

"What are you surprised at?"

"Why, everything. I can understand the police officer who simply obeys orders, but the prosecutor drawing up an indictment of that kind? An educated man——"

"That is where the mistake lies. We are in the habit of considering public prosecutors and judges in general to be some kind of liberal persons. There was a time when they were such, but now it is quite different. They are just officials, only troubled about pay-day. They get their salaries and want more, and there their principles end. They will accuse, judge, and sentence any one you like."

"Yes; but no laws really exist that can condemn a man to Siberia for reading the Bible with others?"

"Yes, to exile, if you can only prove that in reading the Bible he took the liberty of explaining it to others not as is ordered, and so condemned the explanations given by the Church. Censuring the Greek Orthodox religion in the presence of the common people means, according to Article 196, exile to Siberia."

"Impossible!"

"I assure you it is so. I always tell these gentlemen, the judges," the advocate continued, "that I cannot look at them without gratitude; because if I am not in prison, and you and all of us, it is only owing to their kindness. To deprive us of our privileges and send us all to the less remote parts of Siberia would be an easy thing for them."

"Well, but if that is so and everything depends on the *Procureur* and others who can, at will, either enforce the laws or not, what are the trials for?"

The advocate burst into a hearty laugh. "You do put strange questions. My dear sir, that is philosophy. Well, we might have a talk about that, too. Could you come on Saturday? You will meet men of science, literary men, and artists, at my house, and then we might discuss these abstract questions," said the advocate, pronouncing the words "abstract questions" with ironical sententiousness. "You have met my wife? Do come."

"Thank you; I will try," said Nekhlyudov, and felt that he was telling an untruth, knowing that if he tried to do anything it would be to keep away from the advocate's literary evening, and his circle of men of science, art, and literature.

The laugh with which the advocate met Nekhlyudov's remark that trials could have no meaning if the judges can enforce the laws or not as they like, and the tone in which he pronounced the words "philosophy" and "abstract questions," proved to Nekhlyudov how very differently he and the advocate, and probably the advocate's friends, looked at things; and he felt that great as was the distance that now existed between himself and his former companions, Schonbock and the rest, the distance between himself and the advocate and his circle of friends was still greater.

Chapter XII

THE PRISON was a long way off and it was getting late, so Nekhlyudov hired an *izvozchik*. The *izvozchik*, a middle-aged man with an intelligent, kind face, turned round towards Nekhlyudov as they were driving along one of the streets and pointed to a huge house that was being built there.

"Just see what a tremendous house they are putting up," he said, as if he was concerned in the building of the house and proud of it.

The house was really immense, and the style was complicated and original. Scaffolds of strong pine beams, fastened together with iron ties, surrounded the building, and a hoarding separated it from the street. On the boards of the scaffolding, workmen all bespattered with mortar moved thither and thither like ants. Some were laying bricks, some cutting them, some carrying up the heavy hods and pails and bringing them down empty. A fat and well-dressed gentlemen—probably the architect—stood by the scaffolding, pointing upward and explaining something to a contractor, a peasant from the Vladimir Government, who was listening respectfully. Loaded carts went in through the gate and empty ones came out, passing by the architect and the contractor.

"And how sure they all are—those who do the work as well as those who make them do it—that it must be so; that while their wives at home, who are with child, are labouring beyond their strength, and their children with patchwork caps, doomed soon to death from starvation, smile like old men and contort their little legs, they must be building this stupid and useless palace for some stupid and useless person—one of those who rob and ruin them," thought Nekhlyudov, while looking at the house.

"Yes, it is a stupid house," he said, giving voice to his thought.

"Why stupid?" replied the *izvozchik* in an offended tone. "Thanks to it the people get work; it's not stupid."

"But the work is useless."

"It can't be useless, or why should it be done?" said the *izvozchik*. "The people get bread by it."

Nekhlyudov was silent, especially as it would have been difficult to talk above the clatter the wheels made.

When they came nearer the prison, and the *izvozchik* turned off the cobblestones on to the macadamised road, it became easier to talk and he again turned to Nekhlyudov.

"And what a lot of folk come flocking to town nowadays; it's awful," he said, turning round on his box and pointing to a party of peasant workmen who were coming towards them carrying saws and axes, and with sheepskin coats and bags strapped to their shoulders.

"More than in other years?" Nekhlyudov asked.

"By far. This year every place is crowded, so that it's really terrible. The employers just fling the workmen about like chaff. Not a job to be got."

"Why is that?"

"More of them have come! There's no room for them."

"Well, but why are there more of them? Why do not they stay in the village?"

"There's nothing for them to do in the village. There's no land to be had."

Nekhlyudov felt as one does when a sore place is touched. One feels as if the bruised part were always being hit; but it is only because the place is sore that the touch is felt.

"Is it possible that the same thing is happening everywhere?" he thought, and began questioning the *izvozchik* about the quantity of land in his village, how much land the man himself had, and why he had left the country.

"We have a desyatin per man, sir, and our family have three men's shares." The *izvozchik* began to speak willingly: "My father and a brother are at home and manage the land, and another brother is serving in the army. But there's nothing to manage. My brother has had thoughts of coming to Moscow, too."

"And cannot land be rented?"

"How's one to rent it nowadays? The gentry, such as they were, have squandered all theirs, and business men have got it all into their own hands. One can't rent it from them—they farm it themselves. We have a Frenchman ruling in our place; he bought the estate from our former landlord, and won't let it, and there's an end of it."

"Who is that Frenchman?"

'Dufour is the Frenchman's name. Perhaps you've heard of him. He makes wigs for the actors at the big theatre. It is a good business, so he's made money. He bought the whole of the estate from our lady, and now he has us in his power; he just rides on us as he pleases. The Lord be thanked, he is a good man himself; but his wife, a Russian, is such a brute that—God have mercy on us. She just robs the people. It's awful. Well, here's the prison. Am I to drive you to the entrance? I'm afraid they'll not let us do it, though."

Chapter XIII

WHEN HE rang the bell at the front entrance Nekhlyudov's heart failed him at the thought of the state he might find Maslova in to-day, and at the mystery he felt to be in her, and in the people that were collected in the prison. He asked the jailer who opened the door for Maslova. After making some inquiry the jailer informed him that she was at the hospital. There a kindly old man, the hospital doorkeeper, let Nekhlyudov in at once, and, after asking him whom he wanted, directed him to the children's ward.

A young doctor, saturated with carbolic acid, came out to Nekhlyudov in the passage and asked him sternly what he wanted. This doctor was always making things easier for the prisoners, and was therefore continually coming into conflict with the prison authorities and even with the head doctor. Fearing that Nekhlyudov would demand something illegal, and wishing to show that he made no exceptions for any one, he pretended to be cross. "There are no women here; this is the children's ward," he said.

"Yes, I know; but a prisoner has been taken here as assistant nurse."

"Yes, there are two such here. Which of them do you want?"

"I am closely connected with one of them, named Maslova," Nekhlyudov answered, "and I should like to speak to her. I am going to Petersburg to hand in an appeal to the Senate about her case and should like to give her this. It is only a photograph," Nekhlyudov said, taking an envelope out of his pocket.

"All right, you may do that," said the doctor, relenting, and turning to an old woman in a white apron he told her to call the prisoner Maslova. "Will you take a seat here or go into the waiting-room?" he asked.

"Thank you," said Nekhlyudov, and profiting by the doctor's favourable change in manner towards him he asked how they were satisfied with Maslova in the hospital.

"Oh, she is all right. She works fairly well, if you take into account the conditions of her former life. But here she is!"

The old nurse came in at one of the doors, followed by Maslova, who wore a blue striped dress, a white apron, and a kerchief that quite covered her hair. When she saw Nekhlyudov her face flushed, and she stopped as if hesitating; then she frowned, and with downcast eyes came quickly towards him along the strip of carpet in the middle of the passage. When she came up to Nekhlyudov she did not wish to give him her hand, but then gave it, flushing redder still.

Nekhlyudov had not seen her since the day when she begged his forgiveness for having been in a passion, and he expected to find her the same as she was then. But to-day she was quite different. There was something new in the expression of her face, something reserved and shy, and also, it seemed to him, something inimical towards him. He told her what he had already said to the doctor—that he was going to Petersburg—and he handed her the envelope with the photograph he had brought from Panovo.

"I found this in Panovo—it's an old photo; perhaps you would like it. Take it."

Raising her dark eyebrows, she looked at him with surprise in her squinting eyes, as if asking, "What is this for?" and without saying a word she took the photograph and put it in the bib of her apron.

"I saw your aunt there," said Nekhlyudov.

"Did you?" she said indifferently.

"Are you all right here?" Nekhlyudov asked.

"Oh yes, it's all right," she replied.

"Not too difficult?"

"Oh no. But I am not used to it yet."

"I am glad, for your sake. Anyhow, it is better than there."

"Than there—where?" she asked, her face flushing again.

"There—in the prison," Nekhlyudov hastened to answer.

"Why better?" she asked.

"I think the people are better. Here are none such as there must be there."

"There are many good ones there," she said.

"I have been seeing about the Menshovs, and hope they will be liberated," said Nekhlyudov.

"God grant they may. Such a splendid old woman," she said, again repeating her opinion of the old woman, and smiling slightly.

"I am going to Petersburg to-day. Your case will come on soon, and I hope the sentence will be revoked."

"Revoked or not revoked, it's all the same now," she said.

"Why now?"

"Well?—" she said, looking with a quick questioning glance into his eyes.

Nekhlyudov understood the word and the look to mean that she wished to know whether he still kept firm to his decision or had accepted her refusal.

"I do not know why it's all the same to you," he said. "So far as I am concerned it certainly is all the same whether you are acquitted or not. I am ready in any case to do what I told you," he said decidedly.

She lifted her head, and her black squinting eyes remained fixed on him and beyond him, and her face shone with joy. But the words she spoke were very different to what her eyes said.

"You'd better not say that," she said.

"I am saying it so that you should know."

"Everything has been said about that, and there's no more to say," she said, with difficulty repressing a smile.

A sudden noise came from the hospital ward, and the sound of a child crying.

"I think they are calling me," she said, and looked round uneasily.

"Well, good-bye, then," he said.

She pretended not to see his extended hand, and without taking it she turned away and hastily walked along the strip of carpet, trying to hide the elation she felt.

"What is going on in her? What is she thinking? What does she feel?

Does she mean to test me, or can she really not forgive me? Is it that she cannot or that she will not express what she feels and thinks? Has she softened or hardened?" he asked himself, and could find no answer. He only knew that she had altered and that an important change was going on in her soul, and this change united him not only to her but also to Him for whose sake that change was being wrought. And this union touched and joyously excited him.

When she returned to the ward, in which stood eight small beds, Maslova began, in obedience to the nurse's orders, to arrange one of the beds; and, bending over too far with the sheet, she slipped and nearly fell.

A convalescent little boy with a bandaged neck, who was looking at her, laughed. Maslova could no longer contain herself and burst out into loud laughter, which was so contagious that several of the children also burst out laughing, and one of the sisters rebuked her angrily.

"What are you giggling at? Do you think you are where you used to be? Go and fetch the food."

Maslova became silent, and taking the crockery went where she was sent; but, catching the eye of the bandaged boy who was forbidden to laugh, she again gave a smothered laugh.

Whenever she was alone Maslova again and again pulled the photograph partly out of the envelope and looked at it admiringly; but only in the evening when she was off duty and alone in the bedroom she shared with the nurse did she take it quite out of the envelope, and, motionless, caressing with her eyes every detail of faces and clothing, the steps of the veranda, and the bushes which served as a background to her and his and his aunts' faces, she gazed long at the faded yellow photograph and could not help admiring it, especially herself with her pretty young face with the curly hair round the forehead. She was so absorbed that she did not hear her fellow-nurse come into the room.

"What's that he's given you?" said the good-natured, fat nurse, stooping over the photograph. "Who's this?—You?"

"Who else?" said Maslova, looking into her companion's face with a smile.

"And is that he himself?—and that, his mother?"

"No, his aunt. Would you not have known me?"

"Never. The whole face is altered. Why, it must be ten years ago."

"Not years, but a lifetime," said Maslova. And suddenly her animation vanished, her face grew gloomy, and a deep line appeared between her brows.

"Why so? Your way of life must have been an easy one."

"Easy, indeed," Maslova repeated, closing her eyes and shaking her head. "Worse than hell."

"Why, what makes it so?"

"What makes it so! From eight till four in the morning, and every night the same!"

"Then why don't they give it up?"

"They can't give it up if they want to. But what's the use of talking?" Maslova cried, jumping up and throwing the photograph into the drawer of the table. And with difficulty repressing angry tears, she ran out into the passage, slamming the door behind her.

While looking at the group she imagined herself such as she had been there, and dreamt of her happiness then and of the possibility of happiness with him now. But her companion's words reminded her of what she was now and what she had been, and brought back all the horrors of that life, which she had felt but vaguely and never dared to allow herself to realise.

It was only now that the memory of all those horrible nights came vividly back to her, especially one during the carnival when she was expecting a student who had promised to buy her out. She recalled how—wearing her low-necked silk dress stained with wine, a red bow in her untidy hair, wearied, weak, half-tipsy, having seen her visitors off—about two o'clock in the morning she sat down during an interval in the dancing, by the piano, beside the bony pianiste with the blotchy face, who accompanied the violin, and began complaining of her hard fate; and how this pianiste said that she, too, was feeling her position very heavily and would like to change it; and how Bertha suddenly came up to them; and how they all three decided to change their life. They thought that the night was over, and were about to go away, when suddenly the noise of tipsy voices was heard in the ante-room. The violinist struck up the tune and the pianiste began hammering out on the piano the first figure of a quadrille set to the tune of a most merry Russian song. A small, perspiring man, smelling of spirits, with a white tie and swallow-tail coat, which he took off after the first figure, came to her, hiccoughing, and caught her up, while another, a fat man with a beard, and also in a dresscoat (they had come straight from a ball), caught Bertha up, and for a long time they turned, danced, screamed, drank. . . . And so it went on for another year, and another, and a third. How could she help changing? And he was the cause of it all!

And, suddenly, all her former bitterness against him reawoke; she wished to revile, to reproach him. She regretted having neglected the opportunity to-day of repeating to him once more that she knew him, and would not give in to him—would not let him make use of her spiritually as he had done physically. And she longed for drink in order to stifle the feeling of pity for herself and the useless feeling of reproach to him. She would have broken her word if she had been in the prison;

here, however, she could not get any spirits except by applying to the medical assistant; but she was afraid of him because he made up to her, and intimate relations with men were disgusting to her now. After sitting a while on a form in the passage she returned to her little room, and without paying any heed to her companions' words, she cried a long time over her wrecked life.

Chapter XIV

NEKHLYUDOV HAD four matters to attend to in Petersburg: Maslova's petition at the Senate; Theodosia Birukova's case at the Committee of Petitions; and Vera Dukhova's requests—to try to get her friend Shustova released from prison, and at the office of the gendarmerie to get permission for a mother to visit her son in prison. These two requests, about which Vera Dukhova had written him, Nekhlyudov counted as one matter.

The fourth thing he meant to attend to was the case of the sectarians who had been separated from their families and exiled to the Caucasus because they read and discussed the Gospels. It was not so much to them as to himself that he had promised to do all he could to clear up this affair.

Since his last visit to Maslennikov, and especially since he had been in the country, Nekhlyudov, while not exactly forming a resolution on the matter, felt with his whole being a loathing for the society in which he had lived till then: that society which so carefully hides the sufferings borne by millions to assure ease and pleasure to a small minority, that the people comprising it do not and cannot see these sufferings nor the cruelty and wickedness of their own lives. Nekhlyudov could no longer move in this society without feeling ill at ease and reproaching himself. And yet all the ties of relationship and friendship and his own habits were drawing him back to it. Besides, that which alone interested him now, his desire to help Maslova and the other sufferers, necessitated asking for help and service from persons belonging to that society, persons whom not only he could not respect but who often aroused in him indignation and contempt.

When he came to Petersburg and stayed with his aunt—his mother's sister, the Countess Charskaya, wife of a former Minister—Nekhlyudov at once found himself in the very midst of that aristocratic circle which had grown so foreign to him. This was very unpleasant, but there was no possibility of escaping it. To put up at an hotel instead of at his aunt's house would have been to offend his aunt, and, besides, she had important connections and might be extremely useful in the matters he had to attend to.

"What is this I hear of you? All sorts of marvels," said the Countess Catherine Ivanovna Charskaya, as she gave him coffee immediately after his arrival. "*Vous posez pour un Howard*[1]—helping criminals, going the round of prisons, setting things right."

"Oh no, not at all."

"Why not? It is a good thing, but there seems to be some romantic story connected with it. Tell me all about it."

Nekhlyudov told her the whole truth about his relations to Maslova.

"Yes, yes, I remember your poor mother telling me about it. That was when you were staying with those old women. I believed they wished to marry you to their ward" (the Countess Catherine Ivanovna had always despised Nekhlyudov's aunts on his father's side). "So it's she. *Elle est encore jolie?*"[2]

Catherine Ivanovna was a strong, bright, energetic, talkative woman of sixty. She was tall and very stout, and had a decided black moustache. Nekhlyudov was fond of her, and even as a child had felt infected by her energy and mirth.

"No, *ma tante*, that's at an end. I only wish to help her because she is innocently accused. I am the cause of it and the cause of her fate being what it is. I feel it my duty to do all I can for her."

"But what is this I have heard about your intending to marry her?"

"Yes, it was my intention, but she does not wish it."

Catherine Ivanovna looked at her nephew in silent amazement with raised brows and drooping eyes. Suddenly her face changed, and with a pleased look she said:—

"Well, she is wiser than you. Dear me, you are a fool. And you would have married her?"

"Most certainly."

"After her having been what she was?"

"All the more, since I was the cause of it."

"Well, you are a simpleton," said his aunt, repressing a smile—"a terrible simpleton; but it is just because you are such a terrible simpleton that I love you." She repeated the word, evidently liking it—it seemed to convey to her mind the correct idea of her nephew's moral state. "Do you know—what a lucky chance! Aline has a wonderful home—the Magdalen Home. I went there once. They are terribly disgusting. After

---

[1] You pose as a Howard.
[2] Is she still pretty?

that I washed and washed. But Aline is devoted to it, body and soul, so we shall place her there—yours, I mean."

"But she is condemned to Siberia. I have come on purpose to appeal about it. This is one of my requests to you."

"Dear me, and where do you appeal to in this case?"

"To the Senate."

"Ah, the Senate! Yes, my dear Cousin Leo is in the Senate, but he is in the heraldry department and I don't know any of the real ones. They are all some kind of Germans: Gay, Fay, Day—*tout l'alphabet*—or else all sorts of Ivanovs, Simonovs, Nikitines, or else Ivanenkos, Simonenkos, Nikitenkos, *pour varier. Des gens de l'autre monde.*[3] Well, all the same, I'll tell my husband; he knows them. He knows all sorts of people. I'll tell him, but you will have to explain—he never understands me. Whatever I say, he always maintains that he does not understand it. *C'est un parti pris:*[4] every one understands, only not he."

At this moment a footman in knee-breeches came in with a note on a silver salver.

"There now, from Aline herself. You'll have a chance of hearing Kiesewetter."

"Who is Kiesewetter?"

"Kiesewetter? Come this evening, and you will find out who he is. He speaks in such a way that the most hardened criminals sink on their knees and weep and repent."

The Countess Catherine Ivanovna, however strange it may be and however little in keeping with the rest of her character, was a staunch adherent to that teaching which holds that the essence of Christianity lies in a belief in the Redemption. She went to meetings where this teaching, then in fashion, was being preached, and assembled "the faithful" in her own house. Though this teaching repudiated all ceremonies, icons, and sacraments, Catherine Ivanovna had icons in every room, and even one on the wall above her bed, and observed all that the Church prescribed, without noticing any contradiction.

"There now; if your Magdalen could hear him she would be converted," said the Countess. "Do stay at home to-night; you will hear him. He is a wonderful man."

"It does not interest me, *ma tante.*"

"But I tell you that it is interesting, and you must come home. Now you may go. What else do you want of me? *Videz votre sac.*"[5]

"The next is in the fortress."

---

[3] For variety. People of another world.
[4] That's a fixed point.
[5] Empty your sack, *i.e.* let's have it all.

"In the fortress? I can give you a note for that to Baron Kriegsmuth. *C'est un très brave homme.*[6] Oh, but you know him; he was a comrade of your father's. *Il donne dans le spiritisme.*[7] But that does not matter, he is a good fellow. What do you want there?"

"I want to get leave for a mother to visit her son who is imprisoned there. But I was told that this did not depend on Kriegsmuth but on Chervyansky."

"I do not like Chervyansky, but he is Mariette's husband; we might ask her. She will do it for me. *Elle est très gentille.*"[8]

"I have also to petition for a woman who is imprisoned there without knowing what for."

"No fear; she knows well enough. They all know it very well, and it serves them right, those short-haired ones."

"I do not know whether it serves them right or not. But they suffer. You are a Christian and believe in the Gospel teaching and yet you are so pitiless."

"That has nothing to do with it. The Gospels are the Gospels, but what is disgusting remains disgusting. It would be worse if I pretended to love Nihilists, especially short-haired women Nihilists, when I cannot bear them."

"Why can you not bear them?"

"You ask why, after the 1st of March."[9]

"They did not all take part in the 1st of March affair."

"Never mind; they should not meddle with what is no business of theirs. It's not women's business."

"Yet you consider that Mariette may take part in business."

"Mariette? Mariette is Mariette, and these are goodness knows what. They want to teach everybody."

"Not to teach, but simply to help the people."

"One knows whom to help and whom not to help without them."

"But the peasants are in great need. I have just returned from the country. Is it necessary that the peasants should work to the very limit of their strength and never have enough to eat, while we are living in the greatest luxury?" said Nekhlyudov, who was involuntarily led on by his aunt's good-nature into telling her what was in his mind.

"What do you want, then? That I should work and not eat anything?"

"No, I do not wish you not to eat," said Nekhlyudov, smiling involuntarily; "I only wish that we should all work and all eat."

---

[6] He is a capital man.

[7] He goes in for spiritualism.

[8] She is very nice.

[9] The Emperor Alexander II was assassinated on the 1st of March 1881 (old style).

Again raising her brow and drooping her eyes his aunt looked at him curiously.

"*Mon cher, vous finirez mal,*"[10] she said.

"But why?"

Just then the General and former Minister, Countess Charskaya's husband, a tall, broad-shouldered man, entered the room.

"Ah, Dmitry, how d'you do?" he said, turning his freshly shaved cheek to Nekhlyudov to be kissed. "When did you arrive?" And he silently kissed his wife on the forehead.

"*Non, il est impayable,*"[11] the Countess said, turning to her husband. "He wants me to go and wash clothes and live on potatoes. He is an awful fool, but all the same do what he is going to ask you. A terrible simpleton," she added. "Have you heard? Kamensky's mother is in such despair that they fear for her life," she said to her husband. "You should go and call there."

"Yes; it is dreadful," said her husband.

"Go along, now, and talk to him. I must write some letters."

Hardly had Nekhlyudov stepped into the room next to the drawing-room when she called him back.

"Shall I write to Mariette, then?"

"Please, *ma tante.*"

"I shall leave a blank for what you want to say about the short-haired one, and she will give her husband his orders, and he'll do it. Do not think me wicked; they are all so disgusting, your protégées, but *je ne leur veux pas de mal,*[12] bother them. Well, go, but be sure to stay at home this evening to hear Kiesewetter, and we shall have some prayers. And if only you do not resist *ça vous fera beaucoup de bien.*[13] I know your poor mother and all of you were always very backward in these things. Good-bye for the present."

Chapter XV

COUNT IVAN MIKHAYLICH had been a Minister, and was a man of strong convictions. His convictions consisted in the belief that just as it was natural for a bird to feed on worms, to be clothed in feathers and down,

---

[10] My dear, you will end badly.
[11] Oh, he's inimitable.
[12] I don't wish them any harm.
[13] It will do you much good.

and to fly in the air, so it was natural for him to feed on the choicest and most expensive food, prepared by highly paid cooks, to wear the most comfortable and most expensive clothing, to drive with the best and fastest horses; and that, therefore, all these things should be ready found for him. Besides this, Count Ivan Mikhaylich considered that the more money he could get out of the Treasury by all sorts of means, the more Orders he had, up to and including the diamond-mounted insignia of something or other, and the oftener he spoke to highly placed individuals of both sexes, so much the better it was.

Everything else, compared to these dogmas, Count Ivan Mikhaylich considered insignificant and uninteresting. Everything else might be as it was, or just the reverse. Count Ivan Mikhaylich had lived and acted according to these lights for forty years, and at the end of that time he reached the position of a Minister of State.

The chief qualities that enabled him to reach that position were, first, his capacity for understanding the meaning of documents and laws, and for drawing up, though clumsily, intelligible State papers, and for spelling them correctly; secondly, his very stately appearance, which enabled him, when necessary, to seem not only extremely proud, but unapproachable and majestic, while at other times he could be abjectly and almost passionately servile; and, thirdly, the absence of any general principles or rules of morality either personal or administrative, this making it possible for him either to agree or disagree with anybody according to what was wanted at the time. When acting thus, his only endeavour was to sustain the appearance of good breeding, and not to seem too plainly inconsistent. Whether his actions were moral or not in themselves, and whether they would result in the highest welfare or the greatest evil for the whole of the Russian Empire, or even the entire world, was quite indifferent to him.

When he became a Minister, not only those dependent on him (and there were a great many of them) and people connected with him, but many strangers and even he himself, were convinced that he was a very clever statesman. But after some time had passed and he had accomplished nothing and elucidated nothing, and when, in accordance with the law of the struggle for existence, others like himself, stately and unprincipled officials who had learnt to write and understand documents, displaced him, it became plain to every one that he was not only far from clever, but was, in fact, a shallow, badly educated, self-assured man, whose ideas scarcely reached the level of the leading articles in the Conservative papers. It became evident that there was nothing in him to distinguish him from those other badly educated and self-assured officials who had elbowed him out; and he himself saw this. But it did not shake his conviction that he had to receive a great deal of money from the Treasury every year, and new decorations for his dress-clothes. This conviction was so firm that no one had the courage to refuse him these things, and he received yearly, partly in the form of a pension, partly as salary for being a member of a Government institution and chairman of all kinds of committees and councils, several tens of thousands of rubles, besides the right—highly prized by him— of sewing all sorts of new cords to his shoulders and trousers, and receiving ribbons and enamelled stars to fix on his dress-clothes. In consequence of this Count Ivan Mikhaylich had very high connections.

Count Ivan Mikhaylich listened to Nekhlyudov as he was wont to listen to the reports of the permanent secretary of his department, and, having heard him, said he would give him two notes, one of them to Senator Wolf, of the Appeal Department.

"All sorts of things are reported of him, but *dans tous les cas c'est un homme très comme il faut*,"[1] he said. "He is indebted to me, and will do all he can."

The other note Count Ivan Mikhaylich gave Nekhlyudov was to an influential member of the Petition Committee. The story of Theodosia Birukova as told by Nekhlyudov interested him very much. When Nekhlyudov said that he thought of writing to the Empress about it, the Count replied that it certainly was a very touching story, and might, if occasion presented itself, be told her, but he could not promise. Let the petition be handed in in proper form. Should there be an opportunity, and if a *petit comité* were called for Thursday, he thought he would tell her the story. As soon as Nekhlyudov had received these two notes, and a note to Mariette from his aunt, he at once set off to the different addresses.

First he went to Mariette's. He had known her as a girl in her teens, the daughter of an aristocratic but not wealthy family, and knew she had married a man whom Nekhlyudov had heard badly spoken of, but who was making a career; and, as usual, he felt it hard to ask a favour of a man he did not respect. In such cases he always experienced an inner dissension and dissatisfaction, and wavered whether to ask the favour or not; and always decided to ask. Besides feeling in a false position among a set he no longer considered he belonged to, but who yet regarded him as being one of themselves, he now felt himself again in an old accustomed rut, and, in spite of himself, yielded to the thoughtless and immoral tone reigning in that circle. He felt this already at his aunt's, and when speaking to her about most serious matters had dropped into a bantering tone.

---

[1] In any case he is a thorough gentleman.

Petersburg, where he had not been for a long time, in general affected him with its usual physically invigorating and morally dulling effect.

Everything was so clean, so comfortably and well arranged, and the people were so lenient in moral matters, that life seemed very easy.

A fine, clean, and polite *izvozchik* drove him past fine, clean, polite policemen, along the fine, clean, watered streets, past fine, clean houses, to the house in which Mariette lived.

At the front door stood a pair of English horses with English harness, and an English-looking coachman in livery, with whiskers half down his cheeks, sat on the box, proudly holding a whip.

The doorkeeper, dressed in wonderfully clean livery, opened the door into the hall, where in still cleaner livery with gold cords stood the footman, with splendid whiskers well combed out, and an orderly on duty in a brand-new uniform.

"The General does not receive, and her Excellency does not receive either. She is just going to drive out."

Nekhlyudov took out Catherine Ivanovna's letter, and going up to a table on which lay a visitors' book began to write that he was sorry not to have been able to see any one. Then the footman went up the staircase, the doorkeeper went out and shouted to the coachman, and the orderly stood rigid with his arms at his side, following with his eyes a little, slight lady, who was coming down the stairs with rapid steps not at all in keeping with her grandeur.

Mariette had on a large hat with feathers, a black dress and cape, and new black gloves. Her face was covered by a veil. When she saw Nekhlyudov she raised the veil from a very pretty face with bright eyes that looked inquiringly at him.

"Ah, Prince Dmitry Ivanich Nekhlyudov," she said, with a soft, pleasant voice. "I should have known——"

"What! you even remember my name?"

"I should think so. Why, I and my sisters were even in love with you," she said in French. "But dear me, how you have altered. . . . Oh, what a pity I have to go out. Let us go up again," she said, and stopped, hesitating. Then she looked at the clock. "No, I can't. I am going to the Kamenskys' to attend a mass for the dead. The mother is terribly afflicted."

"Who are the Kamenskys?"

"Have you not heard? The son was killed in a duel. He fought Posen. He was the only son. Terrible! The mother is so afflicted."

"Yes, I heard something of it."

"No, I had better go, and you must come again to-night or to-morrow," she said, and went to the door with quick, light steps.

"I cannot come to-night," he said, going out after her; "but I have a request to make to you," and he looked at the pair of bays that were drawing close to the front door.

"What is it?"

"This is a letter from my aunt to you," said Nekhlyudov, handing her a narrow envelope with a large crest. "You'll find all about it there."

"I know Countess Catherine Ivanovna thinks I have some influence with my husband in his affairs. She is mistaken. I can do nothing and do not like to interfere. But, of course, for the Countess and you I am willing to break my rule. What is this business about?" she said, searching in vain for her pocket with her little black-gloved hand.

"There is a girl imprisoned in the fortress, and she is ill and innocent."

"What is her name?"

"Shustova—Lydia Shustova. It's in the note."

"All right; I'll try what I can do," she said, and she jumped lightly into her small, softly upholstered, open carriage, its brightly varnished splash-guards glistening in the sunshine, and opened her parasol. The footman got on the box and signed to the coachman to start. The carriage moved, but at that moment she touched the coachman with her parasol, and those slim-legged beauties, the bay mares, stopped, arching their beautiful necks tightened by bearing reins, and stepping from foot to foot.

"But you must come; only, please, without interested motives," and she looked at Nekhlyudov with a smile, the force of which she well knew; and, as if the performance was over and she were drawing the curtain, she dropped the veil over her face again. "All right," and she again touched the coachman with her parasol.

Nekhlyudov raised his hat, and the thoroughbred bays, slightly snorting, set off, their hoofs clattering on the stones, and the carriage rolled quickly and smoothly on its new rubber tyres, only now and then giving a jump over some unevenness of the road.

Chapter XVI

WHEN NEKHLYUDOV remembered the smile that had passed between him and Mariette, he shook his head.

"You have hardly had time to turn round before you are again drawn into this life," he thought, feeling that discord and doubt which usually oppressed him when he had to curry favour with people he did not respect.

After considering where to go next, so as not to have to retrace his steps, Nekhlyudov set off for the Senate. There he was shown into the office, where in the midst of a magnificent apartment he found a great many very polite and very clean officials. Nekhlyudov was told by the officials that Maslova's petition had been received and had been passed on, for consideration and report, to that same Senator Wolf to whom Nekhlyudov had a letter from his uncle.

"There will be a meeting of the Senate this week," one of the officials said to Nekhlyudov, "but Maslova's case will hardly come before that meeting unless by special request, in which case it might possibly be taken on Wednesday."

During the time Nekhlyudov waited in the office while the case was being looked up, the conversation in the Senate office was all about the duel, and he heard a detailed account of how the young man, Kamensky, had been killed. It was here he first heard the full facts of this case, which was the talk of all Petersburg. The story was this. Some officers were eating oysters and, as usual, drinking very much, when one of them said something ill-natured about the regiment to which Kamensky belonged, and Kamensky called him a liar. The other hit Kamensky. The next day they fought. Kamensky was wounded in the stomach and died two hours later. The murderer and the seconds were arrested, but it was said that though they were under arrest in the guard-house they would be set free in a couple of weeks.

From the Senate Nekhlyudov drove to see an influential member of the Petition Committee, Baron Vorobev, who lived in a splendid house belonging to the Crown. The doorkeeper told Nekhlyudov in a severe tone that the Baron could not be seen except on his reception days; that he was with His Majesty the Emperor to-day, and the next day he would again have to deliver a report. Nekhlyudov left his uncle's letter with the doorkeeper and went on to see Senator Wolf.

Wolf had just had lunch when Nekhlyudov entered, and was, in his customary manner, helping digestion by smoking a cigar and pacing up and down the room. Vladimir Vasilich Wolf was certainly *un homme très comme il faut*, and prized this quality very highly, and regarded every one else from that altitude. He could not but esteem this quality of his very highly, because thanks to it alone he had made a brilliant career, the very career he desired—that is, by marriage he had obtained a fortune which brought him in eighteen thousand rubles a year, and by his own exertions he secured the post of a Senator. He considered himself not only *un homme très comme il faut* but also a man of knightly honour. By honour he understood not accepting secret bribes from private individuals. But he did not consider it dishonest to importune the Government for all sorts of allowances, fares, and travelling expenses, and to do anything the Government might require of him in return. To ruin hundreds of innocent people, to cause them to be imprisoned and exiled because they loved their own people and the religion of their fathers, as he had done when Governor of one of the provinces of Poland, he did not consider dishonourable, but even thought it noble, manly, and patriotic. Nor did he consider it dishonest to appropriate everything that belonged to his wife (who was in love with him) and his sister-in-law. On the contrary, he thought it a very wise way of arranging his family affairs. His family consisted of his commonplace wife, his sister-in-law, whose fortune he had appropriated by selling her estate and putting the money to his own account, and his meek, frightened, plain daughter, who lived a lonely, weary life, from which she had lately begun to look to Evangelicalism for relaxation: attending meetings at Aline's, and the Countess Catherine Ivanovna's. Wolf's son, an easy-going fellow, who at fifteen had grown a beard and begun to drink and to lead a fast life (which he continued to do until, when he was twenty, his father turned him out for not completing his studies), moved in a low set and compromised his father by making debts. His father had once paid a debt of two hundred and thirty rubles for him, then another of six hundred rubles, but this time warned the son that he did it for the last time, and that if he did not reform he would be turned out of the house and all further intercourse between him and his family would cease. The son did not reform, but made a debt of a thousand rubles, and took the liberty of telling his father that life at home was a torment anyhow. Then Wolf announced to his son that he might go where he pleased—that he was no son of his any longer. Since then Wolf pretended he had no son, and no one at home dared speak to him about his son, and Vladimir Vasilich Wolf was firmly convinced that he had arranged his family life in the best way.

When Nekhlyudov was shown in, Wolf stopped pacing up and down his study, and greeted Nekhlyudov with a friendly though slightly ironical smile, which was his involuntary way of showing how *comme il faut* he was, and how superior to the majority of men. He read the note which Nekhlyudov handed to him.

"Please take a seat, and excuse me if, with your permission, I continue to walk up and down," he said, putting his hands into his coat-pockets, and beginning again to walk with light soft steps across his large study furnished in a severely correct style.

"Very pleased to make your acquaintance, and of course very glad to do anything that Count Ivan Mikhaylich wishes," he said, blowing the fragrant blue smoke out of his mouth and removing his cigar carefully so as not to drop the ash.

"I should only like to ask that the case might come on soon, so that if the prisoner has to go to Siberia she might set off early," said Nekhlyudov.

"Yes, yes, with one of the first steamers from Nizhny. I know," said

Wolf, with his patronising smile, always knowing in advance whatever one wanted to tell him. "What is the prisoner's name?"

"Maslova."

Wolf went up to the table and looked at paper that lay with other business papers on a file.

"Yes, yes, Maslova. All right, I will ask the others. We will hear the case on Wednesday."

"Then may I telegraph to the advocate?"

"The advocate! What's that for? But if you like, why not?"

"The causes for appeal may be insufficient," said Nekhlyudov, "but I think the case will show that the sentence was passed owing to a misunderstanding."

"Yes, yes; it may be so, but the Senate cannot decide the case on its merits," said Wolf severely, looking at the ash of his cigar. "The Senate only considers the exactness of the application of the laws and their right interpretation."

"But this, I think, is an exceptional case."

"I know, I know! All cases are exceptional. We shall do our duty. That's all." The ash was still holding on, but there was a crack and it was in danger of falling.

"Are you often in Petersburg?" said Wolf, holding his cigar so that the ash should not fall. But the ash began to shake, and Wolf carefully carried it to the ashpan, into which it fell.

"What a terrible thing this Kamensky affair is," he said. "A splendid young man. The only son. . . . Especially the mother's position," he went on, repeating almost word for word what every one in Petersburg was at that time saying about Kamensky. Wolf spoke a little about the Countess Catherine Ivanovna and her enthusiasm for the new religious teaching, of which he neither approved nor disapproved, but which was evidently needless to him who was so *comme il faut*, and then he rang the bell.

Nekhlyudov bowed.

"If it is convenient, come and dine on Wednesday, and I will give you a decisive answer," said Wolf, extending his hand.

It was late, and Nekhlyudov returned to his aunt's.

Chapter XVII

THE COUNTESS Catherine Ivanovna's dinner-hour was half-past seven, and the dinner was served in a way quite new to Nekhlyudov. After they had placed the dishes on the table the footmen left the room and the diners helped themselves. The men would not let the ladies undergo any exertion, but, as befitted the stronger sex, manfully took on themselves the burden of helping the ladies and themselves to food and drink. When one course was finished the Countess pressed the button of an electric bell fitted to the table, and the footmen stepped in noiselessly, quickly carried away the dishes, changed the plates, and brought in the next course. The dinner was very choice, the wines very costly, A French *chef* was working in the large, light kitchens, with two white-clad assistants. There were six persons at dinner: the Count and Countess, their son (a surly officer in the Guards who sat with his elbows on the table), Nekhlyudov, a French companion, and the Count's chief steward, who had come up from the country. Here, too, the conversation was about the duel, and opinions were expressed as to the Emperor's view of the case. It was known that the Emperor was very much grieved for the mother's sake—and all were grieved for her; and as it was also known that the Emperor did not mean to be very severe with the murderer, who had defended the honour of his uniform, everybody was also lenient to the officer who had defended the honour of his uniform. Only the Countess Catherine Ivanovna, with her free thoughtlessness, expressed her disapproval.

"They get drunk, and kill unobjectionable young men. I should not forgive them on any account," she said.

· "Now, that's a thing I cannot understand," said the Count.

"I know that you never can understand what I say," the Countess began, and turning to Nekhlyudov, she added: "Everybody understands, except my husband. I say I am sorry for the mother, and I do not wish that he should kill and then be satisfied."

Then her son, who had been silent up to this point, took the murderer's part, and rudely attacked his mother, arguing that an officer could not behave in any other way, because his fellow-officers would condemn him and turn him out of the regiment. Nekhlyudov listened to the conversation without joining in. Having been an officer himself, he understood, though he did not agree with, young Charsky's arguments, and at the same time he could not help contrasting with the fate of the officer that of a handsome young convict whom he had seen in the prison, condemned to the mines for killing a man in a fight. Both had become murderers through drunkenness. The one, the peasant, having killed a man in a moment of passion, is parted from his wife and family, has chains on his legs, and with shaven head is going to hard labour in Siberia; while the officer sits in a fine room in the guard-house, eating a good dinner, drinking good wine, and reading books, and will be set free in a day or two to live as before, having become only more interesting by the affair.

Nekhlyudov said what he had been thinking, and at first his aunt, Catherine Ivanovna, seemed to agree with him, but a last she became as silent as the rest were, and Nekhlyudov felt that he had committed some kind of impropriety.

In the evening, soon after dinner, the large ballroom—with its high-backed carved chairs arranged in rows as for a meeting, and an arm-chair placed next to a little table with a bottle of water on it for the speaker—began to fill with people come to hear the foreigner, Kiese-wetter, preach.

Elegant equipages stopped at the front entrance. In the richly fur-nished room sat ladies in silks and velvets and lace, with false hair and laced in and padded figures, and with them were men in uniform and evening-dress, and some half-dozen common people: two men-servants, a shopkeeper, a footman, and a coachman.

Kiesewetter, a thick-set, grizzly man, spoke in English, and a thin young girl, wearing a pince-nez, translated into Russian promptly and well.

He said that our sins were so great, the punishment for them so great and so unavoidable, that it was impossible to live anticipating such punishment.

"Beloved brothers and sisters, let us for a moment consider what we are doing: how we are living, how we have offended against the all-loving Lord, and how we make Christ suffer; and we cannot but under-stand that there is no forgiveness possible for us, no escape, no salva-tion: that we are all doomed to destruction. A terrible fate—everlasting torment—awaits us," he said, with tears in his trembling voice. "Oh, how can we be saved, brothers? How can we be saved from this terri-ble, unquenchable fire? The house is in flames; there is no escape."

He was silent for a while, and real tears flowed down his cheeks. For about eight years now, every time he reached this part of his address, which he himself liked so well, he felt a choking in his throat and an irritation in his nose, and tears came into his eyes; and these tears touched him still more.

Sobs were heard in the room. The Countess Catherine Ivanovna sat with her elbows on an inlaid table, leaning her head on her hands, and her fat shoulders were shaking. The coachman looked with fear and surprise at the German, feeling as if he with the pole of his carriage were about to run him down and the foreigner would not move out of his way. All sat in attitudes similar to that which Catherine Ivanovna had assumed. Wolf's daughter, a thin, fashionably-dressed girl, very like her father, knelt with her face in her hands.

The orator suddenly uncovered his face, and smiled a very real-looking smile, such as actors express joy with, and began again in a sweet, gentle voice:—

"Yet there is a way to be saved. Here it is—a joyful, easy way. Salvation is in the blood shed for us by the only Son of God, who gave Himself up to torments for our sake. His sufferings, His blood, will save us. Brothers and sisters," he said, again with tears in his voice, "let us praise the Lord, who has given His only begotten Son for the redemption of the world. His holy blood——"

Nekhlyudov felt so deeply disgusted that he rose silently, and, frowning and keeping back a groan of shame, he left on tiptoe and went to his room.

Chapter XVIII

NEXT DAY, as soon as Nekhlyudov had finished dressing, and was about to go to down, the footman brought him a card from the Moscow advocate. The advocate had come to Petersburg on business of his own, and also, if Maslova's case was to be heard soon, to be present when it was considered by the Senate. Nekhlyudov's telegram had crossed him on the way. Having found out from Nekhlyudov when the case was going to be heard, and which Senators were to be present, he smiled.

"Exactly, all the three types of Senators," he said. "Wolf is a Petersburg official; Skovorodnikov is a theoretical jurist; and Bay a practical jurist—and therefore the most alive of them all," said the advocate. "There is most hope of him. Well, and how about the Petition Committee?"

"Oh, I'm going to Baron Vorobev to-day. I could not get an audience with him yesterday."

"Do you know why he is 'Baron' Vorobev?" said the advocate, noticing the slightly ironical stress Nekhlyudov placed on this foreign title in connection with so very Russian a surname. "It is because the Emperor Paul rewarded the grandfather—I think he was a Court footman—by giving him this title. He managed to please him in some way, so he made him a Baron. 'It's my wish, so don't gainsay me!' And so there's a 'Baron' Vorobev, and very proud of the title. He is a dreadful old humbug."

"Well, I'm going to see him," said Nekhlyudov.

"That's good; we can go together. I will give you a lift."

As they were starting, a footman met Nekhlyudov in the ante-room, and handed him a note from Mariette: —

Pour vous faire plaisir, j'ai agi tout à fait contre mes principes, et j'ai intercédé auprés de mon mari pour votre protégée. Il se trouve que cette personne peut être relâchée immédiatement. Mon mari a écrit au commandant. Venez donc disinterestedly. *Je vous attends.*[1]   ˉ M."

"Just fancy!" said Nekhlyudov to the advocate. "Is this not dreadful? A woman whom they have kept in solitary confinement for seven months turns out to be quite innocent, and only a word was needed to get her released."

"That's always so. Well, anyhow, you have succeeded in getting what you wanted."

"Yes, but this success grieves me. Just think what must be going on there. Why have they been keeping her?"

"Oh, it's best not to look too deeply into it. Well, then, shall I give you a lift?" said the advocate, as they left the house, and a fine carriage that the advocate had hired drove up to the door. "It's Baron Vorobev you are going to see?"

The advocate told the driver where to go, and the two fine horses quickly brought Nekhlyudov to the house in which the Baron lived. The Baron was at home. A young official in uniform, with a long, thin neck, a very prominent Adam's apple, and an extremely light walk, was in the first room with two ladies.

"Your name, please?" asked the young man with the Adam's apple, stepping across from the ladies to Nekhlyudov with extreme lightness and grace.

Nekhlyudov gave his name.

"The Baron has spoken about you. In a moment," said the young man, the Baron's adjutant, and went out through an inner door. He returned, leading a weeping lady dressed in mourning. With her bony fingers the lady was trying to pull her tangled veil over her face in order to hide her tears.

"Come in, please," said the young man to Nekhlyudov, lightly stepping up to the door of the study and holding it open. When Nekhlyudov entered he saw before him a thick-set man of medium height, with short hair, in a frock-coat, sitting in an armchair opposite a large writing-table, with a jovial expression.

The kindly, rosy-red face, striking by its contrast with the white hair, moustache, and beard, turned towards Nekhlyudov with a friendly smile.

---

[1] To please you I have acted quite against my principles, and have interceded with my husband for your protégée. It turns out that this person can be set free immediately. My husband has written to the Commander. Come then, disinterestedly. I expect you.

"Very glad to see you. Your mother and I were old acquaintances and friends. I have seen you as a boy, and later on as an officer. Sit down and tell me what I can do for you. . . . Yes, yes," he said, shaking his cropped white head, while Nekhlyudov was telling him Theodosia's story. "Go on, go on. I quite understand. It is certainly very touching. And have you handed in the petition?"

"I have got the petition ready," Nekhlyudov said, getting it out of his pocket; "but I thought of speaking to you first in hopes that the case would then get special attention."

"You have done very well. I shall certainly report it myself," said the Baron, unsuccessfully trying to put an expression of pity on his merry face. "Very touching! It is clear she was but a child; the husband treated her roughly and this repelled her, but as time went on they fell in love with each other. Yes, I will report the case."

"Count Ivan Mikhaylich was also going to speak about it."

Nekhlyudov had hardly got these words out when the Baron's face changed.

"You had better hand in the petition to the office, after all, and I will do what I can," he said.

At this moment the young official again entered the room, evidently showing off his elegant manner of walking.

"That lady is asking if she may say a few words more."

"Well, ask her in. . . . Ah, *mon cher*, how many tears we have to see shed! If only we could dry them all. One does all one can."

The lady entered.

"I forgot to ask you that he should not be allowed to give up his daughter, because he is ready——"

"I have already told you that I will do all I can."

"Baron, for the love of God! You will save a mother."

She seized his hand and began kissing it.

"Everything shall be done."

When the lady went out Nekhlyudov also began to take leave.

"We will do what we can. I will speak about it at the Ministry of Justice, and when we get their answer we will do what we can."

Nekhlyudov left the study, and went into the office again. Just as in the Senate office, he saw, in a splendid apartment, a number of very elegant officials—clean, polite, severely correct, and distinguished in dress and in speech.

"How many there are of them; how very many, and how well fed they all look. And what clean shirts and hands they all have, and how well all their boots are polished. Who does it for them? How comfortable they all are, as compared not only with the prisoners but even with the peasants!" These thoughts again involuntarily entered Nekhlyudov's mind.

Chapter XIX

THE MAN on whom it depended to ease the fate of the Petersburg prisoners was an old General of repute, a baron of German descent, who, as people said of him, had outlived his wits. He had received a profusion of Orders, but wore only one of them—the Order of the White Cross. He had received this Order, which he greatly prized, while serving in the Caucasus, because a number of Russian peasants, with cropped hair, dressed in uniforms and armed with guns and bayonets, had killed at his command more than a thousand men who were defending their liberty, their homes, and their families. Later on he served in Poland, and there also made Russian peasants commit many different crimes, and got more Orders and decorations for his uniform. Then he served somewhere else, and now that he was a weak old man he held this position, which ensured him a good house, an income, and respect. He strictly observed all the regulations which were prescribed "from above," and was very zealous in the fulfilment of these regulations, to which he ascribed a special importance, considering that everything else in the world might be changed except the regulations prescribed "from above." His duty was to keep political prisoners—men and women—in solitary confinement in such a way that half of them perished within ten years: some going out of their minds, some dying of consumption, some committing suicide by starving themselves, cutting their veins with bits of glass, hanging themselves, or burning themselves to death.

The old General was not ignorant of this, for it all happened before his eyes; but these things no more touched his conscience than accidents caused by thunderstorms, floods, etc. These things followed as a consequence of the fulfilment of regulations prescribed "from above" by His Imperial Majesty. These regulations had inevitably to be fulfilled, and hence it was absolutely useless to think of the consequences of that fulfilment. The old General did not even allow himself to think of such things, counting it his patriotic duty as a soldier not to think of them for fear of becoming weak in the execution of the obligations that seemed to him so very important. Once a week the old General made the round of the cells—one of the duties of his position—and asked the prisoners if they had any requests to make. The prisoners had all sorts of requests. He listened to them quietly in impenetrable silence, and never fulfilled any of their requests, because they were all incompatible with the regulations.

Just as Nekhlyudov drove up to the old General's house, the chime of treble bells in the belfry clock rang out "How great is the Lord," and then struck two. The sound of these chimes brought back to Nekhlyudov's mind what he had read in the memoirs of the Decembrists,[1] of how this sweet music, repeated every hour, re-echoes in the hearts of those imprisoned for life.

Meanwhile the old General was sitting in his darkened drawing-room at an inlaid table, turning a tea-saucer on a sheet of paper with the aid of a young artist, the brother of one of his subordinates. The thin, moist, weak fingers of the artist were pressed against the wrinkled and stiff-jointed fingers of the old General, and the hands joined in this manner were moving together with the saucer over a sheet of paper on which all the letters of the alphabet were written. The saucer was answering questions put by the General as to how souls will recognize each other after death.

When Nekhlyudov sent in his card by an orderly acting as footman, the soul of Joan of Arc was speaking by the aid of the saucer. The soul of Joan of Arc had already spelt, letter by letter, these words: "They will know each other by," and these words had been written down. When the orderly came in the saucer had stopped on *b* and on *y*, and had then began jerking about hither and thither. This jerking was caused by the General's opinion that the next letter should be *b*—that Joan of Arc ought to say that the souls will know each other by "being cleansed" of all that is earthly, or something of that sort; clashing with the opinion of the artist, who thought the next letter should be *l*—that is, that the souls should know each other by "light" emanating from their astral bodies. The General, with his bushy grey eyebrows gravely contracted, sat gazing at the hands on the saucer, and, imagining that it was moving of its own accord, kept pulling the saucer towards *b*. The pale-faced young artist, with his thin hair combed back behind his ears, was looking with his lifeless blue eyes into a dark corner of the drawing-room, nervously moving his lips and pulling the saucer towards *l*.

The General made a wry face at the interpretation, but after a moment's pause he took the card, put on his pince-nez, and, uttering a groan, rose, in spite of the pain in his loins, to his full height, rubbing his numb fingers.

"Ask him into the study."

"With your excellency's permission I will finish alone," said the artist, rising. "I feel the presence."

"All right, finish alone," the General said, severely and decidedly,

---

[1] The Decembrists were a group who attempted to put an end to absolutism in Russia by means of a military revolt, at the time of the accession of Nicholas the First, in December 1825.

and stepped quickly, with big, firm, and measured strides, into his study.

"Very glad to see you," said the General to Nekhlyudov, uttering the friendly words in a gruff tone and pointing to an armchair by the side of the writing-table. "Have you been in Petersburg long?"

Nekhlyudov replied that he had only just arrived.

"Is the Princess, your mother, well?"

"My mother is dead."

"Pardon me; I am very sorry. My son told me he had met you."

The General's son was making the same kind of career for himself that the father had done, and, having passed the Military Academy, was now serving in the Inquiry Office, and was very proud of his duties there. He had the management of the Government spies.

"Why, I served with your father. We were friends—comrades. And you; are you also in the service?"

"No, I am not."

The General bent his head disapprovingly.

"I have a request to make, General."

"Ver—y pleased. In what way can I be of service to you?"

"If my request is out of place, pray pardon me. But I am obliged to make it."

"What is it?"

"There is a certain Gurkevich imprisoned in the fortress; his mother asks for an interview with him, or at least to be allowed to send him some books."

The General expressed neither satisfaction nor dissatisfaction at Nekhlyudov's request, but bending his head on one side he closed his eyes as if considering. In reality he was not considering anything, and was not even interested in Nekhlyudov's requests, well knowing that he would answer them according to the law. He was simply resting mentally and not thinking at all.

"You see," he said at last, "this does not rest with me. There is a regulation, confirmed by his Majesty, concerning interviews; and as to books, we have a library of suitable books, and they may have what is permitted."

"Yes, but he wants scientific books; he wishes to study."

"Don't you believe it," growled the General, and was silent for a while. "It is not study he wants; it is merely restlessness."

"But what is to be done? They must occupy their time somehow in their hard condition," said Nekhlyudov.

"They are always complaining," said the General. "We know them."

He spoke of them in a general way, as of a specially bad race of men.

"They have conveniences here which can be found in few places of confinement," said the General. And as though justifying himself he begun to enumerate the comforts the prisoners enjoyed, as if the aim of the institution were to give those imprisoned there a comfortable home.

"It is true it used to be rather rough, but now they are very well kept here," he continued. "They have three courses for dinner—and one of them meat: cutlets or rissoles. On Sundays they get a fourth—a sweet dish. God grant every Russian may live as well as they do."

Like all old people, the General, having once got on to a familiar topic, enumerated the various proofs he had often given before of the unreasonableness of the prisoners' demands and of their ingratitude.

"They get books on religious subjects, and old journals. We have a library. But they rarely read. At first they seem interested, later on the new books remain with not half the pages cut, and the old ones with their leaves unturned. We tried them," said the old General, with the dim likeness of a smile. "We put bits of paper in on purpose, and they remained just as they had been placed. Writing, too, is not forbidden," he continued. "A slate is provided, and a slate pencil, so that they can write as a pastime. They can wipe the slate and write again. But they don't write, either. Oh, they very soon get quite tranquil. At first they seem restless, but later on they even grow fat and become very quiet." Thus spoke the General, never suspecting the terrible meaning of his words.

Nekhlyudov listened to the hoarse old voice, looked at the stiff limbs, the lustreless eyes under the grey brows, at the old, clean-shaven, flabby jaw supported by the collar of the military uniform, at the white cross this man was so proud of, chiefly because he had gained it by exceptionally cruel and extensive slaughter—and knew that it was useless to reply to the old man or to explain to him the meaning of his own words. He made another effort, and asked about the prisoner Shustova, for whose release, as he was informed that morning, orders had been given.

"Shustova—Shustova? I cannot remember all their names, there are so many of them," he said, as if reproaching them because they were so many. He rang, and ordered his secretary to be called. While waiting for the latter, he began persuading Nekhlyudov to enter the service, saying that "honest noblemen" (counting himself among the number) "were particularly needed by the Tsar,—and the country," he added, evidently only to round off his sentence. "I am old, yet I am serving still as well as my strength allows."

The secretary, a dry, emaciated man, with restless, intelligent eyes, came in and reported that Shustova was imprisoned in some strange fortified place, and that he had received no orders concerning her.

"When we get the order we shall let her out the same day. We do not want to keep them; we do not value their visits so much," said the General, with another attempt at a playful smile, which only distorted his old features.

Nekhlyudov rose, trying to keep from expressing the mixed feelings of repugnance and pity which he felt towards this terrible old man. The old man on his part felt that he must not be too severe on the thoughtless and evidently misguided son of his old comrade, and should not let him go without advice.

"Good-bye, my dear fellow; do not take it amiss. It is my affection that makes me say it. Do not keep company with such people as we have here. There are no innocent ones among them. All these people are most immoral. We know them," he said, in a tone that admitted no possibility of doubt.

And he did not doubt; not because the thing was so, but because if it were not so, he would have to admit himself to be, not a noble hero living out the last days of a good life, but a scoundrel, who had sold, and still in his old age continued to sell, his conscience.

"Best of all, go and serve," he continued; "the Tsar needs honest men,—and the country," he added. "Why, supposing I and the others refused to serve, as you are doing? Who would be left? Here we are finding fault with the order of things, and yet not wishing to help the Government."

With a deep sigh Nekhlyudov made a low bow, shook the large, bony hand condescendingly stretched out to him, and left the room.

The General shook his head disapprovingly, and, rubbing his loins, he returned to the drawing-room where the artist was waiting for him. The answer given by the soul of Joan of Arc was already written down. The General put on his pince-nez and read: "They will know each other by light emanating from their astral bodies."

"Ah," said the General with approval, and closed his eyes. "But how is one to recognise them, if the light of all is alike?" he asked, and again crossed fingers with the artist on the saucer.

The *izvozchik* drove Nekhlyudov out of the gate.

"It's dull here, sir," he said, turning to Nekhlyudov. "I almost wished to drive off without waiting for you."

Nekhlyudov agreed; "Yes, it is dull," and he took a deep breath, and looked with a sense of relief at the grey clouds that were floating in the sky, and at the glistening ripples made by the boats and steamers on the Neva.

Chapter XX

THE NEXT day Maslova's case was to be heard at the Senate, and Nekhlyudov and the advocate met at the majestic entrance to the building, where several carriages were waiting. Ascending the magnificent and imposing staircase to the first floor, Fanarin, who knew all the ins and outs of the place, turned to the left and entered through a door which bore above it the date of the introduction of the Code of Laws.

After taking off his overcoat in a narrow room he found out from the attendant that the Senators were all there, the last to arrive having just come in. Fanarin, in his swallow-tail coat, a white tie above the white shirt-front, and a self-confident smile on his lips, passed into the next room, where to the right were a large cupboard and a table, and to the left a winding staircase, which an elegant official in uniform with a portfolio under his arm was descending. In this room an old man with long white hair and a patriarchal appearance attracted every one's attention. He wore a short coat and grey trousers. Two attendants stood respectfully beside him. The old man with white hair entered the cupboard and shut himself in.

Fanarin noticed a fellow-advocate dressed in the same way as himself, with a white tie and dress-coat, and at once entered into animated conversation with him. Nekhlyudov was meanwhile examining the people in the room. The public consisted of about fifteen persons, of whom two were ladies—a young one with a pince-nez, and an old, grey-haired one.

A case of libel was to be heard that day, and therefore the public were more numerous than usual—chiefly persons belonging to the journalistic world.

The usher, a red-cheeked, handsome man in a splendid uniform, came up to Fanarin with a paper in his hand and asked him his business. When he heard that it was Maslova's case he noted something down and walked away. Then the cupboard door opened and the old man with the patriarchal appearance stepped out, no longer in a short coat, but with glittering metal plates on his breast and in a gold-trimmed attire which made him look like a bird.

This funny costume seemed to make the old man himself feel uncomfortable, and walking faster than his wont he hurried out of the door opposite the entrance.

"That is Bay, a most estimable man," Fanarin said to Nekhlyudov, and then, having introduced him to his colleague, he explained the case that was about to be heard, which he considered very interesting.

The hearing of the case soon began, and Nekhlyudov, with the rest of the audience, went to the left and entered the Senate chamber. They all, including Fanarin, took their places behind a railing. Only the Petersburg advocate went up to a desk in front of the railing.

The Senate chamber was not as big as the Criminal Court, and was more simply furnished, though the table in front of the Senate was covered with crimson gold-trimmed velvet instead of green cloth; but the attributes of all places of judgment were there: the mirror of justice; the icon, the emblem of hypocrisy; and the Emperor's portrait, the emblem of servility.

The usher announced, in the usual solemn manner, "The Court is coming." Every one rose in the usual way, and the Senators, in their uniforms, entered and sat down on high-backed chairs and leant on the table trying to appear natural, just in the same way as way as the judges in the Criminal Court. There were four Senators present—Nikitin, who took the chair, a clean-shaven man with a narrow face and steely eyes; Wolf, with significantly compressed lips, and small white hands, with which he kept turning over the pages of the business papers; Skovorodnikov, a heavy, fat, pock-marked man—the learned jurist; and Bay, the patriarchal-looking man who had arrived last.

With the Senators entered the chief secretary and public prosecutor, a lean, clean-shaven young man of medium height, very dark complexion, and sad, black eyes. Nekhlyudov knew him at once, in spite of his curious uniform and the fact that he had not seen him for six years. He had been one of Nekhlyudov's best friends in their student days.

"The public prosecutor, Selenin?" Nekhlyudov asked, turning to the advocate.

"Yes. Why?"

"I know him well. He is a fine fellow."

"And a good public prosecutor too—business-like. Now, he is the man you should have interested."

"He will act according to his conscience in any case," said Nekhlyudov, recalling the intimate relation and friendship between himself and Selenin, and his attractive qualities—purity, honesty, and good breeding in its best sense.

"Yes. It is too late now, anyhow," whispered Fanarin, who was listening to the report of the case that had commenced.

The case was an appeal against a judgment given by the Court of Appeal, which had confirmed a decision given in a District Court.

Nekhlyudov listened and tried to make out the meaning of what was going on; but, just as in the Criminal Court, so now, his difficulty was that it was not the evidently chief point but some side-issues which were being discussed. The case was that of a newspaper which had published an exposure of a fraud arranged by a director of a limited liability company. It would seem that the only important point was whether the director of the company really was abusing his trust, and, if so, to stop him from doing it. But the questions under consideration were whether the editor had a legal right to publish this article, and what he had been guilty of in publishing it—slander or libel,—and in what way slander included libel, or libel included slander, and something rather incomprehensible to ordinary people about all sorts of statues and resolutions passed by some General Department.

The only things clear to Nekhlyudov were, that, in spite of what Wolf had so strenuously insisted on the day before (that the Senate could not try a case on its merits), he was evidently in this case strongly in favour of repealing the decision of the Court of Justice, and that Selenin, contrary to his characteristic reserve, stated the opposite opinion with quite unexpected warmth. The warmth evinced by the usually self-controlled Selenin, which surprised Nekhlyudov, was due to his knowledge of the director's shadiness in money matters, and to the fact, which had accidentally come to his ears, that Wolf had been to a grand dinner-party at the swindler's house only a few days before.

Now, when Wolf reported the case, guardedly enough but with evident bias, Selenin became excited, and expressed his opinion with too much nervous irritation for an ordinary case. It was clear that Selenin's speech offended Wolf. He grew red, moved in his chair, made silent gestures of surprise, and retired with the other Senators to the debating-room looking very dignified and offended.

"What case is it you have come about?" the usher asked again, addressing Fanarin.

"I have already told you: Maslova's case."

"Yes, just so. It is to be heard to-day, but——"

"But what?" the advocate asked.

"Well, you see, they did not expect to hear any argument upon it, so that the Senators will hardly come out again after pronouncing their decision on the present case. But I will inform them."

"What do you mean?"

"I'll inform them; I'll inform them." And the usher again put something down on his paper.

The Senators really had intended to pronounce their decision in the libel case, and then, without leaving the debating-room, to finish the other business, including Maslova's case, over their tea and cigarettes.

Chapter XXI

AS SOON as the Senators were seated round the table in the debating-room, Wolf with great animation began to bring forward all the reasons in favour of a repeal. The president, an ill-natured man at best, was in a particularly bad humour that day. His thoughts were concentrated on the words he had written down in his diary on the occasion when not he but Viglanov was appointed to an important post he had long coveted. It was the president Nikitin's honest conviction that his opinions of the officials of the two higher grades, with which he was in connection, would furnish valuable material to future historians. He had written a chapter the day before in which certain officials of those two highest grades were soundly rated for preventing him, as he expressed it, from averting the ruin towards which the present rulers of Russia were driving the country; which simply meant that they had prevented his getting a higher salary. And now he was considering what a new light for posterity this chapter would shed on events.

"Yes, certainly," he said, in reply to the words addressed to him by Wolf, without listening to them.

Bay was listening to Wolf with a sad face, and drawing a garland on the paper that lay before him. Bay was a Liberal of the very first water. He held sacred the Liberal traditions of the sixth decade of this century, and if he ever overstepped the limits of strict neutrality it was always in the direction of Liberalism. So in this case: besides the fact that the swindling director who was appealing was a bad lot, the prosecution of a journalist for libel, tending as it did to restrict the freedom of the press, in itself inclined Bay to reject the appeal.

When Wolf concluded his arguments Bay stopped drawing his garland, and in a sad and gentle voice (he was sad to feel himself obliged to demonstrate such truisms) showed concisely, simply, and convincingly that the appellant had no case, and then, bending his white head, he continued drawing on his garland.

Skovorodnikov, who sat opposite Wolf, and with his fat fingers kept stuffing his beard and moustache into his mouth, stopped chewing his beard as soon as Bay was silent, and said with a loud grating voice that, notwithstanding the fact of the director being a terrible scoundrel, he would have been in favour of repealing the sentence had there been any legal grounds for it, but as there were none he was of Bay's opinion. He was glad to put this spoke in Wolf's wheel.

The president agreed with Skovorodnikov, and the appeal was rejected.

Wolf was dissatisifed, especially because it was like being caught acting with dishonest partiality; so he pretended to be indifferent, and unfolding the document dealing with Maslova's case he became engrossed in it. Meanwhile the Senators rang and ordered tea, and began talking about the event that, together with the duel, was occupying all Petersburg. It was the case of the chief of a

Government department, who was accused of the crime provided for in Article 995.

"What nastiness," said Bay, with disgust.

"Why, where is the harm of it? I can show you a Russian book containing the project of a German writer, openly proposing that it should not be considered a crime, and that men should be allowed to marry men," said Skovorodnikov, drawing in greedily the fumes of the crumpled cigarette which he held between his fingers close to the palm; and he laughed boisterously.

"Impossible!" said Bay.

"I will show it you," said Skovorodnikov, giving the full title of the book, and even the date and place of its publication.

"I hear he has been appointed governor to some town in Siberia."

"That's splendid! The bishop will meet him with a crucifix. They ought to appoint a bishop of the same sort," said Skovorodnikov. "I could recommend them one," and he threw the end of his cigarette into his saucer, and again stuffed as much of his beard and moustache as he could into his mouth and began chewing them.

The usher came in and reported the advocate's and Nekhlyudov's desire to be present at the examination of Maslova's case.

"This case," said Wolf, "is quite romantic," and he told them what he knew about Nekhlyudov's relations with Maslova. When they had talked a little about it and finished their tea and cigarettes, the Senators returned to the Senate chamber and proclaimed their decision in the libel case, and then began to hear Maslova's appeal.

Wolf, with his thin voice, reported Maslova's appeal very fully, but again not without some bias and an evident wish for the repeal of the sentence.

"Have you anything to add?" the chairman said, turning to Fanarin. Fanarin rose, and standing with his broad white chest expanded, proved point by point with wonderful exactness and persuasiveness how the Criminal Court had in six points strayed from the exact meaning of the law; and besides this he touched, though briefly, on the merits of the case and on the crying injustice of the sentence. The tone of his short but strong speech was one of apology to the Senators, who, with their penetration and judicial wisdom, could not help seeing and understanding it all better than he, his speech being only necessary in order to fulfil the duty he had undertaken.

After Fanarin's speech one might have thought that there could not remain the least doubt that the Senate ought to repeal the decision of the Court. When he had concluded his speech, Fanarin looked round with a smile of triumph, seeing which Nekhlyudov felt sure that the case was won. But when he looked at the Senators he saw that Fanarin smiled and triumphed alone. The Senators and the public prosecutor did not smile or triumph, but looked like people who were wearied and thinking "We have often heard the like of you—it is all in vain," and were only too glad when he stopped and ceased uselessly detaining them. Immediately after the end of the advocate's speech the president turned to the public prosecutor. Selenin briefly and clearly expressed himself in favour of leaving the decision of the court unaltered, finding all the reasons for revision inadequate. After this the Senators retired to the debating-room. They were divided in their opinion. Wolf was in favour of allowing the appeal. Bay, when he understood the case, took up the same side with fervour, vividly presenting to his companions the scene at the Court as he himself clearly saw it. Nikitin, who was always on the side of severity and formality, took the other side. All depended on Skovorodnikov's vote, and he voted for rejecting the appeal, chiefly because Nekhlyudov's determination to marry the woman on moral grounds was extremely repugnant to him.

Skovorodnikov was a materialist and a Darwinian, and counted every manifestation of abstract morality, or, worse still, religion, not only as despicable folly but as a personal affront to himself. All this bother about a prostitute, with the presence of a celebrated advocate and Nekhlyudov in the Senate, were in the highest degree repugnant to him. So he stuffed his beard into his mouth and made faces, and very skilfully pretended to know nothing of this case, excepting that the reasons for the appeal were insufficient, and that he, therefore, agreed with the president that the decision of the Court should remain unaltered.

So the sentence remained unrepealed.

Chapter XXII

"TERRIBLE," SAID Nekhlyudov, as he went out into the waiting-room with the advocate, who was arranging the papers in his portfolio. "In a matter which is perfectly clear they attach importance only to the form, and decline to interfere. Terrible!"

"The case was spoiled in the Criminal Court," said the advocate.

"And Selenin, too, was in favour of the rejection. Terrible! terrible!" Nekhlyudov repeated. "What is to be done now?"

"We will appeal to His Imperial Majesty, and you can hand in the petition yourself while you are here. I will write it for you."

At this moment little Wolf, with his stars and uniform, came out into the waiting-room and approached Nekhlyudov. "It could not be helped, dear Prince. The reasons for an appeal were insufficient," he said, shrugging his narrow shoulders and closing his eyes, and then he went off.

After Wolf, Selenin came out too, having heard from the Senators that his old friend Nekhlyudov was there.

"Well, I never expected to see you here," he said, coming up to Nekhlyudov, and smiling only with his lips, while his eyes remained sad. "I did not know you were in Petersburg."

"And I did not know you were *Ober-Procureur.*"

"Assistant," corrected Selenin. "But how is it you are here in the Senate? I had heard, by the way, that you were in Petersburg. But what are you doing here?"

"Here? I am here because I hoped to find justice and save a woman innocently condemned."

"What woman?"

"The one whose case has just been decided."

"Oh! the Maslova case," said Selenin, suddenly remembering it. "The appeal had no grounds whatever."

"It is not the appeal; it's the woman, who is innocent, and is being punished."

Selenin sighed. "That may well be, but——"

"Not may be, but it is——"

"How do you know?"

"Because I was on the jury. I know how we made the mistake."

Selenin became thoughtful. "You should have made a statement at the time," he said.

"I did make a statement."

"It should have been put down in an official report. If this had been added to the petition for the appeal——"

"Yes, but still, as it is, the verdict is evidently absurd."

"The Senate has no right to say so. If the Senate took upon itself to revise the decisions of the Law Courts according to its own views as to whether those decisions were just in themselves, the verdict of the jury would lose all its meaning, not to mention that the Senate would have no basis to rest upon, and would run the risk of infringing justice rather than upholding it," said Selenin, calling to mind the case that had just been heard.

"All I know is that this woman is quite innocent, and that almost the last hope of saving her from an unmerited punishment is gone. The grossest injustice has been confirmed by the highest Court."

"It has not been confirmed. The Senate did not and cannot enter into the merits of the case itself," said Selenin, blinking his eyes. Always busy and rarely going out into society, he had evidently heard nothing of Nekhlyudov's romance. Nekhlyudov noticed this, and made up his mind that it was best to say nothing about his personal relations with Maslova.

"I suppose you are staying with your aunt," Selenin remarked, apparently wishing to change the subject. "She told me yesterday you were here, and invited me to meet you in the evening, when some foreign preacher was to give an address," and Selenin again smiled only with his lips.

"Yes, I was there, but left in disgust," said Nekhlyudov crossly, vexed that Selenin had changed the subject.

"Why with disgust? After all, it is a manifestation of religious feeling, though one-sided and sectarian," said Selenin.

"Why, it's only a kind of whimsical folly."

"Oh dear no. The curious thing is that we know the teaching of our own Church so little that we see some new kind of revelation in what are, after all, our own fundamental dogmas," said Selenin, as if hurrying to let his old friend know his present views.

Nekhlyudov looked at Selenin searchingly and with surprise, and Selenin dropped his eyes, in which appeared an expression not only of sadness but also of ill-will.

"Do you, then, believe in the dogmas of the Church?" Nekhlyudov asked.

"Of course I do," replied Selenin, gazing straight into Nekhlyudov's eyes with a lifeless look.

Nekhlyudov sighed. "It is strange," he said.

"However, we can have a talk some other time," said Selenin. . . . "I am coming," he added, in answer to the usher, who had respectfully approached him. "Yes, we must meet again," he went on with a sigh. "But shall I be able to find you? You will always find me in at seven o'clock dinner. My address is Nadezhdinskaya," and he gave the number. "Ah, time does not stand still," and he turned to go, smiling only with his lips.

"I will come if I can," said Nekhlyudov, feeling that a man once near and dear to him had, by this brief conversation, suddenly become strange, distant, and incomprehensible, if not hostile.

Chapter XXIII

WHEN NEKHLYUDOV knew Selenin as a student, he was a good son, a true friend, and for his years an educated man of the world with much tact, always elegant, handsome, and yet unusually truthful and honest. He learnt well, without much exertion and no pedantry, receiving gold medals for his essays. He considered the service of mankind, not only in words but in acts, to be the aim of his young life. He saw no other way of being useful to humanity than by serving the State. Therefore, as soon as he had completed his studies, he systematically examined all the activities to which he might devote his life, and deciding that he could be most useful in the Second Department of the Chancellery, where the laws are drawn up, he entered that branch of the public service. But, in spite of the most scrupulous and exact discharge of the duties demanded of him, this service did not satisfy his desire to be useful, nor could he awaken in himself the consciousness that he was doing "the right thing."

This dissatisfaction was so much increased by friction with his very small-minded and vain superior that he left the Chancellery and entered the Senate. It was better there, but the same dissatisfaction still pursued him; he felt it to be very different from what he had expected and from what ought to be.

While he was in the Senate his relations obtained for him the post of Gentleman of the Bedchamber, and he had to go in a carriage, dressed in an embroidered uniform and a white linen apron, to thank all sorts of people for having placed him in the position of a lackey. However much he tried, he could find no reasonable explanation for the existence of this post, and felt, more even than in the Senate, that it was not "the right thing"; and yet he could not refuse it for fear of offending those who felt sure they were giving him much satisfaction by this appointment, and because it flattered the lower part of his nature. It pleased him to see himself in a mirror dressed in his gold-embroidered uniform, and to accept the deference paid him by some people because of his position.

Something of the same kind happened when he married. A very brilliant match from a worldly point of view was arranged for him; and he married, chiefly because by refusing he would have hurt the feelings both of the young lady who wished to be married to him and of those who arranged the affair, and also because a marriage with a nice young girl of noble birth flattered his vanity and gave him pleasure. But this marriage very soon proved to be even less "the right thing" than the Government service and his position at Court.

After the birth of her first child the wife decided to have no more, and began leading that luxurious worldly life in which he now had to participate whether he liked it or not.

She was not particularly good-looking, was faithful to him, and seemed, in spite of all the efforts it cost her, to derive nothing but weariness from the life she led; yet she perseveringly continued to lead it, though it was poisoning her husband's life. And all his efforts to alter this life were shattered, as against a stone wall, by her convictions, which all her friends and relations supported, that all was as it should be.

The child, a little girl with bare legs and long golden curls, was a being perfectly foreign to him, chiefly because she was brought up quite otherwise than he wished her to be. There sprang up between the husband and wife the usual misunderstandings, reluctance to understand each other, and then a silent warfare, hidden from outsiders and tempered by decorum. All this made his life at home a burden, and it became even less "the right thing" than his service and his post.

But, above all, it was his attitude towards religion which was not "the right thing." Like every one of his set and his time, by the growth of his reason he broke without the least effort the fetters of the religious superstitions in which he was brought up, and was not even aware of the exact time when he gained his freedom. Being earnest and upright he did not, during his youth and intimacy with Nekhlyudov as a student, conceal his rejection of the State religion. But as years went on and he rose in the service, and especially at the time of the Conservative reaction in society, his spiritual freedom stood in his way. Apart from family pressure—especially when his father died and memorial services were held for him—and besides his mother's wish, partly backed by public opinion, that he should fast and prepare for communion, the Government service required that he should be present at all sorts of services, consecrations, thanksgivings, and the like. Hardly a day passed without some outward religious form having to be observed. With reference to these services he had to do one of two things: either pretend belief in something he did not believe in—and being truthful he could not do that—or, having made up his mind that all these external forms are false, so to alter his life that he should not be obliged to be present at such ceremonials. But to do what seemed so simple would have cost a great deal. Besides encountering the perpetual hostility of all those who were near to him, he would have to give up his whole position: throw up the service, and sacrifice all the usefulness which he thought he was now rendering to humanity by that service, and which he hoped to increase in the future. To make such a sacrifice one would have to be firmly convinced of being right. And he was firmly convinced he was right, as no educated man of our time can help being convinced who knows a little history, and knows how the religions, and especially Church-Christianity, originated. He could not but know that he was right in not acknowledging the truth of the Church teaching.

But under the stress of his daily life he, a truthful man, allowed a small falsehood to creep in. He said that in order to do justice to an unreasonable thing one has to study that unreasonable thing. It was a small falsehood, but it sank him into the big falsehood in which he was now engulfed.

Before putting to himself the question whether the orthodoxy in which he was born and bred contained the truth—that same orthodoxy which every one expected him to accept, and without which he could not continue his activity so useful to man—he had already decided the answer. And so, to clear up the question, he did not read Voltaire, Schopenhauer, Herbert Spencer, or Comte, but he read the philosophical works of Hegel and the religious works of Vinet and Homyakov, and he naturally found in them what he was looking for—something like peace of mind, and a vindication of that religious teaching in which he had been educated, which his reason had long ceased to accept, but without which his whole life was filled with unpleasantness that could all be removed by accepting the teaching.

And so he adopted all the usual sophisms which go to prove that a single human intellect cannot know the truth; that the truth is only revealed to an association of men, and can only be known by revelation, which revelation is kept by the Church, etc., and from that time forth, without being conscious of the lie, he managed, with a quiet mind, to be present at prayers and masses for the dead, to confess, to make signs of the cross in front of icons, and to continue in the service which gave him the feeling of being useful, and afforded him some relief from his joyless family life. Although he believed thus, he felt with his entire being that this religion of his, more than all else, was not "the right thing," and that is why his eyes always looked sad. And seeing Nekhlyudov whom he had known before all these lies had taken root within him, reminded him of what he had been; and, especially after he had hastily hinted at his present religious views, he felt more strongly than ever that all this was not "the right thing," and he became painfully sad. Nekhlyudov felt this also after the first joy of meeting his old friend had passed.

And so, though they promised each other to meet, they did not take any steps towards an interview, and did not again see each other during Nekhlyudov's stay in Petersburg.

Chapter XXIV

LEAVING THE Senate, Nekhlyudov and the advocate walked on together, the advocate having given the driver of his carriage orders to follow them. The advocate told Nekhlyudov the story of the chief of a Government department, about whom the Senators had been talking: how the thing was found out, and how the man, who according to law should have been sent to the mines, had been appointed governor of a town in Siberia. Having finished this story, with all its nastiness, he went on to relate with particular pleasure how several influential persons stole a lot of money collected for the erection of the ever unfinished monument they had passed that morning; also how the mistress of So-and-so won millions on the Stock Exchange, and how So-and-so agreed with So-and-so to sell him his wife. The advocate also began another story about a swindle and all sorts of crimes committed by persons in high places, who instead of being in prison sat on presidential chairs in different Government institutions. These tales, of which the advocate seemed to have an inexhaustible supply, gave him much pleasure, showing as they did with perfect clearness that his way of getting money was quite just and innocent compared to the means used by the highest officials in Petersburg. The advocate was therefore surprised when Nekhlyudov took an *izvozchik* before hearing the end of the story, said good-bye, and left him.

Nekhlyudov felt very sad. He was saddened chiefly by the rejection of the appeal by the Senate, confirming the senseless torments that the innocent Maslova was enduring, and also by the fact that this rejection made it still harder for him to unite his fate with hers. The terrible stories about existing evils, which the advocate had recounted with such relish, heightened his sadness, and so also did the cold, unkind look that the once sweet-natured, frank, noble Selenin had given him, a look which kept recurring to his mind.

On his return the doorkeeper handed him a note, and said, rather scornfully, that some kind of woman had written it in the hall. It was a note from Shustova's mother. She wrote that she had come to thank her daughter's benefactor and saviour, and to implore him to come to see them on the Vasilyevsky, 5th Line, house No. —. This was very necessary because of Vera Dukhova. He need not be afraid that they would weary him with expressions of gratitude. They would not speak their gratitude, but simply be glad to see him. Would he not come next morning, if possible?

There was also a note from Bogatirev, a former fellow-officer, aide-de-camp to the Emperor, whom Nekhlyudov had asked to hand personally to the Emperor the petition on behalf of the sectarians. Bogatirev wrote, in his large firm hand, that he would put the petition into the Emperor's own hands as he had promised; but that it had occurred to him that it might be better for Nekhlyudov first to go and see the person on whom the matter depended.

After the impressions received during the last few days, Nekhlyudov felt perfectly hopeless of getting anything done. The plans he had formed in Moscow seemed now something like the dreams of youth, which are inevitably followed by disillusion when life comes to be faced. Still, being in Petersburg, he considered it his duty to do all he had intended, and he resolved that he would next day, after consulting Bogatirev, follow his advice and see the person on whom the case of the sectarians depended.

He took the sectarians' petition from his portfolio and began reading it over, when there came a knock at his door, and a footman entered with a message from the Countess Catherine Ivanovna, asking him to come up and have a cup of tea with her.

Nekhlyudov said he would come at once, and having put the papers back into the portfolio went up to his aunt's sitting-room. Looking out of a window on his way, and seeing Mariette's pair of bays standing in front of the house, he suddenly brightened and felt inclined to smile.

Mariette, with a hat on her head, not in black but in a light dress of many colours, sat with a cup in her hand beside the Countess's easy-chair, prattling about something while her beautiful laughing eyes glistened. When Nekhlyudov entered the room Mariette had just uttered something so funny, and indecently funny—as he knew by the kind of laughter—that the good-natured, moustached Countess Catherine Ivanovna's fat body was shaking with laughter, while Mariette, with her smiling mouth slightly drawn to one side, her head a little bent, and a peculiarly mischievous expression on her merry, energetic face, sat silently looking at her companion.

From a few words he had overheard, Nekhlyudov guessed that they were talking of the second piece of Petersburg news, the episode of the new Siberian governor, and that it was about this that Mariette had said something so funny that the Countess could not control herself for a long time.

"You will kill me," she said, coughing.

After saying "How do you do?" Nekhlyudov sat down. He was about to censure Mariette in his mind for her levity, when she, noticing the serious and even slightly dissatisfied look in his eyes, suddenly changed not only the expression of her face, but also the attitude of her mind; for she felt the wish to please him as soon as she looked at him. She suddenly turned serious, dissatisfied with her life, as if seeking and striving after something; it was not that she pretended, but she really reproduced in herself the very same state of mind that he was in, although it would have been impossible for her to express in words what was the state of Nekhlyudov's mind at that moment.

She asked him how he had got on with his various concerns. He told her about his failure in the Senate and of his meeting Selenin.

"Ah, what a pure soul! He is, indeed, a *chevalier sans peur et sans reproche*.[1] A pure soul!" said both ladies, using the epithet commonly applied to Selenin in Petersburg society.

"What is his wife like?" Nekhlyudov asked.

"His wife? Well, I do not wish to judge, but she does not understand him."

"Is it possible that he, too, was for rejecting the appeal?" Mariette asked, with real sympathy. 'It is dreadful. How sorry I am for her," she added, with a sigh.

He knitted his brows, and in order to change the subject began to speak about Shustova, who had been imprisoned in the fortress and was now set free through Mariette's intervention. He thanked her for her trouble, and was going on to say how dreadful he thought it that this woman and the whole of her family had suffered merely because no one had reminded the authorities about them; but Mariette interrupted him and expressed her own indignation.

"Don't speak to me about it," she said. "When my husband told me she could be set free, it was this that struck me, 'Why was she kept in prison at all if she is innocent?'" She went on expressing what Nekhlyudov was about to say. "It is revolting—revolting."

Countess Catherine Ivanovna noticed that Mariette was coquetting with her nephew, and this amused her. "I'll tell you what," she said, when they were silent. "Suppose you come to Aline's to-morrow night. Kiesewetter will be there. And you, too," she said, turning to Mariette.

"*Il vous a remarqué*,"[2] she went on to her nephew. "He told me that what you said (I repeated it all to him) is a very good sign, and that you will certainly come to Christ. You absolutely must come. Tell him to, Mariette, and come yourself."

"In the first place, Countess, I have no right whatever to offer the Prince any kind of advice," said Mariette, and gave Nekhlyudov a look that somehow established a full understanding between them of their attitude towards the Countess's words and to evangelicalism in general: "secondly, I do not much care, you know . . ."

"Yes, I know, you always do things the wrong way round, and according to your own ideas."

"My own ideas? I believe like the commonest peasant woman," said

---

[1] A knight without fear and without reproach.
[2] He noticed you.

Mariette, with a smile. "And, thirdly, I am going to the French Theatre
to-morrow night."

"Ah! And have you seen that—What's her name?" asked the
Countess Catherine Ivanovna of Nekhlyudov. Mariette gave the name
of a celebrated French actress.

"You must go, most decidedly; she is wonderful."

"Whom am I to hear first, *ma tante*: the actress or the preacher?"
Nekhlyudov said, with a smile.

"Please don't quibble."

"I should think the preacher first and then the actress, or else the
desire for a sermon might vanish altogether," said Nekhlyudov.

"No; better begin with the French Theatre and do penance afterwards."

"Now, now, you are not to make fun of me. The preacher is the
preacher, and the theatre is the theatre. One need not pull a long face
and weep in order to be saved. One must believe, and then one is sure
to be gay."

"You, *ma tante*, preach better than any preacher."

"I'll tell you," said Mariette. "Come to my box to-morrow."

"I am afraid I shall not be able——"

The footman interrupted the conversation by announcing a visitor.
It was the secretary of a philanthropic society of which the Countess
was president.

"Oh, he is the dullest of men. I think I will receive him out there,
and return to you later on. Mariette, give him some tea," said the
Countess, and left the room with her usual quick waddle.

Mariette took the glove off her firm, rather flat hand, the fourth finger of which was covered with rings.

"Have some?" she said, taking hold of the silver tea-kettle, under
which a spirit-lamp was burning, and holding her little finger out in a
curious manner.

Her face looked sad and serious.

"It is always terribly painful to me to notice that people whose opinion I value confound me with the position I am placed in."

She seemed ready to cry as she said these last words. And though
these words, if one were to analyse them, had no meaning, or at any
rate only a very indefinite meaning, they seemed to be of exceptional
depth, meaning, and goodness to Nekhlyudov, so much was he
attracted by the look of the bright eyes which accompanied the words
of this young, beautiful, and well-dressed woman.

Nekhlyudov looked at her in silence, and could not take his eyes off
her face.

"You think I do not understand you and all that goes on in you. Why,

everybody knows what you are doing. *C'est le secret de polichinelle.*[3]
And I am delighted with your work, and approve of it."

"Really, there is nothing to be delighted with; I have done so little as
yet."

"No matter. I understand your feelings, and I understand her. All
right, all right, I will say nothing more about it," she said, noticing dis-
pleasure on his face. "But I also understand that after seeing all that suffering and horror in the prisons," Mariette went on, wishing to attract
him, and guessing with her woman's instinct what was dear and important to him, "you wish to help the sufferers: those who are made to suffer so terribly by other men's cruelty and indifference. I understand the
willingness to give one's life, and could give mine in such a cause, but
we each have our own fate."

"Are you, then, dissatisfied with your fate?"

"I?" she asked, as if struck with surprise that such a question could
be put to her. "I have to be satisfied, and am satisfied. But there is a
worm that wakes up——"

"And he must not be allowed to fall asleep again. It is a voice that
must be obeyed," Nekhlyudov said, falling into the snare.

Many a time afterwards Nekhlyudov remembered with shame his
talk with her. He remembered her words, which were not so much lies
as imitations of his own, and her face, which seemed looking at him
with sympathetic attention when he told her about the horrors of the
prison and of his impressions in the country.

When the Countess returned they were talking not merely like old
friends but like exclusive friends who amidst a crowd of indifferent people alone understood one another.

They talked of the injustice of power, of the sufferings of the unfortunate, the poverty of the people; yet in reality, in the midst of the
sound of their talk, their eyes, gazing at each other, kept asking, "Can
you love me?" and answering, "I can," and the sex-feeling, taking the
most unexpected and attractive forms, drew them to each other.

As she was going away, she told him that she would always be willing to serve him in any way she could, and asked him to come and see
her in the theatre next day, if only for a moment, as she had a very
important thing to tell him.

"Yes, and who knows when I shall see you again?" she added with a
sigh, carefully drawing the glove over her jewelled hand. "So say you
will come."

Nekhlyudov promised.

That night, when Nekhlyudov was alone in his room, and lay down

[3] It is an open secret.

after putting out his candle, he could not sleep. While he was thinking of Maslova, the Senate's decision, his decision in any case to follow her, and his renunciation of his land—suddenly Mariette's face appeared with her sigh and glance as she said: "When shall I see you again?" and her smile was so vivid that he smiled back as though he saw her. "Shall I be doing all right in going to Siberia? And have I done right in giving up my wealth?" he asked himself.

And the answers to these questions on this Petersburg night, on which the light streamed into the window from under the blind, were quite indefinite. All seemed confused. He recalled his former state of mind, and the former sequence of his thoughts, but they no longer had their former force or validity.

"And supposing I have invented all this, and am unable to live it through—supposing I repent of having acted rightly," he thought; and, unable to answer, he was seized with such anguish and despair as he had long not felt, and fell into a heavy sleep, such as he had formerly slept after a heavy loss at cards.

Chapter XXV

NEKHLYUDOV AWOKE next morning feeling as if he had been guilty of some iniquity the day before. He began considering. He could not remember having done anything wrong, he had committed no evil act. But he had had evil thoughts. He had thought that all his present resolutions, to marry Katusha and to give up his land, were unachievable dreams; that he should be unable to bear it, that it was artificial, unnatural, and that he would have to go on living as he lived before.

He had committed no evil action, but, what was far worse than an evil action, he had entertained evil thoughts, whence evil actions proceed.

An evil action may not be repeated, and can be repented of; but evil thoughts generate all evil actions.

An evil action only smooths the path for other evil acts; evil thoughts uncontrollably drag one along that path.

When Nekhlyudov repeated in his mind the thoughts of the day before, he was surprised that he could have believed them for a moment. However new and difficult it might be to do what he had decided on, he knew that it was the only possible way of life for him now; and however easy and natural it might be to return to his former state, he knew that state to be death. Yesterday's temptation seemed like the feeling when one awakes from deep sleep, and, without feeling sleepy, wants to lie comfortably in bed a little longer, knowing nevertheless that it is time to rise and begin the glad and important work that awaits one.

On that, his last day in Petersburg, he went in the morning to the Vasilyevsky Ostrov to see Shustova.

Shustova lived on the second floor; and having been shown the back stairs Nekhlyudov entered straight into the hot kitchen, which smelt strongly of food. An elderly woman, with turned-up sleeves, apron, and spectacles, stood by the fire stirring something in a steaming pan.

"Whom do you want?" she asked sternly, looking at him over her spectacles.

Nekhlyudov had hardly time to give his name, when an expression of alarm and joy appeared on her face.

"Oh, Prince!" she exclaimed, wiping her hands on her apron. "But why have you come the back way? Our benefactor. I am her mother. They have nearly killed my little girl. You have saved us," she said, catching hold of Nekhlyudov's hand and trying to kiss it.

"I went to see you yesterday. My sister asked me to. She is here. This way, this way, please," said Shustova's mother, as she led the way through a narrow door and a dark passage, arranging her hair and pulling at her tucked-up skirt. "My sister's name is Kornilova. You must have heard of her," she added in a whisper, stopping before a closed door. "She was mixed up in a political affair. An extremely clever woman!"

Shustova's mother opened the door and showed Nekhlyudov into a small room, where on a sofa with a table before it sat a plump, short girl with fair hair that curled round her pale, round face, which was very like her mother's. She had a striped cotton blouse on.

Opposite her in an armchair, leaning forward, so that he was nearly bent double, sat a young fellow with a slight black beard and moustache, and wearing a Russian embroidered shirt. They were so engrossed in their conversation that they only turned round after Nekhlyudov had entered the room.

"Lydia, Prince Nekhlyudov! the same one . . ." the mother said.

The pale girl jumped up, nervously pushing back a lock of hair behind her ear, and gazed at the new-comer with a frightened look in her large grey eyes.

"So you are that dangerous woman whom Vera Dukhova wished me to intercede for?" Nekhlyudov asked, with a smile.

"Yes, I am," said Lydia Shustova, her broad, kind, childlike smile disclosing a row of beautiful teeth. "It was aunt who was so anxious to see you. Aunt!" she called out in a pleasant, gentle voice through a door.

"Your imprisonment grieved Vera Dukhova very much," said Nekhlyudov.

"Take a seat here, or better here," said Lydia, pointing to the battered easy-chair from which the young man had just risen.

"My cousin, Zakharov," she said, noticing that Nekhlyudov looked at the young man.

The young man greeted the visitor with a smile as kindly as Lydia's, and when Nekhlyudov sat down he brought himself another chair and sat by his side. A fair-haired schoolboy, of about sixteen, also came into the room and silently sat down on the window-sill.

"Vera Dukhova is a great friend of my aunt's, but I hardly know her myself," said Shustova.

Then a woman with a very pleasant face, wearing a white blouse and leather belt, came in from the next room.

"How do you do? Thanks for coming," she began as soon as she had taken the place next to Lydia on the sofa.

"Well, and how is Vera? You have seen her? How does she bear her fate?"

"She does not complain," said Nekhlyudov. "She says her feelings are Olympian."

"Ah, that's like Vera. I know her," said the aunt, smiling and shaking her head. "One has to know her. She has a fine character. Everything for others, nothing for herself."

"No, she asked nothing for herself, but only seemed concerned about your niece. What seemed to trouble her most was, as she said, that your niece was imprisoned for nothing."

"Yes, that's true," said the aunt. "It is a dreadful business. It was really on account of me that she suffered."

"Not at all, aunt. I should have taken the papers without you all the same."

"Allow me to know better," said the aunt. "You see," she went on to Nekhlyudov, "it all happened because a certain person asked me to keep his papers for a while; and I, having no house at the time, brought them to her. And that very night the police searched her room and took her and the papers, and kept her till now, demanding that she should tell from whom she had them."

"But I never told them," said Lydia quickly, pulling nervously at a lock of hair that was not even out of place.

"I never said you did," answered the aunt.

"If they took Mitin up, it was certainly not through me," said Lydia, blushing, and looking round uneasily.

"Don't speak about it, Lydia, dear," said her mother.

"Why not? I should like to tell it," said Lydia, no longer smiling nor pulling at her lock of hair, but twisting it round her finger and getting redder.

"Don't forget what happened yesterday when you began talking about it."

"Not at all—Leave me alone, mamma. . . . I did not tell, I only kept quiet. When he examined me about Mitin and about aunt, I said nothing, and told him I would not answer."

"Then this . . . Petrov——"

"Petrov is a spy, a gendarme, and a blackguard," put in the aunt, to explain her niece's words to Nekhlyudov.

"Then he began persuading," continued Lydia, excitedly and hurriedly. "'Anything you tell me,' he said, 'can harm no one; on the contrary, if you tell me, we may be able to set free innocent people whom we may be uselessly tormenting.' Well, I still said I would not tell. Then he said, 'All right, don't tell, but do not deny what I am going to say.' And he named Mitin."

"Don't talk about it," said the aunt.

"Oh aunt, don't interrupt . . ." and she went on pulling the lock of hair and looking round: "and then, only fancy, the next day I hear—they let me know by tapping on the wall—that Mitin is arrested. Well, I think I have betrayed him, and this tormented me so—it tormented me so that I nearly went mad."

"And it turned out that it was not at all because of you he was taken up?"

"Yes, but I didn't know. I think, 'There now, I have betrayed him.' I walk and walk from wall to wall, and cannot help thinking. I think, 'I have betrayed him.' I lie down and wrap myself up, and hear something whispering, 'Betrayed! betrayed Mitin! Mitin betrayed!' I know it is an hallucination, but cannot help listening. I wish to fall asleep, I cannot. I wish not to think, and cannot stop thinking. It was terrible!" and as Lydia spoke she got more and more excited, twisted and untwisted the lock of hair round her finger, and kept looking round.

"Lydia, dear, be calm," the mother said, touching her shoulder.

But Shustova could not stop herself.

"It was all the more terrible . . ." she began again, but did not finish, and jumping up with a cry rushed out of the room.

Her mother turned to follow her.

"They ought to be hanged, the rascals!" said the schoolboy, who was sitting on the window-ledge.

"What's that?" said the mother.

"I only said . . . Oh, it's nothing," the schoolboy answered, and taking a cigarette that lay on the table he began to smoke.

Chapter XXVI

"YES, THAT solitary confinement is terrible for the young," said the aunt, shaking her head, and also lighting a cigarette.

"I should say for any one," Nekhlyudov replied.

"No, not for all," answered the aunt. "For the real revolutionists, I have been told, it is rest and quiet. A man who is wanted by the police lives in a state of continual anxiety and material want, in fear for himself and others and for his cause; and at last, when he is taken and it is all over, and all responsibility is off his shoulders, he can sit and rest. I have been told they actually feel glad when arrested. But the young and innocent—they always first arrest the innocent, like Lydia—for them the first shock is terrible. It is not the loss of freedom, and the bad food and bad air—all that is nothing. Three times as many privations might be easily borne if it were not for the moral shock when one is first taken."

"Have you, then, experienced it?"

"I? I was twice in prison," she answered, with a sad gentle smile. "When I was arrested for the first time I had done nothing. I was twenty-two, had a child, and was expecting another. Though the loss of freedom and the parting with my child and husband were hard, they were nothing compared with what I felt when I found out that I had ceased to be a human being and had become a thing. I wished to say good-bye to my little daughter. I was told to go and get into an *izvozchik's* trap. I asked where I was being taken to. The answer was that I should know when I got there. I asked what I was accused of, but got no reply. When, after I had been examined, and they had undressed me and put numbered prison clothes on me, they led me to a vault, opened a door, pushed me in, locked the door again, and left me alone—a sentry with a loaded rifle pacing up and down in front of my door and every now and then looking in through a crack—I felt terribly depressed. What struck me most at the time was that the gendarme officer who examined me offered me a cigarette. So he knew that people like to smoke, and must also have known that they like freedom and light, and that mothers love their children, and children their mothers. Then how could they tear me pitilessly from all that was dear to me, and lock me up in prison like a wild animal? That sort of thing could not be borne without evil effects. Any one who believes in God and man, and believes that men love one another, will cease to believe it after going through all that. I have ceased to believe in humanity since then, and have grown embittered," she concluded, with a smile.

Lydia's mother came in at the door through which her daughter had gone out, and reported her very much upset and unable to return.

"And what has this young life been ruined for?" said the aunt. "What is especially painful to me is that I am the involuntary cause of it."

"She will recover in the country, God willing," said the mother. "We shall send her to her father."

"But for you she would have perished altogether," said the aunt. "Thank you! But what I wished to see you for was this: I wished to ask you to take a letter to Vera Dukhova," and she got the letter out of her pocket. "The letter is not sealed; you may read it and tear it up, or hand it to her, as your principles may prompt you," she said. "It contains nothing compromising."

Nekhlyudov took the letter, and having promised to give it to Vera Dukhova he said good-bye and went away. He sealed the letter without reading it, meaning to deliver it as asked.

Chapter XXVII

THE LAST thing that kept Nekhlyudov in Petersburg was the case of the sectarians, whose petition he intended to get handed to the Tsar through his former fellow-officer, the aide-de-camp Bogatirev. He arrived at Bogatirev's in the morning, and found him still at breakfast, though ready to go out. Bogatirev was not tall, but was firmly built and wonderfully strong (he could bend a horseshoe): a kind, honest, straight, and even liberal man. In spite of these qualities, he was intimate at Court and very fond of the Tsar and his family, and by some strange means he managed, while living in that highest circle, to see nothing but the good in it and take no part in its evil and corruption. He never condemned anybody nor any measure—always either keeping silent or speaking in a bold, loud voice, almost shouting what he had to say, and often laughing in the same boisterous manner. And he did this, not for diplomatic reasons, but because such was his character.

"Ah, that's right that you have come. Would you like some breakfast? Sit down, the beefsteaks are excellent! I always begin with something substantial—begin and finish, too. Ha! ha! ha! Well then, have a glass of wine," he shouted, pointing to a decanter of claret. "I have been thinking of you. I will hand on the petition. I will put it into his own hands. You may count on that, only it occurred to me that it would be best for you to see Toporov first."

Nekhlyudov made a wry face at the mention of Toporov.

"It all depends on him. He will be consulted anyhow. And perhaps he may himself meet your wishes."

"If you advise it I will go."

"That's right. Well, and how does Petersburg agree with you?" shouted Bogatirev. "Tell me. Eh?"

"I feel myself getting hypnotised," replied Nekhlyudov.

"Hypnotised!" Bogatirev repeated, and burst out laughing. "You won't have anything? Well, just as you please," and he wiped his moustache with his napkin. "Then you'll go? Eh? If he won't do it, give the petition to me and I will hand it on to-morrow." Shouting these words, he rose, crossed himself just as unconsciously as he had wiped his mouth, and began buckling on his sword.

"And now good-bye; I must go."

"We are both going out," said Nekhlyudov, and shaking Bogatirev's strong, broad hand with the sense of pleasure which the impression of something healthy and unconsciously fresh always gave him, he parted from him on the doorstep.

Though he expected no good result from his visit, still, following Bogatirev's advice, Nekhlyudov went to see Toporov, on whom the fate of the sectarians depended.

The position occupied by Toporov, involving as it did an incongruity of purpose, could only be held by a man who was dull and morally obtuse. Toporov possessed both these negative qualities. The incongruity of the position he occupied was this. It was his duty to maintain, and to defend by external measures not excluding violence, that Church which, by its own declaration, was established by God himself and could not be shaken by the gates of hell nor by any human effort. This divine and immutable God-established institution had to be sustained and defended by a human institution—the Holy Synod—managed by Toporov and his officials. Toporov did not see this incongruity, nor did he wish to see it, and he was therefore much concerned lest some Romish priest, some pastor, or some sectarian, should destroy that Church against which the gates of hell could not prevail. Toporov, like all those who are quite destitute of the fundamental religious feeling which recognises the equality and brotherhood of man, was fully convinced that the common people were creatures entirely different from himself, and that the people needed what he could very well do without; for at the bottom of his heart he believed in nothing, and found such a state very convenient and pleasant. Yet he feared lest the people might also come to such a state, and looked upon it as his sacred duty, as he called it, to save them from it.

A certain cookery book states that crabs like to be boiled alive. In the same way he thought and spoke as if the people liked to be kept in superstition; only he meant it literally, whereas the cookery book does not.

His position towards the religion he was upholding was the same as that of a poultry-keeper towards the carrion he feeds his fowls on: carrion is very disgusting, but fowls like it and eat it, therefore it is right to feed fowls on carrion.

Of course all this worship of the images of the Iberian, Kazan, and Smolensk "Mothers of God" is gross idolatry, but the people like it and believe in it, and therefore the superstition must be kept up. Thus thought Toporov, not considering that the people only like superstition because there always have been, and still are, cruel men like himself who, being enlightened, instead of using their light to help others to struggle out of their dark ignorance, use it to plunge them yet deeper into it.

When Nekhlyudov entered the reception-room, Toporov was in his cabinet talking with an abbess, a lively and aristocratic lady, who was spreading the Greek Orthodox faith in Western Russia among the Uniates, who acknowledge the Pope of Rome, but upon whom the Orthodox faith is being forced.

An official who was in the reception-room inquired Nekhlyudov's business, and when he heard that Nekhlyudov meant to hand in a petition to the Emperor, he asked if he would allow the petition to be read first. Nekhlyudov gave it him and the official took it into the cabinet. The abbess, with her hood and flowing veil, and her long train trailing behind, left the cabinet and went out, her white hands (with their well-tended nails) holding a topaz rosary. Nekhlyudov was not immediately asked to enter. Toporov was reading the petition and shaking his head. He was unpleasantly surprised by the clear and emphatic wording of it.

"If it gets into the hands of the Emperor it may cause misunderstandings, and unpleasant questions may be asked," he thought, as he read. Then he put the petition on the table, rang, and ordered that Nekhlyudov should be asked in.

He remembered the case of these sectarians; he had had a petition from them before. The case was this. These Christians, fallen away from the Greek Orthodox Church, after first being exhorted, were tried by law but acquitted. Then the bishop and the governor arranged, on the plea that their marriages were illegal, to exile these sectarians, separating the husbands, wives, and children. These fathers and wives were now petitioning that they should not be parted. Toporov recol-

lected that when the case came to his notice he had at the time hesitated whether he had not better put a stop to it. But then he thought
that no harm could result from his confirming the decision to separate
and exile the different members of the sectarian families, whereas
allowing the peasant sect to remain where it was might have a bad
effect on the rest of the inhabitants of the place and cause them to fall
away from Orthodoxy. And then the affair also proved the bishop's zeal,
so he decided to let the case proceed along the lines it had taken.

But now that they had an advocate such as Nekhlyudov, who had
some influence in Petersburg, the case might be personally pointed out
to the Emperor as something cruel, or it might get into the foreign
papers. Therefore he at once took an unexpected decision.

"How do you do?" he said, with the air of a very busy man, receiving
Nekhlyudov standing, and at once starting on the business. "I know this
case. As soon as I saw the names I recollected this unfortunate business," he said, taking up the petition and showing it to Nekhlyudov.
"And I am much indebted to you for reminding me of it. It is the over-
zealousness of the provincial authorities."

Nekhlyudov stood silent, looking with no kindly feelings at the
immovable, pale mask of a face before him.

"And I shall give orders for these measures to be revoked and the
people reinstated in their homes."

"So that I need not make use of this petition?"

"I promise you most assuredly," answered Toporov, laying a stress on
the word I, evidently quite convinced that *his* honesty, *his* word was the
very best guarantee. "It will be best if I write at once. Take a seat,
please."

He went up to the table and began to write. Nekhlyudov, not sitting
down, looked at the narrow, bald skull, at the fat, blue-veined hand that
was swiftly guiding the pen, and wondered why this evidently unfeel-
ing man was doing what he did, and why he was doing it with such
care.

"Well, here you are," said Toporov, sealing the envelope; "you may
let your clients know," and he stretched his lips to imitate a smile.

"Then why did these people suffer?" Nekhlyudov asked, as he took
the envelope.

Toporov raised his head and smiled, as if Nekhlyudov's question gave
him pleasure. "That I cannot tell you. All I can say is that the interests
of the people guarded by us are so important, that excess of zeal in matters of religion is not so dangerous or harmful as the indifference which
is now spreading——"

"But how is it that in the name of religion the very first demands of
righteousness are violated—families separated?"

Toporov continued to smile patronisingly, evidently thinking what Nekhlyudov said very pretty. Anything that Nekhlyudov could say he would have considered very pretty and very one-sided, from the height of what he considered his own far-reaching political outlook.

"It may seem so from the point of view of a private individual," he said, "but from an administrative point of view it appears in a rather different light. However, I must bid you good-bye now," said Toporov, bowing his head and holding out his hand.

Nekhlyudov pressed it in silence and hurriedly went out, repenting of having taken that hand.

"The interests of the people! Your interests, you mean!" thought Nekhlyudov as he went out. And he ran over in his mind the people on whom is exercised the activity of the institutions that uphold religion and educate the people. He began with the woman punished for the illicit sale of spirits, the boy for theft, the tramp for tramping, the incendiary for arson, the banker for fraud, and that unfortunate Lydia Shustova, imprisoned only because from her they might get information they wanted. Then he thought of the sectarians punished for violating Orthodoxy, and Gurkevitch for wanting constitutional government; and Nekhlyudov clearly saw that all these people were arrested, locked-up, exiled, not really because they infringed justice or behaved unlawfully, but only because they were an obstacle, hindering the officials and the rich from enjoying the property they had taken away from the people. And the woman who sold wine without having a licence, and the thief knocking about the town, and Lydia Shustova hiding proclamations, and the sectarians upsetting superstitions, and Gurkevitch desiring a constitution, were a real hindrance. It seemed perfectly clear to Nekhlyudov that all these officials, beginning with his aunt's husband, the Senators, and Toporov, down to those clean, correct, and important gentlemen who sat at Ministerial tables, were not at all troubled by the fact that under such conditions innocent people suffered, but were only concerned how to get rid of the really dangerous.

So not only was the rule disregarded, that ten guilty should escape rather than one innocent be condemned, but, on the contrary, for the sake of getting rid of one really dangerous person, ten who were not dangerous were punished, just as, when cutting a rotten piece out of anything, one cuts away also some that is good.

This explanation seemed very simple and clear to Nekhlyudov; but its very simplicity and clearness made him hesitate to accept it. Was it possible that so complicated a phenomenon could have so simple and terrible an explanation? Was it possible that all these words about justice, law, religion, and God, and so on, were mere words, veiling the coarsest cupidity and cruelty?

Chapter XXVIII

NEKHLYUDOV WOULD have left Petersburg that same evening, but he had promised Mariette to see her at the theatre; and, though he knew that he ought not to keep that promise, he deceived himself into the belief that it would be wrong to break his word.

"Am I capable of withstanding these temptations?" he asked himself, not quite sincerely. "I will try for the last time."

In evening dress, he arrived at the theatre during the second act of the eternal *Dame aux Camélias*, in which a foreign actress once again, and in a novel manner, showed how consumptive women die.

The theatre was quite full. On Nekhlyudov's asking for it, Mariette's box was immediately and very respectfully pointed out to him. A liveried servant stood in the corridor outside; he bowed to Nekhlyudov as to one he knew, and opened the door of the box.

All the people who sat or stood in the boxes on the opposite side, those who sat near and those who were in the parterre—with their grey, grizzly, bald, or curly heads—all were absorbed in watching the thin, bony actress who, dressed in silks and laces, was wriggling before them and speaking in an unnatural voice.

Some one called "Hush!" when the door opened, and two streams, one of cool, the other of hot air, swept over Nekhlyudov's face.

In the box were Mariette, a lady with a red cape and heavy head-dress whom he did not know, and two men: Mariette's husband the General, a tall, handsome man with a severe, inscrutable countenance, a Roman nose, and a uniform padded round the chest, and a fair man with a bit of shaved chin between pompous whiskers.

Mariette, graceful, slight, elegant, her low-necked dress showing her firm, shapely, sloping shoulders, with a little black mole where they joined her neck, immediately turned, and with a smile of welcome and gratitude, and, as it seemed to him, full of meaning, motioned with her fan to Nekhlyudov to take the chair behind her.

The husband looked at him in the quiet way in which he did everything, and bowed. In the look he exchanged with his wife, the master, the owner of a beautiful woman, was to be seen at once.

When the monologue was over, the theatre resounded with the clapping of hands. Mariette rose and, holding her rustling silk skirt, went into the back of the box and introduced Nekhlyudov to her husband. The General, without ceasing to smile with his eyes, said he was very pleased, and then sat inscrutably silent.

"I ought to have left to-day had I not promised," said Nekhlyudov to Mariette.

"If you do not care to see me," said Mariette, in answer to what his words implied, "you will see a wonderful actress. Was she not splendid in the last scene?" she asked, turning to her husband.

The husband nodded his head.

"This sort of thing does not touch me," said Nekhlyudov. "I have seen so much real suffering to-day that——"

"Yes, sit down and tell me."

The husband listened, his eyes smiling more and more ironically.

"I have been to see that woman whom they have set free, and who has been kept in prison so long; she is quite broken down."

"That is the woman I spoke to you about," Mariette said to her husband.

"Oh yes, I was very glad that she could be set free," said the husband quietly, nodding, and smiling with open irony under his moustache, as it seemed to Nekhlyudov. "I will go out and have a smoke."

Nekhlyudov sat waiting to hear what the something was that Mariette had to tell him. She said nothing, and did not even try to say anything, but spoke and joked about the performance, which she thought ought specially to touch Nekhlyudov.

Nekhlyudov saw that she had nothing to tell, but only wished to show herself to him in all the splendour of her evening dress, with her shoulders and the little mole; and this was pleasant and yet repulsive to him.

The veil of charm that had covered all this sort of thing for Nekhlyudov's eyes was not removed, but it was as if he could see what lay beneath. Looking at Mariette he admired her; and yet he knew that she was a liar, living with a husband who was making his career by means of the tears and lives of hundreds and hundreds of people, that she was quite indifferent about it, that all she had said the day before was untrue, and that what she wanted—neither he nor she knew why—was to make him fall in love with her. This both attracted and disgusted him. Several times he took up his hat, meaning to go, but still stayed on.

But at last, when her husband returned with a strong smell of tobacco-smoke on his thick moustache and looked at Nekhlyudov with a patronising, contemptuous air, as if not recognising him, Nekhlyudov left the box before the door was closed again, got his overcoat, and went out of the theatre.

As he was walking home along the Nevsky, he could not help noticing a tall, shapely and aggressively well-dressed woman, who was quietly walking in front of him along the broad asphalt pavement. The consciousness of her detestable power was noticeable in her face and whole figure. All who met or passed that woman looked at her.

Nekhlyudov walked faster than she did, and he, too, involuntarily looked at her in the face. The face, which was probably painted, was handsome, and the woman looked at him with a smile and her eyes sparkled. And, curiously enough, Nekhlyudov was suddenly reminded of Mariette, because, just as he had done in the theatre, he again felt both attracted and disgusted.

Having hurriedly passed her, Nekhlyudov, vexed with himself, turned off on to the Morskaya, and passed along the embankment, where, to the surprise of a policeman, he began pacing up and down the pavement.

"The other one gave me just such a smile when I entered the theatre," he thought, "and the meaning of both smiles was the same. The only difference is, that this one said plainly and openly, 'If you want me, take me; if not, go your way,' and the other one pretended that she was not thinking of this, but living in some high and refined state—while the same thing was really at the root. This one was at least truthful, but that one lied. Besides, this one was driven to it by necessity, while the other amused herself by playing with that enchanting, disgusting, frightful passion. This woman of the street is like stagnant putrid water offered to those whose thirst is greater than their disgust; that other one in the theatre is like a poison which, unnoticed, poisons everything it touches."

Nekhlyudov recalled his affair with the wife of the *Maréchal,* and shameful memories rose before him.

"The animalism of the brute nature in man is disgusting," he thought, "but as long as it remains in its naked form we observe it from the height of our spiritual life and despise it; and—whether one has fallen or resisted—one remains what one was before. But when that same animalism hides under a cloak of poetry and æsthetic feeling and demands our worship—then we are swallowed up by it completely and worship animalism, no longer distinguishing good from evil. Then it is awful!"

Nekhlyudov now perceived all this as clearly as he saw the palace, the sentries, the fortress, the river, the boats, and the Stock Exchange. And just as on this northern summer night there was no soothing, restful darkness on the earth, but only a dismal, dull light coming from an invisible source, so in Nekhlyudov's soul there was no longer the restful darkness of ignorance.

Everything was clear. It was clear that everything considered important and good was insignificant and repulsive, and that all this glamour and luxury hid the old, well-known crimes, which not only remained unpunished but were adorned with all the splendour men can devise.

He wished to forget all this, not to see it, but he could no longer help seeing it. Though he could not see the source of the light which revealed it to him any more than he could see the source of the light which lay over Petersburg; and though the light appeared to him dull, dismal, and unnatural, yet he could not help seeing what it revealed, and he felt both joyful and anxious.

Chapter XXIX

ON HIS return to Moscow, Nekhlyudov went at once to the prison hospital to take Maslova the sad news that the Senate had confirmed the decision of the Court, and that she must prepare to go to Siberia. He had little hope of success with the petition to the Emperor which the advocate had written, and which Nekhlyudov now brought with him for Maslova to sign. And, strange to say, he did not at present even wish it to succeed; he had got used to the thought of going to Siberia and living among the exiled and the convicts, and he could not easily picture to himself how his life and Maslova's would shape themselves if she were acquitted. He remembered the thought of the American writer, Thoreau, who at the time when the slavery existed in America said that "under a government which imprisons any unjustly, the true place for a just man is also a prison." Nekhlyudov, especially after his visit to Petersburg and all he discovered there, thought in the same way.

"Yes, the only place befitting an honest man in Russia at the present time is a prison," he thought, and even felt that this applied to him personally, when he drove up to the prison and entered its walls.

The doorkeeper of the hospital recognised Nekhlyudov, and told him at once that Maslova was no longer there.

"Where is she, then?"

"She is in the prison again."

"Why has she been removed?" Nekhlyudov asked.

"Oh, your excellency, what are such people?" said the doorkeeper, smiling contemptuously. "She carried on with the medical assistant, so the head doctor ordered her back."

Nekhlyudov had had no idea how much Maslova and the state of her mind meant to him. He was stunned by the news.

He felt as one feels at the news of a great and unforeseen misfortune, and his pain was very keen. His first feeling was one of shame. He, with his joyful idea of the change he imagined was going on in her soul, now seemed ridiculous in his own eyes. He thought that all her words about not wishing to accept his sacrifice, all her reproaches and tears, were only the devices of a depraved woman, who wished to use him to the best advantage. He seemed to remember having seen signs of obduracy at his last interview with her. All this flashed through his mind as he instinctively put on his hat and left the hospital.

"What am I to do now? Am I still bound to her? Has this action of hers not set me free?" But when he put these questions to himself, he knew at once that if he considered himself free and threw her up, he would be punishing, not her, which was what he wished to do, but himself, and he was seized with fear.

"No, what has happened cannot alter—it can but strengthen—my resolve. Let her do what flows from the state that her mind is in. If it is carrying on with the medical assistant, let her carry on with the medical assistant; that is her affair. I must do what my conscience demands of me. And my conscience demands that I should sacrifice my freedom. My resolution to marry her, if only in form, and to follow wherever she may be sent, remains unalterable." Nekhlyudov said all this to himself with vicious obstinacy, as he left the hospital and walked with resolute steps towards the big gates in the prison.

He asked the warder on duty at the gate to inform the inspector that he wished to see Maslova. The warder knew Nekhlyudov, and speaking as to an acquaintance told him the important prison news. The old inspector had been superseded, and a new, very severe official appointed in his place.

"They are so strict nowadays, it's just awful," said the jailer. "He is in here, and shall be told at once."

The new inspector was in the prison and soon came out to Nekhlyudov. He was a tall, angular man, with high cheek bones, morose, and very slow in his movements.

"Interviews are allowed in the visiting-room on the appointed days," he said, without looking at Nekhlyudov.

"But I have a petition to the Emperor which I want signed."

"You can give it to me."

"I must see the prisoner myself. I was always allowed to do so before."

"Yes, that was before," replied the inspector, with a furtive glance at Nekhlyudov.

"I have a permission from the governor," insisted Nekhlyudov, and took out his pocket-book.

"Allow me," said the inspector, still without looking him in the eyes, and he took the paper from Nekhlyudov with his long, dry, white fingers, on the first of which was a gold ring, and read the paper slowly, "Step into the office, please," he said.

This time the office was empty. The inspector sat down by the table, and began sorting some papers that lay on it, evidently intending to be present at the interview.

When Nekhlyudov asked whether he might see the political prisoner Dukhova, the inspector answered shortly that he could not.

"Interviews with political prisoners are not permitted," he said, and again fixed his attention on his papers. With a letter to Dukhova in his pocket, Nekhlyudov felt as if he had been trying to commit some offence and his plans been discovered and frustrated.

When Maslova entered the room the inspector raised his head, and, without looking either at her or Nekhlyudov, remarked: "You may talk," and went on sorting his papers.

Maslova again had on the white jacket, petticoat, and kerchief. When she came up to Nekhlyudov and saw his cold, hard look she blushed scarlet, and crumpling the hem of her jacket with her hand, she cast down her eyes.

Her confusion seemed to Nekhlyudov to confirm the hospital door-keeper's words.

Nekhlyudov had meant to treat her in the same way as before, but could not bring himself to shake hands with her, so repugnant was she to him now.

"I have brought you bad news," he said in a monotonous voice, without looking at her or taking her hand. "The Senate has rejected the appeal."

"I knew they would," she said in a strange tone, as if she were gasping for breath.

Formerly Nekhlyudov would have asked why she said she knew they would; now he only looked at her. Her eyes were full of tears.

But this did not soften him; it roused his irritation against her even more.

The inspector rose and began pacing up and down the room.

In spite of the repugnance Nekhlyudov was feeling towards her at the moment, he considered it right to express his regret at the Senate's decision.

"You must not despair," he said. "The petition to the Emperor may meet with success, and I hope——"

"I'm not thinking of that," she said, looking piteously at him with her wet squinting eyes.

"What then?"

"You have been to the hospital, and they have most likely told you about me that——"

"What of that? That is your affair," said Nekhlyudov coldly, and frowned. The cruel feeling of wounded pride that had quieted down rose with renewed force when she mentioned the hospital.

He, a man of the world, whom any girl of the best families would think it happiness to marry, offered himself as a husband to this woman; and she could not even wait, but began intriguing with the medical assistant, he thought, with a look of hatred.

"Well, sign this petition," he said, taking a large envelope from his pocket, and laying the paper on the table. She wiped her tears with a corner of her kerchief, and asked what to write and where.

He showed her, and she sat down, arranging the cuff of her right sleeve with her left hand. He stood behind her, silently looking at her back, which shook with suppressed emotion; and evil and good feelings were fighting in his breast: feelings of wounded pride, and of pity for her who was suffering—and the last feeling was victorious.

He could not remember which came first; did pity for her first enter his heart, or did he first remember his own sins—his own repulsive actions, the very same for which he was condemning her? Anyhow, he both felt himself guilty and pitied her.

Having signed the petition and wiped her inky finger on her petticoat, she got up and looked at him.

"Whatever happens, whatever comes of it, my resolve remains unchanged," said Nekhlyudov. The thought that he had forgiven her heightened his feelings of pity and tenderness for her, and he wished to comfort her. "I will do what I have said; wherever they take you I shall be with you."

"What's the use?" she interrupted hurriedly, though her whole face lit up.

"You had better think of what you will want on the way."

"I don't know of anything in particular, thank you."

The inspector came up, and without waiting for any remark from him Nekhlyudov took leave, and went out with such peace, joy, and love towards everybody in his heart as he had never felt before. The certainty that no action of Maslova's could change his love for her, filled him with joy, and raised him to a height which he had never before attained. Let her intrigue with the medical assistant; that was her affair. He loved her not for his own, but for her sake and for God's.

And this intrigue, for which Maslova was turned out of the hospital, and of which Nekhlyudov believed her really guilty, consisted of the following.

Maslova was sent by the head nurse to get some herb-tea from the dispensary at the end of the corridor, and there, all alone, she found the medical assistant, a tall man with a pimply face, who had long been bothering her. In trying to get away from him Maslova gave him such a push that he knocked his head against a shelf, from which two bottles fell and broke.

The head doctor, who was passing at that moment, heard the sound of breaking glass, and seeing Maslova run out quite flushed, shouted to her angrily—

"Ah, my good woman, if you start intriguing here, I'll send you about your business. . . . What is the meaning of this?" he went on, addressing the medical assistant and looking at him sternly over his spectacles.

The assistant smiled, and began to justify himself. The doctor did not heed him, but, lifting his head so that he now looked through his spectacles, he entered the ward. He told the inspector the same day to send a more sedate assistant nurse in Maslova's place.

And this was her "intrigue" with the medical assistant. Being turned out for a love intrigue was particularly painful to Maslova, because connections with men, which had long been repulsive to her, had become specially disgusting since meeting Nekhlyudov. The thought that, judging her by her past and present position, every man, the pimply assistant among them, considered he had a right to insult her and to be surprised at her refusal, hurt her deeply, and made her pity herself and brought tears to her eyes. When she went out to Nekhlyudov this time she wished to clear herself of the false charge of which she knew he must surely have heard. But when she began to justify herself, she felt he did not believe her and that her excuses would only strengthen his suspicions; and tears choked her and she was silent.

Maslova still thought and continued to persuade herself that she had not forgiven him, and hated him, as she told him at their second interview, but in reality she loved him again, loved him so that she involuntarily did all he wished her to do: left off drinking, smoking, coquetting, and entered the hospital because she knew he wished it. And if every time he reminded her of it she refused as decidedly as ever to accept his sacrifice and marry him, it was because she liked repeating the proud words she had once uttered, and also because she knew that a marriage with her would be a misfortune for him. She had resolutely made up her mind that she would not accept his sacrifice, and yet the thought that he despised her and believed that she still was what she had been and did not notice the change that had taken place in her, was very painful. That he was perhaps still thinking she had done wrong while in the hospital, tormented her more than the news that her sentence was confirmed.

Chapter XXX

MASLOVA MIGHT be sent off with the first gang of prisoners, so Nekhlyudov got ready for his departure. But there was so much to be done that he felt that he could not finish it all, however much time he might have. It was quite different now from what it had been. Formerly he used to be obliged to invent occupations, the interest of which always centered in one person, *i.e.* Dmitry Ivanich Nekhlyudov; and yet, though every interest of his life was thus centred, all these occupations were very wearisome. Now all his occupations related to other people and not to Dmitry Ivanich, and they were all interesting and attractive, and there was no end to them. Nor was this all. Formerly Dmitry Ivanich Nekhlyudov's occupations always made him feel vexed and irritable; now they produced a joyful state of mind.

The business at present occupying Nekhlyudov could be divided under three heads. He himself, with his usual pedantry, divided it in that way, and accordingly kept the papers referring to it in three different portfolios.

The first referred to Maslova, and was chiefly that of taking steps to secure attention for her petition to the Emperor, and preparing for her probable journey to Siberia.

The second was the arrangement of the affairs on his estates. In Panovo he had given the land to the peasants on condition that they paid rent to be devoted to their own communal use. But he had to confirm this transaction by a legal deed, and to make his will in accordance with it. In Kusminsky the state of things was still as he had first arranged it: he was to receive the rent; but the terms had to be fixed, and also how much of the money he would use to live upon, and how much he would leave for the peasants' use. As he did not know what his journey to Siberia might cost him he had not yet made up his mind to forfeit this income altogether, though he reduced it by half.

The third part of his business was to help the prisoners, who applied to him more and more often.

At first when he came in contact with the prisoners and they appealed to him for help, he at once began interceding for them, hoping to lighten their fate; but he soon had so many applications that he felt the impossibility of attending to all of them, and this naturally led him to take up another piece of work, which at last roused his interest even more than the three first.

This new business consisted in the solution of the questions: what was this strange institution called criminal law, which occasioned that prison whose inmates he had to some extent got to know, and numbers of other places of confinement, from the Petropavlovsky Fortress in Petersburg to the island of Sakhalin, where hundreds and thousands of victims of this, to him extraordinary, criminal law, were pining: why did it exist? where did it come from?

From his personal relations with the prisoners, from notes by some of those in confinement, and by questioning the advocate and the prison priest, Nekhlyudov came to the conclusion that the prisoners, the so-called criminals, could be divided into five classes. The first were quite innocent people, condemned by judicial blunders. Such were the Menshovs, supposed to be incendiaries, Maslova, and others. There were not many of these—according to the priest's estimate only seven per cent—but their condition excited particular interest.

The second class consisted of people condemned for actions done in peculiar circumstances: passion, jealousy, or drunkenness; circumstances in which those who judged them would surely have committed the same actions. According to Nekhlyudov's observations, more than half of all the criminals belonged to this category.

The third class consisted of people punished for having committed actions which, according to their own ideas, were quite natural and even good, but which those other people, the men who made the laws, considered to be crimes. Such were those who sold spirits without a licence, smugglers, those who gathered grass and wood on large estates, and in the forests belonging to the Crown, the mountain robbers,[1] and those unbelievers who robbed churches.

To the fourth class belonged those who were imprisoned only because they stood morally higher than the average level of society. Such were the sectarians; such were the Poles and the Circassians, rebelling in order to regain their independence; such were the political prisoners, the Socialists, and the strikers. According to Nekhlyudov's observations a very large percentage belonged to this class, and among them were some of the best of men, condemned for resisting the authorities.

The fifth class consisted of persons who were far more sinned against than sinning in their relations with society. These were the castaways, stupefied by continual oppression and temptation, such as the boy who had stolen the mats, and hundreds of others whom Nekhlyudov had seen in the prison and out of it. The conditions under which they lived seemed to lead on systematically to those actions which are termed crimes. A great many thieves and murderers with whom he had lately come in contact belonged, in Nekhlyudov's estimation, to this class. To this class also he assigned those depraved, demoralised creatures, whom the new school of criminology classify as the criminal type, the existence of which is considered to be the chief proof of the necessity for criminal law and punishment. This demoralised, depraved, abnormal type was, according to Nekhlyudov, exactly the same as that against

---

[1] Presumably the mountain robbers alluded to are those natives of the Caucasus who, though the country has long been subdued by Russia, still pride themselves on plundering the caravans of traders, and raiding any Russian flocks or herds they can.

whom society had sinned, only here society had sinned, not directly against them, but against their parents and forefathers.

Among this latter class Nekhlyudov was specially struck by one Okhotin, an inveterate thief, the illegitimate son of a prostitute, brought up in a doss-house, who, up to the age of thirty, had apparently never met any one whose morality was above that of a policeman, and who had got into a band of thieves when quite young. He was gifted with an extraordinary sense of humour, by means of which he made himself very attractive. He asked Nekhlyudov to intercede for him, at the same time making fun of himself, the lawyers, the prison, and laws human and divine. Another was the handsome Fedorov, who, with a band of robbers of whom he was the chief, had robbed and murdered an old man, an official. Fedorov was a peasant whose father had been unlawfully deprived of his house, and who, later on, when serving as a soldier, had suffered in consequence of falling in love with an officer's mistress. He had a fascinating, passionate nature, that longed for enjoyment at any cost. He had never met anybody who restrained himself for any cause whatever, and had never heard a word about any aim in life save enjoyment. Nekhlyudov distinctly saw that both these men were richly endowed by nature, but had been neglected and crippled like uncared-for plants. He had also met a tramp and a woman, who had repelled him by their dulness and seeming cruelty, but even in them he could find no trace of the criminal type written about by the Italian school, but saw in them only people who were repulsive to him personally just in the same way as some he had met outside the prison—in tailed coats, wearing epaulettes, or bedecked with lace.

And so the investigation of the reasons why all these very different persons were put to prison, while others just like them were going about free, and even judging them, formed a fourth task for Nekhlyudov.

He hoped to find an answer to this question in books, and bought all that dealt with it. He obtained the works of Lombroso, Garofalo, Ferri, Liszt, Maudsley, Tarde, and read them carefully. But as he read he became more and more disappointed. It happened to him as it always happens to those who turn to science, not in order to play a rôle in it, nor to write, nor to dispute, nor to teach, but simply to get an answer to an everyday question of life. Science answered thousands of other very subtle and ingenious questions touching criminal law, but not the one he was trying to solve.

He asked a very simple question: "Why, and by what right, do some people lock up, torment, exile, flog, and kill others, while they are themselves just like those whom they torment, flog, and kill?" And in answer he got deliberations as to whether human beings had free-will or not; whether or not signs of criminality could be detected by measuring the skull; what part heredity played in crime; whether immorality could be inherited; what madness is, what degeneration is, and what temperament is; how climate, food, ignorance, imitativeness, hypnotism, or passion affect crime; what society is; what its duties are—and so on.

These disquisitions reminded Nekhlyudov of the answer he once got from a little boy whom he met coming home from school. Nekhlyudov asked him if he had learnt to spell.

"Yes, I can spell," answered the boy.

"Well then, tell me, how do you spell 'leg'?"

"A dog's leg, or what kind of leg?" answered the boy, with a sly look.

Just such answers in the form of questions were what Nekhlyudov found in the scientific books, in reply to his one fundamental inquiry. There was much that was wise, learned, and interesting; but there was no answer on the chief point: "By what right do some people punish others?"

Not only was this not answered, but all the arguments brought forward were employed to explain and vindicate punishment, the necessity of which was taken as an axiom.

Nekhlyudov read much, but only in snatches, and, putting down his failure to this superficial way of reading, hoped to find the answer later on. He would not allow himself to believe in the truth of the answer which began, more and more often, to present itself to him.

Chapter XXXI

THE GANG of convicts among whom was Maslova was to start on the 5th of July, and Nekhlyudov arranged to start the same day.

The day before, Nekhlyudov's sister and her husband came to town to see him.

Nekhlyudov's sister, Nataly Ivanovna Rogozhinskaya, was ten years older than her brother. Nekhlyudov had grown up partly under her influence. She had been very fond of him when he was a boy, and later on, before her marriage, they grew very near to each other, as if they were equals, she being a young woman of twenty-five, he a lad of fifteen. At that time she was in love with his friend, Nikolenka Irtenyev, since dead. They both loved Nikolenka, and loved in him and in themselves that which is good, and which unites all men.

Since then they had both been depraved: he by military service and a vicious life, she by marrying a man whom she loved with a sensual love, and who not only did not care for the things that had once been so dear and holy to her and to her brother, but did not even understand the meaning of those aspirations towards moral perfection and the service of mankind which once constituted her life, and put them down to ambition and a wish to show off—that being the only explanation comprehensible to him.

Nataly's husband, a man without name or fortune but very adroit at his profession, by artfully manœuvring between Liberalism and Conservatism and utilising whichever of the two currents best suited his purpose at the given time and occasion, and specially through some quality which pleased women, had made a comparatively brilliant judicial career. While travelling abroad when he was no longer in his first youth, he made Nekhlyudov's acquaintance and managed to make Nataly, who was also no longer young, fall in love with him—rather against her mother's wishes, who considered a marriage with him to be a mésalliance for her daughter.

Nekhlyudov, though he tried to hide it from himself, and though he fought against it, hated his brother-in-law.

Nekhlyudov's strong antipathy towards him was caused by the vulgarity of Rogozhinsky's feelings and his self-assured narrowness, but arose chiefly on account of Nataly, who in spite of the narrowness of her husband's nature was able to love him so passionately, so selfishly, and so sensually, stifling for his sake all the good there had been in her.

It always hurt Nekhlyudov to think of Nataly as the wife of that hairy, self-assured man with a shiny bald patch on his head. He could not even master a feeling of revulsion towards their children, and when he heard that she was again going to have a baby, he felt a kind of sorrow that she had once more been infected with something bad by this man who was so foreign to him.

The Rogozhinskys had come to Moscow alone—having left their two children, a boy and a girl, at home—and had taken the best rooms in the best hotel. Nataly at once went to her mother's old house, but hearing from Agrafena Petrovna that her brother had left and was living in lodgings, she drove there. The dirty servant met her in the stuffy passage, dark but for a lamp which burnt there all day. He told her that the Prince was out.

Nataly asked to be shown into his rooms as she wished to leave a note for him, and the man showed her up.

Nataly carefully examined her brother's two little rooms. She noticed in everything the love of cleanliness and order she knew so well in him, and was struck by the novel simplicity of the sur-roundings. On his writing--table she saw the paper-weight with the bronze dog on the top which she remembered; the tidy way in which his different portfolios and writing materials were placed on the table was also familiar, and so was the large crooked ivory paper knife which marked the place in a French book by Tarde, which lay with other volumes on punishment and a book in English by Henry George.

She sat down at the table and wrote a note asking him to be sure to come that same day, and, shaking her head in surprise at what she saw, she returned to her hotel.

Two questions regarding her brother now interested Nataly: his marriage with Katusha, which she had heard spoken about in their town—for everybody was speaking about it—and his giving away the land to the peasants, which was also known, and struck many as an action of a political nature and dangerous. The marriage with Katusha pleased her in a way. She admired that resoluteness which was so like him and herself, as they used to be in those happy times before her marriage. And yet she was horrified when she thought of her brother marrying such a dreadful woman. The latter was the stronger feeling of the two, and she decided to use all her influence to prevent him from doing it, though she knew how difficult this would be.

The other matter, the giving up of the land to the peasants, did not touch her so nearly, but her husband was very indignant about it and expected her to influence her brother against it.

Rogozhinsky said that such an action was the height of inconsistency, flightiness, and pride,—the only possible explanation of which was the desire to appear original, to brag, and to be talked about.

"What sense can there be in letting the land to the peasants on condition that they pay the rent to themselves?" he said. "If he was resolved to do such a thing, why not sell the land to them through the Peasants' Bank? There might have been some sense in that. In fact, this act verges on insanity."

And Rogozhinsky began seriously to think about putting Nekhlyudov under legal guardianship, and demanded of his wife that she should speak seriously to her brother about his strange intention.

Chapter XXXII

As soon as Nekhlyudov returned that evening and saw his sister's note on the table, he set off to see her. They had not met since their mother's death. He found Nataly alone; her husband was resting in the next room. She wore a tightly fitting black silk dress, with a red bow in front, and her black hair was crimped and arranged according to the latest fashion.

The pains she took to appear young for the sake of her husband, whose equal she was in years, were very obvious.

When she saw her brother she jumped up, and hurried towards him, her silk dress rustling. They kissed, and looked smilingly at each other. There passed between them that mysterious exchange of looks, full of meaning and truth which cannot be expressed in words. Then came words which were not true.

"You have grown stouter and younger," he said, and her lips puckered up with pleasure.

"And you have grown thinner."

"Well, and how is your husband?" Nekhlyudov asked.

"He is taking a rest; he did not sleep all night."

There was much to say—it was not said in words, but their looks expressed what their words failed to say.

"I have been to your lodgings."

"Yes, I know. I moved because the house is too big for me. I was lonely there, and dull. I want nothing of all that is there, so that you had better take it all. The furniture and things, I mean."

"Yes. Agrafena Petrovna told me. I went there. Thanks, very much. But——"

At this moment the hotel waiter brought in a silver tea-set. While he set the table they were silent. Then Nataly sat down at the table and made the tea, still in silence. Nekhlyudov also said nothing.

At last Nataly began resolutely.

"Well, Dmitry, I know all about it." And she looked at him.

"What of that? I am glad you know."

"How can you hope to reform her after the life she has led?" she asked.

He sat quite straight on a small chair and listened attentively, trying to understand her and to answer rightly. The state of mind called forth in him by his last interview with Maslova still filled his soul with quiet joy and goodwill to all men.

"It is not her but myself I wish to reform," he replied.

Nataly sighed.

"There are other ways than marriage to do that."

"But I think it is the best. Besides, it leads me into a world in which I can be of use."

"I cannot believe you will be happy," said Nataly.

"My happiness is not the point."

"Of course; but if she has a heart she cannot be happy—cannot even wish it."

"She does not wish it."

"I understand; but life . . ."

"Yes—life?"

"Demands something different."

"It demands nothing but that we should do right," said Nekhlyudov, looking into her face, still handsome, though slightly wrinkled round the eyes and mouth.

"I do not understand," she said, and sighed.

"Poor darling, how could she change so?" he thought, calling back to his mind Nataly as she had been before her marriage, and feeling towards her a tenderness woven of innumerable memories of childhood. At that moment Rogozhinsky entered the room, with head thrown back and expanded chest, stepping lightly and softly in his usual manner, his spectacles, his bald patch, and his black beard all glistening.

"How do you do? How do you do?" he said, laying an unnatural stress on his words.

They shook hands, and Rogozhinsky sank softly into an easy-chair.

"I am not interrupting your conversation?"

"No, I do not wish to hide what I am saying or doing from any one."

As soon as Nekhlyudov saw the hairy hands, and heard the patronising, self-assured tones, his meekness left him in a moment.

"Yes, we were talking about his intentions," said Nataly. "Shall I give you a cup of tea?" she added, taking the teapot.

"Thanks. What particular intentions are they?"

"That of going to Siberia with the gang of prisoners among whom is the woman I consider myself to have wronged," uttered Nekhlyudov.

"I hear, not only to accompany her, but more than that."

"Yes, to marry her if she wishes it."

"Indeed! But if you do not mind would you explain your motives? I do not understand them."

"My motives are that this woman . . . that this woman's first step on her way to degradation . . ." Nekhlyudov got angry with himself for being unable to find the right expression. "My motives are that I am the guilty one, and she gets the punishment."

"If she is being punished, she, too, cannot be innocent."

"She is entirely innocent."

And Nekhlyudov related the whole incident with unnecessary warmth.

"Yes, that was a case of carelessness on the part of the president, resulting in a thoughtless answer on the part of the jury. But there is the Senate for cases like that."

"The Senate has rejected the appeal."

"Well, if the Senate has rejected it, there cannot have been sufficient reasons for appealing," said Rogozhinsky, evidently sharing the prevailing opinion that truth is the product of judicial decisions. "The Senate cannot enter into the merits of the case. If there is a real mistake, the Emperor should be petitioned."

"That has been done, but there is no probability of success. They will apply to the Department of the Ministry, the Department will consult the Senate, the Senate will repeat its decision, and, as usual, the innocent will get punished."

"In the first place, the Department of the Ministry won't consult the Senate," said Rogozhinsky, with a condescending smile; "it will give orders for the original documents to be sent from the Law Courts, and if it discovers a mistake it will decide accordingly. And secondly, the innocent are never punished, or only in very rare, quite exceptional cases. It is the guilty who are punished," Rogozhinsky said deliberately, and smiled self-complacently.

"And I am convinced of the contrary," said Nekhlyudov, with a feeling of ill-will towards his brother-in-law, "I am fully convinced that the greater part of those condemned by law are innocent."

"In what sense?"

"Innocent in the literal sense of the word. Just as innocent as this woman is of poisoning any one; as innocent as a peasant I have just come to know is of the murder he never committed; as a mother and son who are now on the point of being condemned for incendiarism committed by the owner of the house that was set on fire."

"Well, of course, there always have been and always will be judicial errors. Human institutions cannot be perfect."

"And besides, there are a great many people convicted who are innocent of doing anything considered wrong by the society they have grown up in."

"Excuse me, that is not so; every thief knows that stealing is wrong, and that we should not steal—that it is immoral," said Rogozhinsky, with the quiet, self-assured, slightly contemptuous smile which specially irritated Nekhlyudov.

"No, he does not know it; they say to him 'don't steal,' and he knows that the master of the factory steals his labour by keeping down his wages; that the Government, through all its officials, robs him continually by taxation."

"Why, this is Anarchism," Rogozhinsky said, quietly defining his brother-in-law's words.

"I can't say what it is; I only say what happens," Nekhlyudov continued. "He knows that the Government robs him, he knows that we landed proprietors have robbed him long since, robbed him of the land which should be the common property of all; and then, if from the land stolen from him he picks up some twigs and branches to light his fire with, we put him in jail and try to persuade him that he is a thief. Of course he knows that not he but those who robbed him of the land are the thieves, and that to obtain any restitution of what has been stolen from him is a duty towards his family."

"I don't understand, or if I do I cannot agree. The land must be somebody's property. If you divided it—" began Rogozhinsky quietly, convinced that Nekhlyudov was a Socialist, and that Socialism demands that all the land should be divided equally, that such a division would be very foolish, and that he could easily prove it so. "If you divided it equally to-day, to-morrow it would again be in the hands of the most industrious and clever."

"No one is thinking of dividing the land equally. The land must not be anybody's property; must not be a thing to be bought and sold or rented."

"The rights of property are inborn in man; without them there would be no incentive to the cultivation of the land. Destroy the rights of property and we lapse into barbarism." Rogozhinsky uttered this authoritatively, repeating the usual argument in favour of private ownership of land, supposed to be irrefutable, and based on the assumption that people's desire to possess land proves their right to possess it.

"On the contrary, only when the land is nobody's property will it cease to lie idle, as it does now while the landlords, like dogs in the manger, unable themselves to put it to use, will not let those use it who are able."

"But Dmitry Ivanich, what you are saying is sheer madness. Is it possible to abolish property in land in our age? I know it is your old hobby. But allow me to tell you frankly," and Rogozhinsky grew pale and his voice trembled: it was evident that this question touched him very nearly—"I should advise you to consider this question well before attempting to solve it practically."

"Are you speaking of my personal affairs?"

"Yes. I hold that we who are placed in special circumstances must bear the responsibilities which spring from such circumstances, must uphold the conditions in which we were born, which we have inherited from our predecessors, and which we ought to pass on to our descendants."

"I consider it my duty——"

"Excuse me," said Rogozhinsky, not permitting the interruption. "I am not speaking for myself or my children. The position of my children is assured: I earn enough for us to live comfortably, and I expect my children will live so too. So that my interest in your action—which, if you will allow me to say so, is not well considered—is not based on personal motives; it is on principle that I cannot agree with you. I should advise you to think it well over, to read——"

"Please allow me to settle my affairs, and to choose what to read and what not to read, myself," said Nekhlyudov, turning pale. Feeling his hands grow cold, and that he was no longer master of himself, he stopped, and began drinking his tea.

Chapter XXXIII

"WELL, AND how are the children?" Nekhlyudov asked his sister when he was calmer. His sister told him that the children had remained with their grandmother. And very glad that the dispute with her husband had come to an end she went on to tell him how her children played that they were travelling, exactly as he used to do with his three dolls, one of them a negro and another which he called the French lady.

"Do you really remember it all?" said Nekhlyudov, smiling.

"Yes; and just fancy, they play in the very same way."

The unpleasant conversation had been brought to an end and Nataly was quieter, but she did not care to talk in her husband's presence of what could be comprehensible only to her brother, so, wishing to start a general conversation, she began talking about the sorrow of Kamensky's mother at losing her only son, who had fallen in a duel; for this Petersburg topic of the day had now reached Moscow. Rogozhinsky expressed disapproval at the state of things that excluded murder in a duel from the ordinary criminal offences.

This remark evoked a rejoinder from Nekhlyudov, and a new dispute arose on the subject. Nothing was fully explained, neither of the antagonists expressed all he had in his mind, each keeping to his conviction, which condemned the other. Rogozhinsky felt that Nekhlyudov condemned him and despised his activity, and he wished to show him the injustice of his opinions.

Nekhlyudov, on the other hand, felt provoked by his brother-in-law's interference in his dealings with the land (knowing in his heart of hearts that his sister, her husband, and their children, as his heirs, had grounds for objecting), and was indignant that this narrow-minded man persisted with calm assurance in regarding as just and lawful what Nekhlyudov no longer doubted was folly and crime. This calm assurance irritated Nekhlyudov.

"What could the law do?" he asked.

"It could sentence one of the two duellists to the mines like an ordinary murderer."

Nekhlyudov's hands grew cold again.

"Well, and what good would that be?" he asked hotly.

"It would be just."

"As if justice were the aim of the law," said Nekhlyudov.

"What else is?"

"The upholding of class interests! The law, in my opinion, is only an instrument for upholding the existing order of things to the advantage of our class."

"This is a perfectly new view," said Rogozhinsky with a quiet smile; "the law is generally supposed to have a totally different aim."

"Yes, so it has in theory, but not in practice, as I have found out. The law aims only at preserving the present state of things, and therefore it persecutes and executes those who stand above the ordinary level and wish to raise it—the so-called political offenders—as well as those who are below the average, the so-called criminal types."

"I do not agree with you. In the first place, I cannot admit that the criminals classed as political are punished because they are above the average. In most cases they are the refuse of society, just as much perverted, though in a different way, as the criminal types whom you consider below the average."

"But I happen to know men who are morally far above their judges; all the sectarians are moral, from——"

But Rogozhinsky, a man not accustomed to be interrupted when he spoke, did not listen to Nekhlyudov, but went on talking at the same time, thereby irritating him still more.

"Nor can I admit that the object of the law is the upholding of the present state of things. The law aims at reforming——"

"A nice kind of reform, in a prison!" Nekhlyudov put in.

"Or removing," Rogozhinsky went on persistently, "the perverted and brutalised persons who threaten society."

"That's just what it doesn't do. Society has not the means of doing either the one thing or the other."

"How is that? I don't understand," said Rogozhinsky, with a forced smile.

"I mean that there are only two reasonable kinds of punishment existing, those used in the old days: corporal punishment and capital punishment, which, as human nature gradually softens, both fall more and more into disuse," said Nekhlyudov.

"Indeed, this is quite new and very strange to hear from your lips."

"Yes, it is reasonable to hurt a man so that he should not do in future what he is hurt for doing, and it is also quite reasonable to cut a man's head off when he is injurious or dangerous to society. These punishments have an intelligible meaning. But where is the sense of locking up in a prison a man perverted by want of occupation and by bad example; to place him in a position where he is provided for, where laziness is imposed on him, and where he is in company with the most perverted of men? Where is the sense of taking a man at public cost (it comes to more than five hundred rubles per head) from the Tula to the Irkutsk Government, or from Kursk——"

"Yes, but all the same, people are afraid of those journeys at public cost, and if it were not for such journeys and the prisons you and I would not be sitting here as we are."

"The prisons cannot ensure our safety, because these people do not stay there for ever, but are set free again. On the contrary, in these establishments men are brought to the greatest vice and degradation, so that the danger is increased."

"You mean to say that the penitentiary system should be improved."

"It cannot be improved. Improved prisons would cost more than all that is now spent on the people's education, and would lay a still heavier burden on the people."

"But the shortcomings of the penitentiary system in nowise invalidate the law itself," Rogozhinsky continued, without heeding his brother-in-law.

"There is no remedy for these shortcomings," said Nekhlyudov, raising his voice.

"What then? Are we to kill them off? Or, as a certain statesman proposed, start putting people's eyes out?" Rogozhinsky remarked.

"Yes, that would be cruel, but it would be effective. What is done now is cruel, and not only ineffective but so stupid that one cannot understand how people in their senses can take part in so absurd and cruel a business as criminal law."

"But I happen to take part in it," said Rogozhinsky, growing pale.

"That is your business. But to me it is incomprehensible."

"I think there are a good many things incomprehensible to you," said Rogozhinsky, with a trembling voice.

"I have seen how one public prosecor did his utmost to get an unfortunate boy condemned who could have evoked nothing but sympathy in an unperverted mind. I know how another cross-examined a sectarian, and managed to make a criminal offence out of the reading of the Gospels: in fact, the whole business of the Law Courts consists in senseless and cruel actions of that sort."

"I should not serve if I thought so," said Rogozhinsky, rising.

Nekhlyudov noticed a peculiar glitter under his brother-in-law's spectacles. "Can it be tears?" he thought. And they really were tears of injured pride. Rogozhinsky, going to the window, got out his handkerchief, and, coughing, began to rub his spectacles, and having taken them off, wiped his eyes also.

When he returned to the sofa he lit a cigar, and did not speak any more.

Nekhlyudov felt pained and ashamed at having offended his brother-in-law and his sister to such a degree, especially as he was going away the next day, and should not see them again.

He parted with them in confusion, and drove home.

"All I have said may be true—anyhow he did not answer it. But it was not said in the right way. How little I must have changed if I can be so carried away by ill-feeling as to offend him and hurt and wound poor Nataly so," he thought.

Chapter XXXIV

THE GANG of convicts among whom was Maslova was to leave Moscow by rail at 3 P.M.; therefore in order to see the gang start and go to the station with the prisoners Nekhlyudov meant to reach the prison before twelve o'clock.

The night before, as he was packing up and sorting his papers, he came upon his diary and read some passages here and there. The last one written before he left for Petersburg ran thus: "Katusha does not wish to accept my sacrifice; she wishes to make a sacrifice herself. She has conquered, and so have I. She makes me happy by the inner change which seems to me, though I fear to believe it, to be going on in her. I fear to believe it, yet she seems to be coming back to life." Then, farther on, he read: "I have lived through something very hard and very joyful. I learnt that she has behaved very badly in the hospital, and I suddenly felt great pain. I never thought that it could be so painful. I spoke to her with loathing and hatred; then suddenly I called to mind how many times I have been, and even still am, though but in thought, guilty of the thing I hated her for; and immediately I became disgusting to myself, and I pitied her and felt happy again. If only we could manage to see the beam in our own eye in time, how kind we should be." Having read this, he wrote: "I have been to see Nataly, and self-satisfaction again made me unkind and spiteful, and a heavy feeling remains. Well, it cannot be helped. To-morrow a new life begins. A final good-bye to the old! Many new impressions have accumulated, but I cannot yet bring them to unity."

When he awoke next morning, Nekhlyudov's first feeling was regret about the affair between himself and his brother-in-law.

"I cannot go away like that," he thought. "I must go and make it up with them." But when he looked at his watch he saw that he had not time to go, but must hurry so as not to be too late for the departure of the gang. He hastily got everything ready, sent the things to the station with a servant and with Taras, Theodosia's husband, who was also going, and then took the first *izvozchik* he could find and drove off to the prison.

The convicts' train started only two hours before the train by which he was going, so Nekhlyudov paid his bill at the lodgings and left for good.

. . . .

It was July, and the weather was unbearably hot. From the stones, the walls, and the iron of the roofs, which the sultry night had not cooled, the heat streamed into the motionless air. When at rare intervals a slight breeze did rise, it brought but a whiff of foul, hot air, filled with dust and smelling of oil-paint.

There were few people in the streets, and those who were out tried to keep on the shady side. Only the sun-burnt peasants with their bronzed faces and with bark shoes on their feet, who were mending the road, sat in the sun, hammering the stones into the burning sand; while the morose policemen, in their holland blouses with revolvers attached by orange cords, stood melancholy and depressed in the middle of the road, shifting from foot to foot; and, with ringing bells, the tramcars kept passing up and down the sunny road, the horses wearing holland hoods with slits for their ears.

When Nekhlyudov drove up to the prison the gang had not yet left the yard. The strenuous work of delivering and receiving the convicts, that had commenced at 4 A.M., was still going on. The gang was to consist of six hundred and twenty-three men and sixty-four women. They had all to be counted, received according to the registry list, the sick and the weak sorted out, and all delivered to the convoy. The new inspector with two assistants, the doctor and medical assistant, the officer of the convoy and the clerk, were sitting in the prison-yard in the shade of a wall at a table, covered with writing-materials and papers. They called the prisoners one by one, examined and questioned them, and took notes.

The rays of the sun had gradually reached the table, and it was growing very hot and oppressive from the stillness of the air and the breath of the crowd of prisoners close by.

"Good heavens, will this never come to an end!" exclaimed the convoy officer, a tall, fat, red-faced man with high shoulders and short arms, who kept puffing the smoke of his cigarette into his thick moustache. He inhaled a big mouthful of smoke. "You are killing me. From where have you got them all? Are there many more?"

The clerk looked it up on the list.

"There are twenty-four men prisoners more besides the women."

"What are you standing there for? Come on," shouted the convoy officer to the prisoners who had not yet passed the inspection, and who stood crowded one behind another. The prisoners had been standing there more than three hours packed in rows in the full glare of the sun, waiting their turn.

While this was going on in the prison-yard, outside the gate (besides the sentry with a rifle, who stood there as usual) about twenty carts were drawn up to carry the luggage of the prisoners and such of the prisoners themselves as were too weak to walk, and at the corner stood a group of relatives and friends waiting to see the prisoners as they came out, to exchange a few words if a chance presented itself, and to give them a few things.

Nekhlyudov took his place in the group. He had stood there about an hour when the clanking of chains, the noise of footsteps, authoritative voices, the sound of coughing, and of the low murmur of a large crowd, became audible.

This continued for about five minutes, during which several jailers went in and out of the gateway. At last the word of command was given. The gates opened with a thundering noise, the clattering of the chains became louder, and the convoy soldiers, dressed in white blouses and carrying rifles, came out into the street and took their places in a large, exact circle in front of the gate. This was evidently a usual, much-practised manœuvre. Then another command was given, and the convicts began coming out in couples, with flat, pancake-shaped caps on their shaven heads and sacks over their shoulders, dragging their chained legs and swinging one arm while the other supported the sack.

First came the men condemned to hard labour, all dressed alike in grey trousers and cloaks with marks on the back. All of them—young and old, thin and fat, pale, red, and dark, bearded and beardless, Russians, Tartars, Jews—came out clanking their chains and swinging their arms briskly as if prepared to go a long distance, but stopped after having taken ten steps, and obediently took their places behind each other, four abreast. Then immediately more shaved men streamed out, dressed in the same manner, with no chains on their legs, but fastened to one another by handcuffs. These were condemned to exile. They came out as briskly and stopped as suddenly, taking their places four in a row. Then came those exiled by their communes.

Then, in the same order, came the women: first those condemned to hard labour, with grey cloaks and kerchiefs; then the exiled women and those following their husbands of their own free will, dressed in their own town or village clothing. Some of the women were carrying babies wrapped in the fronts of their grey cloaks.

With the women came the children, boys and girls, who, like colts in a herd of horses, pressed in among the prisoners.

The men took their places silently, only coughing now and then or making short remarks.

The women talked without intermission. Nekhlyudov thought he saw Maslova among them as they were coming out, but she was at once lost in a large crowd, and he could only see grey creatures—seemingly devoid of all that was human or at any rate of all that was womanly—with sacks on their backs and children round them, taking their places behind the men.

Though all the prisoners had been counted inside the prison walls, the convoy counted them again, comparing the numbers with the list. This took very long, especially as some of the prisoners moved and changed places, which confused the convoy's calculation.

The convoy soldiers shouted at and pushed the prisoners (who complied, though angrily), and counted them over again. When all were counted the convoy officer gave a command, and a commotion arose in the crowd. The weak men and women and children rushed, racing each other, towards the carts, and began placing their bags on them and climbing up. Women with crying babies, merry children scrambling for places, and dull, careworn prisoners, got into the carts.

Several of the prisoners took off their caps and came up to the convoy officer with some request. Nekhlyudov found out later that they were asking for places in the carts. Nekhlyudov saw how the officer, without looking at the prisoners, drew in a whiff from his cigarette, and then suddenly waved his short arm in front of one of the prisoners, who quickly drew his shaved head back between his shoulders as if afraid of a blow and sprang back.

"I will give you a lift that you'll remember. You'll get there on foot right enough," shouted the officer. Only one of the men was granted his request—an old man with chains on his legs—and Nekhlyudov saw him take off his pancake-shaped cap and go up to the cart crossing himself. He could not manage to climb on to the cart because the chains prevented his lifting his weak old legs, but a woman who was sitting in the cart at last helped him, pulling him in by the hand.

When all the sacks were in the carts and those who were allowed to get on were seated, the officer took off his cap, wiped his forehead, his bald head and fat red neck, and crossed himself.

"March!" he commanded. The soldiers' rifles rattled, the prisoners took off their caps and crossed themselves, those who were seeing them off shouted something, the prisoners shouted something back, among the women there was great agitation; and the gang, surrounded by the soldiers in their blouses, moved forward, raising the dust with their chained feet. The soldiers went in front; then came the convicts condemned to hard labour, clattering their chains; then the exiled and those banished by their communes, chained in couples by their wrists; then the women. After them, on the carts loaded with sacks, came the weak ones. High up on one of the carts sat a woman closely wrapped up who kept shrieking and sobbing.

Chapter XXXV

THE PROCESSION was such a long one that the carts with the baggage and the weak prisoners started only when those in front were already out of sight. When the last of the carts started, Nekhlyudov got into the trap that stood waiting for him and told the *izvozchik* to overtake the prisoners in front, so that he could see if he knew any of the men in the gang, and also try to find Maslova among the women, and ask her if she had received the things he sent her.

It was very hot. There was no wind, and a cloud of dust raised by a thousand tramping feet hung all the time over the gang that was moving down the middle of the street. The prisoners were walking quickly, and the slow-going *izvozchik* horse was some time in catching them up. They passed row upon row of those strange and terrible-looking creatures, none of whom Nekhlyudov knew.

On they went, all dressed alike, moving a thousand feet all shod alike, and swinging their free arms as if to keep up their spirits. There were so many of them, they all looked so much alike, and were all placed in such strange unusual conditions, that they seemed to Nekhlyudov to be not men but some sort of peculiar and terrible creatures. This impression passed only when he recognised in the crowd of convicts the murderer Fedorov, and among the exiles Okhotin, the wit, and another tramp who had appealed to him for assistance. Almost all the prisoners turned and looked at the trap that was passing them and at the gentleman inside. Fedorov tossed his head backwards as a sign that he had recognized Nekhlyudov, Okhotin winked, but neither of them bowed, thinking it not permitted.

Catching up the women, Nekhlyudov at once recognised Maslova. She was in the second row. The first in the row was a short-legged, black-eyed, hideous woman, who had her cloak tucked up in her girdle. This was Horoshavka. The next was a pregnant woman who dragged herself along with difficulty. The third was Maslova; she was carrying her sack on her shoulder and looking straight before her. Her face appeared calm and resolute. The fourth in the row was a young, beautiful woman who was walking along briskly, dressed in a short cloak, her kerchief tied peasant fashion. This was Theodosia.

Nekhlyudov got down and approached the women, meaning to ask Maslova if she had received the things he had sent her and inquire how she was feeling, but the convoy sergeant who was walking on that side noticed him at once and ran towards him.

"You must not do that, sir. It's against the regulations to approach the gang," shouted the sergeant as he came up.

But when he recognised Nekhlyudov (whom every one in the prison knew) the sergeant raised his fingers to his cap and, stopping in front of him, said: "Not now, sir; wait till we get to the railway station: here it is not allowed. . . . Don't lag behind there; march!" he shouted to the convicts, and putting on a brisk air he ran back to his place at a trot, in spite of the heat and the elegant new boots on his feet.

Nekhlyudov went on to the pavement, and telling the *izvozchik* to drive behind walked on so as to keep the party in sight. Wherever the gang passed, it attracted attention mixed with horror and compassion. Those who drove past leant out of the vehicles and followed the prisoners with their eyes. Those on foot stopped and looked with fear and surprise at the terrible sight. Some came and gave alms to the prisoners, these being received by the convoy. Some followed the gang as if hypnotised; then stopped, shook their heads, and followed the prisoners only with their eyes. Everywhere people came out of the gates and doors and called others to come out too, or leant out of the windows looking, silent and immovable, at the frightful procession. At a crossroad a fine carriage was stopped by the procession. A fat shiny-faced coachman, with two rows of buttons on his back, sat on the box; a married couple sat facing the horses—the wife a pale thin woman in a light-coloured bonnet and with a bright sunshade in her hand, and the husband in a top hat and well-cut, light-coloured dust-coat. On the seat in front sat their children—a well-dressed little girl with loose fair hair, and as fresh as a flower, also holding a bright parasol, and an eight-year-old boy with a long, thin neck and sharp collar-bones, wearing a sailor hat with long ribbons.

The father angrily scolded the coachman for not passing in front of the gang when he had the chance, and the mother frowned and half closed her eyes with a look of disgust, shielding herself from the dust and the sun with the silk sunshade which she held close to her face.

The fat coachman frowned angrily at the unjust rebukes of his master—who had himself given the order to drive along that street—and with difficulty held in the glossy black horses, lathering under their harness and fretting to go on.

The policeman wished with all his soul to please the owner of the fine equipage by stopping the gang, yet felt that the dismal solemnity of the procession must not be broken even for so rich a gentleman. He only raised his fingers to his cap to show his respect for riches, and looked severely at the prisoners as if promising in any case to protect the owners of the carriage from them. So the carriage had to wait till the whole of the procession had passed, and could only move on when the last of the carts laden with sacks and prisoners rattled by. The hysterical woman who sat on one of the carts, and who had grown calm, again began shrieking and sobbing when she saw the elegant carriage. Then the coachman touched the reins slightly, and the black trotters, their shoes ringing on the cobbles, drew the softly-swaying carriage on its rubber tyres towards the country house where the husband, the wife, the girl and the boy with the sharp collar-bones, were going to amuse themselves.

Neither the father nor the mother gave the girl and boy any explanation of what they had seen, so that the children had themselves to find out the meaning of this curious sight.

The girl, taking the expression of her father and mother's faces into consideration, solved the problem by deciding that these people were quite another kind of men and women than her parents and their acquaintances; that they were bad people, and therefore had to be treated in this way. Therefore the girl felt nothing but fear, and was glad when she could no longer see those people.

But the boy with the long, thin neck, who had looked at the processions of prisoners without taking his eyes off them, solved the question differently. For he knew, firmly and without any doubt, having it straight from God, that these people were just the same kind of people as he was, and like all other people, and that therefore some one had done these people a wrong, something that ought not to have been done; and he was sorry for them and felt dread both at those who were shaved and chained and at those who had shaved and chained them. And so the boy's lips pouted more and more, and he made greater and greater efforts not to cry, thinking it a shame to cry about such a matter.

Chapter XXXVI

NEKHLYUDOV KEPT up with the quick pace of the convicts. Though lightly clothed he felt dreadfully hot, and it was difficult to breathe in the stifling, motionless, burning air filled with dust.

When he had walked about a quarter of a mile he again got into the trap, but it felt still hotter in the middle of the street. He tried to recall last night's conversation with his brother-in-law, but the recollections no longer excited him as they had done in the morning. They were overcome by the impressions made by the starting of the gang and its march, and especially by the intolerable heat.

On the pavement, in the shade of some trees overhanging a fence, he saw two schoolboys standing over a kneeling vender of ices. One of the boys was already sucking a horn spoon and enjoying his ice, the other was waiting for a glass that was being filled with something yellowish.

"Where could I get something to drink here?" Nekhlyudov asked his *izvozchik*, feeling an insurmountable desire for some refreshment.

"There is a good place close by," the *izvozchik* answered, and, turning a corner, drove up to a door with a large sign-board. The plump shopman in a Russian shirt who stood behind the counter, and the waiters in their once-white clothing who sat at the tables (there being hardly any customers), looked with curiosity at the unusual visitor and rose to wait on him. Nekhlyudov asked for a bottle of seltzer water and sat down some way from the window at a small table covered with a dirty cloth. Two men sat at another table with tea-things and a white bottle in front of them, mopping their foreheads and calculating something in a friendly manner. One of them was dark and bald and had just such a fringe of hair at the back of his head as Rogozhinsky. This sight again reminded Nekhlyudov of yesterday's talk with his brother-in-law and of his wish to see him and Nataly.

"I shall hardly be able to do it before the train starts," he thought; "I'd better write." He asked for paper, an envelope and a stamp, and as he was sipping the cool, effervescing water he considered what he should say. But his thoughts wandered, and he could not manage to compose a letter.

"'My dear Nataly,—I cannot go away with the heavy impression that yesterday's talk with your husband has left,'" he began. . . . "What next? Ask him to forgive me for what I said yesterday? But I only said what I felt. He will think that I am taking it back. Besides, his interference in my private matters. . . . No, I cannot . . ." and again he felt hatred rising in his heart towards that man who was so foreign to him. He folded the unfinished letter and put it in his pocket, paid, went out, and again got into the trap to overtake the gang.

It had grown still hotter. The stones and the walls seemed to be breathing out hot air, the pavement seemed to scorch the feet, and Nekhlyudov felt a burning sensation in his hand when he touched the lacquered mud-guard of the trap.

The horse was jogging along at a weary trot, striking the uneven, dusty road monotonously with its hoofs; the *izvozchik* kept falling into a doze. Nekhlyudov sat without thinking of anything, gazing indifferently before him.

In front of the gates of a big house, where the road sloped to the gutter, a group of people had collected and a convoy soldier stood by.

Nekhlyudov stopped the driver. "What has happened?" he inquired of a porter.

"Something is the matter with a convict."

Nekhlyudov got down and approached the group. On the rough stones of the gutter, with his head lower than his feet, lay a broad-shouldered, elderly convict, with red beard and flat nose, and very red in the face. He had on a grey cloak and grey trousers, and lay on his back with the palms of his freckled hands downwards, his bloodshot eyes fixed on the sky; and at long intervals his broad, high chest heaved, and he groaned. By him stood a cross-looking policeman, a pedlar, a postman, a clerk, an old woman with a parasol, and a short-haired boy with an empty basket.

"They are weak. They get weak sitting locked up in prison, and then they are taken through the most broiling heat," said the clerk, addressing Nekhlyudov, who had just come up.

"Probably he'll die," said the old woman with the parasol, in a doleful tone.

"His collar should be loosened," said the postman.

The policeman began, with his thick, trembling fingers, clumsily to untie the tapes that fastened the shirt round the red, sinewy neck. He was evidently excited and confused, but still thought it necessary to address the crowd.

"What have you collected here for? It is hot enough without your keeping the air off."

"They should have been examined by a doctor and the weak ones left behind. He has been sent out more dead than alive," said the clerk, showing off his knowledge of the law.

The policeman, having undone the tapes of the shirt, rose and looked round.

"Move on, I tell you. It is not your business, is it? What's there to stare at?" he said, and turned to Nekhlyudov for sympathy, but not finding any in his face he turned to the convoy soldier.

But the soldier stood aside examining the down-trodden heel of his boot, and was quite indifferent to the policeman's perplexity.

"Those whose business it is don't care. . . . Is it right to do men to death like this? . . . A convict is a convict, but still he is a man," voices were heard saying in the crowd.

"Raise his head higher and give him some water," said Nekhlyudov.

"Water has been sent for," said the policeman, and taking the prisoner under the arms he with difficulty pulled his body a little higher up.

"Now then, what's this crowd here for?" said a decided, authoritative voice, and a police officer with a wonderfully clean, shiny blouse and still more shiny top-boots came up to the assembled crowd.

"Move on. No standing about here," he shouted to the crowd, before he knew what had attracted it.

When he came near and saw the dying convict, he made a sign of approval with his head as if he had quite expected it, and turning to the policeman said, "How is this?"

The policeman said that as a gang of prisoners was passing, one of the convicts had fallen down and the convoy officer had ordered him to be left behind.

"Well, that's all right. He must be taken to the police station. Call an *izvozchik*."

A porter has gone for one," said the policeman, with his fingers to his cap.

The shopman began saying something about the heat.

"Is it your business, eh? Move on," said the police officer, and looked so severely at him that the clerk was silenced.

"He ought to have a little water," said Nekhlyudov. The police officer looked severely at Nekhlyudov also, but said nothing. When the porter brought a mug full of water, the officer told the policeman to offer some to the convict. The policeman raised the drooping head and tried to pour a little water into the mouth, but the prisoner could not swallow it and it ran down his beard, wetting his jacket and his coarse, dirty, linen shirt.

"Pour it on his head," ordered the officer; and the policeman took off the pancake-shaped cap, and poured the water over the red curls and the bald part of the prisoner's head. His eyes opened wide as if in fear, but his position remained unchanged.

Streams of dirt trickled down his dusty face, but the mouth continued to gasp in the same regular way and his whole body shook.

"Look here! Take this one," said the police officer, pointing to Nekhlyudov's *izvozchik*. "You there, drive up!"

"I am engaged," said the *izvozchik* dismally, and without looking up.

"It is my *izvozchik*; but take him. I will pay you," added Nekhlyudov, turning to the *izvozchik*.

"Well, what are you waiting for?" shouted the officer. "Catch hold."

The policeman, the porter, and the convoy soldier lifted the dying man and carried him to the trap, and put him on the seat. But he could not sit up; his head fell back and the whole of his body glided off the seat.

"Lay him down," ordered the officer.

"It's all right, your honour; I'll get him to the police station like this," said the policeman, getting the dying man by his side on the seat, and clasping his strong right arm round the body under the arms. The convoy soldier lifted the stockingless feet in their prison shoes and placed them in the trap.

The police officer looked round, and noticing the convict's pancake-shaped cap lifted it up and put it on the wet, drooping head.

"Go on," he ordered.

The *izvozchik* looked angrily round, shook his head, and accompanied by the convoy soldier started slowly back towards the police station. The policeman, sitting beside the convict, kept dragging up the body that was continually sliding down from the seat, while the head swung from side to side.

The convoy soldier, who was walking by the side of the trap, kept putting the legs in position. Nekhlyudov followed the trap.

Chapter XXXVII

THE TRAP passed the fireman who stood sentry at the entrance,[1] drove into the yard of the police station and stopped at one of the doors.

In the yard several firemen with their sleeves tucked up were washing

---

[1] The fire brigade and police stations are generally together in Moscow.

some kind of cart and talking loudly. When the trap stopped, several policemen surrounded it, and seizing the lifeless body of the convict under the arms, lifted it out of the trap which creaked under the weight.

The policeman who had brought the body got down, shook his numbed arm, took off his cap, and crossed himself. The body was carried through the door and up the stairs. Nekhlyudov followed. Four beds stood in the small, dirty room to which the body was taken. On two of them sat a couple of sick men in dressing-gowns, one with a crooked mouth and bandaged neck, the other a consumptive. Two of the beds were empty; the convict was laid on one of them. A little man with glistening eyes and continually moving brows, with only his underclothes and stockings on, came up with quick, soft steps, looked at the convict and then at Nekhlyudov, and burst into loud laughter. This was a madman who was being kept in the police hospital.

"They wish to frighten me, but no, they won't succeed," he said.

The policemen who carried the corpse were followed by a police officer and a medical assistant.

The medical assistant came up to the body and lifted the freckled hand which, though still soft, was deadly pale and had already grown cold. He held it for a moment and then let it drop. It fell lifelessly on the dead man's stomach.

"He's done for," said the medical assistant, but, evidently to be quite in order, he undid the wet, unbleached shirt, and tossing back his curly hair put his ear to the convict's yellowish, broad, immovable chest. All were silent. The medical assistant raised himself again, shook his head, and touched with his fingers first one lid and then the other over the open, fixed, blue eyes.

"I'm not frightened, I'm not frightened," the madman kept repeating, spitting in the direction of the medical assistant.

"Well?" asked the police officer.

"Well?" replied the medical assistant, "he must be put into the mortuary."

"Be careful! Are you sure?" said the police officer.

"It's time I should know," said the medical assistant, drawing the shirt over the chest of the corpse. "However, I will send for Matthew Ivanich and let him have a look. Petrov, call him," and the medical assistant stepped away from the body.

"Take him to the mortuary," said the police officer. "And then you must come into the office and sign," he added to the convoy soldier who had not left the convict for a moment.

"Yes, sir," said the soldier.

The policemen lifted the body and carried it down again. Nekhlyudov wished to follow but the madman kept him back.

"You are not in the conspiracy, so give me a cigarette," he said. Nekhlyudov got out his cigarette case and gave him one.

The madman, quickly moving his brows all the time, began relating how they tormented him by thought-suggestion.

"Why, they are all against me, and torment and torture me through their mediums."

"Excuse me," said Nekhlyudov, and without listening any further he left the room and went out into the yard, wishing to see where the body would be put.

The policemen with their burden had already crossed the yard and were entering the door of a cellar. Nekhlyudov wished to go up to them, but the police officer stopped him.

"What do you want?"

"Nothing."

"Nothing? Then go."

Nekhlyudov obeyed, and returned to his *izvozchik*, who was dozing. He woke him and they drove back towards the railway station.

They had not gone a hundred yards before they met a cart accompanied by a convoy soldier with a rifle. On the cart lay another convict, who was evidently already dead. The convict lay on his back in the cart, his shaven head (from which the pancake-shaped cap had slid over the black-bearded face down to the nose) shaking and thumping at every jolt. The driver, in his heavy boots, walked by the side of the cart holding the reins; a policeman followed on foot. Nekhlyudov touched his *izvozchik's* shoulder.

"Just look what they are doing!" said the *izvozchik*, stopping his horse.

Nekhlyudov got down, and, following the cart, again passed the sentry and entered the gate of the police station. By this time the firemen had finished washing the cart, and instead of them a tall, bony man, with a blue band round his cap, the captain of the fire brigade, stood with his hands in his pockets, looking severely at a fat-necked, well-fed, bay stallion that was being led up and down before him by a fireman. The stallion was lame on one of his forefeet, and the fire brigade captain was angrily saying something to a veterinary surgeon who stood by.

The police officer was also standing there. Seeing another corpse he went up to the convoy soldier.

"Where did you pick him up?" he said, shaking his head disapprovingly.

"On the Gorbatovskaya," answered the policeman.

"A prisoner?" asked the fire brigade captain.

"Yes. It's the second to-day."

"Well, I must say they make some queer arrangements. Though of course it's a broiling day," said the chief of the fire brigade; then, turning to the fireman who was leading the lame stallion, he shouted:—

"Put him in the corner stall. And as to you, you hound, I'll teach you how to cripple horses worth more than you are, you scoundrel!"

The dead man was taken from the cart by the policemen just in the same way as the first had been, and carried upstairs into the hospital. Nekhlyudov followed them as if he were hypnotised.

"What do you want?" asked one of the policemen. But Nekhlyudov did not answer, and followed where the body was being carried. The madman, sitting on a bed, was greedily smoking the cigarette Nekhlyudov had given him.

"Ah, you've come back," he said, and laughed. When he saw the body he made a face, and said: "Again! I am sick of it. I am not a boy, am I, eh?" and he turned to Nekhlyudov with a questioning smile.

Nekhlyudov was looking at the dead man, whose face, which had been hidden by his cap, was now visible. This convict was as handsome in face and body as the other was ugly. He was a man in the full bloom of life. Notwithstanding the disfigurement from half of his head being shaved, the straight, though not high forehead, slightly arched above the black, lifeless eyes, was very fine, and so was the nose above the thin, black moustache. There was a smile on the lips that were already growing blue, a small beard outlined the lower part of the face, and on the shaven side of the head one noticed a firm, well-shaped ear. The expression of his face was calm, serious, and kind.

One could see that possibilities of a higher life had been destroyed in this man, while the fine bones of his hands and shackled feet, the strong muscles of all his well-proportioned limbs, showed what a beautiful, strong, agile human animal he had been. Merely as an animal he had been far more perfect of his kind than the bay stallion about the laming of which the captain of the fire brigade was so angry.

Yet he had been done to death; and not only was no one sorry for him as a human being, no one was even sorry that so fine a working animal had perished. The only feeling evinced was one of annoyance at the bother caused by the necessity of getting this body, threatened with putrefaction, out of the way. The doctor and his assistant entered the hospital, accompanied by the inspector of the police station. The doctor was a thick-set man, dressed in a pongee silk coat, and trousers of the same material closely fitting his muscular thighs. The inspector was a little fat fellow, with a red face as round as a ball, which he made still redder and rounder by a habit he had of filling his cheeks with air and slowly letting it out again. The doctor sat down on the bed by the side of the dead man, lifted the hands in the same way as his assistant had done, put his ear to the heart, and rose, pulling his trousers straight.

"Could not be more dead," he said.

The inspector filled his mouth with air and slowly let it out again.

"What prison is he from?" he asked the convoy soldier.

The soldiers told him, and reminded him of the chains on the dead man's feet.

"I'll have them taken off; we have got a smith about, the Lord be thanked," said the inspector, and having filled his cheeks again he went towards the door slowly letting out the air.

"Why has this happened?" Nekhlyudov asked the doctor.

The doctor looked at him through his spectacles.

"Why has what happened? Why they die of sunstroke, you mean? This is why. They sit all through the winter without exercise and without light, and they are suddenly taken out into the sunshine on a day like this: they march in a crowd so that they get no air, and sunstroke results."

"Then why are they sent out?"

"Oh, as to that, go and ask those who send them. But may I ask who you are?"

"I am a stranger."

"Oh! Well, good afternoon; I have no time." The doctor was vexed; he gave his trousers a downward pull, and went towards the beds of the sick.

"Well, how are you getting on?" he asked the pale man with the crooked mouth and bandaged neck.

Meanwhile the madman sat on a bed, and, having finished his cigarette, kept spitting in the direction of the doctor.

Nekhlyudov went down into the yard and out of the gate, passing the firemen's horses and some hens and the sentry in his brass helmet, and got into the trap, the driver of which had again fallen asleep.

Chapter XXXVIII

WHEN NEKHLYUDOV arrived at the station the prisoners were all seated in railway carriages with grated windows. Some people, who had come to see them off, stood on the platform, but were not allowed to approach the carriages. The convoy was much troubled that day. On the way from the prison to the station, besides the two Nekhlyudov had seen, three other prisoners had fallen and died of sunstroke. One was taken to the nearest police station like the first two, and the others died at the railway station.[1] The convoy men were not troubled because five men who might have been alive died while in their charge. This did not trouble them, but they were concerned lest anything that the law required in such cases should be omitted. To convey the bodies to the places appointed, to deliver up their papers and belongings, to take them off the list of those to be conveyed to Nizhny—all this was very troublesome, especially on such a hot day.

It was this that occupied the convoy men, and until it was all accomplished Nekhlyudov and the others who asked for permission to do so were not allowed to go up to the carriages. Nekhlyudov, however, tipped the convoy sergeant, and was soon allowed to go up. The sergeant let Nekhlyudov pass, but asked him to be quick and get his talk over before any of the officials noticed him. There were eighteen carriages in all, and, except one for the officials, they were all quite full of prisoners. As Nekhlyudov passed the carriages he listened to what was going on in them. In all the carriages was heard the clanking of chains and the sound of bustle mixed with loud and senseless language, but not a word was being said about their dead fellow-prisoners. The talk was all about sacks, drinking-water, and the choice of seats.

Looking into one of the carriages, Nekhlyudov saw two convoy soldiers taking the manacles off the hands of the prisoners. The prisoners held out their arms, and one of the soldiers unlocked the manacles with a key and took them off, and the other collected them.

Passing all the men's carriages Nekhlyudov came up to the women's. From the second of these he heard a woman's groans: "Oh, oh, oh! O God! Oh, oh! O God!"

Nekhlyudov passed this carriage and went up to a window of the third carriage, which a soldier had pointed out to him. When he put his face near the window he felt the hot air, heavy with the smell of human perspiration, coming out of it, and heard distinctly the shrill sound of women's voices.

All the seats were filled with red, perspiring, loudly talking women, dressed in prison cloaks and white jackets. Nekhlyudov's face at the window attracted their attention. Those nearest stopped talking and drew towards him. Maslova, in her white jacket and with her head uncovered, sat by the opposite window. The fair, smiling Theodosia sat a little nearer to him. Recognising Nekhlyudov, she nudged Maslova and pointed to the window.

---

[1] In Moscow, about 1880, five convicts died of sunstroke in one day on their way from the Boutirsky prison to the Nizhny railway station.—L. T.

Maslova rose hurriedly, threw her kerchief over her black hair, and with a smile on her hot red face came up to the window and took hold of one of the bars.

"Well, it is hot," she said with a glad smile.

"Did you get the things?"

"Yes, thank you."

"Is there anything more you want?" asked Nekhlyudov, while the air came out of the hot carriage as from an oven.

"I want nothing, thank you."

"If we could get a drink," said Theodosia.

"Yes, if we could get a drink," repeated Maslova.

"Why, have you not got any water?"

"They put some in, but it is all gone."

"I will ask one of the convoy men directly. We shall not see each other now till we get to Nizhny."

"Why, are you coming?" said Maslova, as if she did not know it, and looked joyfully at Nekhlyudov.

"I am coming by the next train."

Maslova said nothing, but only sighed deeply.

"Is it true, sir, that twelve convicts have been done to death?" said a severe-looking old prisoner with a deep voice like a man's.

It was Korableva.

"I did not hear of twelve; I have seen two," said Nekhlyudov.

"They say there are twelve they've killed. And will nothing be done to them? To think of it! The devils!"

"And have none of the women fallen ill?" Nekhlyudov asked.

"Women are stronger," said another of the prisoners—a short little woman—and laughed; "only there's one that has taken it into her head to be delivered. There she goes," she said, pointing to the next carriage, whence proceeded the groans.

"You ask if we want anything," said Maslova, trying to keep the smile of joy from her lips; "could not this woman be left behind, suffering as she is? There now, if you would tell the authorities——"

"Yes, I will."

"And one thing more; could she not see her husband—Taras?" she added, pointing with her eyes to the smiling Theodosia. "He is going with you, is he not?"

"Sir, you must not talk," said a convoy sergeant.

He was not the one who had let Nekhlyudov pass. Nekhlyudov left the carriage and went in search of an official to whom he might speak about the woman in travail and about Taras, but could neither find him, nor for a long time get an answer from any of the convoy. They were all in a bustle; some were leading a prisoner somewhere or other, others running to get themselves provisions, some were placing their things in the carriages or attending on a lady who was accompanying the convoy officer, and they answered Nekhlyudov's questions unwillingly.

Nekhlyudov found the convoy officer only after the second bell[2] had been rung.

The short-armed officer was wiping with his stumpy hand the moustache that covered his mouth, and, shrugging his shoulders, was reproving a corporal for something or other.

"What is it you want?" he asked Nekhlyudov.

"You've got a woman there who is being confined, so I thought it would be——"

"Well, let her be confined; we'll see to it afterwards," and briskly swinging his short arms he ran up to his carriage.

At this moment the guard passed with a whistle in his hand, and from the people on the platform and from the women's carriages there arose a sound of weeping and words of prayer.

Nekhlyudov stood on the platform by the side of Taras, and watched how the carriages with the shaved heads of the men at the grated windows glided past him one after the other. Then came the first of the women's carriages, with women's heads at the windows, some covered with kerchiefs, some bareheaded; then the second, from whence the groans still proceeded; then the carriage in which Maslova was. She stood with the others at the window and looked at Nekhlyudov with a pathetic smile.

Chapter XXXIX

THERE WERE still two hours before the passenger train, by which Nekhlyudov was going, would start. He had thought of using this interval to see his sister again; but after the impressions of the morning he felt so excited and done up that, sitting down on a sofa in the first-class refreshment room, he quite unexpectedly found himself so drowsy that he turned over on his side and at once fell asleep with his head on his hand.

A waiter in a dress-coat with a napkin in his hand woke him.

---

[2] In Russia it is usual at a terminus to ring a first bell fifteen or twenty minutes before a train starts, a second bell, say, ten minutes before, and a third bell just before. At intermediate stations the intervals are shorter.

"Please, sir, are you not Prince Nekhlyudov? A lady is looking for you."

Nekhlyudov started up, and, rubbing his eyes, recollected where he was and all that had happened in the morning.

He saw in imagination the procession of prisoners, the dead bodies, the railway carriages with barred windows and women locked up in them, one of whom was lacking assistance though tortured in travail, while another was pathetically smiling at him through the bars.

The reality before his eyes was very different: a table with vases, candlesticks and crockery, and agile waiters moving round it; and, at the end of the room, a cupboard, an array of bottles, and bowls of fruit, a barman, and the backs of passengers standing at the bar.

When Nekhlyudov had risen, and sat gradually collecting his thoughts, he noticed that everybody in the room was inquisitively looking at something occurring in the doorway. He also looked, and saw a procession of people carrying a chair on which sat a lady whose head was wrapped in some kind of airy fabric. Nekhlyudov thought he knew the footman who was supporting the chair in front, and the man behind, with gold cord on his cap, was a familiar doorkeeper. An elegant lady's-maid with a fringe and an apron, who was carrying a parcel, a parasol, and something in a round leather case, was walking behind the chair. Then came Prince Korchagin with his thick lips and apoplectic neck, and with a travelling cap on his head: behind him Missy, her cousin Misha, and an acquaintance of Nekhlyudov's—the long-necked diplomatist, Osten, with his protruding Adam's-apple and his unvarying merry mood and expression. He was saying something very emphatically, though jokingly, to the smiling Missy. The doctor was walking behind, angrily puffing at a cigarette. The Korchagins were moving from their estate near the city to an estate of the Princess's sister on the Nizhny railway.

The procession—the men carrying the chair, the maid, and the doctor—vanished into the ladies' waiting room, evoking a feeling of curiosity and respect in the onlookers. But the old Prince remained, and, sitting down at the table, called the waiter and ordered food and drink. Missy and Osten also remained in the refreshment room, and were about to sit down when they saw an acquaintance in the doorway and went up to her. It was Nataly Rogozhinskaya.

Nataly came into the refreshment room accompanied by Agrafena Petrovna, and both looked round the room. Nataly noticed, at the same moment, both her brother and Missy. She merely nodded to her brother, first going up to Missy; but having kissed her, she at once turned to him.

"At last I have found you," she said. Nekhlyudov rose to greet Missy,

Misha, and Osten, and to say a few words to them. Missy told him of a fire at their country house, which necessitated their moving to her aunt's. Osten began relating a funny story about a fire.

Nekhlyudov paid no attention, and turned to his sister.

"How glad I am that you have come."

"I have been here a long time," she said. "Agrafena Petrovna is with me." And she pointed to Agrafena Petrovna, who, in a waterproof and with a bonnet on her head, stood some way off and bowed to him with kindly dignity and some confusion, not wishing to intrude.

"We looked for you everywhere."

"And I had fallen asleep here. How glad I am you have come," repeated Nekhlyudov. "I had begun to write to you."

"Really?" she said, looking frightened. "What about?"

Missy and the gentlemen, noticing that an intimate conversation was about to commence between the brother and sister, went away. Nekhlyudov and his sister sat down by the window on a velvet-covered sofa, on which lay a rug, a box, and a few other things.

"After I left you yesterday, I felt inclined to return and express my regret, but I did not know how your husband would take it," said Nekhlyudov. "I spoke hastily to him, and it troubled me."

"I knew, I was sure, that you did not mean it," said his sister. "Oh, you know!" and the tears came to her eyes, and she touched his hand.

The sentence was not clear, but he understood it perfectly, and was touched by what it expressed. Her words meant that, besides the love for her husband which held her in its sway, she prized and considered important the love she had for him, her brother, and that every misunderstanding between them caused her deep suffering.

"Thank you, thank you. Oh! what I have seen to-day!" he said, suddenly recalling the second of the dead convicts. "Two prisoners have been killed."

"Killed? How?"

"Yes, killed. They led them out in this heat, and two died of sunstroke."

"Impossible! What, to-day? Just now?"

"Yes, just now. I have seen their corpses."

"But why killed? Who killed them?" asked Nataly.

"Those who forced them to go killed them," said Nekhlyudov with irritation, feeling that she looked at this, too, with her husband's eyes.

"O God!" said Agrafena Petrovna, who had come up to them.

"Yes, we have not the slightest idea of what is being done to those unfortunate beings. But it ought to be known," added Nekhlyudov, and looked at old Korchagin, who, sitting with a napkin tied round his neck and a bottle before him, turned round to Nekhlyudov just then.

"Nekhlyudov," he called out, "won't you join me and take some refreshment? It is a good thing before a long journey."

Nekhlyudov declined and turned away.

"But what are you going to do?" Nataly continued.

"What I can. I don't know, but I feel I must do something. And I shall l do what I can."

"Yes, I understand. And how about them?" she continued, with a smile and a look towards Korchagin. "Is it possible that it is all over?"

"Completely, and I think without any regrets on either side."

"It is a pity, and I am sorry. I am fond of her. However, supposing it is so, why do you wish to bind . . . to bind yourself?" she added shyly. "Why are you going?"

"I go because I must," answered Nekhlyudov, seriously and dryly, as if wishing to put a stop to this conversation. But at once he felt ashamed of his coldness. "Why not tell her all I am thinking, and let Agrafena Petrovna also hear it?" he thought, with a look at the old servant, whose presence made the wish to repeat his decision to his sister even stronger.

"You mean my intention to marry Katusha? Well, you see, I made up my mind to do it, but she refused definitely and firmly," he said, and his voice shook, as it always did when he spoke of this. "She does not wish to accept my sacrifice, but she is herself sacrificing what in her position means much, and I cannot accept this sacrifice if it is only a momentary impulse. So I am going to with her, and shall be where she is, and shall try to lighten her fate as much as I can."

Nataly said nothing. Agrafena Petrovna looked at her with a questioning look and shook her head. At this moment the same procession reappeared from the ladies' room. The same handsome footman (Philip) and the door-keeper were carrying the Princess Korchagina. She stopped the men who were carrying her and motioned Nekhlyudov to approach, and with a pitiful, languishing air extended her white, ringed hand, anticipating and fearing the firm pressure of his hand.

"*Epouvantable!*"[1] she said, meaning the heat. "I cannot stand it! *Ce climat me tue!*"[2] And, after a short talk about the horrors of the Russian climate, and inviting Nekhlyudov to visit them, she gave the men a sign to go on.

"Be sure and come to see us," she added, turning her long face towards Nekhlyudov as she was borne away.

The procession with the Princess turned to the right towards the first-

---

[1] Horrible!
[2] This climate is killing me.

class carriages. Nekhlyudov with the porter who was carrying his
things, and Taras with his sack, turned to the left.

"This is my companion," said Nekhlyudov to his sister, pointing to
Taras, whose story he had told her before.

"Surely not third-class?" said Nataly, when Nekhlyudov stopped in
front of a third-class carriage and Taras and the porter with the things
got in.

"Yes, I prefer it. I am going with Taras," he said. "One thing more,"
he added; "up to now I have not given the Kusminsky land to the peasants; so that in case of my death your children will inherit it."

"Dmitry, don't!" said Nataly.

"If I do give it away, all I can say is that everything else will be theirs,
as it is not likely I shall marry; and if I do marry I shall have no children, so that——"

"Dmitry, don't talk like that!" said Nataly. But Nekhlyudov noticed
that she was glad to hear him say it.

Higher up, by the side of a first-class carriage, there stood a group of
people still looking at the carriage into which the Princess Korchagina
had been carried. Most of the passengers were already seated. Some of
the late comers hurriedly clattered along the boards of the platform; the
guard was closing the doors and asking passengers to get in and others
to come out.

Nekhlyudov entered the hot, smelly carriage, but at once stepped
out again on to the small platform at the end of the carriage.

Nataly in her fashionable bonnet and cape stood near the carriage by
the side of Agrafena Petrovna, and was evidently trying to find something to say.

She could not ever say "*écrivez*,"[3] because they always used to laugh
at this word, habitually used by those about to part. The conversation
about money matters had in a moment destroyed the tender brotherly
and sisterly feelings that had filled their hearts. They felt estranged, so
that Nataly was glad when the train moved and she could only say,
nodding her head with a sad and tender look, "Good-bye, good-bye,
Dmitry."

But as soon as the carriage had passed her she thought of how she
should repeat to her husband the conversation with her brother, and
her face became serious and troubled.

Nekhlyudov, too, though he had nothing but the kindest feelings for
his sister, and had hidden nothing from her, now felt depressed and
uncomfortable with her, and was glad to part. He felt that the Nataly
who had once been so near to him no longer existed, and in her place

---

[3] Write to me.

was only the slave of a strange, unpleasant, dark, hairy man. He saw it clearly when her face lit up with peculiar animation as he spoke of what would particularly interest her husband—the giving up of the land to the peasants and the inheritance.

And this made him sad.

Chapter XL

THE HEAT in the large third-class carriage, which had been standing in the burning sun all day, was so great that Nekhlyudov did not go in but stayed on the little platform behind. But there was not a breath of fresh air there either, and Nekhlyudov breathed freely only when the train had passed the buildings and a draught blew across the platform.

"Yes, killed," he said, repeating to himself the words he had used to his sister. And in his imagination, in the midst of all other impressions, there arose with wonderful clearness the beautiful face of the second dead convict, with the smile on the lips, the severe expression of brows, and the small, firm ear below the shaven, bluish skull.

"And what seems terrible," he thought, "is that while he has been murdered, no one knows who murdered him. Yet he has been murdered. He was led out by Maslennikov's orders like all the rest of the prisoners. Maslennikov probably gave the usual order, signing with his stupid flourish a paper with a printed heading, and most certainly did not consider himself guilty. Still less will the careful doctor who examined the convicts. He performed his duty accurately, and separated the weak. How could he foresee this terrible heat, or the fact that they would start so late in the day and in such crowds? The prison inspector? But the inspector has only carried into execution the order that on a given day a certain number of exiles and convicts—men and women—were to be sent off. The convoy officer cannot be guilty either, for his business was to receive a certain number of persons at a certain place and to deliver up the same number. He conducted them in the usual manner, and could not foresee that two such strong men as those I saw would be unable to stand it, and would die. No one is guilty, and yet the men have been murdered by these people who are not guilty of their death.

"All this comes," thought Nekhlyudov, "from the fact that all these people—governors, inspectors, police officers, and policemen—consider that there are circumstances when human relations are not necessary between human beings. All these men, Maslennikov, and the inspector, and the convoy officer, if they were not governor, inspector, officer, would have considered twenty times before sending such a mass of people out in such heat—would have stopped twenty times on the way, and seeing a man growing weak, gasping for breath, would have led him into the shade, would have given him water and let him rest, and if an accident had still occurred, they would have expressed pity. But not only did they not do this, but they hindered others from doing it, because they thought not of men and their duty towards them but only of the office they themselves filled, and considered the obligations of that office to be above human relations. That is the whole matter," Nekhlyudov continued. "If once we admit—be it only for an hour or in some exceptional case—that anything can be more important than a feeling of love for our fellows, then there is no crime which we may not commit with easy minds, free from feelings of guilt."

Nekhlyudov was so engrossed by his thoughts that he did not notice a change in the weather. The sun was covered by a low-hanging, ragged cloud. A compact, light-grey cloud was rapidly coming up from the west, and far in the distance heavy, driving rain was already falling on the fields and woods. Moisture, coming from the cloud, mixed with the air. Now and then the cloud was rent by flashes of lightning, and peals of thunder mingled more and more often with the rattling of the train. The cloud came nearer and nearer, and slanting raindrops driven by the wind began to spot the platform and Nekhlyudov's coat. Stepping to the other side of the carriage platform, and inhaling the fresh moist air filled with the smell of corn and wet earth that had long been waiting for rain, he stood looking at the gardens, the woods, the yellow rye-fields, the green oat-fields, the dark green strips of potatoes in bloom, that glided past. Everything looked varnished: the green turned greener, the yellow yellower, the black blacker.

More! more!" said Nekhlyudov, gladdened by the sight of gardens and fields revived by the beneficent shower. The heavy shower did not last long. Part of the cloud came down in rain, part passed over, and soon the last fine drops were falling straight to the moist earth. The sun reappeared, everything began to glisten, and in the east—not very high above the horizon—appeared a bright rainbow broken only at one end, the violet tint being very distinct.

"Yes, what was I thinking about?" Nekhlyudov asked himself when all these changes in nature were over, and the train ran into a cutting with high, sloping sides.

"Oh! I was thinking that all those people: inspector, convoy men—all those in the service—are for the greater part kind people, cruel only because they serve."

He recalled Maslennikov's indifference when he told him of what was being done in the prison, the inspector's severity, and the cruelty of the convoy officer in refusing places on the carts to those who asked for them, and paying no attention to the fact that there was a woman in travail in the train. All these people were evidently invulnerable by and impermeable to the simplest feelings of compassion only because they held offices. "As officials they are as impermeable to the feelings of humanity as this paved earth is impermeable to the rain," thought Nekhlyudov, as he looked at the sides of the cutting paved with stones of different colours, down which the water was running in streams instead of soaking into the earth. "Perhaps it is necessary to pave slopes with stones, but it is sad to look at earth deprived of vegetation, when it might be yielding corn, grass, bushes, or trees like those on the top of this cutting.

"And it is the same thing with men," thought Nekhlyudov. "Perhaps these governors, inspectors, policemen are needed; but it is terrible to see men deprived of the chief human attribute: love and sympathy for one another. The thing is," he continued, "that these people acknowledge as law what is not law, and do not acknowledge as law at all, the eternal, immutable law written by God in the hearts of men. That is why I feel so depressed when I am with these people. I am simply afraid of them. And really they are terrible, more terrible than robbers. A robber might, after all, feel pity, but they can feel no pity; they are inured against pity as these stones are against vegetation. That is what makes them so terrible. It is said that the Pugatchevs and the Razins[1] are terrible. These are a thousand times more terrible," he continued in his thoughts.

"If a psychological problem were set to find means of making men of our time—Christian, humane, simple, kind people—perform the most horrible crimes without feeling guilty, only one solution could be devised: simply to go on doing what is being done now. It is only necessary that these people should be governors, inspectors, policemen; that they should be fully convinced that there is a kind of business, called Government service, which allows men to treat other men as things without having human brotherly relations with them; and that they should be so linked together by this Government service that the responsibility for the results of their deeds should not fall on any one of them individually. Without these conditions the terrible acts I witnessed to-day would be impossible in our times. It all lies in the fact that men think there are circumstances when one may deal with human beings without love. But there are no such circumstances. We

---

[1] Leaders of rebellions in Russia: Stenka Razin in the seventeenth and Pugatchev in the eighteenth century.

may deal with things without love—we cut down trees, make bricks, hammer iron without love—but we cannot deal with men without it, just as one cannot deal with bees without being careful. If one deals carelessly with bees one will injure them and will one's self be injured. And so with men. It cannot be otherwise, because mutual love is the fundamental law of human life. It is true that a man cannot force another to love him as he can force him to work for him, but it does not follow that one may deal with men without love, especially if one demands or expects anything from them. If you feel no love, sit still," Nekhlyudov thought; "occupy yourself with things, with yourself, with anything you like, only not with men. Just as you can only eat without injuring yourself when you are hungry, so you can only usefully and without injury deal with men when you love. Only let yourself deal with a man without love, as I did yesterday with my brother-in-law, and there are no limits to the suffering you will bring on yourself, as all my life proves. Yes, yes, it is so," thought Nekhlyudov; "it is true; yes, it is true," he repeated, enjoying the freshness after the torturing heat, and conscious of having attained the fullest clearness on a question that had long occupied him.

Chapter XLI

THE CARRIAGE in which Nekhlyudov had taken his place was half-filled with people. There were servants, working-men, factory hands, butchers, Jews, shopmen, workmen's wives, a soldier, two ladies (a young one, and an old one with bracelets on her bare arms), and a severe-looking gentleman with a cockade in his black cap. The bustle of taking their places was long over, and all these people were sitting quietly; some cracking and eating sunflower seeds, some smoking, some talking.

Taras sat to the right of the gangway, looking very happy, keeping a place for Nekhlyudov and carrying on an animated conversation with a muscular man in a cloth coat who sat opposite him, and who was, as Nekhlyudov afterwards found out, a gardener going to a new place. Before reaching Taras, Nekhlyudov stopped in the gangway near a patriarchal old man with a white beard and a nankeen coat, who was talking with a young woman in peasant dress. Next to the woman, cracking sunflower seeds incessantly, sat a little, seven-year-old girl dressed in a new peasant costume with a kerchief over her very fair hair.

The old man turned round, and, seeing Nekhlyudov, gathered up the skirts of his coat to make room for him on the shiny seat, and said in a friendly manner:—

"Please: here's a seat."

Nekhlyudov thanked him and took the seat. As soon as he was seated, the woman continued the interrupted conversation.

She was returning to her village, and told how her husband, whom she had been visiting, had received her in town.

"I was there during the Carnival, and now, by the Lord's help, I've been again," she said. "Then, God willing, at Christmas I'll go again."

"That's right," said the old man with a look at Nekhlyudov, "it's the best way to go and see him, else a young man can easily go to the bad, living in a town."

"Oh no, sir, mine is not such a man. No nonsense of any kind about him; his life is like a young maiden's. All the money he earns he sends home to a kopeyk. And as to our girl here, he was so glad to see her there are no words for it," said the woman, and smiled.

The little girl, who sat cracking her seeds and spitting out the husks, listened to her mother's words and, as if to confirm them, looked up with calm, intelligent eyes into the faces of Nekhlyudov and the old man.

"Well, if he's so wise that's better still," said the old man. "None of that sort of thing?" he added, with a look towards a couple, evidently factory hands, who sat at the other side of the carriage. The husband, with his head thrown back, was pouring vodka down his throat out of a bottle, and the wife, holding a bag out of which they had taken the bottle, sat watching him intently.

"No, mine neither drinks nor smokes," said the woman who was conversing with the old man, glad of the opportunity of praising her husband once more. "No, sir, the earth holds few like him." And, turning to Nekhlyudov, she added, "That's the sort of man he is."

"What could be better?" said the old man, looking at the factory worker. The man had had his drink and had passed the bottle to his wife. She laughed, shook her head, and also raised the bottle to her lips. Noticing Nekhlyudov and the old man looking at them, the factory worker addressed Nekhlyudov.

"What is it, sir? Because we are drinking? Ah, how we work no one sees, but every one sees how we drink. I have earned it, and I am drinking and treating my wife, and no one else."

"Yes, yes," said Nekhlyudov, not knowing what to say.

"True, sir. My wife is a steady woman. I am contented with my wife, because she can feel for me. Is it right what I'm saying, Mavra?"

"There you are, take it, I don't want any more," said the wife returning the bottle to him. "And what are you jawing like that for?" she added.

"There now! She's good—that good; and then suddenly she'll begin squeaking like a wheel that wants greasing. Mavra, is it right what I'm saying?"

Mavra laughed, and moved her hand with a tipsy gesture.

"Oh my, he's at it again."

"There now! She's that good—that good; but only let her get her tail over the reins, and you can't tell what she'll be up to. . . . Is it right what I'm saying? You must excuse me, sir; I've had a drop! What's to be done?" said the factory worker, and preparing to go to sleep he put his head on the lap of his smiling wife.

Nekhlyudov sat a while with the old man, who told him all about himself. The old man was a stove-builder who had been working for fifty-three years, and had built so many stoves that he had lost count. Now he wanted to rest but could not spare time. He had been to town and found employment for the young ones, and was now going to the country to see the people at home. After hearing the old man's story, Nekhlyudov went to the place that Taras was keeping for him.

"It's all right, sir; sit down, we'll put the sack here," said the gardener who sat opposite Taras, in a friendly tone, looking up into Nekhlyudov's face.

"Rather a tight fit, but no matter since we are friends," said Taras smiling; and lifting the sack weighing more than five stone as if it were a feather, he carried it across to the window.

"Lots of room; besides, one can stand a bit, or even get under the seat. We're quite comfortable. Why pretend not to be?" he said, beaming with friendliness and kindness.

Taras used to say of himself that he could not talk unless he had had a drink; drink, he said, helped him to find the right words, and then he could express everything. And, actually, when he was sober Taras kept silent; but when he had been drinking, which happened rarely and only on special occasions, he became very pleasantly talkative. Then he spoke a great deal, spoke well and very simply and truthfully, and especially with great kindliness, which shone in his gentle blue eyes and in the friendly smile that never left his lips.

He was in such a state to-day. Nekhlyudov's approach interrupted the conversation; but when he had put the bag in its place, Taras sat down again, and with his strong hands folded in his lap, and looking straight into the gardener's face, he continued his story. He was telling his new acquaintance about his wife, giving all the details: what she was being sent to Siberia for, and why he was now following her.

Nekhlyudov had never heard a detailed account of this affair, so he listened with interest. When he came up, the story had reached the point when the attempt to poison was already an accomplished fact, and the family had discovered that it was Theodosia's doing.

"It's about my troubles that I'm talking," said Taras, addressing Nekhlyudov with cordial friendliness. "I have chanced to some across such a hearty man and we've got into conversation, and I'm telling him all."

"I see," said Nekhlyudov.

"Well then, in this way, my friend, the business becomes known. Mother, she takes the cake. 'I'm going,' says she, 'to the police officer.' My father is a just old man. 'Wait, wife,' says he, 'the little woman is a mere child, and did not herself know what she was doing. We must have pity. She may come to her senses.' But, dear me, mother would not hear of it. 'While we keep her here,' she says, 'she may make away with us all like cockroaches.' Well, friend, so she goes off for the police officer. He bounces in upon us at once. Calls for witnesses."

"Well, and you?" asked the gardener.

"Well, I, you see, friend, roll about with the pain in my stomach, and spew. All my in'ards are turned inside out; I can't even speak. Well, so father he goes and harnesses the mare, and puts Theodosia into the cart, and is off to the police station and then to the magistrate's. And she, you know, just as she had done from the first, so also there, confesses all to the magistrate—where she got the arsenic, and how she kneaded the cake. 'Why did you do it?' says he. 'Why?' says she. 'Because he's hateful to me. I prefer Siberia to a life with him.' That's me," and Taras smiled.

"Well, so she confessed all. Then, naturally—the prison, and father comes back home alone. And harvest time just coming on, and mother the only woman at home, and she no longer strong. So we think what we are to do. Could we not get her out on bail? So father goes and sees an official. No go! Then another. I think he went to five of them, and we thought of giving it up. Then we happened to come across a clerk—such an artful one as you don't often find. 'You give me five rubles, and I'll get her out,' says he. He agreed to do it for three. Well, and what do you think, friend? I went and pawned the linen she herself had woven, and gave him the money. As soon as he had written that paper," drawled out Taras, just as if he were speaking of a shot, "it came off at once. I was up by that time and went to fetch her myself."

"Well, friend, so I go to town, put up the mare, take the paper out and go to the prison. 'What do you want?' 'This is what I want,' says I; 'you've got my wife here in prison.' 'And have you got a paper?' I gave him the paper. He gave it a look. 'Wait,' says he. So I sat down on a bench. It was already past noon by the sun. An official comes out. 'Are you Birukov?' 'I am.' 'Well, take her.' The gates opened, and they led her out in her own clothes, quite all right. 'Well, come along.' 'You have not come on foot?' 'No, I came with the horse.' So I went and paid the ostler and harnessed the mare, put in all the hay that was left, and covered it with sacking for her to sit on. She got in and wrapped her shawl round her, and off we drove. She says nothing, and I say nothing. Just as we were coming to the house she says, 'And how's mother; is she alive?' 'Yes, she's alive.' 'And father; is he alive?' 'Yes, he is.' 'Forgive me, Taras,' she says, 'for my folly. I did not know myself what I was doing.' So I say, 'Words won't mend matters. I have forgiven you long ago.' She said no more. We got home, and she just fell at mother's feet. Mother says, 'The Lord will forgive you.' And father said, 'How d'you do?' and 'What's past is past. Live as best you can. Now,' says he, 'is not the time for all that; there's the harvest down at Skorodino to be gathered in,' he says. 'Down on the manured acre, by the Lord's help, the ground has borne such rye that the sickle can't tackle it. It's all tangled and heavy, and has sunk beneath its weight; it must be reaped. You and Taras had better go and see to it to-morrow.' Well, friend, from that moment she took to the work and worked so that every one wondered. At that time we rented three desyatins, and by God's help we had a wonderful crop both of oats and rye. I mow, and she binds the sheaves, and sometimes we both of us reap. I am good at work and not afraid of it, but she's better still at whatever she takes up. She's a smart woman, young and full of life; and as to work, friend, she'd grown that eager that I had to stop her. We get home, our fingers swollen, our arms aching, and she, instead of resting, rushes off to the barn to make binds for the sheaves next day. Such a change!"

"Well, and had she grown kinder to you?" asked the gardener.

"That's certain. She clung to me as if we were one soul. Whatever I think, she understands. Even mother, angry as she was, could not help saying: 'It's as if our Theodosia had been transformed; she's quite a different woman now!' We were once going to cart the sheaves with two carts. She and I were in the first, and I say, 'How could you think of doing that, Theodosia?' and she says, 'How could I think of it? It was this way, I did not wish to live with you. I thought I'd rather die than live with you!' I say, 'And now?' and she says, 'Now you're in my heart!'" Taras stopped, and smiled joyfully, shook his head as if surprised. "Hardly had we got the harvest home, I went to soak the hemp, and when I got home"—he stopped and paused for a moment—"there was a summons: she must go to be tried. And we had forgotten all about the matter that she was to be tried for."

"It can only be the evil one," said the gardener. "Could any man of himself think of destroying a living soul? We had a fellow once"—and the gardener was about to begin a story when the train slackened.

"It seems we are coming to a station," he said. "I'll go and have a drink."

The conversation stopped, and Nekhlyudov followed the gardener out of the carriage on to the wet platform of the station.

Chapter XLII

BEFORE NEKHLYUDOV got out he had noticed several elegant equipages in the station yard, some with three, some with four, well-fed horses with tinkling bells on their harness. When he stepped out on the dark, wet boards of the platform, he saw a group of people in front of the first-class carriage, among whom were conspicuous a stout lady, wearing a waterproof, with costly feathers in her hat, and a tall thin-legged young man in a cycling suit. The young man had by his side an enormous, well-fed dog with an expensive collar. Behind them stood footmen, holding wraps and umbrellas, and a coachman—also come to meet the train.

On the whole of the group, from the fat lady down to the coachman who stood holding up his long coat, there lay the stamp of wealth and quiet self-assurance. An inquisitive and servile crowd rapidly gathered round this group—the station-master in his red cap, a gendarme, a thin young lady in a Russian costume, with beads round her neck (who, all through the summer, made a point of seeing the trains come in), a tele-graph clerk, and passengers, men and women.

In the young man with the dog Nekhlyudov recognised young Korchagin, the gymnasium student. The fat lady was the Princess's sis-ter, to whose estate the Korchagins were now moving. The guard, with his gold cord and shiny top-boots, opened the door of the railway car-riage and stood holding it as a sign of deference, while Philip and a porter with a white apron carefully carried out the long-faced Princess in her folding chair. The sisters greet each other, and French sentences began to fly about. Would the Princess go in a closed or an open car-riage? At last the procession started towards the exit, the lady's-maid with her curly fringe, parasol, and leather case in the rear.

Nekhlyudov, not wishing to meet them and to have to take leave over again, stopped before he got to the door, waiting for the whole procession to pass.

The Princess, her son, Missy, the doctor, and the maid, went out first, the old Prince and his sister-in-law remaining behind. Nekhlyudov was too far off to catch anything but a few disconnected French sentences of their conversation. As often happens, one of the sentences, uttered by the Prince, for some unaccountable reason remained in his memory with all its intonations and the sound of the voice.

"*Oh, il est du vrai grand monde, du vrai grand monde,*"[1] said the Prince about some one, in his loud, self-assured tone, as he went out of the station with his sister-in-law, accompanied by the respectful guards and porters.

At this moment from behind the corner of the station suddenly appeared a crowd of workmen in bark shoes, carrying their sheep-skin coats and sacks on their backs. The workmen went up to the nearest carriage with soft yet resolute steps, and were about to get in, but were at once driven away by a guard. Without stopping, the workmen passed on, hurrying and jostling one another, to the next carriage, and began getting in, catching their sacks against the corners and door of the carriage; but another guard caught sight of them from the door of the station, and shouted at them severely. The workmen, who had already got in, hurried out again, and went on still farther, with the same soft and firm steps, to the next carriage—the one in which Nekhlyudov sat. A guard was again going to stop them, but Nekhlyudov said there was plenty of room inside, and that they had better get in. They obeyed and got in, followed by Nekhlyudov. The workmen were about to take their seats, when the gentleman with the cockade and the two ladies, looking at this attempt to settle in their carriage as a personal affront to themselves, indignantly protested and wanted to turn them out. The workmen—there were twenty of them, old men and quite young ones, all of them with wearied, sunburnt, haggard faces—began at once to move on through the carriage, their sacks catching the seats, the walls, and the doors. They evidently felt they were to blame, and seemed ready to go on to the world's end and sit wherever they might be told to—even on spikes.

"Where are you pushing to, you devils? Sit down here," shouted another guard whom they met.

"*Voilà encore des nouvelles,*"[2] exclaimed the younger of the two ladies, quite convinced that she would attract Nekhlyudov's attention by her good French.

The lady with the bracelets kept sniffing and making faces, and remarked something about the pleasure of sitting with smelly peasants.

The workmen, experiencing the joy and calm felt by people who have escaped some kind of danger, jerked their heavy sacks off their shoulders and stowed them away under the seats.

The gardener, who had left his own seat to talk with Taras, now went

---

[1] Oh, he is of the best society, the best society.
[2] Here is something new.

back, so that there were two seats unoccupied opposite Taras, and one next to him. Three of the workmen took these seats, but when Nekhlyudov came up to them in his gentleman's clothing, they got so confused that they rose to leave them; but Nekhlyudov asked them to stay, and himself sat down on the arm of the seat next the gangway down the middle of the carriage.

One of the workmen, a man of about fifty, exchanged a surprised and even frightened look with a younger man. That Nekhlyudov, instead of scolding and driving them away as was natural to a gentleman, should give up his seat to them, astonished and perplexed them. They even feared that this might have some evil consequences.

However, they soon saw that there was no underlying plot when they heard Nekhlyudov talking quite simply with Taras. Feeling at ease, they told a lad to sit down on his sack and insisted that Nekhlyudov should resume his place. At first the elderly workman who sat opposite Nekhlyudov shrank and drew back his legs for fear of touching the gentleman, but after a while he grew quite friendly, and, in talking to him and Taras, even slapped Nekhlyudov familiarly on the knee when he wanted to draw special attention to what he was saying.

He told them all about his affairs, and of his work in the peat bogs, whence he was now returning home. He had been working there for two and a half months, and was bringing home his wages, which only came to ten rubles, since part had been paid in advance when he was hired. He explained how they worked, up to their knees in water from sunrise to sunset, with two hours' interval for dinner.

"Those who are not used to it find it hard, of course," he said; "but when one's hardened it doesn't matter, if only the food is right. At first the food was bad. Later the people complained and they got good food, and then it was easy to work."

Then he told them how for twenty-eight years he had gone out to work and sent all his earnings home: first to his father, then to his eldest brother, and now to his nephew, who was at the head of the household. On himself he spent only two or three rubles of the fifty or sixty he earned a year, just for luxuries—tobacco and matches.

"But I'm a sinner; and when tired I even drink a little vodka sometimes," he added with a guilty smile.

Then he told them how the women did the work at home; how the contractor had treated them (the men) to half a pail of vodka before they started to-day, how one of them had died and another was returning home ill. The sick workman he was talking about was in a corner of the same carriage. He was a young lad, with a pale, sallow face and bluish lips. He was evidently worn out by ague. Nekhlyudov went up to him, but the lad looked up with such a severe and suffering expression that Nekhlyudov did not care to trouble him with questions, but advised the elder man to buy him quinine and wrote the word down for him. He wished to give him money for it, but the old workman said he would pay for it himself.

"Well, much as I have travelled, I have never met such a gentleman before. Instead of punching your head, he actually gives up his place to you," said the old man to Taras. "It seems there are all sorts of gentlefolk, too."

"Yes, this is quite a new and different world," thought Nekhlyudov, looking at these spare, sinewy limbs, coarse, home-made garments, and sunburnt, kindly, though weary-looking faces, and feeling himself surrounded on all sides with new people and the serious interests, joys, and sufferings of a life of labour.

"Here is *le vrai grand monde*," thought Nekhlyudov, remembering the words of Prince Korchagin, and reminding himself of all that idle, luxurious world to which the Korchagins belonged, with their petty, mean interests. And he felt the joy of a traveller discovering a new, unknown, and beautiful world.

BOOK THREE

Chapter I

THE GANG of prisoners to which Maslova belonged had gone about three thousand miles. She and the other prisoners condemned for criminal offences had travelled by rail and steamboat as far as the town of Perm. It was only here that Nekhlyudov succeeded in obtaining permission for her to travel with the political prisoners, as Vera Dukhova, who was among the latter, had advised.

The journey to Perm had been very trying to Maslova, both physically and morally: physically, because of the overcrowding, the dirt, and the disgusting vermin which gave her no peace; morally, because of the equally disgusting men. The men, like the vermin, though they changed at each halting-place, were everywhere alike importunate. They swarmed round her, giving her no rest. Among the women prisoners and the men prisoners, jailers, and convoy soldiers, the habit of a kind of cynical debauchery was so firmly established that unless a female prisoner was willing to utilise her womanhood she had to be constantly on her guard. To be continually in a state of fear and strife was very trying, and Maslova was specially exposed to attacks, her appearance being attractive and her past known to every one. The resolute resistance with which she now met the importunities of all the men seemed offensive to them, and awakened another feeling, that of ill-will, towards her. But her position was made a little easier by her intimacy with Theodosia and with Taras, who, having heard of the molestations his wife was subject to, had been arrested at his own desire in Nizhny Novgorod in order to be able to protect her, and was now travelling with the gang as a prisoner.

Maslova's position became much more bearable in every way when she was allowed to join the political prisoners. Besides that political prisoners were provided with better accommodation and better food, and were treated less rudely, Maslova's condition was much improved by her being no longer molested by the men, and being able to live without being reminded of that past which she was so anxious to forget. But the chief advantage of the change lay in the fact that she made the acquaintance of several persons who exercised a decided and most beneficial influence on her character.

Maslova was allowed to be with the political prisoners at all the halting-places; but, being a strong and healthy woman, she was obliged to march with the criminal convicts. In this way she walked all the way from Tomsk. Two political prisoners also marched with the gang: Mary Pavlovna Shchetinina, the beautiful girl with the hazel eyes who had attracted Nekhlyudov's attention when he visited Dukhova in prison, and one Simonson, the dishevelled, dark young fellow with deep-set eyes whom Nekhlyudov had also noticed during the same visit, and who was now on his way to exile in the Yakutsk district. Mary Pavlovna was walking because she had given up her place on the cart to a woman criminal who was pregnant; and Simonson because he did not think it right to avail himself of a class privilege. These three used to start with the criminals early in the morning, before the rest of the political prisoners, who came on in the carts later; and this was the arrangement followed on the last march before reaching a certain big town, where a fresh convoy officer took charge of the gang.

It was early on a wet September morning. A cold wind blew in sudden gusts, and rain and snow kept falling by turns. The whole gang of prisoners (some four hundred men and fifty women) was already assembled in the court of the halting-place. Some of them were crowding round the chief of the convoy, who was giving to specially-appointed prisoners money for two days' keep to distribute among the rest; while others were purchasing food from women hawkers who had been let into the courtyard. One could hear the voices of the prisoners counting their money and making their purchases, and the shrill voices of the women selling the food.

Katusha and Mary Pavlovna, both wearing high boots and short fur cloaks and with shawls tied round their heads, came out of the building into the courtyard, where the saleswomen sat sheltered from the wind by the northern wall of the yard and vied with one another in offering their goods: hot meat-pies, fish, vermicelli, buck-wheat porridge, liver, beef, eggs, milk—one had even a roast pig to offer.

Simonson, in his rubber jacket and wearing rubber overshoes fastened with string over his worsted stockings (he was a vegetarian and did not use the skins of slaughtered animals), was also in the courtyard waiting for the gang to start. He stood by the porch jotting down in his notebook a thought that had occurred to him. This was what he wrote: "If a bacterium observed and examined a human nail, it would pronounce it inorganic matter; and thus we, with reference to the globe, examine its crust and pronounce it inorganic. This is incorrect."

Having bought eggs, bread, fish, and rusks, Maslova was putting them into her bag while Mary Pavlovna was paying the women, when a movement occurred among the convicts. All became silent, and began taking their places. The officer came out and gave the final orders before starting.

Everything was done as usual. The prisoners were counted, and the chains on their legs examined, and those who were to march in couples were linked together with manacles. But suddenly the angry authoritative voice of the officer shouting something was heard, and the sound of a blow as well as the crying of a child. All were silent for a moment, and then came a hollow murmur from the crowd. Maslova and Mary Pavlovna went towards the spot whence the noise came.

Chapter II

THIS IS what Mary Pavlovna and Katusha saw when they reached the scene. The officer, a sturdy fellow with fair moustaches, frowning, and uttering words of coarse abuse, stood rubbing the palm of his right hand, which he had hurt by striking a prisoner in the face. Before him stood a tall thin convict with half his head shaven, and dressed in a cloak too short for him and trousers much too short, wiping his bleeding face with one hand and holding a shrieking little girl wrapped in a shawl with the other.

"I'll give it you [foul abuse]. I'll teach you to argue [more abuse]. You're to give her to the women!" shouted the officer. "Now then, on with them!"

The convict (who was exiled by his village commune) had been carrying his little daughter all the way from Tomsk, where his wife had died of typhus. The officer had now ordered him to be manacled. The exile's explanations that he could not carry the child if he were manacled irritated the officer, who happened to be in a bad temper, and he gave the troublesome prisoner a beating for not obeying at once.[1]

A convoy soldier stood near the injured convict, together with a black-bearded prisoner with manacles on one hand, who looked gloomily from under his brows, now at the officer, now at the injured

---

[1] An incident described by D. A. Linyev in *Transportation.* —L. T.

prisoner with the little girl. The officer repeated his order to the soldier to take away the girl. The murmur among the prisoners grew louder.

"All the way from Tomsk they were not put on," came a hoarse voice from some one in the rear. "It's a child, and not a puppy."

"What's he to do with the lassie? That's not the law," said some one else.

"Who's that?" shouted the officer, as if he had been stung, and rushed into the crowd. "I'll teach you the law. Who spoke? You? You?"

"Everybody says so, because——" said a short, broad-faced prisoner.

Before he had finished speaking the officer hit him in the face with both hands. "Mutiny is it? I'll show you what mutiny means. I'll have you all shot like dogs, and the authorities will be only too thankful. Take the girl."

The crowd was silent. One convoy soldier pulled away the girl, who was screaming desperately, while another manacled the prisoner, now submissively holding out his hand.

"Take her to the women," shouted the officer, arranging his sword-belt.

The little girl, whose face had turned quite red, was trying to disengage her arms from under the shawl and screamed unceasingly. Mary Pavlovna stepped out from among the crowd and came up to the officer.

"Will you allow me to carry the little girl?" she said.

"Who are you?" asked the officer.

"A political prisoner."

Mary Pavlovna's handsome face with the beautiful prominent eyes (he had noticed her before, when the prisoners were given into his charge) evidently produced an effect on the officer. He looked at her in silence as if considering, then said: "I don't mind; carry her if you like. It is easy for you to show pity! But if he escaped, who would answer for it?"

"How could he run away with the child in his arms?" said Mary Pavlovna.

"I have no time to talk with you. Take her if you like."

"Shall I give her up?" asked the soldier.

"Yes, give her up."

"Come to me," said Mary Pavlovna, trying to coax the child to come to her.

But the child in the soldier's arms stretched herself towards her father and continued to scream, and would not go to Mary Pavlovna.

"Wait a bit, Mary Pavlovna," said Maslova, getting a rusk out of her bag, "she will come to me."

The little girl knew Maslova, and when she saw her face and the rusk she let herself be taken by her.

All became quiet. The gates were opened, and the gang went outside and formed in rows. The convoy counted the prisoners over again. The sacks were packed on the carts, and the weak prisoners seated on the top. Maslova, with the child in her arms, took her place next to Theodosia among the women. Simonson, who had all the time been watching what was going on, stepped with long determined strides up to the officer—who having given his orders was just getting into a trap—and said:—

"You have behaved badly."

"Get to your place; it is no business of yours."

"It is my business to tell you that you have behaved badly, and I have told you," said Simonson, looking intently into the officer's face from under his bushy eyebrows.

"Ready? March!" the officer called out, paying no heed to Simonson; and, taking hold of his driver's shoulder, he got into the trap. The gang started, spreading out as it came on to the muddy high road with ditches on each side, which led through a dense forest.

Chapter III

IN SPITE of their hard conditions, life among the political prisoners seemed very good to Katusha after the six years of depraved, luxurious, and effeminate life she had led in town, and after the several months' imprisonment with criminal prisoners. The fifteen to twenty miles covered each day, with good food and one day's rest after two days' marching, strengthened her physically; and the fellowship with her new companions opened out a life full of interests such as she had never dreamt of. People so wonderful (so she expressed it) as those whom she was now with, she had not only never met but could not even have imagined.

"There now! and I cried when I was sentenced," she said. "Why, I must thank God for it all the days of my life. I have learnt to know what I never should have found out otherwise."

She understood easily and without effort the motives that guided these people, and being of the people herself fully sympathised with them. She understood that they were for the people and against the upper classes, and, though themselves belonging to the upper classes, had sacrificed their privileges, their liberty, and their lives for the people. This especially made her value and admire them.

She was delighted with all her new companions, but particularly with Mary Pavlovna; whom she was not only delighted with, but loved with a peculiar, respectful, and devoted love. She was struck by the fact that this beautiful girl, who could speak three languages, the daughter of a rich general, gave away all that her rich brother sent her, lived like the simplest working girl, and dressed not only simply but poorly, paying no heed to her appearance. This trait, a complete absence of coquetry, was particularly surprising and therefore attractive to Maslova.

Maslova could see that Mary Pavlovna knew, and was even pleased to know, that she was beautiful, yet the effect her appearance had on men was not at all pleasing to her: she was even afraid of it, and had an absolute disgust and fear of all falling in love. Her men companions knew this, and never fell in love with her—or, at any rate, concealed it if they did—and behaved to her as they would to a man; but with strangers, who often molested her, the great physical strength on which she prided herself stood her in good stead.

"It happened once," she told Katusha, laughing, "that a man followed me in the street and would not leave me on any account. At last I gave him such a shaking that he was frightened and ran away!"

She became a revolutionist, as she said, because she had felt a dislike for the life of the well-to-do from childhood up, and loved the life of common people. She was always being scolded for spending her time in the servants' hall, in the kitchen or the stables, instead of in the drawing-room.

"But I found it amusing to be with the cooks and coachmen, and very dull with the ladies and gentlemen," she said. "Then, when I came to understand things, I saw that our life was altogether wrong. I had no mother and was not fond of my father, so I left home when I was nineteen, and went to work as a factory hand with a girl friend."

After she left the factory she lived in a village, then returned to town and lived in a lodging where they had a secret printing press. There she was arrested, and she was sentenced to hard labour. She said nothing about it herself, but Katusha heard from others that Mary Pavlovna was sentenced because, after the lodging was searched by the police and one of the revolutionists fired a shot in the dark, she pleaded guilty to the shot.

As soon as she had learned to know Mary Pavlovna, Katusha noticed that, whatever conditions she found herself in, Mary Pavlovna never thought of herself, but was always anxious to serve: to help some one, in things small or great. One of her present companions, Novodvorov, said of her that she devoted herself to the sport of philanthropy. And this was true. The interest of her whole life lay in searching for opportunities to serve others just as the sportsman searches for game. And the sport had become the habit, the business, of her life, and she did it all so naturally that those who knew her were no longer grateful, but simply expected it of her.

When Maslova first came among them, Mary Pavlovna felt repelled and disgusted. Katusha noticed this; but she also noticed that, having made an effort to overcome these feelings, Mary Pavlovna became particularly tender and kind to her. The tenderness and kindness of so uncommon a being touched Maslova so much that she gave her whole heart to her; and, unconsciously accepting her views, could not help imitating her in everything. And Mary Pavlovna was in her turn moved by this devoted love of Katusha's, and learned to reciprocate it. They were also united by the repulsion both felt from sexual love. The one loathed that love, having experienced all its horrors; the other, never having experienced it, looked on it as something incomprehensible, and at the same time as something repugnant and offensive to human dignity.

Chapter IV

MARY PAVLOVNA'S influence was one of the influences to which Maslova submitted herself. It arose from the fact that Maslova loved Mary Pavlovna. Another influence was that of Simonson. This influence arose from the fact that Simonson loved Maslova.

All men live and act partly according to their own, partly according to other people's ideas. The extent to which they do the one or the other is one of the chief things that differentiate men. To some, thinking is a kind of mental game: they treat their reason, in most cases, as if it were a driving-wheel without a connecting strap, and are guided in their actions by other people's ideas, by custom, by tradition, or by law. Some consider their own ideas the chief motive power of all their actions, listen to the dictates of their own reason and submit to it, only accepting other people's opinions occasionally and after weighing them critically. Simonson was such a man; he settled and verified everything according to his own reason, and acted on the decisions thus arrived at.

Having come to the conclusion, when a schoolboy, that his father's income as paymaster in a Government office was dishonestly earned, he told his father that it ought to be given to the people. When his father instead of listening to him gave him a scolding, he left the house and would no longer avail himself of his father's means. Having come

to the conclusion that all existing evils resulted from the people's ignorance, he joined the People's Party as soon as he left the University, took
a post as a village schoolmaster, and boldly taught and explained to his
pupils and to the peasants what he considered to be just, and openly
repudiated what he considered unjust.

He was arrested and tried.

During his trial he came to the conclusion that his judges had no
right to judge him, and told them so. When the judges paid no heed to
his words but went on with the trial, he decided not to answer them,
and remained resolutely silent when they questioned him.

He was exiled to the Government of Archangel. There he formulated a religious teaching which governed all his activity. This teaching
was founded on the theory that everything in the universe lives, that
nothing is dead, and that all the objects we consider lifeless, or inorganic, are but parts of an enormous organic body which we cannot
compass, and that the task of man, as part of that huge organism, is to
sustain its life and that of all its living parts. And therefore he considered it a crime to destroy life, and was against wars, capital punishment,
and every kind of killing, not only of human beings but also of animals.
Concerning marriage, too, he had his own theory: he thought that pro-
creation was a lower function of man, the higher function being to
serve already existing lives. He found support for this theory in the fact
that there exist phagocytes in the blood. Celibates, according to his
opinion, were like phagocytes, whose mission it is to help the weak and
sick parts of the organism. From the moment he came to this conclusion he lived accordingly, though in his youth he had been dissipated;
and he considered himself, and Mary Pavlovna as well, to be human
phagocytes.

His love for Katusha did not infringe this conception, because he
loved her platonically, and such love, he considered, could not hinder
his activity as a phagocyte, but, on the contrary, acted as an inspiration.

He decided in his own way not only moral questions but also the
most practical ones. He had a theory of his own about all practical matters: had rules respecting how many hours to work, how many to rest,
as to the kind of food to eat, how best to dress, and to heat and light
houses.

With all this Simonson was very shy and modest; but, when he had
once made up his mind, nothing could shake him.

And this man, through his love for her, had a decided influence on
Maslova. With a woman's instinct Maslova very soon found out that he
loved her, and the fact that she could awaken love in such a man raised
her in her own esteem. Nekhlyudov offered to marry her from magna-
nimity and because of what had happened in the past, but Simonson

loved her as she was now, and simply because he loved her. And she felt that Simonson considered her to be an exceptional woman, having peculiarly high moral qualities. She was not quite sure what the qualities were he attributed to her, but in order to be on the safe side and that he should not be disappointed in her, she tried with all her might to awaken in herself all the highest qualities she could conceive, and to be as good as possible.

This had begun while they were still in prison, when, one general visiting day, she had noticed his kindly dark-blue eyes gazing fixedly at her from under his projecting brows. Even then she had noticed too that this was a peculiar man and that he was looking at her in a peculiar manner; and she had also noticed the striking combination of sternness, which the unruly hair and the frowning forehead gave to his appearance, with the childlike kindness and innocence of his look. She saw him again in Tomsk, where she joined the political prisoners. And though not a word had passed between them, the look they exchanged was an admission of remembrance and of their importance to each other. Even after that there were no serious conversations between them, but Maslova felt that when he spoke in her presence his words were addressed to her, and that he spoke for her sake, trying to express himself as clearly as possible. But it was when he started walking with the criminal prisoners that they grew specially near to one another.

Chapter V

UNTIL THEY left Perm, Nekhlyudov managed to see Katusha only twice—once in Nizhny Novgorod, before the prisoners were embarked on a barge on which they were caged in with wire netting, and again in Perm in the prison office. At both these interviews he found her reserved and unkind. His questions whether she was in want of anything and whether she was comfortable, she answered evasively and bashfully, and, as he thought, with the same feeling of hostile reproach which she had shown several times before. Her depressed state of mind—which was only the result of the molestations she was undergoing at the time from the men—tormented Nekhlyudov. He feared lest, influenced by the hard and degrading circumstances in which she was placed during the journey, she should again fall into that state of despair and discord with herself which formerly made her irritable with him, and which had caused her to drink and smoke to gain oblivion. But he was unable to help her in any way during this part of the journey, for he could never see her. It was only when she joined the political prisoners that he saw how unfounded his fears were, and at each interview he noticed that inner change he so strongly desired to see in her becoming more and more definite. The first time they met in Tomsk she was again just as she had been when leaving Moscow. She did not frown or become confused when she saw him, but met him joyfully and simply, thanking him for what he had done for her, especially for bringing her among the people with whom she now was.

After two month's march with the gang the change that had taken place within her became apparent in her appearance. She grew sunburnt and thinner, and seemed older; wrinkles appeared on her temples and round her mouth. She had no ringlets on her forehead now, and her hair was covered by her kerchief. In the way it was arranged, as well as in her dress and manner, there was no trace of coquetry left. And this change which had taken place and was still unceasingly going on in her made Nekhlyudov very happy.

He felt for her something he had never experienced before. This feeling had nothing in common with his first poetic love for her, still less with the sensual love that had followed, or even with the satisfaction of a duty fulfilled (not unmixed with self-admiration) with which, after the trial, he decided to marry her. The present feeling was simply one of pity and tenderness. He had felt it when he met her in prison for the first time, and again when, after conquering his repugnance, he forgave her the imagined intrigue with the medical assistant in the hospital (the injustice done her had since been discovered). It was the same feeling he now had, only with this difference: that whereas formerly it was momentary, now it became permanent. Whatever he thought of now, whatever he did, a feeling of pity and tenderness dwelt with him, and pity and tenderness not only for her but for every one. This feeling seemed to have opened the floodgates of love which had found no outlet in Nekhlyudov's soul, and the love now flowed out to every one he met.

During the journey Nekhlyudov's feelings were so stimulated that he could not help being attentive and considerate to everybody from the coachmen and the convoy soldiers to the prison inspectors and governors with whom he had to deal.

Now that Maslova was among the political prisoners Nekhlyudov naturally became acquainted with many of them; first in Ekaterinburg where they had a good deal of freedom and were kept all together in a large cell, and then on the road with the five men and four women to whose company she was transferred. Coming into contact in this way with political exiles caused Nekhlyudov to change his mind completely about them.

From the very beginning of the revolutionary movement in Russia, but especially since that 1st of March (O.S.) when Alexander II was murdered, Nekhlyudov had regarded the revolutionists with dislike and contempt. He was revolted by the cruelty and secrecy of the methods they employed in their struggles against the Government, especially by the cruelty of the murders they committed; he also disliked the air of self-importance which was a prominent characteristic of theirs. But having come to know them more intimately, and learned all they had suffered at the hands of the Government, he saw that they could not be other than they were.

Terrible and senseless as were the torments inflicted on the so-called criminal prisoners, there was at least some semblance of justice shown them before and after they were sentenced; but in the case of the political prisoners there was not even that semblance, as Nekhlyudov saw in the case of Shustova and of many of his new acquaintances. These people were dealt with like fish caught in a net; everything that gets into the net is pulled ashore, and then the big fish which are required are sorted out, and the little ones are left to perish unheeded on the shore. Having captured hundreds who were evidently guiltless, and who could not be dangerous, the Government kept them in prison for years, where they became consumptive, went out of their minds, or committed suicide; keeping them only because the officials had no inducement to set them free, but thought that safe in prison they might possibly be of use to elucidate some question at a judicial inquiry. The fate of these persons, often innocent even from the Government point of view, depended on the whim, leisure, or humour of some police officer, or spy, or public prosecutor, or magistrate, or governor, or minister. Some one of these officials feels dull, or inclined to make himself prominent, and orders a number of arrests, and imprisons or sets free, according to his own fancy or that of the higher authorities. And the higher official for like motives, or influenced by his relations to a minister, exiles men to the other side of the world, keeps them in solitary confinement, condemns them to Siberia, to hard labour, to death, or sets them free at the request of some lady.

They were dealt with as in war, and they naturally employed the same means as were used against them. And just as military men live in an atmosphere of public opinion that not only conceals from them the guilt of their actions but represents these actions as feats of heroism, so these political offenders were also constantly surrounded by an atmosphere of public opinion which made the cruel actions they committed in the face of danger and at the risk of liberty and life and all that is dear to men, seem not wicked but glorious. Nekhlyudov found in this the explanation of the surprising phenomenon that men of the mildest character who seemed incapable of witnessing the suffering of any living creature, much more of inflicting pain, should be quietly prepared to murder men; almost all of them considering murder lawful and just on certain occasions: as a means of self-defence, for the attainment of high aims, or for the general welfare. The importance the revolutionists attributed to their cause, and consequently to themselves, flowed naturally from the importance the Government attached to their actions, and the cruelty of the punishments it inflicted on them. They had to have a high opinion of themselves to be able to bear what they were made to suffer.

When Nekhlyudov came to know them better he became convinced that they were neither the downright villains that some imagined them to be, nor the complete heroes that others thought them, but quite ordinary people, among whom, as everywhere, there were some good, some bad, and some middling.

Some among them had turned revolutionists because they honestly considered it their duty to fight existing evils, but there were also some who chose this activity from selfish ambitious motives. The majority, however, were attracted to the revolutionary idea by the thirst for danger, for risk, and the enjoyment of playing with one's life: feelings which, as Nekhlyudov knew from his own military experience, are quite common to the most ordinary people while they are young and full of energy. But they differed from ordinary people favourably in that their conception of morality was higher. They considered not only self-control, hard living, truthfulness and disinterestedness as their duty, but held it their duty even to be ready to sacrifice everything, including life itself, for the common cause. Therefore the best of them stood on a moral level that is not often reached, while the worst were far below the ordinary level, many of them being untruthful and hypocritical and at the same time self-confident and proud. So that Nekhlyudov learned to respect some of his new acquaintances, and even to love them with all his heart, while to others he remained more antipathetic than indifferent.

Chapter VI

NEKHLYUDOV GREW especially fond of Kriltsov, a consumptive young man condemned to hard labour, and belonging to the same party as Katusha. Nekhlyudov made his acquaintance in Ekaterinburg, and after that talked with him several times on the road. Once during the summer Nekhlyudov spent almost a whole day with him at a halting-station, and Kriltsov, having started talking, told him his story and explained how he had become a revolutionist. His story up to the time of his imprisonment was soon told. He lost his father, a rich landed proprietor in the south of Russia, when still a child. He was the only son, and his mother brought him up. He learnt easily both at school and at the university, and was first in the mathematical set of his year. He had the offer of a scholarship from the university to enable him to study abroad. But he delayed coming to a decision. He was in love, and had thoughts of marriage, and of taking part in the rural administration. He wanted to do everything, and could not decide which course to take. At this juncture some fellow-students at the university asked him for money for a popular cause. He knew that this cause was the revolutionary cause, a thing he was not interested in at that time, but he gave the money from a sense of comradeship and vanity, and lest it should be thought he was afraid. Those who received the money were caught, and a note was found which proved that the money had been given by Kriltsov. He was arrested, taken first to the police station, then imprisoned.

"They were not specially strict in that prison," Ktriltsov went on (he was sitting on the high bed-shelf, his elbows on his knees, with sunken chest, the beautiful eyes with which he looked at Nekhlyudov glistening feverishly). "We managed to converse—in other ways besides tapping the walls—and we could walk about the corridors, share our provisions and our tobacco, and in the evenings we even sang in chorus. I had a fine voice. Yes; if it had not been for mother—she was terribly grieved—it would have been all right, even pleasant and interesting. There I made the acquaintance of the famous Petrov, who afterwards killed himself with a piece of glass in the fortress, and of others. But I was not yet a revolutionist. I also became acquainted with two neighbours in cells near mine. They had both been caught in the same affair, and arrested with Polish proclamations in their possession, and were tried for attempting to escape from the convoy on their way to the railway station. One was a Pole, Lozinsky, the other a Jew, Rozovsky. Yes. Well, this Rozovsky was quite a boy. He said he was seventeen, but he looked fifteen. Thin, small, active, with black sparkling eyes, and, like most Jews, very musical. His voice was still breaking, and yet he sang beautifully. Yes. I saw them both taken to be tried. They were taken in the morning. They returned in the evening, and said they were condemned to death. No one had expected it. Their case was so unimportant; they only tried to get away from the convoy and did not even wound any one. And then it was so unnatural to execute such a child as Rozovsky. And we in prison all came to the conclusion that it was only done to frighten them, and would not be confirmed. At first we were excited, and then we comforted ourselves, and life went on as before. Yes. Well, one evening the watchman comes to my door and tells me mysteriously that the carpenters had come and were putting up the gallows. At first I did not understand. What's that? What gallows? But the old watchman was so excited that I saw at once it was for our two. I wished to tap and communicate with my comrades, but was afraid those two would hear. The comrades were also silent. Evidently everybody knew. In the corridor and in the cells everything was as still as death all that evening. We did not tap the walls nor sing. At ten the watchman came again and announced that a hangman had arrived from Moscow. He said this and went away. I began calling him back. Suddenly I hear Rozovsky shouting to me across the corridor, 'What's the matter? Why do you call him?' I answered something about his bringing me some tobacco, but he seemed to guess, and asked me, 'Why did we not sing to-night; why did we not tap the walls?' I do not remember what I said, but I stepped back so as not to speak to him. Yes; it was a terrible night. I listened to every sound all night. Suddenly, towards morning, I heard doors opening and somebody walking—many persons. I went up to the slot in my door. There was a lamp burning in the corridor. The first to pass was the inspector. He was a stout man, and usually seemed resolute and self-confident, but now he was ghastly pale, downcast, and seemed frightened; then came his assistant, gloomy, but resolute: and, behind all, the watchman. They passed my door and stopped at the next, and I heard the assistant calling out in a strange voice, "Lozinsky, get up, and put on clean linen!" Yes. Then I heard the creaking of the door. They entered his cell. Then I heard Lozinsky's steps going to the opposite side of the corridor. I could only see the inspector. He stood quite pale, and buttoned and unbuttoned his coat, shrugging his shoulders. Yes. Then as if frightened of something he moved out of the way. It was Lozinsky, who passed him and came up to my door. A handsome young fellow he was, you know, of that Polish type: broad-shouldered, his head covered with fair, fine curly hair as with a cap, and with beautiful blue eyes. So blooming, so fresh, so healthy. He stopped in front of my slot, so that I could see the whole of his face. A dreadful, gaunt, livid face. 'Kriltsov, have you any cigarettes?' I wished to pass him some, but the assistant hurriedly pulled out his cigarette case and passed it to him. He took one, the assistant struck a match; he lit the cigarette and began to smoke, and seemed to be thinking. Then, as if he had remembered something, he began to speak. 'It is cruel and unjust. I have committed no crime. I——' I saw something quiver in his white young throat, from which I could not take my eyes, and he stopped.

Yes. At that moment I heard Rozovsky shouting in his high-pitched Jewish voice. Lozinsky threw away the cigarette, and stepped from the door. And Rozovsky appeared at my slot. His childish face, with the limpid black eyes, was red and moist. He also had clean linen on. The trousers were too wide, and he kept pulling them up, and was trembling all over. He approached his pitiful face to my slot. 'Kriltsov, it's true that the doctor has prescribed cough mixture for me, is it not? I am not well. I'll take some more of the mixture.' No one answered, and he looked inquiringly, now at me, now at the inspector. What he meant to say I never made out. Yes. Suddenly the assistant put on a stern expression, and called out, again in a kind of squeaking tone. 'Now then, what jokes are these? Let us go.' Rozovsky seemed incapable of understanding what awaited him, and hurried, almost ran, in front of all along the corridor. But then he drew back, and I could hear his shrill voice and his cries. Then the tramping of feet and general hubbub. He was shrieking and sobbing. The sounds came fainter and fainter, and at last the door rattled, and all was quiet. . . . Yes. They were hanged. Both throttled with a rope. A watchman, another one, saw it done, and told me that Lozinsky did not resist; but Rozovsky struggled for a long time, so that they had to pull him on to the scaffold and to force his head into the noose. Yes. This watchman was a rather stupid fellow. He said: 'They told me, sir, that it would be frightful: but it was not at all frightful. When they were hanging they only shrugged their shoulders twice — like this,' — he showed how the shoulders convulsively rose and fell — 'then the hangman pulled a bit, so as to tighten the noose, and it was all up, and they never budged.'"

And Kriltsov repeated the watchman's words, "Not at all frightful," and tried to smile, but burst into sobs instead.

For a long time after that he remained silent, breathing heavily, and repressing the sobs that were choking him.

"From that time I became a revolutionist. Yes," he said when he was quieter, and he finished his story in a few words.

He belonged to the Narodovolstvo, and was even at the head of the "Disorganising Group" whose object was to terrorise the Government so that it should resign its power of its own accord. In connection with this object he travelled to Petersburg, to Kief, to Odessa, and abroad, and was everywhere successful. A man in whom he had full confidence betrayed him. He was arrested, tried, and, after being kept in prison for two years, was condemned to death, but the sentence was mitigated to one of hard labour for life.

He fell into consumption while in prison, and in the conditions in which he was now placed he could scarcely live more than a few months. This he knew, but did not repent, saying that if he had another life he would use it in the same way, to destroy the conditions which made possible such things as he had witnessed.

This man's story, and intimacy with him, explained much to Nekhlyudov that he had not understood before.

Chapter VII

ON THE day when the convoy officer had the encounter about the child with the prisoners at the halting-station, Nekhlyudov, who had spent the night at the village inn, awoke late, and was some time writing letters to post at the next Government town; so that he left the inn later than usual and did not overtake the gang on the road as he had done on previous occasions, but reached the village where the next halting-station was when it was growing dusk.

Having dried himself at the inn, which was kept by an elderly woman with an extraordinarily fat white neck, he had his tea in a clean room, decorated with a great number of icons and pictures, and then hurried away to ask the officer for an interview with Katusha. At the last six halting-stations he could not get this permission from any of the officers. Though they had been changed several times, not one of them would allow Nekhlyudov inside the stations, so that he had not seen Katusha for more than a week. This strictness was occasioned by the fact that an important prison official was expected to pass that way. Now that this official had passed by without looking at the gang after all, Nekhlyudov hoped that the officer who had taken charge of the gang that morning would allow him an interview with the prisoners, as former officers had done.

The landlady offered Nekhlyudov a trap to drive to the halting-place situated at the farther end of the village, but Nekhlyudov preferred to walk. A labourer, a broad-shouldered young Hercules with enormous high boots freshly blackened with strongly smelling tar, offered himself as a guide.

A dense mist obscured the sky, and it was so dark that when the young fellow was three steps in advance Nekhlyudov could not see him unless the light of some window happened to fall on him, but he could hear the heavy boots squelching through the deep, sticky slush. After passing the open space in front of the church and the long street with its rows of windows shining brightly in the darkness, Nekhlyudov followed his guide to the outskirts of the village, where it was pitch dark. But here, too, rays of light, streaming through the mist from the lamps in front of the halting-station, soon became discernible in the darkness. The reddish spots of light grew bigger and bigger. At last the stakes of the palisade, the moving figure of the sentry, a post painted with white and black stripes, and the sentry-box, became visible.

The sentry called his usual, "Who goes there?" as they approached, and seeing they were strangers was so strict that he would not even allow them to wait by the palisade. But Nekhlyudov's guide was not abashed by this strictness.

"Halloo, lad! why so fierce? You go and rouse your boss while we wait here."

The sentry gave no answer, but shouted something in at the gate and stood looking at the broad-shouldered young labourer scraping the mud off Nekhlyudov's boots with a chip of wood by the light of the lamp. From behind the palisade came the hum of male and female voices. In about three minutes something rattled, the gate opened, and a sergeant with his cloak thrown over his shoulders stepped out of the darkness into the lamplight.

The sergeant was not as strict as the sentry, but he was extremely inquisitive. He insisted on knowing what Nekhlyudov wanted the officer for, and who he was, evidently scenting a tip and anxious not to let it escape. Nekhlyudov said he had come on special business, and would show his gratitude; and would the sergeant take a note for him to the officer? The sergeant took the note, nodded, and went away.

Some time after, the gate rattled again, and women, carrying baskets, boxes, jugs, and sacks, came out, loudly chattering in their peculiar Siberian dialect as they stepped over the threshold of the gate. None of them wore peasant costumes; all were dressed in town fashion, with jackets and fur-lined cloaks. Their skirts were tucked up high, and their heads were wrapped in shawls. They examined Nekhlyudov and his guide curiously by the light of the lamp. One of them showed evident pleasure at the sight of the broad-shouldered fellow, and affectionately administered to him a dose of Siberian abuse.

"You demon, what are you doing here? The devil take you!" she said, addressing him.

"I've been showing this traveller here the way," answered the young fellow. "And what have you been bringing here?"

"Dairy stuff, and I am to bring more in the morning."

"They didn't want to keep you for the night, eh?" asked the young fellow.

"You be damned, you liar!" she called out, laughing. "Eh, but come along with us as far as the village."

The guide said something in answer that made not only the women but also the sentry laugh; then, turning to Nekhlyudov, he said: —

"You'll find your way alone? Won't get lost, will you?"

"I shall find it all right."

"When you have passed the church it's the second from the two-storeyed house. Oh, and here, take my stick," he said, handing Nekhlyudov the staff he was carrying, which was longer than himself; and splashing through the mud with his enormous boots he disappeared in the darkness together with the women.

His voice, mingling with the voices of the women, was still to be heard through the mist, when the gate again rattled and the sergeant appeared and invited Nekhlyudov to follow him to the officer.

Chapter VIII

THIS HALTING-STATION, like all such stations along the Siberian road, was surrounded by a courtyard fenced round with a palisade of sharp-pointed stakes, and consisted of three one-storyed houses. One of them, the largest, with grated windows, was for the prisoners; another for the convoy soldiers; and the third, in which was the office, for the officer. There were lights in the windows of all the three houses, and, like all such lights, they promised (here in a specially deceptive manner) something cosy within. Lamps were burning before the porches of the houses, and along the walls about five more lamps lit up the yard. Leading Nekhlyudov along a plank which lay across the yard, the sergeant went up to the porch of the smallest of the houses. When he had gone up the three steps of the porch he let Nekhlyudov pass before him into the ante-room, in which a small lamp was burning, and which was filled with smoky fumes. By the stove a soldier in a coarse shirt, with a necktie and black trousers, and with one top-boot on, stood blowing the charcoal in a samovar, using the other boot as a bellows.[1] When he saw Nekhlyudov, the soldier left the samovar, helped Nekhlyudov off with his leather coat, and then went into an inner room.

"He has come, your honour."

"Well, ask him in," came an angry voice.

"Go in at the door," said the soldier, and busied himself at the samovar again.

In the next room, which was lighted by a hanging lamp, the officer, with fair moustaches and a very red face, dressed in an Austrian jacket

---

[1] The long boots worn in Russia have concertina-like sides, and when held to the chimney of the samovar can be used instead of bellows to make the charcoal in it burn up.

that closely fitted his broad chest and shoulders, sat at a covered table on which were the remains of his dinner and two bottles. There was a strong smell of tobacco and of some very strong, cheap scent in the warm room. On seeing Nekhlyudov the officer rose and gazed ironically and suspiciously, as it seemed, at the new-comer.

"What is it you want?" he asked; and not waiting for a reply he shouted through the open door, "Bernov! the samovar! What are you about?"

"Coming at once."

"I'll give you 'at once' so that you'll remember it," shouted the officer, and his eyes flashed.

"I'm coming," shouted the soldier, and brought in the samovar.

Nekhlyudov waited while the soldier placed the samovar on the table. When the officer had followed the soldier out of the room with his cruel little eyes, which looked as if they were aiming where best to hit him, he made tea and got a square decanter and some Albert biscuits out of his travelling case. Having placed all this on the cloth he again turned to Nekhlyudov.

"Well, how can I be of service to you?"

"I should like to be allowed to visit a prisoner," said Nekhlyudov, without sitting down.

"A political one? That's forbidden by law," said the officer.

"The woman I mean is not a political prisoner," said Nekhlyudov.

"Yes; but pray take a seat," said the officer.

Nekhlyudov sat down.

"She is not a political one, but at my request she has been allowed by the higher authorities to join the political prisoners——"

"Oh yes, I know," interrupted the officer. "A little dark one! Well, yes, that can be managed. Won't you smoke?"

He moved a box of cigarettes towards Nekhlyudov, and having carefully poured out two tumblers of tea he passed one to Nekhlyudov, and said, "Allow me."

"Thank you, I should like to see——"

"The night is long. You'll have plenty of time. I shall order her to be sent out to you."

"But could I not see her where she is? Why need she be sent for?" Nekhlyudov said.

"In to the political prisoners? It is against the law."

"I have been allowed to go in several times. If there is any danger of my passing anything in to them, I could do it just as well through her."

"Oh no, she would be searched," said the officer, and laughed in an unpleasant manner.

"Well, why not search me?"

"All right, we'll manage without that," said the officer, opening the decanter and holding it out towards Nekhlyudov's tumbler of tea. "May I give you some? No? Well, just as you like. When one is living here in Siberia, one is only too glad to meet an educated person. Ours is very sad work, as you know, and when one is used to better things it is very hard. The idea people have of us is that convoy officers are coarse, uneducated men, and no one seems to remember that we may have been born for a very different position."

This officer's red face, his scent, his rings, and especially his unpleasant laughter, disgusted Nekhlyudov very much; but to-day, as during the whole of his journey, he was in that serious, attentive state which did not allow him to behave slightingly or disdainfully towards any man, but made him feel the necessity of speaking to every one "entirely," as he expressed to himself this relation to men. When he had heard the officer and understood his state of mind, he said in a serious manner:—

"I think that in your position, too, some comfort could be found in helping the suffering people."

"What are their sufferings? You don't know what those people are."

"They are not special people, said Nekhlyudov. "They are just such people as others, and some of them are quite innocent."

"Of course, there are all sorts among them, and naturally one pities them. Some of us won't relax anything, but I try to lighten their condition where I can. Rather let me suffer than they. Others keep to the law in every detail, even as far as to shoot; but I show pity. . . . Allow me— have another," he said, pouring out another tumbler of tea for Nekhlyudov. "And who is she, this woman that you want to see?" he asked.

"She is an unfortunate woman who got into a brothel and was there falsely accused of poisoning, but she is a very good woman," Nekhlyudov answered.

The officer shook his head.

"Yes, it happens. I can tell you about a certain Emma who lived in Kazan. She was a Hungarian by birth, but she had quite Persian eyes," he continued, unable to restrain a smile at the recollection. "There was so much *chic* about her that she might have been a countess——"

Nekhlyudov interrupted the officer and returned to the former topic of conversation.

"I think that you could lighten the conditions of the people while they are in your charge, and in acting that way I am sure you would find great joy," said Nekhlyudov, trying to pronounce the words as distinctly as possible, as if talking to a foreigner or a child.

The officer looked at Nekhlyudov with sparkling eyes, impatiently waiting for him to stop, so that he might continue the tale about the Hungarian with Persian eyes, who evidently presented herself very vividly to his imagination and quite absorbed his attention.

"Yes, of course, this is all quite true," he said, "and I do pity them; but I should like to tell you about this Emma. What do you think she did——"

"It does not interest me," said Nekhlyudov, "and I must tell you frankly that though I was myself very different at one time, I now hate that kind of relation to women."

The officer gave Nekhlyudov a frightened look.

"Won't you take some more tea?" he said.

"No, thank you."

"Bernov!" the officer called, "take the gentleman to Vakulov. Tell him to let him into the separate political room; he may remain there till the inspection."

Chapter IX

ACCOMPANIED BY the orderly, Nekhlyudov went out into the courtyard dimly lit up by the red light of the lamps.

"Where to?" asked a convoy soldier, addressing the orderly.

"Into the separate one, No. 5."

"You can't pass here, it's locked. You must go the other way round."

"Why's that?"

"The boss has gone to the village and taken the key with him."

"Well then, come this way."

The soldier led Nekhlyudov along some boards to another entrance. While still in the yard Nekhlyudov could hear the din of voices and the general commotion going on inside, as in a beehive when the bees are preparing to swarm; but when he came nearer and the door opened, the din grew louder and changed into the distinct sounds of shouting, abuse, and laughter. He heard the clatter of chains and smelt the well-known foul air.

As always, this din of voices, the clatter of chains and the close smell, flowed into one tormenting sensation and produced in Nekhlyudov a feeling of moral nausea which grew into physical nausea, the two feelings mingling with and heightening each other.

The first thing Nekhlyudov saw on entering was a large, stinking tub, on the edge of which sat a woman, while in front of her stood a man, with his pancake-shaped cap on the side of his shaved head. They were talking about something. When he saw Nekhlyudov the man winked and remarked:—

"The Tsar himself cannot hold back the water."

But the woman pulled down the skirts of her cloak and seemed abashed.

From the entrance ran a corridor into which several doors opened. The first was the family room, then came the bachelors' room, and at the very end two small rooms were set apart for the political prisoners.

The building, which was arranged to hold one hundred and fifty prisoners, was so crowded now that there were four hundred and fifty there, so that the prisoners could not all get into the rooms, but filled the passage also. Some were sitting or lying on the floor, some were going out with empty teapots or bringing them back filled with boiling water. Among the latter was Taras. He overtook Nekhlyudov and greeted him affectionately. The kind face of Taras was disfigured by dark bruises on his nose and under his eye.

"What has happened to you?" asked Nekhlyudov.

"Well, something has happened," Taras said with a smile.

"Yes, they're always fighting," said the convoy soldier.

"All because of the woman," added a prisoner, who followed Taras. "He's had a row with blind Fedka."

"And how's Theodosia?"

"She's all right. I'm bringing the water for her tea now," Taras answered, and went into the family room.

Nekhlyudov looked in at the door. The room was crowded with women and men, some of whom were on, and some under, the bed-shelves; it was full of steam from the wet clothes that were drying, and the chatter of women's voices was unceasing. The next door led into the bachelors' room. This room was still more crowded; even the doorway and the passage in front of it were blocked by a noisy crowd of men in wet garments, busy doing or deciding something or other. The convoy sergeant explained that the prisoner appointed to buy the provisions was paying out of the food-money what was owing to a sharper (who had won from, or lent money to, the prisoners), and receiving back little tickets made of playing-cards. When they saw the convoy soldier and a gentleman, those who were nearest became silent and followed them with looks of ill-will. Among them Nekhlyudov noticed the criminal Fedorov, whom he knew, and who always kept beside him a miserable lad with a swollen appearance and raised eyebrows; and also a disgusting, noseless, pock-marked tramp, who was notorious among the prisoners because he had killed a comrade in the marshes while trying to escape, and had, it was said, fed on his flesh. The tramp stood in the passage with his wet

cloak thrown over one shoulder, looking mockingly and boldly at
Nekhlyudov, and did not move out of the way. Nekhlyudov passed
him by.

Though this kind of scene had become quite familiar to him,
though during the last three months he had seen these four hundred criminal prisoners over and over again in many different circumstances—in the heat, enveloped in clouds of dust raised by the
dragging of their chained feet along the road; at the resting-places
by the way; inside the halting-stations; and out in the courtyards in
warm weather, where the most horrible scenes of barefaced
debauchery had occurred—yet every time he came among them
and felt their attention fixed on him as it was now, shame and the
consciousness of his sin against them tormented him. To this sense
of shame and guilt was added an unconquerable feeling of loathing
and horror. He knew that, placed in a position such as theirs, they
could not be other than they were, and yet he was unable to stifle
his disgust.

"It's well for them grub-suckers," Nekhlyudov heard some one way
in a hoarse voice, as he approached the room of the political prisoners.
The speaker added some words of obscene abuse, and a roar of spiteful, mocking laughter followed.

Chapter X

WHEN THEY had passed the bachelors' room the sergeant who had
accompanied Nekhlyudov left him, promising to come for him before
the inspection. As soon as the sergeant was gone, a prisoner, quickly
stepping with his bare feet and holding up his chains, came close to
Nekhlyudov, enveloping him in a strong acid smell of perspiration, and
said in a mysterious whisper:—

"Take the case in hand, sir. They have quite befooled the lad; they've
made him drunk, and to-day at the inspection he's already given his
name as Karmanov. Stop it, sir; we dare not, or they'll kill us," and looking uneasily round, he turned away.

This is what had happened. The criminal Karmanov had persuaded
a young fellow, who was sentenced to exile and who resembled him in
appearance, to change names with him and go to the mines in his
place, letting him (Karmanov) go to exile instead.

Nekhlyudov knew about this intended exchange. Some convict had
told him of it the week before. He nodded as a sign that he understood

and would do what he could, and continued his way without looking round.

Nekhlyudov knew the convict who spoke to him, and was surprised by his action. When in Ekaterinburg this convict had asked Nekhlyudov to get permission for his wife to follow him. He was a man of the most ordinary peasant type, of medium size, about thirty years old, and was condemned to hard labour for an attempt to murder and rob. His name was Makar Devkin. His crime was a very curious one. In the account he gave of it to Nekhlyudov, he said it was not his own (Makar's), but *his*, the devil's, doing. He said that a traveller had come to his father's house and hired a sleigh to drive to a village twenty-six miles off. Makar's father told him to drive the stranger. Makar harnessed the horse, dressed, and sat down to drink tea with the stranger. The stranger related at the tea-table that he was going to be married, and that he had with him five hundred rubles which he had earned in Moscow. When he had heard this, Makar went out into the yard and put an axe into the sleigh under the straw.

"And I did not myself know why I was taking the axe," he said. "'Take the axe,' says *he*, and I took it. We got in and started. We drove along all right. I even forgot about the axe. Well, we were getting near the village—only about four miles more to go. The way from the cross-road to the high-road was uphill, and I got out. I walked behind the sleigh, and *he* whispers to me, 'What are you thinking about? When you get to the top of he hill you will meet people along the highway, and then there's the village. He will carry the money away; if you mean to do it, now's the time.' I stooped over the sleigh as if to arrange the straw, and the axe seemed to jump into my hand of itself. The man turned round, 'What are you doing?' I lifted the axe and tried to knock him down, but he was quick, jumped out, and took hold of my hands. 'What are you doing, you villain?' He threw me down into the snow, and I did not even struggle, but gave in at once. He bound my arms with his sash, threw me into the sleigh, and took me straight to the police station. I was imprisoned and tried. The commune gave me a good character: said I was a good man, and that nothing wrong had been noticed about me. The masters for whom I had worked also spoke well of me, but we had no money to engage a lawyer, and so I was condemned to four years' hard labour."

It was this man who, wishing to save a fellow-villager, though he knew that by speaking he risked his own life, nevertheless revealed a prisoners' secret to Nekhlyudov, for which, if they discovered what he had done, they would certainly strangle him.

Chapter XI

THE POLITICAL prisoners were kept in two small rooms, the doors of which opened into a part of the passage partitioned off from the rest. On entering this part of the passage Nekhlyudov saw Simonson in his rubber jacket and with a log of pinewood in his hands crouching in front of a stove, the door of which trembled, drawn by the heat inside.

When he saw Nekhlyudov he looked up at him from under his protruding brow, and gave him his hand without rising.

"I am glad you have come. I want to speak to you," he said, looking Nekhlyudov straight in the eyes with a significant expression.

"Yes. What is it?" Nekhlyudov asked.

"It will do later on. I am busy just now." And Simonson turned again towards the stove, which he was heating according to a theory of his own so as to lose as little heat-energy as possible.

Nekhlyudov was about to enter at the first door, when Maslova, stooping, and pushing a large heap of rubbish and dust towards the stove with a birch-broom with no handle, came out of the other. She had a white jacket on, her skirt was tucked up, and a kerchief drawn down to her eyebrows protected her hair from the dust. When she saw Nekhlyudov she drew herself up, flushing and animated, let go the broom, wiped her hands on her skirt, and stopped just in front of him.

"You are tidying up the premises, I see," said Nekhlyudov, shaking hands.

"Yes, my old occupation," and she smiled: "but the dust! You can't imagine what it is. We have been cleaning and cleaning! Well, is the plaid dry?" she asked, turning to Simonson.

"Almost," Simonson answered, giving her a peculiar look which Nekhlyudov noticed.

"All right, I'll come for it, and bring the cloaks to dry. . . . Our people are all in there," she said to Nekhlyudov, pointing to the first door as she went in at the second.

Nekhlyudov opened the door and entered a little room dimly lit by a small tin lamp which was standing low down on a shelf affixed to the wall to serve as a bedstead. It was cold in the room, and there was a smell of dust (which had not had time to settle), of damp, and of tobacco smoke. The little tin lamp threw a bright light on those near it, but the beds were in the shade, and dark shadows flickered on the walls.

Two men appointed as caterers, who had gone to fetch boiling water and provisions, were away, but most of the political prisoners were gathered together in this small room. Here was Nekhlyudov's old acquaintance, Vera Dukhova, thinner and yellower than ever, with her large, frightened eyes, short hair, and a swollen vein on her forehead. She was wearing a grey jacket, and with a newspaper spread out in front of her sat rolling cigarettes with a jerky movement of her hands.

Emily Rantseva, whom Nekhlyudov considered the pleasantest of the political prisoners, was also here. She looked after the housekeeping and managed to spread a feeling of home comfort and attractiveness even in the midst of the most trying surroundings. She sat beside the lamp with her sleeves rolled up, wiping cups and mugs, and placing them, with her deft, red, sunburnt hands, on a cloth that was spread on the bed-shelf. Rantseva was a plain-looking young woman with a clever and mild expression of face, which when she smiled had a way of suddenly becoming merry, animated, and captivating. It was with such a smile that she now welcomed Nekhlyudov.

"Why, we thought you had gone back to Russia," she said.

Here in a dark corner was also Mary Pavlovna, busy with a little fair-haired girl who kept prattling in her sweet childish accents.

"How nice that you have come," Mary Pavlovna said to Nekhlyudov. "Have you seen Katusha? We have a visitor here," and she pointed to the little girl.

Here also was Anatole Kriltsov, with felt boots on, sitting doubled up and shivering in a far corner with his feet under him, his arms folded in the sleeves of his cloak, and looking at Nekhlyudov with feverish eyes. Nekhlyudov was going up to him, but to the right of the door a man with spectacles and reddish curls, dressed in a rubber jacket, sat talking to the pretty smiling Grabets. This was the celebrated revolutionist, Novodvorov. Nekhlyudov hastened to greet him; he was in a particular hurry about it because this man was the only one among all the political prisoners whom he disliked. Novodvorov's blue eyes glistened through his spectacles as he looked frowningly at Nekhlyudov and held out his narrow hand to him.

"Well, are you having a pleasant journey?" he asked with evident irony.

"Yes, there is much that is interesting," Nekhlyudov answered, as if he did not notice the irony but took the question for politeness, and he passed on to Kriltsov.

Though Nekhlyudov appeared indifferent, he was really far from being so, and these words of Novodvorov, showing his evident desire to say or do something unpleasant, interfered with the state of kindliness in which Nekhlyudov found himself, and he felt depressed and sad.

"Well, how are you?" he asked, pressing Kriltsov's cold and trembling hand.

"Pretty well, only I cannot get warm; I got wet through," Kriltsov answered, quickly replacing his hands in the sleeves of his cloak. "And here it's also beastly cold. There, look, the window panes are broken," and he pointed to the broken panes behind the iron bars. "And how are you? Why have you not been to see us?"

"I was not allowed to come, the authorities were so strict; but to-day the officer is lenient."

"Lenient, indeed!" Kriltsov remarked. "Ask Mary what he did this morning."

Mary Pavlovna, from her place in the corner, related what had happened about the little girl when they left the halting-station that morning.

"I think it is absolutely necessary to make a collective protest," said Vera Dukhova in a determined tone, and yet glancing now at one now at another, with a frightened, undecided look. "Vladimir Simonson did protest, but that is not sufficient."

"What protest do you want?" muttered Kriltsov, cross and frowning. Her lack of simplicity, her artificial manner, and her nervousness, had evidently long been irritating him.

"Are you looking for Katusha?" he asked, addressing Nekhlyudov. "She is working all the time. She has cleaned this—the men's room—and now she has gone to clean the women's. Only it is not possible to clean away the fleas—they eat one alive. And what is Mary doing there?" he asked, nodding towards the corner where Mary Pavlovna sat.

"She is combing out her adopted daughter's hair," replied Rantseva.

"But won't she let the insects loose on us?" asked Kriltsov.

"Oh no; I am very careful. She is a clean little girl now. You take her," said Mary, turning to Rantseva, "while I go and help Katusha, and I will also bring him his plaid."

Rantseva took the little girl on her lap, pressing the plump, bare little arms to her bosom with a mother's tenderness, and gave her a bit of sugar.

As Mary Pavlovna left the room, two men came in with boiling water and provisions.

Chapter XII

ONE OF the new-comers was a short, thin young man, wearing a cloth-covered sheepskin coat and high boots. He stepped lightly and quickly, carrying two steaming teapots, and holding under his arm a loaf wrapped in a cloth.

"Well, so our Prince has put in an appearance again," he said, as he placed the teapots beside the cups and handed the bread to Rantseva. "We have bought wonderful things," he continued, as he took off his sheepskin and flung it over the heads of the others on to the bed-shelf. "Markel has bought milk and eggs; why, we'll have a regular ball to-night. And Rantseva is diffusing her aesthetic cleanliness," he said, and looked with a smile at Rantseva; "and now she will make tea."

The whole presence of this man: his movements, his voice, his look, seemed to breathe vigour and merriment. The other new-comer was just the reverse; he looked despondent and sad. He was short and bony and had very prominent cheek-bones, a sallow complexion, thin lips, and beautiful light hazel eyes, rather far apart. He wore an old wadded coat, long boots and galoshes, and was carrying two pots of milk and two round boxes made of birch bark, which he placed in front of Rantseva. He bowed to Nekhlyudov, bending only his neck and keeping his eyes fixed on him. Then having reluctantly given him his damp hand to shake he began to take out the provisions.

Both these political prisoners were of the people. The first was Nabatov, a peasant; the second, Markel Kondratyev, a factory hand. Markel did not get among the revolutionists till he was quite a man; Nabatov joined them when only eighteen. After leaving the village school Nabatov gained a place at the high school, owing to his exceptional talents, earned his living by giving lessons all the time he studied there, and on finishing won the gold medal. He did not go to the university because, while still in the top class of the high school, he made up his mind to go among the people and enlighten his neglected brethren. This he did, first getting a place as a Government clerk in a large village. He was soon arrested, because he read to the peasants and arranged a co-operative industrial association among them. The authorities kept him imprisoned for eight months, and then set him free, but he remained under police supervision. As soon as he was liberated he went to another village, got a place as schoolmaster, and did the same as he had done in the first village. He was again taken up, and kept fourteen months in prison, where his political convictions became yet stronger.

After that he was exiled to the Perm Government, from whence he escaped. Then he was put in prison for seven months, and after that he was exiled to Archangel. Again he tried to escape, but was re-arrested and condemned to be exiled to the Yakutsk Government; so that half his life since he reached manhood had been passed in prison and in exile. All these adventures did not embitter him and did not weaken his energy, but rather stimulated it. He was a lively young fellow, with a splendid digestion; always active, gay, and vigorous. He never repented

of anything, never looked far ahead, and used all his powers, his clev-
erness, and his practical knowledge to act in the present. When free, he
worked towards the aim he had set himself—the enlightening and the
uniting of the working-men, especially the country labourers. When in
prison he was just as energetic and practical in finding means to come
in contact with the outer world, and in arranging his own life and the
life of his group as comfortably as circumstances permitted. Above all
things he was social—a member of a Commune. He wanted, as it
seemed to him, nothing for himself, and contented himself with very
little, but demanded very much for the group of his comrades, and
could work for it either physically or mentally, day and night, without
sleep or food. As a peasant he was industrious, observant, and clever at
his work; he was also naturally self-controlled, polite without any effort,
and attentive not only to the wishes but also to the opinions of others.
His widowed mother, an illiterate superstitious old peasant woman, was
still living, and Nabatov helped her, and used to visit her while he was
free. During the time he spent at home he entered into all the interests
of his mother's life, helped her in her work, continued his intercourse
with former playfellows, smoked in their company cheap tobacco in
"dog's-foot cigarettes,"[1] took part in their fisticuffs, and explained to
them how they were all being deceived by the State, and how they
ought to disentangle themselves from the deception they were kept in.
When he thought or spoke of what a revolution would do, he always
imagined the people, from whom he had himself sprung, left in very
nearly the same conditions as before, only with sufficient land and
without the gentry and officials. The revolution, according to him—
and in this he differed from Novodvorov and Novodvorov's follower,
Markel Kondratyev—should not alter the fundamental forms of the life
of the people, should not break down the whole edifice, but should
only alter the inner walls of the beautiful, strong, colossal old structure
he loved so dearly.

He was also a typical peasant in his views on religion: never thinking
about metaphysical questions, about the origin of all origins, or about
the future life. God was to him (as to Arago)[2] an hypothesis which
he had as yet not needed. He was not concerned about the origin of the
world, and did not care whether Moses or Darwin were right.
Darwinism which seemed so important to his companions was to him
only the same kind of plaything of the mind as the creation in six days.
The question how the world originated did not interest him, just

---

[1] Dog's-foot is a kind of cigarette that the peasants smoke, made with a bit of paper bent
at one end into a hook.—L. T.
[2] [François Jean Dominique Arago (1786–1853) was a French physicist.]

because the question how best to live in this world was ever before him. He never thought about a future life, always bearing in the depth of his soul the firm and quiet conviction, inherited from his forefathers and common to all labourers on the land, that just as in the world of plants and animals nothing ceases to exist, but each thing continually changes its form—the manure into grain, the grain into food, the tadpole into a frog, the caterpillar into a butterfly, the acorn into an oak—so man also does not perish, but only undergoes change. He believed in this, and therefore always looked death straight in the face and bravely bore the sufferings that led towards it, but did not care and did not know how to speak about it. He loved work and was always employed on some practical business, and he spurred on his comrades in the same direction.

The other political prisoner from among the people, Markel Kondratyev, was a very different kind of man. He began to work at the age of fifteen, and took to smoking and drinking in order to stifle a vague sense of being wronged. He first realised he was wronged one Christmas, when they (the factory children) were invited to a Christmas tree arranged by the employer's wife. There he received a farthing whistle, an apple, a gilded walnut, and a fig, while the employer's children had presents given them which seemed gifts from fairyland, and had cost, as he afterwards heard, more than fifty rubles. When he was thirty, a noted revolutionist came to their factory to work as a factory girl, and noticing his superior abilities she began giving Kondratyev books and pamphlets, and talked to him, explaining his position and the remedy for it. When the possibility of freeing himself and others from oppression became clear in his mind, the injustice of the present state of things appeared more cruel and more terrible than ever, and he longed passionately, not only for freedom but also for the punishment of those who arranged and who maintain this cruel injustice. It was knowledge, he was told, that gave this possibility; and Kondratyev devoted himself passionately to the acquisition of knowledge. It was not clear to him how knowledge would bring about the realisation of the socialist ideal, but he believed that the knowledge that had shown him the injustice of the conditions in which he lived would also abolish the injustice itself. Besides, knowledge would in his opinion raise him above others. Therefore he left off smoking and drinking, and devoted all his leisure time to study.

The revolutionist gave him lessons, and his thirst for every kind of knowledge, and the facility with which he absorbed it, surprised her. In two years he had mastered algebra, geometry, and history (of which he was specially fond), and had made acquaintance with poetry and fiction and critical, and especially socialistic, literature.

The revolutionist was arrested, and Kondratyev with her, forbidden books having been found in their possession, and they were imprisoned and then exiled to the Vologda Government. There Kondratyev became acquainted with Novodvorov, read a great deal more revolutionary matter, remembered it all, and became still firmer in his socialistic views. After his exile he became a leader in a large strike which ended in the destruction of a factory and the murder of the director. He was again arrested and condemned to Siberia.

His religious views were of the same negative nature as his views of existing economic conditions. Having seen the absurdity of the religion in which he was brought up, and having freed himself from it with great effort—at first with fear but later with rapture—he, as if wishing to revenge himself for the deception that had been practised on him and on his ancestors, was never tried of venomously and angrily ridiculing priests and religious dogmas.

He was ascetic by habit, contenting himself with very little, and, like all who have been used to work from childhood and whose muscles have been developed, he could work much and easily and was quick at any manual labour; but what he valued most was the leisure in prisons and at the halting-stations, which enabled him to continue his studies. He was now studying the first volume of Karl Marx, and carefully hid the book in his sack, as if it were a great treasure. He behaved with reserve and indifference to all his comrades except Novodvorov, to whom he was greatly attached, and whose arguments on all subjects he accepted as irrefutable truths.

He had an infinite contempt for women, whom he looked upon as a hindrance in all useful activity. But he pitied Maslova and was gentle with her, for he considered her an example of the way in which the lower are exploited by the upper classes. The same reason made him dislike Nekhlyudov, so that he talked little with him and never pressed his hand, but when greeting him only held out his own to be pressed.

Chapter XIII

THE FIRE had burnt up, and the stove was warm; the tea was made, poured out into cups and mugs, and milk was added to it; and rusks, fresh rye and wheaten bread, butter, hard-boiled eggs, and calf's head and feet were placed on the cloth. Every one had moved towards the part of the bed-shelf which served as a table, and sat eating and talking. Rantseva sat on a box pouring out tea. The rest crowded round her except Kriltsov, who had taken off his wet cloak, wrapped himself in his dry plaid, and lay in his own place talking to Nekhlyudov.

After the cold damp march, and the dirt and disorder they had found here, after the pains they had taken to get things tidy, and after having eaten, and drunk hot tea, they were all in the best and brightest of spirits.

The fact that the tramp of feet and the screams and abuse of the criminals reached them through the wall, reminding them of their surroundings, seemed only to increase the sense of cosiness. As on an island in the midst of the sea these people felt themselves for a brief space not swamped by the degradation and sufferings which surrounded them. This raised their spirits and excited them. They talked about everything except about their present position and that which awaited them. As generally happens among young men and women — especially if they are forced to remain together as these people were — all sorts of agreements and disagreements and attractions (curiously blended) had sprung up among them. Almost all of them were in love. Novodvorov was in love with the pretty smiling Grabets. This was a young, thoughtless girl, who had gone in for a course of study, was perfectly indifferent to revolutionary questions, but, succumbing to the influence of the day, compromised herself in some way and was exiled. The chief interest of her life during the time of her trial and in prison and exile was her success with men, just as it had been when she was free. Now, on the journey, she consoled herself with the fact that Novodvorov had taken a fancy to her, and she too fell in love with him. Vera Dukhova, who was very prone to fall in love herself but did not awaken love in others, though she was always hoping for mutual love, was sometimes drawn to Nabatov and sometimes to Novodvorov. Kriltsov felt something like love for Mary Pavlovna. He loved her with a man's love, but knowing how she regarded this sort of love hid his feelings under the guise of friendship and gratitude for the tenderness with which she attended to his wants. Nabatov and Rantseva were attached to each other by very complicated ties. As Mary Pavlovna was a perfectly chaste maiden, so Rantseva was perfectly virtuous as her own husband's wife.

When a school-girl of only sixteen she fell in love with Rantsev, a student of the Petersburg University, and married him before he left the university, she being then nineteen years old. During his fourth year at the university her husband became involved in some student disturbances, was exiled from Petersburg, and turned revolutionist. She gave up the medical courses she was attending and followed him, and she also turned revolutionist. If she had not considered her husband the cleverest and best of men she would not have fallen in love with him, and if she had not fallen in love she would not have married him; but having fallen in love and married him whom she thought the best and cleverest of men, she naturally looked upon life and its aims in the way that this best and cleverest man looked at them. At first he thought the aim of life was to learn, and she therefore looked upon study as the aim of life. He became a revolutionist and so did she. He could demonstrate very clearly that the existing state of things could not go on, and that it is everybody's duty to combat this state and to try to bring about conditions in which the individual could develop freely, and so on; and she imagined that she really thought and felt all this, but in reality she only regarded everything her husband thought as absolute truth, and only sought for perfect agreement, perfect identification of her own soul with his, that being the only condition which could give her full moral satisfaction.

The parting with her husband and their child (whom her mother took) was very hard to bear, but she bore it firmly and quietly since it was for her husband's sake, and for a cause which she had not the slightest doubt was good, since he served it. She was always with her husband in thought, and did not and could not love anyone else now, any more than she could when with him. But Nabatov's devoted and pure love touched and excited her. This moral, firm man, her husband's friend, tried to treat her as a sister, but something more appeared in his behaviour to her, and this rather frightened them both, yet gave colour to their life of hardship.

So that in all this circle only Mary Pavlovna and Kondratyev were quite free from love affairs.

Chapter XIV

EXPECTING TO have a private talk with Katusha as usual after tea, Nekhlyudov sat by Kriltsov's side conversing with him. Among other things he told him the story of Makar's crime and about Makar's request to him. Kriltsov listened attentively, gazing at Nekhlyudov with glistening eyes.

"Yes," he said suddenly, "I often think that here we are going side by side with them—and who are they? The very people for whose sake we are going, and yet we not only do not know them, but do not even wish to know them. And they are even worse, they hate us and look upon us as enemies. Is it not terrible?"

"There is nothing terrible about it," broke in Novodvorov, overhearing the conversation. "The masses always worship power and power only. The Government has the power now, and they worship it and hate us. Tomorrow we shall have the power and they will worship us," he said.

At that moment a volley of abuse and a rattle of chains sounded from behind the wall. Something was heard thumping against it, and screams and shrieks. Some one was being beaten, and some one was calling out, "Murder! help!"

"Hear them, the beasts! What intercourse can there be between us and such as they?" quietly remarked Novodvorov.

"You call them beasts, and Nekhlyudov was just telling me about such an action," irritably retorted Kriltsov; and went on to say how Makar was risking his life to save a fellow villager. "That is not the action of a beast: it is heroism."

"Sentimentality!" Novodvorov ejaculated scornfully. "It is difficult for us to understand the emotions of these people and the motives on which they act. You see generosity, but it may be simply jealousy of that other criminal."

"How is it that you never wish to see anything good in another?" Mary Pavlovna said, suddenly flaring up.

"But how can one see what does not exist?"

"Of course it exists when a man takes the risk of a terrible death."

"I think," said Novodvorov, "that if we want to do something, the first condition is——" (here Kondratyev put down the book he was reading by the lamplight and began to listen attentively to his teacher's words) "that we should not give way to fantasy but look at things as they are. We should do all in our power for the masses, and expect nothing in return. The masses can only be the object of our activity, they cannot be our fellow-workers as long as they remain in the state of inertia they are in at present." He went on as if delivering a lecture. "Therefore to expect help from them before there has taken place the process of development—that process we are preparing them for—is delusive."

"What process of development?" Kriltsov began, flushing up. "We say that we are against arbitrary despotism; and yet is not this the most awful despotism?"

"No despotism whatever," quietly rejoined Novodvorov. "I am only saying that I know the path that the people must travel, and can show them that path."

"But how can you be sure that the path you show is the true path? Is this not the same kind of despotism that lay at the bottom of the perse-cutions of the Inquisition and the French Revolution? They too knew the one true way by means of science."

"That they erred is no proof that I am going to err. Besides, there is a great difference between the ravings of ideologues and facts based on sound economic science."

Novodvorov's voice filled the room, he alone continued to speak, all the rest were silent.

"They are always disputing," Mary Pavlovna said when there was a moment's silence.

"And you yourself, what do you think about it?" Nekhlyudov asked her.

"I think Kriltsov is right when he says we should not force our views on the people."

"And you, Katusha?" asked Nekhlyudov with a smile, and waited anxiously for her answer, fearing she would say something awkward.

"I think the common people are wronged," she said, and blushed scarlet; "I think they are dreadfully wronged."

"That's right, Maslova, quite right," cried Nabatov. "They are terribly wronged—the people—and they must not be wronged, and therein lies our whole task."

"A curious idea of the object of revolution," Novodvorov remarked crossly, and began to smoke in silence.

"I cannot talk with him," said Kriltsov in a whisper, and was silent.

"And it is much better not to," said Nekhlyudov.

Chapter XV

ALTHOUGH NOVODVOROV was highly esteemed by all the revolutionists, and though he was very learned and considered very wise, Nekhlyudov reckoned him among those who being revolutionists and yet below the average moral level were much below it. The intellectual powers of the man—his numerator—were great; but his opinion of himself—his denominator—was immeasurably greater, and had far outgrown his intellectual powers.

He was a man of a nature just the contrary to that of Simonson. Simonson was one of those people, chiefly of a masculine type, whose actions follow the dictates of their reason and are determined by it. Novodvorov belonged, on the contrary, to the class of people of a feminine type, whose reason is directed partly towards the attainment of aims set by their feelings, partly to the justification of acts instigated by their feelings.

The whole of Novodvorov's revolutionary activity, though he could explain it very eloquently and very convincingly, appeared to Nekhlyudov to be founded on nothing but ambition and the desire for supremacy. At first his capacity for assimilating the thoughts of others and expressing them correctly had given him a position of supremacy among the pupils and teachers in the high school and the university where qualities such as his are highly prized, and he was satisfied. But when he had finished his studies and received his diploma, and that supremacy was over, he suddenly altered his views in order (so Kriltsov, who did not like him, said) to gain supremacy in another sphere, and from being a moderate Liberal he became a rabid adherent of the Narodovolstov.

Being devoid of those moral and aesthetic qualities which call forth doubts and hesitation, he very soon acquired a position in the revolutionary world which satisfied him—that of leader of a party. Having once chosen a direction, he never doubted or hesitated, and was therefore certain that he never made a mistake. Everything seemed quite simple, clear, and certain. And the narrowness and one-sidedness of his views did make everything seem simple and clear; one only had to be logical, as he said. His self-assurance was so great that it either repelled people or made them submit to him. As he carried on his activity among very young people who mistook his boundless self-assurance for depth and wisdom, the majority did submit to him and he had great success in revolutionary circles. His activity was directed to the preparation of a rising in which he was to usurp power and call together a council. A programme composed by him was to be put before this council, and he felt sure that this programme of his solved every problem, and that it would be inevitably carried out.

His comrades respected but did not love him. He did not love anyone, and looked upon all men of note as rivals, and could he have done it would willingly have treated them as old male monkeys treat young ones. He would have torn all mental power, all capacity, from other men, so that they should interfere with the display of his talents. He behaved well only to those who bowed before him. Now, on the journey, he behaved well to Kondratyev (who was influenced by his propaganda), and to Vera Dukhova and pretty little Grabets (who were both in love with him). Although in principle he was in favour of the women's movement yet in the depths of his soul he considered all women stupid and insignificant except those with whom he was sentimentally in love (as he was now in love with Grabets), and such women he considered to be exceptional, he alone being capable of discerning their merits.

The question of the relation of the sexes also he looked upon as thoroughly solved by accepting free union.

He had one nominal wife, and one real wife from whom he was separated, having come to the conclusion that there was no real love between them, and he now thought of entering into a free union with Grabets. Novodvorov despised Nekhlyudov for "playing the fool," as he termed it, with Maslova, but especially for the freedom Nekhlyudov took in considering the defects of the existing system and the methods of correcting those defects, not only not as Novodvorov viewed them but in a way that was Nekhlyudov's own: a prince's (that is, a fool's) way. Nekhlyudov felt this relation of Novodvorov's towards him, and knew to his sorrow that in spite of the general state of goodwill in which he found himself on this journey he could not help paying this man in his own coin, and could not stifle the strong antipathy he felt towards him.

Chapter XVI

THE VOICES of officials sounded from the next room. All the prisoners were silent, and a sergeant followed by two convoy soldiers entered. The time for the inspection had come. The sergeant counted every one, and when Nekhlyudov's turn came he addressed him with kindly familiarity.

"You must not stay after the inspection, Prince. You must go now."

Nekhlyudov knew what this meant, went up to the sergeant, and put a three-ruble note into his hand.

"Ah, well; what is one to do with you? Stay a bit longer if you like." The sergeant was about to go when another sergeant, followed by a convict, a spare man with a thin beard and a bruise under his eye, came in.

"It's about the girl I have come," said the convict.

"Here's daddy come!" came a child's ringing accents, and a flaxen head appeared from behind Rantseva, who with Katusha's and Mary Pavlovna's help was making a new garment for the child out of one of Rantseva's own petticoats.

"Yes, daughter, it's me," said the prisoner, Buzovkin, tenderly.

"She is quite comfortable here," said Mary Pavlovna, looking with pity at Buzovkin's bruised face. "Let her stay with us."

"The ladies are making me new clothes," said the girl, pointing to Rantseva's sewing. "Ni-i-ice, re-ed ones!" she went on prattling.

"Do you wish to sleep with us!" asked Rantseva, caressing the child.

"Yes, I wish. And daddy too?"

A smile lit up Rantseva's face.

"No, daddy can't. We'll keep her then," she said, turning to the father.

"Yes, you may leave her," said the first sergeant, and went out with the other.

As soon as they were out of the room Nabatov went up to Buzovkin, slapped him on the shoulder, and said: "I say, old fellow, is it true that Karmanov wants to exchange?"

Buzovkin's kindly, gentle face turned suddenly sad, and a veil seemed to dim his eyes.

"We have heard . . . nothing," he said slowly, and with the same dimness still over his eyes he turned to the child.

"Well, Aksutka, it seems you're to make yourself comfortable with the ladies," he said, and hurried away.

"It is true about the exchange, and he knows it very well," said Nabatov. "What are you going to do?"

"I shall tell the authorities in the next town. I know both prisoners by sight," said Nekhlyudov.

All were silent, fearing a recommencement of the dispute.

Simonson, who had been lying with his arms thrown behind his head and not speaking, rose and walked up to Nekhlyudov with decision, carefully passing round those who were sitting.

"Could you listen to me now?"

"Certainly," and Nekhlyudov rose and followed him.

Katusha looked up with an expression of surprise, and, meeting Nekhlyudov's eyes she blushed and shook her head as if perplexed.

"What I want to speak to you about is this," Simonson began when they had come out into the passage. In the passage the din of the criminals' voices and shouts sounded louder. Nekhlyudov made a face, but Simonson did not seem confused by it. "Knowing your relations to Katusha Maslova," he began, seriously and frankly, with his kind eyes looking straight into Nekhlyudov's face, "I consider it my duty——" He was obliged to stop because two voices were heard disputing and shouting, both at once, close to the door.

"I tell you, blockhead, they were not mine," one voice shouted.

"May you choke, you devil," shouted the other.

At this moment Mary Pavlovna came out into the passage.

"How can one talk here?" she said. "Go in there; Vera is alone," and she went in at the second door and entered a tiny room, evidently meant for a solitary cell, which was now placed at the disposal of the women political prisoners. Vera Dukhova lay covered up, head and all, on the bed.

"She has a headache, and is asleep, so she cannot hear you, and I will go away," said Mary Pavlovna.

"On the contrary, stay here," said Simonson. "I have no secrets from any one—certainly not from you."

"All right," said Mary Pavlovna, and moving her whole body from side to side like a child, to get farther back on the bed-shelf, she settled down to listen, her beautiful hazel eyes seeming to look somewhere far away.

"Well, then, this is my business," Simonson repeated. "Knowing your relations to Katusha Maslova, I consider myself bound to explain to you my relations to her."

Nekhlyudov could not help admiring the simplicity and frankness with which Simonson spoke to him.

"What do you mean?" he asked.

"I mean that I should like to marry Katusha Maslova."

"How strange!" said Mary Pavlovna, fixing her eyes on Simonson.

"And so I made up my mind to ask her to be my wife," Simonson continued.

"What can I do? It depends on her," said Nekhlyudov.

"Yes, but she will not come to any decision without you."

"Why?"

"Because as long as your relations with her are unsettled, she can't make up her mind."

"As far as I am concerned it is finally settled. I want to do what I consider to be my duty, and also to lighten her fate; but on no account would I wish to put any restraint on her."

"Yes, but she does not wish to accept your sacrifice."

"It is no sacrifice."

"And I know that this decision of hers is final."

"Well, then, there is no need to speak to me," said Nekhlyudov.

"She wants you to acknowledge that you think as she does."

"How can I acknowledge that I must not do what I consider to be my duty? All I can say is that I am not free, but she is."

Simonson was silent; then after thinking a little he said:—

"Very well then, I'll tell her. You must not think I am in love with her," he continued; "I love her as a splendid, unique human being who has suffered much. I want nothing from her. I have only a profound longing to help to lighten her——"

Nekhlyudov was surprised to hear a tremor in Simonson's voice.

"To lighten her position," Simonson continued. "If she does not wish to accept your help, let her accept mine. If she consents I shall ask to be sent to the place where she will be imprisoned. Four years are not an eternity. I would live near her and perhaps might lighten her fate, . . ." and he again stopped, too agitated to continue.

"What am I to say?" said Nekhlyudov. "I am very glad she has found such a protector as you——"

"That's what I wanted to know," Simonson interrupted. "I wanted to know if, loving her, wishing her happiness, you would consider it good for her to marry me?"

"Oh yes," Nekhlyudov said decidedly.

"It all depends on her. I only wish that this suffering soul should find rest," said Simonson, with a childlike tenderness no one could have expected from so morose-looking a man.

Simonson rose, went up to Nekhlyudov, smiled shyly, and kissed him.

"So I shall tell her," he said, and went away.

Chapter XVII

"WHAT DO you think of that?" said Mary Pavlovna. "In love, quite in love! Now that's a thing I never should have expected of him—that Vladimir Simonson should be in love, and in the silliest and most boyish way! It is strange and, to tell the truth, it is sad," and she sighed.

"But she—Katusha? How do you think she looks at it?" Nekhlyudov asked.

"She?" Mary Pavlovna paused, evidently wishing to give give as exact an answer as possible. "She? Well, you see, in spite of her past, she has a most moral nature—and such fine feelings. She loves you, loves you rightly, and is happy to be able to do you even the negative good of not letting you get entangled with her. Marriage with you would be a terrible fall for her, worse than all that's past; and therefore she will never consent to it. And yet your presence agitates her."

"Well, what am I to do? Ought I to vanish?"

Mary Pavlovna smiled her sweet, childlike smile, and said—

"Yes, partly."

"How is one to vanish partly?"

"I am talking nonsense. But as for her. I should like to tell you that she probably sees the silliness of his rapturous kind of love—he has not spoken to her—and is both flattered and afraid of it. I am not competent to judge in such affairs, you know; still, I believe that on his part it is the most ordinary man's feeling, though it is masked. He says that his love arouses his energy, and is platonic, but I know that, even if it is exceptional, still at the bottom of it lies the same nastiness . . . the same as between Novodvorov and Grabets."

Mary Pavlovna had wandered from the subject, having started on her pet theme.

"Well, what am I to do?" Nekhlyudov asked.

"I think you should tell her everything. It is always best that everything should be clear. Have a talk with her. I will call her. Shall I?" said Mary Pavlovna.

"Yes, if you please," said Nekhlyudov.

Mary Pavlovna went out.

A strange feeling came over Nekhlyudov when he was alone in the little room with the sleeping Vera Dukhova, listening to her soft breathing, broken now and then by moans, and to the incessant din that came through the two doors that separated him from the criminals. What Simonson had told him freed him from the self-imposed duty which had seemed hard and strange to him in his weak moments, yet he now felt something that was not merely unpleasant but painful. He had a feeling that this offer of Simonson's destroyed the exceptional character of his sacrifice, and therefore lessened its value in the eyes of himself and others. If so good a man who was not bound to her by any kind of tie wanted to join his fate to hers, then this sacrifice was not so great. There may have been an admixture of ordinary jealousy also. He had got so used to her love that he did not like to admit that she could love another.

Then it also upset the plans he had formed of living near her while she was serving her term. If she married Simonson his presence would be unnecessary and he would have to form new plans.

Before he had time to analyse his feelings the loud din of the prisoners' voices came in with a rush (something special was going on among them to-day) as the door opened to admit Katusha.

She came close up to him, stepping briskly.

"Mary Pavlovna has sent me," she said.

"Yes, I must have a talk with you. Sit down. Vladimir Simonson has been speaking to me."

She had sat down, folding her hands in her lap, and seemed quite calm, but hardly had Nekhlyudov uttered Simonson's name when she flushed crimson.

"What did he say?" she asked.

"He told me he wanted to marry you."

Her face suddenly puckered up with pain, but she said nothing, only cast down her eyes.

"He is asking for my consent, or my advice. I told him it depends entirely on you—that you must decide."

"Oh, what does it all mean? Why?" she muttered, and looked in his eyes with the peculiar squint that always strangely affected him. They sat silent for a few seconds, looking into each other's eyes, and this look told much to both.

"You must decide," Nekhlyudov repeated.

"What am I to decide? Everything has long been decided."

"No, you must decide whether you will accept Vladimir Simonson's offer," said Nekhlyudov.

"What sort of a wife can I be—I, a convict? Why should I ruin Vladimir Simonson too?" she said, with a frown.

"Well, but if the sentence should be remitted?"

"Oh, let me alone. There is nothing more to be said," she said, and rose to leave the room.

Chapter XVIII

WHEN, FOLLOWING Katusha, Nekhlyudov returned to the men's room he found every one in a state of excitement. Nabatov, who went about everywhere, got to know everybody, and noticed everything, had just brought news which staggered them all. The news was that he had discovered, on one of the walls, a note written by the revolutionist Petlin, who had been sentenced to hard labour, and who every one thought had long since reached the Kara; and now it turned out that he had passed this way quite recently, the only political prisoner among criminal convicts.

"On the 17th of August," so ran the note, "I was sent off alone with criminals. Neverov was with me, but hanged himself in the lunatic asylum in Kazan. I am well and in good spirits and hope for the best."

All were discussing Petlin's position and the possible reasons of Neverov's suicide. Only Kriltsov sat silent and preoccupied, his glistening eyes gazing fixedly in front of him.

"My husband told me that Neverov had a vision while still in the Petropavlovsky," said Rantseva.

"Yes, he was a poet, a dreamer; these people cannot stand solitary confinement," said Novodvorov. "Now when I was in solitary confinement I never let my imagination run away with me, but arranged my days most systematically, and therefore always bore it very well."

"One can bear pretty nearly anything. Why! I used to be quite glad when they locked me up," said Nabatov cheerfully, wishing to dispel the general depression. "A fellow's afraid of everything: of being

arrested himself and of entangling others and spoiling the whole business, and then he gets locked up, and all responsibility ends and he can
rest—he can just sit and smoke."

"You knew him well?" asked Mary Pavlovna, glancing anxiously at
the altered, haggard expression of Kriltsov's face.

"Neverov a dreamer?" Kriltsov suddenly began, panting for breath as
if he had been shouting or singing for a long time. "Neverov was a man
'such as the earth bears few of,' as our doorkeeper used to express it.
Yes . . . he had a nature like crystal; you could see right through him.
He could not lie; he could not even dissemble. Not merely thin-
skinned, but with all his nerves laid bare, as if he were flayed. Yes . . .
his was a complex, rich nature, not such a . . . But what is the use of
talking?" He paused, and then added, with an angry frown: "We dispute
whether we must first educate the people and then alter the forms of
social life, or first alter the forms of life; and then we dispute how we
are to struggle: by peaceful propaganda or by terrorism? We dispute.
But *they* do not dispute, they know their business: they do not care
whether dozens, hundreds of men perish. And what men! No, that the
best should perish is just what they want. Yes, Herzen said that when
the Decembrists were withdrawn from circulation the average level of
our society sank. I should think so, indeed. Then Herzen himself and
his fellows were withdrawn, and now the Neverovs. . . ."

"They can't all be got rid of," said Nabatov in his cheerful tones.
"There will always be enough left to continue the breed."

"No, there won't, if we show any pity to *them*," Kriltsov continued,
raising his voice, and not letting himself be interrupted. "Give me a cigarette."

"Oh, Anatole, it is not good for you," said Mary Pavlovna. "Please do
not smoke."

"Ah, leave me alone," he said angrily, and lit a cigarette, but at once
began to cough and to retch as if he were going to be sick. Having
expectorated he went on:—

"What we have been doing is not the thing at all. Not to argue, but
all to unite . . . to destroy them."

"But they are also human beings," said Nekhlyudov.

"No, they are not human: men who can do what they are doing . . .
No . . . It is said that some kind of bombs and balloons have been
invented. Well, one ought to go up in a balloon, and sprinkle them
with bombs, as if they were bugs, till they are all exterminated. . . . Yes.
Because . . ." He tried to continue, but turning red he began coughing
worse than before, and a stream of blood rushed from his mouth.
Nabatov ran to get some snow. Mary Pavlovna brought valerian drops
and offered them to him, but, breathing quickly and heavily, he pushed

her away with his thin white hand, and kept his eyes closed. When the snow and cold water had eased him a little, and he had been put to bed, Nekhlyudov having said goodnight to everybody, went out with the sergeant, who had been waiting for him some time.

The criminals were quiet now, and most of them asleep. Though the people were lying on and under the bedshelves and in the spaces between, they could not all be placed inside the rooms, and some of them lay in the passage with their sacks under their heads and covered with their wet cloaks. Snores, moans, and sleepy voices came through the open doors and sounded through the passage. Everywhere lay compact heaps of human beings covered with prison cloaks. The only persons awake were a few men who were sitting in the bachelors' room by the light of a candle-end (which was put out when they noticed the sergeant), and an old man who sat naked under the lamp in the passage picking vermin off his shirt. The foul air in the political prisoners' rooms seemed pure compared with the foul closeness here. The smoking lamp shone dimly as through a mist, and it was difficult to breathe. Stepping along the passage one had to look carefully for an empty space, and, having put down one foot, a place had to be found for the other. Three persons who had evidently found no room even in the passage lay in the ante-room close to the stinking and leaking tub. One of these was an old idiot, whom Nekhlyudov had often seen marching with the gang; another was a boy of about twelve, who lay between the two other convicts, his head on the leg of one of them.

When he had passed out of the gate, Nekhlyudov took a deep breath, and long continued to breathe in deep draughts of the frosty air.

Chapter XIX

IT HAD cleared up and the stars were shining. Except in a few places the mud was frozen hard when Nekhlyudov returned to his inn and knocked at one of its dark windows. The broad-shouldered labourer came bare-footed to open the door and let him in. Through a door on the right, leading to the back premises, came the gruff loud snores of the carters who slept there, and from the yard came the sound of many horses chewing oats. The front room, where a red lamp was burning in front of the icons, smelt of wormwood and perspiration, and some one with mighty lungs was snoring behind a partition. Nekhlyudov undressed, put his leather travelling-pillow on the oilcloth sofa, and spreading out his rug lay down thinking over all he had heard and seen that day. The boy with his head on the convict's leg, sleeping on the liquid that oozed from the stinking tub, seemed more dreadful than all else.

Unexpected and important as his conversation with Simonson and Katusha that evening had been, he did not dwell on it. His position in that matter was so complicated and indefinite that he drove the thought of it from his mind. But the picture of those unfortunate beings, inhaling the noisome air, and lying in liquid oozing from the foul tub, especially the innocent face of the boy asleep on the leg of a criminal, recurred all the more vividly to his mind, and he could not get rid of it.

Merely to know that somewhere, far away, there are men who torture other men by inflicing all sorts of humiliations and inhuman degradations and sufferings on them; and for three months constantly to look on while these defilements and tortures were being inflicted, are two very different things; and Nekhlyudov felt this. More than once during these three months he asked himself: "Am I mad that I see what others do not, or are they mad who do these things that I see?" Yet they (and there were so many of them) did what seemed so astonishing and terrible to him, with such quiet assurance that what they were doing was necesary, and was important and useful work that it was hard to believe they were mad; nor could he—conscious of the clearness of his thoughts—believe he was mad. This kept him in a continual state of perplexity.

This is how the things he saw during these three months impressed him:—

From among all the people who were free, those who were the most nervous, the most hot-tempered, the most excitable, the most gifted, and the strongest, but the least careful and cunning, were selected by means of trials or by administrative orders. These people, not a whit more dangeous than many of those who remained free, were first locked up in prisons, and then transported to Siberia, where they were provided for and kept for months and years in complete idleness, away from nature, their families, and useful work—that is, from all conditions necesary for a natural and moral life. This, firstly.

Secondly, these people were subjected to all sorts of unnecessary indignities in these establishments: chains, shaven heads, and shameful clothing; that is, they were deprived of the chief motives that induce weak people to live good lives—regard for public opinion, a sense of shame, and the consciousness of human dignity.

Thirdly, their lives being in continual danger from the infectious diseases common in places of confinement, from exhaustion and from blows (not to mention exceptional cases of sunstroke, drowning, and fires), these people lived continually in a condition in which the best and most moral men are led by feelings of self-preservation to commit (and excuse others who commit) the most terribly cruel actions.

Fourthly, these people were forced to associate with others who were particularly depraved by life, and especially by these very institutions: with debauchees, murderers, and scoundrels, who acted on those not yet corrupted as leaven acts on dough.

And fifthly, the fact that all sorts of violence, cruelty, and inhumanity, are not only tolerated but even sanctioned by Government when it suits its purpose, was impressed on all these people most forcibly by the inhuman treatment they were subjected to: by the sufferings inflicted on children, women, and old men; by floggings with rods and whips; by rewards offered for bringing a fugitive back, dead or alive; by the separation of husbands and wives, and their union, for sexual intercourse, with the wives and husbands of others; and by shootings and hangings. Therefore acts of violence on the part of those who were deprived of their freedom, and who were in want and misery, could not help seeming even more permissible.

All these institutions seemed purposely devised for the production of depravity and vice, and for spreading this condensed depravity and vice broadcast among the whole population to an extent no other conditions could equal.

"It is just as if a problem had been set: to find the best, the surest means of depraving the greatest number of people!" thought Nekhlyudov, while getting an insight into the deeds that were being done in the prisons and halting-stations. Every year hundreds of thousands were brought to the highest pitch of depravity, and when completely depraved they were liberated to spread broadcast the moral disease they had caught in prison.

In the prisons of Tumen, Ekaterinburg, Tomsk, and at the halting-stations, Nekhlyudov saw how successfully the object society seemed to have set itself was attained. Ordinary simple men holding the social and Christian morality of the ordinary Russian peasant, lost this conception, and formed a new prison-bred one, founded chiefly on the idea that any outrage to or violation of human beings is justifiable if it seems profitable. After living in prison those people became conscious with the whole of their being that, judging by what was happening to themselves, all those moral laws of respect and sympathy for others preached by the Church and by the moral teachers, were set aside in real life, and that therefore they, too, need not keep these laws. Nekhlyudov noticed this effect of prison life in all the prisoners he knew—in Fedorov, in Makar, and even in Taras, who after two months among the convicts struck Nekhlyudov by a lack of morality in his arguments. He learnt during his journey that tramps who escape into the marshes will persuade comrades to escape with them, and will then kill them and feed on their flesh. (He saw a living man who was acccused of this, and acknowledged the act.) And the most terrible thing was that this was not a solitary case of cannibalism, but that the thing was continually recurring.

Only by a special cultivation of vice such as was carried on in these establishmens, could a Russian be brought to the state of these tramps, who excelled Nietzsche's newest teaching, holding everything allowable and nothing forbidden, and spreading this teaching first among the convicts and then among the people in general.

The only explanation of what was being done was that it aimed at the prevention of crime, at inspiring awe, at correcting offenders, and at dealing out to them "lawful vengeance" as the books said. But in reality nothing in the least resembling these results came to pass. Instead of vice being put a stop to, it only spread farther; instead of being frightened, the criminals were encouraged (many a tramp returned to prison of his own free will); instead of correction, every kind of vice was systematically instilled; while the desire for vengance, far from being weakened by the measures of the Government, was instilled into the people, to whom it was not natural.

"Then why is it done?" Nekhlyudov asked himself, and could find no answer.

And what seemed most surprising was that all this was not being done accidentally, nor by mistake, nor only once, but had been done continuously for centuries, with only this difference, that at first people's nostrils used to be slit and their ears cropped; then a time came when they were branded and fastened to iron bars; and now they were manacled, and transported by steam instead of on carts.

The arguments brought forward by those in Government service who said that the things which aroused his indignation were simply due to the imperfect arrangements of the places of confinement, and that they would all be put to rights if prisons of a modern type were built, did not satisfy Nekhlyudov, because he knew that what revolted him was not a consequence of a better or worse arrangement of prisons. He had read of model prisons with electric bells, of executions by electricity as recommended by Tarde, and this refined violence revolted him yet more.

But what revolted him most of all was that there were men in the Law Courts and in the Ministry receiving large salaries taken from the people, for referring to books written by other officials like themselves, actuated by like motives, fitting to this or that statute actions that infringed the laws thus written, and then, in obedience to these statutes, sending those guilty of such actions to places where they saw them no more, but where those people were completely at the mercy of cruel, hardened inspectors, jailers, and convoy soldiers, and where millions of them perished, body and soul.

Now that he had a closer knowledge of prisons, Nekhlyudov found that all the vices which developed among the prisoners—drunkenness, gambling, cruelty, and terrible crimes, even cannibalism—were not casual, nor due to degeneration, nor to the existence of monstrosities of the criminal type (as dull scientists, backing up the Government, explained it), but were an inevitable consequence of the inconceivable delusion that men may punish one another. Nekhlyudov saw that cannibalism did not begin in the marshes, but in the Ministries, Committees, and State Departments, and only came to fruition in the marshes. He saw that his brother-in-law, for example, and in fact all the lawyers and officials from usher to minister, do not care in the least for justice, or the good of the people, about which they talked, but only for the rubles they were paid for doing the things that caused all this degradation and suffering. This was quite evident.

"Can it be, then, that all this is simply due to a misunderstanding? Could it not be arranged that all these officials should have their salaries secured to them and a premium paid them besides, to leave off doing all that they are doing now?" thought Nekhlyudov; and with these thoughts, when the cocks had already crowed the second time, in spite of the fleas that seemed to spring up round him, like water from a fountain, whenever he moved—he fell fast asleep.

Chapter XX

THE CARTERS had left the inn long before Nekhlyudov awoke. The landlady had had her tea, and came in, wiping her fat perspiring neck with her handkerchief, to say that a soldier had brought a note from the halting-station. The note was from Mary Pavlovna. She wrote that Kriltsov's attack was more serious than they had supposed. "We first wished to let him remain here, and to get permission to stop with him, but this has not been allowed, so we shall take him on; but we fear the worst. Please arrange that if he should be left in the next town one of us may remain with him. If in order to get permission to stay I must marry him, I am of course ready to do so."

Nekhlyudov sent the young labourer to the post-station to order horses, and began packing up hurriedly. Before he had drunk his second tumbler of tea the three-horsed post-cart drove up to the porch with ringing bells, the wheels rattling on the frozen mud as on stones. Nekhlyudov paid the fat-necked landlady, hurried out, got into the cart, and gave orders to the driver to go on as fast as possible to overtake the gang. Just past the gates of the communal pasture-ground they overtook the carts laden with sacks and sick prisoners, rattling over the frozen mud that was just beginning to be rolled smooth by the wheels. The officer was not there; he had gone on in front. The soldiers, who had evidently been drinking, followed, chatting merrily, by the side of the road. There were a great many carts. In each of the first carts sat six invalid criminal convicts, closely packed. On each of the last three were three political prisoners: Novodvorov, Grabets, and Kondratyev sat on one, Rantseva, Nabatov, and the woman to whom Mary Pavlovna had given up her own place, on another. On the third cart Kriltsov lay on a heap of hay, with a pillow under his head, Mary Pavlovna sitting by him on the edge of the cart. Nekhlyudov ordered his driver to stop, got out, and went up to Kriltsov. One of the tipsy soldiers waved his hand towards Nekhlyudov, but he paid no attention, and walked on near Kriltsov, holding on to the side of the cart with his hand. Dressed in a sheepskin coat, with a fur cap on his head, and his mouth bound up with a handkerchief, Kriltsov seemed paler and thinner than ever. His beautiful eyes looked very large and brilliant. Shaken from side to side by the jolting of the cart, he lay with his eyes fixed on Nekhlyudov; but when asked about his health he only closed his eyes and angrily shook his head; all his energy seemed to be needed to bear the jolting of the cart. Mary Pavlovna was on the other side. She exchanged a significant glance with Nekhlyudov, which expressed all her anxiety about Krilstov's state, and then she at once began to speak in a cheerful manner.

"It seems the officer is ashamed of himself," she shouted, so as to be heard above the rattle of the wheels. "Buzovkin's manacles have been removed, and he is carrying his little girl himself. Katusha and Simonson are with him, and Vera too. She has taken my place."

Kriltsov said something that could not be heard because of the noise, and frowning in the effort to repress his cough shook his head. Then Nekhlyudov stooped towards him so as to hear, and Kriltsov freeing his mouth from the handkerchief whispered: "Much better now. Only not to catch cold." Nekhlyudov nodded in acquiescence, and again exchanged a glance with Mary Pavlovna.

"How about the problem of the three bodies?" whispered Kriltsov, smiling with great effort. "The solution is diffficult?"

Nekhlyudov did not understand, but Mary Pavlovna explained that he meant the well-known mathematical problem which defines the position of the sun, moon, and earth, to which Kriltsov compared the

relations between Nekhlyudov, Katusha, and Simonson. Kriltsov nodded to show that Mary Pavlovna had explained his joke correctly.

"The solution does not lie with me?" Nekhlyudov said.

"Did you get my note? Will you do it?" Mary Pavlovna asked.

"Certainly," answered Nekhlyudov; and noticing a look of displea-
sure on Kriltsov's face, he returned to his conveyance, got in, and with
both hands holding to the sides of the cart, which jolted him over the
ruts of the rough road, he began passing the gang, which, with its grey
cloaks and sheepskin coats, chains and manacles, stretched over three-
quarters of a mile of the road. On the opposite side of the road
Nekhlyudov noticed Katusha's blue shawl, Vera Dukhova's black coat,
and Simonson's crocheted cap and white worsted stockings, with bands
like those of sandals tied round them. Simonson was walking with the
women and carrying on a heated discussion.

When they saw Nekhlyudov they bowed to him, and Simonson
raised his hat in a solemn manner. Nekhlyudov, having nothing to say,
did not check the driver, and was soon ahead of them. Having again got
on to a smoother part of the road, the driver went along still faster; but
had continually to turn off the beaten track to pass rows of carts that
were moving along the road in both directions.

The road, which was cut up by deep ruts, lay through a thick forest
of pines, mingled with birth trees and larches, bright with the yellow
leaves they had not yet shed. By the time Nekhlyudov had passed about
half the gang he reached the end of the forest. Fields now lay stretched
along both sides of the road, and the crosses and cupolas of a monastery
appeared in the distance. The clouds had dispersed; the weather had
quite cleared up; the leaves, the frozen puddles, and the gilt crosses and
cupolas of the monastery glittered brightly in the sun that had risen
above the forest. A little to the right, mountains began to gleam white
in the blue-grey distance. The vehicle entered a large village. The village street was full of people, both Russian and of other nationalities,
wearing curious caps and cloaks. Drunk and sober men and women
crowded and chattered round booths, public-houses, and carts. The
nearness to a town was noticeable.

Giving a pull and a lash of the whip to the horse on his right, the driver sat down sideways on the right edge of the seat, so that the reins
hung over that side, and with an evident desire to show off drove
quickly down the river, which was crossed by a ferry. The raft was coming towards them and had reached the middle of the stream. About
twenty carts were waiting to cross. Nekhlyudov had not long to wait.
The raft, which had been pulled far up the stream, quickly approached
the landing, carried by the swift current.

The tall, silent, broad-shouldered, muscular ferrymen, dressed in sheepskins, threw the ropes and moored the raft with practised hand, landed the carts that were on it and put on board those that were waiting on the bank. The whole raft was filled with vehicles and with horses that fidgeted at the sight of the water. The broad, swift river splashed against the sides of the ferry boats, tightening the ropes. When the raft was full, and Nekhlyudov's cart, with the horses taken out of it, stood closely surrounded by others on one side of the raft, the ferrymen barred the entrance, and paying no heed to the entreaties of those who had not found room on the raft, unfastened the ropes, and set off.

All was quiet on the raft; one could hear nothing but the tramp of the ferrymen's boots, and the horses stepping from foot to foot.

Chapter XXI

NEKHLYUDOV STOOD at the edge of the raft, looking at the broad river. Two pictures kept rising in his mind. One was the shaking head of Kriltsov, who was dying in anger, the other, Katusha's figure vigorously stepping along the road beside Simonson. The first impression, that of Kriltsov, dying unprepared for death, made a heavy, sorrowful impression on him. The other, that of Katusha, full of energy, having gained the love of such a man as Simonson and found a true and solid path towards righteousness, should have been pleasant, and yet it also created in Nekhlyudov's mind a heavy impression he could not conquer.

The vibrating sounds of a big brass bell reached them from the town. Nekhlyudov's driver, who stood by his side, and the other men on the raft, raised their caps and crossed themselves—all except a short, dishevelled old man who stood close to the railings and whom Nekhlyudov had not noticed before. He did not cross himself, but raised his head and looked at Nekhlyudov. The old man wore a patched coat, cloth trousers, and worn and patched shoes. He had a small wallet on his back and a high cap of much-worn fur on his head.

"Why don't you pray, old chap?" asked Nekhlyudov's driver, as he replaced and straightened his cap. "Aren't you baptized?"

"Who's one to pray to?" asked the tattered old man quickly in a determindedly aggressive tone, pronouncing each syllable.

"To whom? To God of course," said the driver witheringly.

"And you just show me where He is—this God?"

There was something so serious and firm in the old man's expression that the driver felt he had to do with a strong-minded man and was somewhat abashed; but, trying not to show it, and not to be silenced and put to shame before the crowd that was observing them, he answered quickly:—

"Where? In heaven of course."

"And have you been up there?"

"Whether I've been or not, every one knows that one must pray to God."

"No man has ever seen God at any time. The only begotten Son, who is in the bosom of the Father, He hath declared Him," said the old man in the same rapid manner, and with a stern frown.

"It's clear you are not a Christian, but a hole-worshipper. You pray to a hole," said the driver, pushing the handle of his whip into his girdle, and straightening the harness on one of the horses.

Some one laughed.

"What is your faith, dad?" asked a middle-aged man, who stood by his cart on the same side of the raft.

"I have no kind of faith, because I believe no one—no one but myself," said the old man, as quickly and decidedly as before.

"How can you believe yourself?" Nekhlyudov asked, entering into conversation with him. "You might make a mistake."

"Never in my life," the old man said decidedly, with a shake of his head.

"Then why are there different faiths?" Nekhlyudov asked.

"It's just because men believe others, and do not believe themselves, that there are different faiths. I also believed others, and lost myself as in a swamp—lost myself so that I had no hope of finding my way out. Old-Believers and New-Believers, and Judaisers and Hlysty, and Popovtsy and Bezpopovtsy and Avstriaks and Molokans and Skoptsy—every faith praises itself only and so they all creep about like blind puppies. There are many faiths, but the spirit is one—in me, and in you, and in him. So that if every one believes himself, all will be united; every one be himself and all will be as one."

The old man spoke loudly, and often looked round, evidently wishing that as many as possible should hear him.

"And have you long held this faith?"

"I? A long time. This is the twenty-third year that they persecute me."

"Persecute you! How?"

"As they persecuted Christ so they persecute me. They seize me and take me before the courts, and before the priests, the Scribes, and the Pharisees. Once they put me into a madhouse; but they can do nothing, because I am free. They say 'What is your name?' thinking I shall name myself. But I do not give myself a name. I have given up everything; I have no name, no place, no country, no anything. I am just myself. 'What is your name?' 'Man.' 'How old are you?' I say, 'I do not count my years, and cannot count them, because I always was, I always shall be.' 'Who are your parents?' 'I have no parents, except God and Mother Earth. God is my father.' 'And the Tsar? Do you recognise the Tsar?' they say. I say, 'Why not? He is his own Tsar, and I am my own Tsar.' 'Where's the good of talking to him?' say they: and I say, 'I do not ask you to talk to me.' And then they begin tormenting me.'

"And where are you going now?" asked Nekhlyudov.

"Where God may lead me. I work when I can find work, and when I can't, I beg."

The old man noticed that the raft was approaching the bank, and stopped, turning round to the bystanders with a look of triumph.

Nekhlyudov got out his purse, and offered some money to the old man, but he refused, saying:—

"I do not accept that sort of thing; bread I do accept."

"I beg your pardon, then."

"There is nothing to pardon, you have not offended me, and it is not possible to offend me," and the old man replaced on his back the wallet he had taken off.

Meanwhile the post-cart had been landed and the horses harnessed.

"I wonder you should care to talk to him, sir," said the driver, when Nekhlyudov, having tipped the brawny ferrymen, got into the cart again. "He is just a worthless tramp."

Chapter XXII

WHEN THEY got to the top of the bank the driver turned round to Nekhlyudov.

"What hotel am I to drive to?"

"Which is the best?"

"Nothing could be better than the Siberian, but Dukhov's is also good."

"Drive to whichever you like."

The driver again seated himself sideways, and drove faster. The town was like all such towns. The same kind of houses, with attic windows and green roofs, the same kind of cathedral, the same kind of shops and stores in the principal street, and even the same kind of policemen. But almost all the houses were of wood, and the streets were not paved. In one of the chief streets the driver stopped at the door of an hotel, but no room could be had there, so he drove to another. And here Nekhlyudov, after two months, once again found himself in surroundings such as he had been accustomed to, as far as comfort and cleanliness went. Though the room he was shown to was simple enough, yet Nekhlyudov felt greatly relieved to be there, after two months of post-carts, country inns, and halting-stations. His first business was to clean himself from the lice, which he had never been able to get thoroughly rid of after visiting the halting-stations. When he had unpacked he went first to the Russian bath, and then, having put on town attire—a starched shirt, trousers that had got rather creased, a frock coat, and an overcoat—set out to visit the Governor of the district. The hotel-keeper called an *izvozchik*, whose well-fed Kirghiz horse and vibrating trap soon brought Nekhlyudov to the large porch of a big building in front of which stood sentries and a policeman. The house had a garden in front and at the back, where among the aspen and birch trees which spread out their bare branches grew thick dark-green pines and firs. The General was not well and did not receive, but Nekhlyudov asked the footman to hand in his card all the same, and the footman came back with a favourable reply.

"Will you please come in?"

The hall, the footman, the orderly, the staircase, the dancing-room with its well-polished floor, were very much the same as in Petersburg, but more imposing and rather dirtier.

Nekhlyudov was shown into the study.

The General, a bloated man of sanguine disposition, with a bulbous nose, large bumps on his forehead, puffs under his eyes, and a bald head, sat wrapped in a Tartar-silk dressing-gown, smoking a cigarette and sipping his tea out of a tumbler in a silver holder.

"How do you do, my dear sir? Excuse my dressing-gown; it is better so than if I had not received you at all," he said, pulling his dressing-gown over his fat neck, with its deep folds at the nape. "I am not quite well, and do not go out. What has brought you to our remote regions?"

"I am accompanying a gang of prisoners, among whom there is a person closely connected with me," said Nekhlyudov. "And I have come to see your Excellency partly on behalf of this person and partly about another business."

The General took another whiff and a sip of tea, put his cigarette into a malachite ash-pan, and with his narrow eyes fixed on Nekhlyudov, sat listening seriously, only interrupting him once to offer him a cigarette.

The General belonged to the cultured type of military men who believe that liberal and humane views can be reconciled with their profession. But being by nature a kind and intelligent man he soon felt the impossibility of such a reconciliation. So, not to feel the inner discord in which he lived, he gave himself up more and more to the habit

of drinking, so prevalent among military men, and became so addicted
to it that after thirty-five years' military service he had become what
the doctors term an "alcoholic." He was saturated with alcohol, and if
he drank any kind of liquor he became drunk. Yet strong drink was an
absolute necessity to him—he could not live without it—so he was
quite drunk every evening, but had grown so used to this state that he
did not reel or talk any special nonsense. And if he did talk nonsense,
it was accepted as wisdom because of the important and high position
which he occupied. Only in the morning, just at the time Nekhlyudov
came to see him, was he like a reasonable being and able to understand what was said to him, exemplifying more or less aptly a proverb
he was fond of repeating: "He's tipsy but he's wise so he's pleasant in
two ways." The higher authorities knew he was a drunkard, but he was
more educated than the rest—though his education had stopped at
the point at which drunkenness had got hold of him,—he was bold,
adroit, of imposing appearance, showed tact even when drunk, and
therefore was appointed to, and allowed to retain, so public and
responsible a post.

Nekhlyudov told him that the person he was interested in was a
woman, that she was wrongfully convicted, and that a petition had
been sent to the Emperor on her behalf.

"Yes, well?" said the General.

"I was promised in Petersburg that the news concerning her fate
would be sent to me not later than this month, and to this place——"

The General stretched his hand with its stumpy fingers towards the
table and rang a bell, still looking at Nekhlyudov, puffing at his ciga-
rett, and coughing very loudly.

"So I would like to ask that this woman might be allowed to remain
here until the answer to her petition comes."

The footman, an orderly in uniform, came in.

"Ask if Anna Vasilyevna is up," said the General to the orderly, "and
bring some more tea." Then, turning to Nekhlyudov, "Yes, and what
else?"

"My other request concerns a political prisoner who is with the same
gang."

"Is that so?" said the General, with a significant shake of the head.

"He is seriously ill—dying—and he will probably be left here in the
hospital. So one of the political women prisoners would like to stay
behind with him."

"She is no relation of his?"

"No, but she is willing to marry him if that will enable her to
remain."

The General, looking fixedly with twinkling eyes at his interlocutor, and with an evident wish to discomfit him, listened in silence, smoking all the time.

When Nekhlyudov had finished, the General took a book from the table, and wetting his finger quickly turned over the pages and found the statue relating to marriages, and read it.

"What is she sentenced to?" he asked, looking up from the book.

"She? To hard labour."

"Well then, the position of one sentenced to that cannot be bettered by marriage."

"Yes, but——"

"Excuse me. Even if a free man should marry her, she would have to serve her term. The question in such cases is, whose is the heavier punishment, hers or his?"

"They are both sentenced to hard labour."

"Very well; so they are quits," said the General, with a laugh. "She's got the same that he has, but as he is sick he may be left behind, and of course what can be done to lighten his fate shall be done. But as for her, even if she did marry him, she could not remain behind——"

"Her Excellency is having coffee," the footman announced.

The General nodded and continued:—

"However, I will think about it. What are their names? Put them down here."

Nekhlyudov wrote down their names.

Nekhlyudov's request to be allowed to see the dying man the General answered by saying:—

"Neither can I do that. Of course I do not suspect you; but you take an interest in him and in the others, and you have money, and here with us anything can be done with money. They tell me: 'Put down bribery.' But how can I put down bribery when everybody takes bribes? And the lower their rank the more ready they are to be bribed. How can one find it out across more than three thousand miles? Out there any official is a little Tsar, just as I am here," and he laughed. "You have probably been to see the political prisoners: you gave money and got permission, eh?" he said with a smile. "Is it not so?"

"Yes, it is."

"I quite understand that you had to do it. You pity a political prisoner and wish to see him. And the inspector or the convoy soldier accepts because he has a salary of a shilling a day, and a family, and he can't help accepting it. In his place and in yours I should act in the same way as you and he did. But in my position I do not permit myself to swerve an inch from the letter of the law, just because I am a man and might be influenced by pity. I am a member of the executive and I have been placed in a position of trust on certain conditions, and those conditions

I must carry out. . . . Well, so that business is finished. And now let us hear what is going on in the metropolis'; and the General began questioning and relating, with an evident desire both to hear the news and to show off his own knowledge and humanity.

Chapter XXIII

"By THE way, where are you staying?" asked the General, as he was taking leave of Nekhlyudov. "At Dukhov's? Well, it's horrid enough there. Come and dine with us at five o'clock. You speak English?"

"Yes, I do."

"That's good. You see an English traveller has just arrived here. He is studying the transportation question, and examining the prisons of Siberia. Well, he is dining with us to-night, so you must come and meet him. We dine at five, and my wife expects punctuality. Then I will also give you an answer about that woman and about the sick man. Perhaps it may be possible to leave some one behind with him."

Having taken leave of the General, Nekhlyudov drove to the post-office, feeling himself in an extremely animated and energetic frame of mind.

The post–office was a low-vaulted room. Several officials sat behind a counter serving the people, of whom there was quite a crowd. One official sat with his head bent to one side, stamping the letters, which he slipped dexterously under the die. Nekhlyudov had not long to wait. As soon as he had given his name everything that had come for him by post was at once handed over. There was a good deal: several letters, and money and books, and the latest number of the *European Messenger*. Nekhlyudov took all these things to a wooden bench on which a soldier with a book in his hand sat waiting, and sitting down by his side began to sort his letters. Among them was a registered letter in a very good envelope, with a distinctly-stamped bright red seal. He broke the seal, and seeing a letter from Selenin enclosing some official paper he felt the blood rush to his face, and his heart stood still. It was the answer to Katusha's petition. What would that answer be? Surely not a rejection? Nekhlyudov glanced hurriedly through the letter, written in an illegibly small, firm, and cramped hand, and breathed a sigh of relief. The answer was a favourable one.

"Dear Friend," wrote Selenin, "our last talk made a profound impression on me. You were right concerning Maslova. I have looked carefully through the case and see that a shocking injustice has been done her. It could be remedied only by the Committee of Petitions, before which you laid it. I managed to assist at the examination of the case, and I enclose herewith a copy of the mitigation of the sentence. Your aunt, the Countess Catherine Ivanovna, gave me the address to which I am sending this. The original document has been sent to the place where she was imprisoned before her trial, and will from there probably be sent at once to the principal Government office in Siberia. I hasten to communicate this glad news to you, and warmly press your hand. — Yours, SELENIN."

The document ran thus: "His Majesty's Office for the Reception of Petitions addressed to his Imperial Name" (here followed the date and various official technicalities). "By order of the Chief of His Majesty's Office for the Reception of Petitions addressed to His Imperial Name, the peasant woman Katerina Maslova is hereby informed that His Imperial Majesty, with reference to her most loyal petition, condescending to her request, deigns to order that her sentence to hard labour be commuted to one of exile to the less distant districts of Siberia."

This was joyful and important news. All that Nekhlyudov could have hoped for Katusha, and for himself also, had happened. It was true that her new position brought new complications with it. While she was a convict, marriage with her could only be fictitious, and would have had no meaning except that he would be in a position to alleviate her condition. But now there was nothing to prevent their living together; and Nekhlyudov had not prepared himself for that. And besides, what of her relations with Simonson? What was the meaning of her words yesterday? And, if she consented to a union with Simonson, would it be good or bad? He could not unravel all these questions, and gave up thinking about them. "It will all clear itself up later on," he thought. "I must not think about it now, but must convey the glad news to her as soon as possible, and set her free." He thought that the copy of the document he had received would suffice; so when he left the post-office he told the *izvozchik* to drive him to the prison.

Though he had revieved no order from the governor to visit the prison that morning he knew by experience that it was easy to get from the subordinates what the higher officials would not grant, and he meant now to try and get into the prison to give Katusha the joyful news, and perhaps to get her set free, and at the same time to inquire about Kriltsov's health, and tell him and Mary Pavlovna what the General had said.

The prison inspector was a tall, imposing-looking man, with moustache and whiskers that turned towards the corners of his mouth. He received Nekhlyudov very sternly, and told him plainly that he could not grant an outsider permission to interview the prisoners without a special order from his chief. To Nekhlyudov's remark that he had been allowed to visit the prisoners even in the capitals, he answered: —

"That may be so, but I do not allow it," and his tone implied, "You city gentlemen may think to surprise and perplex us, but we in Eastern Siberia also know what the law is, and may even teach it you."

Nor did the copy of a document straight from the Emperor's own office have any effect on the prison inspector. He peremptorily refused to allow Nekhlyudov inside the prison walls. He only smiled contemptuously at Nekhlyudov's naïve conclusion that the copy he had received would suffice to set Maslova free, and declared that a direct order from his own superior would be needed before anyone could be set at liberty. The only things he agreed to do were to communicate to Maslova that a mitigation had arrived for her, and to promise that he would not detain her an hour after the order arrived from his chief to liberate her. He would also give no news of Kriltsov, saying that he could not even tell if there were such a prisoner there. And so having accomplished next to nothing Nekhlyudov got into his trap and drove back to his hotel.

The strictness of the inspector was chiefly due to the fact that an epidemic of typhus had broken out in the prison, owing to twice the number of people it was intended for being crowded into it. The *izvozchik* who drove Nekhlyudov said, "Quite a lot of people are dying in the prison every day. Some kind of pest has attacked them. As many as twenty are buried in a day."

Chapter XXIV

IN SPITE of his non-success at the prison, Nekhlyudov, still in the same vigorous, energetic frame of mind, went to the governor's office to see if the original of the document had arrived for Maslova. It had not arrived, so Nekhlyudov went back to the hotel and wrote about it without delay to Selenin and to the advocate. When he had finished he looked at his watch and saw it was time to go to dinner at the General's.

On the way he again began wondering how Katusha would receive the news of the mitigation of her sentence. Where would she have to live? How should he live with her? What about Simonson? What would his relations with her be? He remembered the change that had taken place in her, and this reminded him of her past.

"I must forget it for the present," he thought, and again hastened to drive her out of his mind. "When the time comes I shall see," he said to himself, and began to think what he ought to say to the General.

· The dinner at the General's, given in the luxurious style to which Nekhlyudov had been accustomed, and which is usual among rich people and high officials, was extremely enjoyable after he had been so long deprived not only of luxury but even of the most ordinary comforts. The mistress of the house was a Petersburg *grande dame* of the old school, a maid of honour at the Court of Nicholas I, who spoke French quite naturally and Russian very unnaturally. She held herself very erect, and kept her elbows close to the waist when moving her hands. She was quietly and somewhat sadly considerate for her husband, and extremely kind to her visitors, though with shades of difference in her behaviour according to who they were. She received Nekhlyudov as if he were one of themselves; and her fine, almost imperceptible, flattery made him once again aware of his virtues, and gave him a sense of satisfaction. She made him feel that she knew of that honest though rather singular step of his which had brought him into Siberia, and that she held him to be an exceptional man. This refined flattery, and the elegance and luxury of the General's house, had the effect of making Nekhlyudov succumb to the enjoyment of the handsome surroundings, the delicate dishes, and the ease and pleasure of intercourse with educated people of his own class, so that the surroundings amid which he had passed the last months seemed a dream from which he now awoke to reality.

Besides those of the household—the General's daughter, her husband, and an aide-de-camp—there were present an Englishman, a merchant interested in the gold mines, and the governor of a distant Siberian town. All these people seemed pleasant to Nekhlyudov.

The Englishman, a healthy man with rosy complexion, who spoke very bad French, but whose command of his own language was very good and oratorically impressive, had seen a great deal, and what he had to say about America, India, Japan, and Siberia was very interesting.

The young merchant interested in the gold mines (the son of a peasant), in evening-dress made in London and with diamond studs in his shirt, possessing a fine library, contributing freely to philanthropic work, and holding liberal European views, seemed pleasant and interesting to Nekhlyudov as a sample of a quite new and good type of civilised and European culture grafted on a healthy, uncultivated peasant stock.

The governor of the distant Siberian town was that same ex-Director of a Government Department who had been so much talked about in Petersburg at the time Nekhlyudov was there. He was plump, with thin, curly hair, soft blue eyes, carefully tended white hands with rings on the fingers, and a pleasant smile; and he was very stout in the lower part of his body. The master of the house valued this governor, because, surrounded by bribe-takers, he alone took no bribes. The mistress of the house, who was very fond of music and a very good pianist herself, valued him because he was a good musician and played duets with her. Nekhlyudov was in such good humour that even this man was not unpleasant to him, in spite of what he knew of his vices.

The bright, energetic aide-de-camp, with his bluey-grey chin, who was continually offering his services, pleased Nekhlyudov by his good nature. But it was the charming young couple, the General's daughter and her husband, who pleased him most. The daughter was a plain-looking, simple-minded young woman, wholly absorbed in her first two children. Her husband, whom she had fallen in love with and had married after a long struggle with her parents, was a Liberal who had taken honours at Moscow University, a modest and intellectual young man in Government service, occupied with statistics, and specially with the native tribes, whom he studied, liked, and tried to save from dying out.

All those people were not only kind and attentive to Nekhlyudov, but evidently pleased to meet him as a new and interesting acquaintance. The General, who came to dinner in uniform and wearing his white cross, greeted Nekhlyudov as he would a friend, and asked the visitors to the side-table to take a glass of vodka and something to whet their appetites. The General asked Nekhlyudov what he had been doing since he left that morning, and Nekhlyudov told him he had been to the post-office and had received news that the sentence of the person he had spoken about in the morning would be mitigated, and he again asked for leave to visit the prison.

The General, evidently displeased that business should be mentioned at dinner, frowned and said nothingg.

"Have a glass of vodka?" he asked, addressing the Englishman, who had just come up to the table.

The Englishman drank a glass, and said he had been to see the cathedral and the factory, but would like to visit the great transportation prison.

"Oh, that will just fit in," said the General to Nekhlyudov; "you will be able to go together. Give them a pass," he added, turning to his aide-de-camp.

"When would you like to go?" Nekhlyudov asked.

"I prefer visiting the prisons in the evening," the Englishman answered: "all are indoors, and there is no preparation; you find them all as they are."

"Ah, he wants to see it in all its glory? Let him do so. I have written about it—but they pay no attention. So let them find out from the foreign press," said the General, and went up to the dinner-table, where the mistress of the house was showing the visitors their places.

Nekhlyudov sat between his hostess and the Englishman. Opposite him sat the General's daughter and the ex-Director of a Department. The conversation at dinner was carried on by fits and starts: now it was India that the Englishman talked about; now the Tonkin Expedition that the General strongly disapproved of; now the universal bribery and corruption in Siberia. All these topics did not interest Nekhlyudov much.

But after dinner, over their coffee, Nekhlyudov, the Englishman, and the hostess began a very interesting conversation about Gladstone, and it seemed to Nekhlyudov that he was saying many clever things which were noticed by his interlocutor. And, after a good dinner, and good wine, he felt it more and more pleasant to be sipping his coffee in an easy chair among amiable, well-bred people. And when at the Englishman's request the hostess went up to the piano with the ex-Director of a Department, and they began to play in well-practised style Beethoven's Fifth Symphony, Nekhlyudov fell into a state of perfect self-satisfaction, to which he had long been a stranger, as though he had only just found out what a good man he was.

The grand piano was a splendid instrument, the symphony was well executed. At least, so it seemed to Nekhlyudov, who knew and liked that symphony. Listening to the beautiful andante, he felt a tickling in his nose, so touched was he by his many virtues.

Nekhlyudov thanked his hostess for the enjoyment he had so long been deprived of, and was about to say good-bye and go when the daughter of the house came up to him with a determined look, and said with a blush:—

"You asked about my children; would you like to see them?"

"She thinks that everybody wants to see her children," said her mother, smiling at her daughter's winning tactlessness. "The Prince is not at all interested."

"On the contrary, I am very much interested," said Nekhlyudov, touched by this overflowing, happy mother-love. "Please let me see them."

"She's taking the Prince to see her babies," the General shouted, laughing from the card-table, where he sat with his son-in-law, the gold miner, and the aide-de-camp. "Go, go, pay your tribute."

The young woman, visibly excited by the thought that judgment was about to be passed on her children, went quickly towards the inner apartments, followed by Nekhlyudov. In the third, a lofty room, papered white, and lit by a shaded lamp, stood two small cots, a nurse with a white cape on her shoulders sitting between; she had a kindly, typical Siberian face with high cheek-bones. She rose and bowed. The mother bent over the first cot, in which a two-year-old girl lay peacefully sleeping with her little mouth open and her long curly hair tumbled over the pillow.

"This is Katie," said the mother, straightening the white and blue crochet coverlet, from under which a tiny white foot had pushed itself out.

"Is she not pretty? She is only two years old, you know."

"Charming!"

"And this is Vasuk, as grandpapa calls him. Quite a different type. A Siberian, is he not?"

"A splendid boy," said Nekhlyudov, as he looked at the little fatty lying asleep on his stomach.

"Yes," said his mother, with a proudly happy smile.

Nekhlyudov recalled to his mind chains, shaven heads, fighting and debauchery, the dying Kriltsov, Katusha and the whole of her past; and he began to feel envious, and to wish for what he saw here, which now seemed to him pure, refined happiness.

After having repeatedly expressed his admiration of the children, thereby at least partially satisfying their mother who eagerly drank in this praise, Nekhlyudov followed her back to the drawing-room, where the Englishman was waiting for him to visit the prison as they had arranged. Having taken leave of their hosts, old and young, the Englishman and Nekhlyudov went out into the porch of the house.

The weather had changed. Snow was falling thickly in large flakes and had already covered the road, the roofs, the trees in the garden, the steps of the porch, the hood of the trap, and the back of the horse.

The Englishman had his own trap, and having told the coachman to drive to the prison, Nekhlyudov called his own *izvozchik*, got in alone with a heavy sense of having to fulfil an unpleasant duty, and followed the Englishman over the soft snow, through which the wheels turned with difficulty.

Chapter XXV

THE DISMAL prison building, with its sentry, and the lamp burning under the gateway, produced by its long row of lighted windows, in spite of the clean white covering that now lay over everything—the porch, the roof, and the walls—an even more dismal impression than in the morning.

The imposing inspector came out to the gate, read by the light of the lamp the pass that had been given to Nekhlyudov and the Englishman, and shrugged his fine shoulders in surprise; but in obedience to the order he asked the visitors to follow him in. He led them through the courtyard, and then in at a door to the right and up a staircase into the office. He offered them seats, and asked what he could do for them; and when he heard that Nekhlyudov would like to see Maslova at once, he sent a jailer to fetch her. Then he prepared himself to answer the questions which the Englishman began to put to him, Nekhlyudov acting as intepreter.

"How many persons is the prison built to hold?" the Englishman asked. "How many are confined in it? . . . How many men? . . . How many women? . . . Children? . . . How many sentenced to the mines? . . . How many exiles? . . . How many sick persons? . . ."

Nekhlyudov translated the Englishman's and the inspector's words without paying any attention to their meaning, and felt an awkwardness he had not in the least expected at the thought of the impending interview. When in the midst of a sentence he was translating for the Englishman, he heard the sound of approaching footseps, and the office door opened, and as had happened many times before a jailer came in followed by Katusha, and he saw her with a kerchief tied round her head and in a prison jacket, a heavy sensation came over him.

"I want to live, I want a family, children, I want a human life." These thoughts flashed through his mind, as she entered the room with rapid steps and downcast eyes.

He rose and made a few steps to meet her, and her face appeared hard and unpleasant to him. It was again as it had been that time when she reproached him. She flushed and turned pale, her fingers nervously twisting a corner of her jacket; she looked up at him, and then cast down her eyes.

"You know that a mitigation has come?"

"Yes, the jailer told me."

"So that as soon as the original document arrives you may come away and decide where to settle. We shall consider——"

She interrupted him hurriedly.

"What have I to consider? Where Vladimir Simonson goes, there I shall follow."

In spite of her excitement she raised her eyes to him and pronounced these words quickly and distinctly, as if she had prepared what she had to say.

"Really?"

"Well, Dmitry Ivanich, you see he wants me to live with him . . ." she stopped, quite frightened, and corrected herself, "he wants me to be near him. What more can I wish for? I must look on it as happiness. What else is there for me? . . ."

"One of two things," thought Nekhlyudov. "Either she has fallen in love with Simonson and does not in the least require the sacrifice I imagined I was making, or she still loves me and refuses me for my own sake, and is burning her ships by uniting her fate with Simonson." And he felt ashamed, and knew that he was blushing.

"And you, yourself, do you love him?" he asked.

"Loving or not loving, what does it matter? I have given up all that. And then Vladimir Simonson is quite an exceptional man."

"Yes, of course," Nekhlyudov began. "He is a splendid man, and I think——"

But she again interrupted him, as if afraid that he might say too much, or that she would not say all.

"No, Dmitry Ivanich, you must forgive me if I am not doing what you wish," and she looked at him with her unfathomable squinting eyes. "Yes, evidently that's how it must be. You, too, must live."

She said just what he had been telling himself a few moments before. But he no longer thought so now, but thought and felt very differently. He was not only ashamed, but felt sorry to lose all he was losing with her.

"I did not expect this," he said.

"Why should you live here and suffer? You have suffered enough," she said, and smiled.

"I have not suffered. It was good for me, and I should like to go on serving you if I could."

"We"—as she said *we* she looked at Nekhlyudov—"we do not want anything. You have done so much for me as it is. If it had not been for you . . ." she wished to say more but her voice trembled.

"You, at any rate, have no reason to thank me," Nekhlyudov said.

"Where is the use of reckoning? God will make up our accounts," she said, and her black eyes began to glisten with tears that filled them.

"What a good woman you are," he said.

"I, good?" she said through her tears; and a pathetic smile lit up her face.

"Are you ready?" the Englishman asked.

"Directly," replied Nekhlyudov, and asked her about Kriltsov.

She mastered her emotion, and quietly told him all she knew. Kriltsov was very weak, and had been sent into the infirmary; Mary Pavlovna was very anxious and had asked to be allowed to enter the infirmary as a nurse, but could not get permission.

"Shall I go?" she asked, noticing that the Englishman was waiting.

"I will not say good-bye; I shall see you again," said Nekhlyudov, holding out his hand.

"Forgive me," she said, so low that he could hardly hear her. Their eyes met, and Nekhlyudov knew by the strange look of her squinting eyes and the pathetic smile with which she said not "Good-bye," but "Forgive me,"[1] that of the two reasons that might have led to her resolution the second was the real one. She loved him, and thought that by uniting herself to him she would be spoiling his life. By going with Simonson she thought she would be setting Nekhlyudov free, and she felt glad that she had done what she meant to do, and yet suffered at parting from him.

She pressed his hand, turned quickly, and left the room.

Nekhlyudov was ready to go, but seeing that the Englishman was noting something down, did not disturb him, but sat down on a wooden seat by the wall; and suddenly a feeling of terrible weariness came over him. It was not the sleepless night, not the journey, not the excitement, that had tired him, but he felt terribly tired of living. He leant against the back of the bench, shut his eyes, and in a moment fell into a deep, heavy sleep.

"Well, would you like to see the cells now?" the inspector asked.

Nekhlyudov looked up and was surprised to find himself where he was. The Englishman had finished his notes, and expressed a wish to see the cells.

Nekhlyudov, tired and indifferent, followed him.

Chapter XXVI

PASSING THROUGH the ante-room and the sickening, foul corridor, in which to their astonishment they saw two prisoners making water on the floor, the Englishman and Nekhlyudov accompanied by the inspector entered the first ward, where those sentenced to hard labour were confined. The prisoners were already lying on the bed-shelves, which occupied the middle of the ward. They lay head to head and side by side. There were about seventy of them. When the visitors entered, all the prisoners jumped up and stood by the beds, excepting

---

[1] The two words *proschayte* (good-bye) and *prostite* (forgive me) are almost interchangeable in Russian, and are etymologically closely akin, but Nekhlyudov detects a meaning in Katusha's choice of the less usual form.

two: a young man in a state of high fever, and an old man who did nothing but groan.

The Englishman asked if the young man had been ill long. The inspector replied that he had been taken ill that morning, but that the old man had been suffering with pains in the stomach for a long time, but could not be removed as the infirmary was over-full. The Englishman shook his head disapprovingly, said he would like to say a few words to these people, and asked Nekhlyudov to interpret. It turned out that besides studying the places of exile and the prisons of Siberia, the Englishman had another object in view, that of preaching salvation by faith and the Redemption.

"Tell them," he said, "that Christ pitied and loved them and died for them. If they believe in this they will be saved." While he spoke all the prisoners stood silent with their arms at their sides. "This book, tell them," he continued, "tells all about it. Can any of them read?"

There were more than twenty who could.

The Englishman took several bound Testaments out of a hand-bag, and many strong hands, with their hard, black nails, stretched out towards him from beneath the coarse shirt sleeves, jostling one another. He gave away two Testaments in this ward.

The same thing happened in the second ward. There was the same foul air, the same icon hanging between the windows, the same tub to the left of the door; they were all lying side by side close to one another, and jumped up in the same manner and stood erect with their arms by their sides—all but three, two of whom sat up, while one remained lying and did not even look at the new-comers. These three were also ill. The Englishman made the same speech, and again gave away two Testaments.

In the third room four were ill. When the Englishman asked why the sick were not put all together into one ward, the inspector said that they did not wish it themselves, that their diseases were not infectious, and that the medical assistant looked after them and did what was necessary.

"He has not set foot here for a fortnight," muttered a voice.

The inspector did not reply, and led the way to the next ward. Again the door was unlocked and all got up and stood silent, and again the Englishman gave away Testaments; it was the same in the fifth and sixth wards, in those to the right, and those to the left.

From those sentenced to hard labour they went on to the exiles; from the exiles to those banished by their commmunes, and those who followed of their own free will. Everywhere men—cold, hungry, idle, diseased, degraded, and confined—were shown off like wild beasts.

The Englishman having given away the appointed number of Testaments stopped giving any more, and made no more speeches. The depressing sights, and especially the stifling atmosphere, quelled even his energy, and he went from cell to cell saying nothing but "All right" to the inspector's report of the prisoners in each ward.

Nekhlyudov followed as in a dream, unable either to refuse to go on, or to go away, and with the same feelings of weariness and hopelessness.

Chapter XXVII

IN ONE of the exiles' wards Nekhlyudov, to his surprise, recognised the strange old man he had seen crossing the ferry that morning. This tattered and wrinkled old man was sitting on the floor by the beds, barefooted, wearing only a dirty cinder-coloured shirt, torn on one shoulder, and similar trousers. He looked severely and inquiringly at the new-comers. His emaciated body, visible through the holes in his dirty shirt, looked miserably weak, but in his face was more concentrated seriousness and animation than even when Nekhlyudov saw him crossing the ferry. As in all the other wards, so here also the prisoners jumped up and stood erect when the official entered, but the old man remained sitting. His eyes glittered and his brow frowned wrathfully.

"Get up!" the inspector called out to him.

The old man did not rise, but only smiled contemptuously.

"Thy servants are standing before thee. I am not thy servant. Thou bearest the seal . . ." said the old man pointing to the inspector's forehead.

"What—a—t?" said the inspector threateningly, and made a step towards him.

"I know this man," Nekhlyudov hastened to say; "what is he imprisoned for?"

"The police have sent him here because he has no passport. We ask them not to send such, but they will do it," said the inspector, casting an angry side-glance at the old man.

"And so it seems thou, too, art one of Antichrist's army?" the old man said to Nekhlyudov.

"No, I am a visitor," said Nekhlyudov.

"What, hast thou come to see how Antichrist tortures men? Here, see. He has locked them up in a cage, a whole army of them. Men should eat bread in the sweat of their brow. But *he* has locked them up with no work to do, and feeds them like swine, so that they should turn into beasts."

"What is he saying?" asked the Englishman.

Nekhlyudov told him the old man was blaming the inspector for keeping men imprisoned.

"Ask him how he thinks one should treat those who do not keep the laws," said the Englishman.

Nekhlyudov translated the question.

The old man laughed strangely, showing his regular teeth.

"The laws?" he repeated with contempt. "First *he* robbed everybody, took all the earth, and all rights away from men—took them all for himself—killed all those who were against him, and then he wrote laws forbidding to rob and to kill. He should have written those laws sooner."

Nekhlyudov translated. The Englishman smiled.

"Well, anyhow, ask him how one should treat thieves and murderers now?"

Nekhlyudov again translated his question.

"Tell him he should take the seal of Antichrist off from himself," the old man said, frowning sternly; "then he will know neither thieves nor murderers. Tell him so."

"He is crazy," said the Englishman, when Nekhlyudov had translated the old man's words; and shrugging his shoulders he left the cell.

"Do thine own business and leave others alone. Every one for himself. God knows whom to execute, whom to pardon, but we do not know," said the old man. "Be your own chief, then chiefs will not be wanted. Go, go," he added, frowning angrily, and looking with glittering eyes at Nekhlyudov, who lingered in the ward. "Hast thou not gazed enough on how the servants of Antichrist feed lice on men? Go! go!"

Nekhlyudov left the ward, and went up to the Englishman, who was standing with the inspector by an open door, asking what that cell was for.

"It is the mortuary."

"Oh," said the Englishman, and expressed a wish to go in.

The mortuary was an ordinary cell, not very large. A small lamp hung on the wall and dimly lit up some sacks and logs that were piled in one corner, and four dead bodies that lay on the bed-shelves to the right. The first body had on a coarse linen shirt and drawers; it was that of a tall man with a small beard, and half his head shaved. The body was already quite rigid; the bluish hands that had evidently been folded on the breast had separated; the legs had also fallen apart, and the bare feet were sticking out. Next to him lay a barefooted and bareheaded old woman, in white petticoat and jacket, her thin plait of hair uncovered, and with a small pinched yellow face and a sharp nose. Beyond her was another man in a mauve coloured garment. This colour reminded Nekhlyudov of something.

He came nearer and looked at the body.

The small pointed beard turned upward, the firm, well-shaped nose, the high, white forehead, the thin, curly hair—he recognised the familiar features, but could scarcely believe his eyes. Yesterday he had seen this face angry, excited, and full of suffering; now it was quiet, motionless and terribly beautiful. Yes, it was Kriltsov, or at any rate the trace of his material existence that remained. "Why had he suffered? Why had he lived? Has he now understood it?" Nekhlyudov thought, and there seemed to be no answer, seemed to be nothing but death, and he felt faint. Without taking leave of the Englishman Nekhlyudov asked the inspector to lead him out into the yard, and feeling the absolute necessity of being alone to think over all that had happened that evening he drove back to his hotel.

Chapter XXVIII

NEKHLYUDOV DID not go to bed but paced up and down his room for a long time. His business with Katusha was at an end. He was not wanted, and this made him sad and ashamed. His other business was not only unfinished, but troubled him more than ever and demanded his activity. All this horrible evil that he had seen and learnt to know lately, and especially to-day in that awful prison,—this evil which had killed that dear Kriltsov,—ruled and was triumphant, and he could see no possibility of conquering it or even of knowing how to conquer it. In his imagination rose up those hundreds and thousands of degraded human beings locked up in noisome prisons by indifferent generals, *procureurs*, and inspectors; he recalled the strange, free old man accusing the officials, and therefore considered mad, and, among the corpses, the beautiful waxen face of Kriltsov, who had died in anger. And again the question whether it was he, Nekhlyudov, who was mad, or those who considered they were in their right minds while they committed all these deeds, came before him with renewed force, demanding an answer.

Tired of pacing up and down, tired of thinking, he sat down on the sofa near the lamp, and mechanically opened a Testament which the Englishman had given him as a remembrance and which he had thrown on the table when he emptied his pockets on coming in.

"It is said one can find an answer to everything here," he thought, and opening the Testament at random he began reading Matthew xviii. 1–4: *"In that hour came the disciples unto Jesus, saying, Who then is greatest in the kingdom of heaven? And he called to him a little child, and set him in the midst of them, and said, Verily I say unto you, Except ye turn, and become as little children, ye shall in no wise enter into the kingdom of heaven. Whosoever therefore shall humble himself as this little child, the same is the greatest in the kingdom of heaven."*

"Yes, yes, that is true," he said, remembering that he had known the peace and joy of life only when he had humbled himself.

"And whoso shall receive one such little child in my name receiveth me: but whoso shall cause one of these little ones which believe on me to stumble, it is profitable for him that a great millstone should be hanged about his neck, and that he should be sunk in the depth of the sea" (Matt. xviii. 5, 6).

"What is this for? — 'Whoso shall receive.' Receive where? And what does 'in my name' mean?" he asked, feeling that these words did not tell him anything. "And why a millstone round his neck? And why the depth of the sea? No, that is not it; it is not exact, not clear"; and he remembered how more than once in his life he had taken to reading the Gospels, and how want of clearness in these passages had repulsed him. He went on to read the 7th, 8th, 9th, and 10th verses about occasions of stumbling, and that they must come, and about punishment by casting men into Gehenna, and some angels who see the face of the Father in heaven. "What a pity that this is so incoherent," he thought; "yet one feels that there is something good in it."

"For the Son of man came to save that which was lost," he went on reading. *"How think ye? if any man have a hundred sheep, and one of them be gone astray, doth he not leave the ninety and nine, and go unto the mountains, and seek that which goeth astray? And if so be that he find it, verily I say unto you, he rejoiceth over it more than over the ninety and nine which have not gone astray.*

"Even so it is not the will of your Father which is in heaven, that one of these little ones should perish."

"Yes, it is not the will of the Father that they should perish, and here they are perishing by hundreds and thousands. And there is no possibility of saving them," thought he, and read farther on.

"Then came Peter, and said to him, Lord, how oft shall my brother sin against me, and I forgive him? until seven times? Jesus saith unto him, I say not unto thee, Until seven times; but, Until seventy times seven.

"Therefore is the kingdom of heaven likened unto a certain king, which would make a reckoning with his servants. And when he had begun to reckon, one was brought unto him which owed him ten thousand talents.

But forasmuch as he had not wherewith to pay, his lord commanded him to be sold, and his wife, and children, and all that he had, and payment to be made. The servant therefore fell down and worshipped him, saying, Lord, have patience with me, and I will pay thee all. And the lord of that servant, being moved with compassion, released him, and forgave him the debt. But that servant went out, and found one of his fellow-servants, which owed him a hundred pence: and he laid hold on him, and took him by the throat, saying, Pay what thou owest. So his fellow-servant fell down and besought him, saying, Have patience with me, and I will pay thee. And he would not: but went and cast him into prison, till he should pay that which was due. So when his fellow-servants saw what was done, they were exceeding sorry, and came and told unto their lord all that was done. Then his lord called him unto him, and saith to him, Thou wicked servant, I forgave thee all that debt, because thou besoughtest me: shouldest not thou also have had mercy on thy fellow-servant, even as I had mercy on thee?" (ver. 21–33).

"And is it only this?" Nekhlyudov suddenly exclaimed aloud, and the inner voice of his whole being said, "Yes, this is all."

And it happened to Nekhlyudov as it often happens to men who are living a spiritual life. The thought that at first seemed strange, paradoxical, or even only a jest, being confirmed more and more often by life's experience, suddenly appeared as the simplest, truest certainty. In this way the idea that the only certain means of salvation from the terrible evil from which men are suffering is, that they should always acknowledge themselves to be guilty before God, and therefore unable to punish or reform others, became clear to him. It became clear to him that all the dreadful evil he had been witnessing in prisons and jails, and the quiet self-assurance of the perpetrators of this evil, resulted from men attempting what was impossible: to correct evil while themselves evil. Vicious men were trying to reform other vicious men, and thought they could do it by using mechanical means. And the result of all this was that needy and covetous men, having made a profession of this pretended punishment and reformation of others, themselves became utterly corrupt, and unceasingly corrupt also those whom they torment. Now he saw clearly whence came all the horrors he had seen, and what ought to be done to put an end to them. The answer he had been unable to find was the same that Christ gave to Peter. It was to forgive always, every one, to forgive an infinite number of times, beause there are none who are not themselves guilty, and therefore none who can punish or reform.

"But surely it cannot be so simple," thought Nekhlyudov; and yet he saw with certainty, strange as it had seemed at first, that it was not only a theoretical but also a practical solution of the question. The usual objection, "What is one to do with the evil-doers? surely not let them go unpunished?" no longer confused him. This objection might have a meaning if it were proved that punishment lessened crime or improved the criminal; but since just the contrary is proved, and it is evident that it is not in the power of some to reform others, the only reasonable thing to do is to cease doing what is not only useless, but harmful, immoral, and cruel. For many centuries people considered to be criminals have been executed. Well, and have they been exterminated? Far from being exterminated, their numbers have been increased, both by criminals corrupted by punishments, and also by those lawful criminals — judges, *procureurs*, magistrates, and jailers — who judge and punish men. Nekhlyudov now understood that society, and order in general, exist, not thanks to these lawful criminals who judge and punish others, but because notwithsanding their depraving influence men still pity and love one another.

Hoping to find a confirmation of this thought in the Gospel Nekhlyudov began reading it from the beginning. When he had read the Sermon on the Mount, which had always touched him, he saw in it to-day for the first time not beautiful abstract thoughts, setting forth for the most part exaggerated and impossible demands, but simple, clear, practical laws, which if carried out in practice (and this is quite possible) would establish perfectly new and surprising conditions of social life, in which the violence that filled Nekhlyudov with such indignation would not only cease of itself, but the greatest blessing attainable by men — the kingdom of heaven on earth — would be reached.

There were five of these laws.

The first law was (Matt. v. 21–26) that man should not kill, and should not even be angry with his brother; should not consider any one "Raca," worthless; and if he has quarrrelled with any one should make it up with him before bringing his gift to God, *i.e.* before praying.

The second law was (Matt. v. 27–32) that man should not commit adultery, and should not even seek for enjoyment in a woman's beauty; and if he has once come together with a woman he should never be faithless to her.

The third law was (Matt. v. 33–37) that man should never bind himself by oath.

The fourth law was (Matt. v. 38–42) that man should not demand an eye for an eye, but when struck on one cheek should offer the other: should forgive an injury and bear it humbly, and never refuse any one a service desired of him.

The fifth law was (Matt. v. 43) that man should not hate his enemies nor fight them, but love them, help them, serve them.

Nekhlyudov sat staring at the lamp, and his heart stood still.

Recalling the monstrous confusion of the life we lead, he distinctly saw what life could be if men were taught to obey these rules; and rapture such as he had long not felt filled his soul. It was as though after long days of weariness and suffering he had suddenly found ease and freedom.

He did not sleep all night, and as happens to many and many a man who reads the Gospels, he understood for the first time the full meaning of words read often before but passed by unnoticed. He drank in all these necessary, important, and joyful revelations as a sponge soaks up water. And all he read seemed quite familiar, and seemed to bring to consciousness and confirm what he had long known but had never fully realised and never quite believed. Now he realised and believed it; and not only realised and believed that if men would obey these laws they would attain the highest blessing possible to them, he also realised and believed that the sole duty of every man is to fulfil these laws, that in this lies the only reasonable meaning of life, and that every deviation from these laws is a mistake which is immediately followed by retribution. This flowed from the whole of the teaching, and was most strongly and clearly illustrated in the parable of the vineyard.

The husbandmen imagined that the vineyard in which they were sent to work for their Master was their own, that all that was in it was made for them, and that their business was to enjoy life in this vineyard, forgetting the Master and killing all those who reminded them of his existence.

"Are we not doing the same," Nekhlyudov thought, "when we imagine ourselves to be masters of our lives, and think that life is given us for enjoyment? For evidently, that is absurd. We were sent here by some one's will and for some purpose. And we have made up our minds that we live only for our own enjoyment, and of course things go ill with us, as they do with labourers when they do not fulfil their master's orders. The Master's will is expressed in these laws. As soon as men fulfil these laws the kingdom of heaven will be established on earth, and men will reach the greatest good they can attain.

"'Seek ye first his kingdom and his righteousness; and all these things shall be added unto you.' But we seek for these things and have evidently failed to obtain them.

"And so here it is—the business of my life. Scarcely have I finished one task, and another has commenced."

A perfectly new life dawned that night for Nekhlyudov; not because he had entered into new conditions of life, but because everything he did after that night had a new and quite different meaning for him. How this new period of his life will end, time alone will prove.

DOVER · THRIFT · EDITIONS

NONFICTION

NARRATIVE OF THE LIFE OF FREDERICK DOUGLASS, Frederick Douglass. 96pp. 28499-9
SELF-RELIANCE AND OTHER ESSAYS, Ralph Waldo Emerson. 128pp. 27790-9
THE LIFE OF OLAUDAH EQUIANO, OR GUSTAVUS VASSA, THE AFRICAN, Olaudah Equiano. 192pp. 40661-X
THE AUTOBIOGRAPHY OF BENJAMIN FRANKLIN, Benjamin Franklin. 144pp. 29073-5
TOTEM AND TABOO, Sigmund Freud. 176pp. (Not available in Europe or United Kingdom.) 40434-X
LOVE: A Book of Quotations, Herb Galewitz (ed.). 64pp. 40004-2
PRAGMATISM, William James. 128pp. 28270-8
THE STORY OF MY LIFE, Helen Keller. 80pp. 29249-5
TAO TE CHING, Lao Tze. 112pp. 29792-6
GREAT SPEECHES, Abraham Lincoln. 112pp. 26872-1
THE PRINCE, Niccolò Machiavelli. 80pp. 27274-5
THE SUBJECTION OF WOMEN, John Stuart Mill. 112pp. 29601-6
SELECTED ESSAYS, Michel de Montaigne. 96pp. 29109-X
UTOPIA, Sir Thomas More. 96pp. 29583-4
BEYOND GOOD AND EVIL: Prelude to a Philosophy of the Future, Friedrich Nietzsche. 176pp. 29868-X
THE BIRTH OF TRAGEDY, Friedrich Nietzsche. 96pp. 28515-4
COMMON SENSE, Thomas Paine. 64pp. 29602-4
SYMPOSIUM AND PHAEDRUS, Plato. 96pp. 27798-4
THE TRIAL AND DEATH OF SOCRATES: Four Dialogues, Plato. 128pp. 27066-1
A MODEST PROPOSAL AND OTHER SATIRICAL WORKS, Jonathan Swift. 64pp. 28759-9
CIVIL DISOBEDIENCE AND OTHER ESSAYS, Henry David Thoreau. 96pp. 27563-9
SELECTIONS FROM THE JOURNALS (Edited by Walter Harding), Henry David Thoreau. 96pp. 28760-2
WALDEN; OR, LIFE IN THE WOODS, Henry David Thoreau. 224pp. 28495-6
NARRATIVE OF SOJOURNER TRUTH, Sojourner Truth. 80pp. 29899-X
THE THEORY OF THE LEISURE CLASS, Thorstein Veblen. 256pp. 28062-4
DE PROFUNDIS, Oscar Wilde. 64pp. 29308-4
OSCAR WILDE'S WIT AND WISDOM: A Book of Quotations, Oscar Wilde. 64pp. 40146-4
UP FROM SLAVERY, Booker T. Washington. 160pp. 28738-6
A VINDICATION OF THE RIGHTS OF WOMAN, Mary Wollstonecraft. 224pp. 29036-0

PLAYS

PROMETHEUS BOUND, Aeschylus. 64pp. 28762-9
THE ORESTEIA TRILOGY: Agamemnon, The Libation-Bearers and The Furies, Aeschylus. 160pp. 29242-8
LYSISTRATA, Aristophanes. 64pp. 28225-2
WHAT EVERY WOMAN KNOWS, James Barrie. 80pp. (Not available in Europe or United Kingdom.) 29578-8
THE CHERRY ORCHARD, Anton Chekhov. 64pp. 26682-6
THE SEA GULL, Anton Chekhov. 64pp. 40656-3
THE THREE SISTERS, Anton Chekhov. 64pp. 27544-2
UNCLE VANYA, Anton Chekhov. 64pp. 40159-6
THE WAY OF THE WORLD, William Congreve. 80pp. 27787-9
BACCHAE, Euripides. 64pp. 29580-X
MEDEA, Euripides. 64pp. 27548-5

DOVER·THRIFT·EDITIONS

PLAYS

DOVER·THRIFT·EDITIONS

FICTION

FLATLAND: A ROMANCE OF MANY DIMENSIONS, Edwin A. Abbott. 96pp. 27263-X

SHORT STORIES, Louisa May Alcott. 64pp. 29063-8

WINESBURG, OHIO, Sherwood Anderson. 160pp. 28269-4

PERSUASION, Jane Austen. 224pp. 29555-9

PRIDE AND PREJUDICE, Jane Austen. 272pp. 28473-5

SENSE AND SENSIBILITY, Jane Austen. 272pp. 29049-2

LOOKING BACKWARD, Edward Bellamy. 160pp. 29038-7

BEOWULF, Beowulf (trans. by R. K. Gordon). 64pp. 27264-8

CIVIL WAR STORIES, Ambrose Bierce. 128pp. 28038-1

"THE MOONLIT ROAD" AND OTHER GHOST AND HORROR STORIES, Ambrose Bierce (John Grafton, ed.) 96pp. 40056-5

WUTHERING HEIGHTS, Emily Brontë. 256pp. 29256-8

THE THIRTY-NINE STEPS, John Buchan. 96pp. 28201-5

TARZAN OF THE APES, Edgar Rice Burroughs. 224pp. (Not available in Europe or United Kingdom.) 29570-2

ALICE'S ADVENTURES IN WONDERLAND, Lewis Carroll. 96pp. 27543-4

THROUGH THE LOOKING-GLASS, Lewis Carroll. 128pp. 40878-7

MY ÁNTONIA, Willa Cather. 176pp. 28240-6

O PIONEERS!, Willa Cather. 128pp. 27785-2

PAUL'S CASE AND OTHER STORIES, Willa Cather. 64pp. 29057-3

FIVE GREAT SHORT STORIES, Anton Chekhov. 96pp. 26463-7

TALES OF CONJURE AND THE COLOR LINE, Charles Waddell Chesnutt. 128pp. 40426-9

FAVORITE FATHER BROWN STORIES, G. K. Chesterton. 96pp. 27545-0

THE AWAKENING, Kate Chopin. 128pp. 27786-0

A PAIR OF SILK STOCKINGS AND OTHER STORIES, Kate Chopin. 64pp. 29264-9

HEART OF DARKNESS, Joseph Conrad. 80pp. 26464-5

LORD JIM, Joseph Conrad. 256pp. 40650-4

THE SECRET SHARER AND OTHER STORIES, Joseph Conrad. 128pp. 27546-9

THE "LITTLE REGIMENT" AND OTHER CIVIL WAR STORIES, Stephen Crane. 80pp. 29557-5

THE OPEN BOAT AND OTHER STORIES, Stephen Crane. 128pp. 27547-7

THE RED BADGE OF COURAGE, Stephen Crane. 112pp. 26465-3

MOLL FLANDERS, Daniel Defoe. 256pp. 29093-X

ROBINSON CRUSOE, Daniel Defoe. 288pp. 40427-7

A CHRISTMAS CAROL, Charles Dickens. 80pp. 26865-9

THE CRICKET ON THE HEARTH AND OTHER CHRISTMAS STORIES, Charles Dickens. 128pp. 28039-X

A TALE OF TWO CITIES, Charles Dickens. 304pp. 40651-2

THE DOUBLE, Fyodor Dostoyevsky. 128pp. 29572-9

THE GAMBLER, Fyodor Dostoyevsky. 112pp. 29081-6

NOTES FROM THE UNDERGROUND, Fyodor Dostoyevsky. 96pp. 27053-X

THE ADVENTURE OF THE DANCING MEN AND OTHER STORIES, Sir Arthur Conan Doyle. 80pp. 29558-3

THE HOUND OF THE BASKERVILLES, Arthur Conan Doyle. 128pp. 28214-7

THE LOST WORLD, Arthur Conan Doyle. 176pp. 40060-3

DOVER · THRIFT · EDITIONS

FICTION

A JOURNAL OF THE PLAGUE YEAR, Daniel Defoe. 192pp. 41919-3
SIX GREAT SHERLOCK HOLMES STORIES, Sir Arthur Conan Doyle. 112pp. 27055-6
SHORT STORIES, Theodore Dreiser. 112pp. 28215-5
SILAS MARNER, George Eliot. 160pp. 29246-0
JOSEPH ANDREWS, Henry Fielding. 288pp. 41588-0
THIS SIDE OF PARADISE, F. Scott Fitzgerald. 208pp. 28999-0
"THE DIAMOND AS BIG AS THE RITZ" AND OTHER STORIES, F. Scott Fitzgerald. 29991-0
MADAME BOVARY, Gustave Flaubert. 256pp. 29257-6
THE REVOLT OF "MOTHER" AND OTHER STORIES, Mary E. Wilkins Freeman. 128pp. 40428-5
A ROOM WITH A VIEW, E. M. Forster. 176pp. (Available in U.S. only.) 28467-0
WHERE ANGELS FEAR TO TREAD, E. M. Forster. 128pp. (Available in U.S. only.) 27791-7
THE IMMORALIST, André Gide. 112pp. (Available in U.S. only.) 29237-1
HERLAND, Charlotte Perkins Gilman. 128pp. 40429-3
"THE YELLOW WALLPAPER" AND OTHER STORIES, Charlotte Perkins Gilman. 80pp. 29857-4
THE OVERCOAT AND OTHER STORIES, Nikolai Gogol. 112pp. 27057-2
CHELKASH AND OTHER STORIES, Maxim Gorky. 64pp. 40652-0
GREAT GHOST STORIES, John Grafton (ed.). 112pp. 27270-2
DETECTION BY GASLIGHT, Douglas G. Greene (ed.). 272pp. 29928-7
THE MABINOGION, Lady Charlotte E. Guest. 192pp. 29541-9
"THE FIDDLER OF THE REELS" AND OTHER SHORT STORIES, Thomas Hardy. 80pp. 29960-0
THE LUCK OF ROARING CAMP AND OTHER STORIES, Bret Harte. 96pp. 27271-0
THE HOUSE OF THE SEVEN GABLES, Nathaniel Hawthorne. 272pp. 40882-5
THE SCARLET LETTER, Nathaniel Hawthorne. 192pp. 28048-9
YOUNG GOODMAN BROWN AND OTHER STORIES, Nathaniel Hawthorne. 128pp. 27060-2
THE GIFT OF THE MAGI AND OTHER SHORT STORIES, O. Henry. 96pp. 27061-0
THE NUTCRACKER AND THE GOLDEN POT, E. T. A. Hoffmann. 128pp. 27806-9
THE ASPERN PAPERS, Henry James. 112pp. 41922-3
THE BEAST IN THE JUNGLE AND OTHER STORIES, Henry James. 128pp. 27552-3
DAISY MILLER, Henry James. 64pp. 28773-4
THE TURN OF THE SCREW, Henry James. 96pp. 26684-2
WASHINGTON SQUARE, Henry James. 176pp. 40431-5
THE COUNTRY OF THE POINTED FIRS, Sarah Orne Jewett. 96pp. 28196-5
THE AUTOBIOGRAPHY OF AN EX-COLORED MAN, James Weldon Johnson. 112pp. 28512-X
DUBLINERS, James Joyce. 160pp. 26870-5
A PORTRAIT OF THE ARTIST AS A YOUNG MAN, James Joyce. 192pp. 28050-0
THE METAMORPHOSIS AND OTHER STORIES, Franz Kafka. 96pp. 29030-1
THE MAN WHO WOULD BE KING AND OTHER STORIES, Rudyard Kipling. 128pp. 28051-9
YOU KNOW ME AL, Ring Lardner. 128pp. 28513-8
SELECTED SHORT STORIES, D. H. Lawrence. 128pp. 27794-1
GREEN TEA AND OTHER GHOST STORIES, J. Sheridan LeFanu. 96pp. 27795-X
THE CALL OF THE WILD, Jack London. 64pp. 26472-6
FIVE GREAT SHORT STORIES, Jack London. 96pp. 27063-7
THE SEA-WOLF, Jack London. 248pp. 41108-7
WHITE FANG, Jack London. 160pp. 26968-X
DEATH IN VENICE, Thomas Mann. 96pp. (Available in U.S. only.) 28714-9
IN A GERMAN PENSION: 13 Stories, Katherine Mansfield. 112pp. 28719-X
THE NECKLACE AND OTHER SHORT STORIES, Guy de Maupassant. 128pp. 27064-5
BARTLEBY AND BENITO CERENO, Herman Melville. 112pp. 26473-4
THE OIL JAR AND OTHER STORIES, Luigi Pirandello. 96pp. 28459-X
THE GOLD-BUG AND OTHER TALES, Edgar Allan Poe. 128pp. 26875-6
TALES OF TERROR AND DETECTION, Edgar Allan Poe. 96pp. 28744-0